REVLENION
AND
THE
GUARDIAN
MANIFESTO

To Prati

Thank you for the love!

REVLENION

AND THE GUARDIAN MANIFESTO

A CURIOUS TALE BY

KALVIN KLAUS

ARTWORK BY FELIPE FLORES

PRODIGY GOLD BOOKS

PHILADELPHIA * LOS ANGELES

PRODIGY
GOLDBOOKS

REVLENION AND THE GUARDIAN MANIFESTO

A Prodigy Gold Book

Text Copyright © 2018 by Kalvin Klaus

Prodigy Gold E-book edition/November 2018

Prodigy Gold Paperback edition/November 2018

Artwork Copyright © 2018 by Felipe Flores

Publisher's Website: www.prodigygoldbooks.com

Author's Website: www.kalvinklaus.com

Library of Congress Catalog Card Number: On File

Ebook ISBN 978-1-939665-93-5

Paperback ISBN 978-1-939665-92-8

Published simultaneously in the US and Canada

PRINTED IN THE UNITED STATES OF AMERICA

For Kaly
The girl who lived and loved this tale first.

THE VENTURE SEQUENCES

CHAPTER ONE
Where the Manifesto Began–1

CHAPTER TWO
The Wonders of Poplar Drive–15

CHAPTER THREE
The Sleuth from Cappa–43

CHAPTER FOUR
The Guardian Manifesto–159

CHAPTER FIVE
The Man in the Mirror–265

CHAPTER SIX
The Macnificent Trio–319

REVLENION
AND
THE
GUARDIAN
MANIFESTO

CHAPTER ONE

WHERE THE MANIFESTO BEGAN

Once upon a time…

Thirteen years ago…

1975

November was ending and it seemed as though the late fall months had barely crept over the hills of the San Luis Obispo valley. The merry seasons were only days away while the husbands across the sprawling seaside town were dreading their in-laws impending holiday. It was a Thursday and had been the rainiest day that week. For the past few days, the town had encountered a vast amount of rain—an inch a day practically. The downtown streets were quiet and lit solely by the bright sidewalk lamps while the old courthouse clock tower quietly ticked to midnight after the heavy rainfall had suddenly come to a halt. Only the soothing echoes of water dripping off shop awnings graced the night and all the brownstone boutiques, cafés, record and bookstores were as tranquil as a mouse in one's house with 'Closed' signs posted in almost every window in sight.

But of course, there's always one hardworking soul that can be found awake at such a still hour of the night. And that only spark of life was in the form of a night-crew janitor, sweeping up the stale popcorn from yet another busy night in the lobby of the majestic Fremont Cinema. Harvey, as it read on his tatty uniform, swept effortlessly along the vast lobby of the Victorian cinema that housed such beautifully aged golden walls lavished with epic murals of great gods and brilliant blue skies. With his handy-dandy FM radio blasting tunes, (a reprieve from the peculiar monotony that one encounters working through such small hours), Harvey set his cleaning supplies aside and turned to the refreshments stands to serve himself a small cup of ice water. Sighing at the thought of the long and insistent list of cleaning tasks he still hadn't completed, Harvey threw his arm out to read his wristwatch: it was break time. As Harvey waddled toward his chair behind the refreshment counter, he snapped his fingers at the sudden flash of recollection; he still needed to shut down the power to the marquee and main lights.

Turning on his booted heel, Harvey marched to the shoebox-like office across from the refreshments as his excitement grew, spurred on by how long he had been waiting to eat whatever his dear wife, Grace, had prepared for him in his favorite tin lunch pail. Click by click: every section of the golden cinema disappeared into the near midnight realm. The lone box-office ticket booth that stood outside, just before the tall lobby doors, went dark with a zap. The purple and red lettered marquee proudly exhorting *The Rocky Horror Picture Show*, having been draped with a massive **SOLD OUT** sign underneath it, suddenly flickered like a set of neon eyes as, it too, fell away into the closing night. Where Harvey now stood, just behind the dimly lit refreshments counter, was but the last trace of light peeking out of the old cinema. At last, Harvey plopped down on his wobbly wooden stool, opened his pail with a flick of his finger, and pulled out his favorite: a turkey and ham sandwich smothered in mayonnaise. With his fingers drenched from his sandwich and tirelessly spinning the tiny cap off his polished whiskey flask, Harvey stretched out his arms and spread his late-night lunch across the counter. Between bites of his gloppy sandwich, Harvey found himself humming along to the late-night tunes that popped from his favorite radio, such as the Simon & Garfunkel song *My Little Town*, which played on. As Harvey stuffed his face with the greatest sandwich he'd ever had, his town seemed almost untouchable and quiet as ever.

Across the street, however, a few remaining blisters of rain clouds above the courthouse suddenly began to take another shape altogether. It was only seconds later when the clouds began to split into phenomenal swirls of roaring wind and flashes of a fantastic blue light. The miniature tornado that took shape slammed like a monstrous fist onto the wet road between the courthouse and the darkened cinema. The roaring whirls then broke from the tornado and gracefully morphed into six-winged creatures. Each of the beings descended to the road, fluttering their long, feathery wings with the chill air as they did. The six of them were robed in the finest satins and masked with silver that looked like it hadn't come from any ordinary place. These creatures stood gallantly in all different heights and sizes and shielded themselves with the polished cuirasses that had been molded to each of their frames. Each of their robes continued to gently sway in the night air as these aerial beings regained their composure and quickly formed a circle. Sitting directly across from the main doors of the cinema (nearly choking on his last bite), Harvey was in a state of pure shock as he dove from his wooden stool and slipped on the greasy floor behind the counter. Panting, Harvey dared to peek over the counter again, his mouth still full. Wiping the crumbs off his thick mustache, Harvey daringly crawled to the wooden column closest to the lobby doors. Our dear Harvey's alarmed eyes watched as these *unbelievable* creatures stood in the wet street. As the winged troupe bowed to one another as though they had not seen each other in several years, one of their numbers gave a quick glance over its broad shoulder to detect any potential eyewitnesses.

"Welcome, my old comrades," said a male Member first, scanning his company with the apparent ability to sense every carefully hidden identity beneath their silvery masks. "Good to have you here, Trevis."

"Good to see you once again, Lawrence," nodded Trevis Sacreen, noticeably the shortest member.

"A pleasure, as always, Ms. Mellya Allowin," said Lawrence,

eyeing his companion. The troupe quickly exchanged their greetings as Lawrence came forward. "It's been exactly ten years," said Lawrence, calmly, "to the date tonight that we, the members of the Divine Seraphion Society, repelled the remaining foul ways of the once feared, Dark Alman—a terrible force that stole the lives of our sacred kind in the most diabolical acts of evil. Together, my fellow grand union, *we* still stand."

"Tonight we look upon only the greatest of all things—the birth of an innocent and healthy baby," said one of their numbers, grandly. The six circling members eyed one another through the thin slits of their masks as a female Seraphion then stepped forward.

"Lawrence is right. We once stood against the *feared one* and its foolish Dark Seethers, we must continue as defenders for the imminent guardian." The woman took a step back as another female member came forward.

"At midnight, birth of the Cherished Guardian will bring a new manifesto for the preservation of the beauty and boundless freedom throughout our sacred Revlenion." The slender masked woman eyed the rest of her comrades, as they nodded in agreement. Lawrence came forward again, his black-gloved hands on his sides.

"What's to be the name of the guardian, Mellya?" asked Lawrence.

"That's still unclear, even from great foretelling—we don't know if it will be a boy or a girl, all that we have come to accept is that the child will be born a *star*," Mellya revealed, while her troupe leaned in with a heightening curiosity, "the very star that our wish will claim tonight. We wish with all our might that the guardian is to be born during the first hour of this land's twenty-eighth day of November."

"Such a blessed wish for the mother and father," agreed Lawrence.

"However, we must not be so quick with this, lest we forget—we're all aware of the bitter one that still lurks. He, along with countless other fiends, will no doubt stalk tonight and the days to come," said Trevis, quickly. "For the birth of our guardian will ignite an unwelcomed strike against us."

"The child's presence is near," said Mellya, eyeing the long ticking hands on the clock tower.

"That is why we have come here tonight," said Lawrence, encouraging his ring, "members, tonight we stand against any foes that may come across us here. We must take a stand for the cherished one, whom has yet to understand its powerful heart and mind. We cannot let the fatal mistakes of our history repeat in any form. We *must* be ready this time. Come together, and let us gift the gentle soul of the Cherished Guardian."

As the members exchanged their last pleasantries, unbeknownst to our winged creatures, a pair of watchful and violent eyes gleamed in the night. Yet so still, and remaining hidden there, the man-with-the-violent-eyes kept crouched atop of the cinema's marquee above the members, listening closely and all while taking in information that it deemed important. Its hot breath misted into the cold night as its fierce eyes quietly observed the Seraphions: extending each of their satin robed arms to the center of the circle, the six hands met as a smoky green rope-like tendril emerged from the air. Roping their wrists together, three elite members began:

"I, Mellya Allowin, present the *first gift* to the Cherished Guardian: whenever you are lost at land and wish to ascend the clouds above, I wish you the ability to soar," she said, nodding to another grand member.

"I, Trevis Sacrecn, present the *second gift* to the Cherished Guardian: whenever you wish to protect others and shield their hearts from darkness, I wish you the Bow of Sagenimus," he said, then nodded.

"And I, Lawrence Efelry, present the *third gift* to the Cherished Guardian: whenever you should have to face a mighty threat and must enter into battle, I wish you the ability to draw your finest Anglix."

After the members wished the final gift, emerald orbs began to slowly swim from each of their silver plated chests, curling in the air like blooming jellyfish. The orbs then melded as one in the center of the circle until their ultimate and luminous piece began to swirl and fuse, but after one, electrifying flash that erupted out of nowhere, the rope binding the members suddenly snapped, sending the entire troupe careening with a blast in all directions on the wet road. The orb of illustrious wishes began to whistle the most startling cry as it swirled once more, mutating into a repulsive sphere of black mold. The rope that had bound our members together fell to the cracked pavement and was nothing more than a snake of ash. Lawrence roared with anger as he and the rest of his troupe balanced themselves with their wings spanned and watched helplessly as their delicate orb evaporated with a hiss into the bitter night air.

"That sweet cry of death, *how I love it,*" a sour voice cracked in the darkness, as the sound of a man's effortless claps echoed while his eyes blazed from the shadows. The Seraphions then turned to the young man standing behind them: the barefooted man emerged from under a thick tree as the sidewalk lamp above him glazed its moon-like palette across his slit-scarred face, and he finally revealed himself from under his tattered, black hood. The members suddenly shifted their bodies, immediately recognizing the disturbed man. "Baffled? You waste of lives—I was hoping to be greeted like an old friend, tonight. Oh, how I've *deeply* missed you all," sneered the scarred-face Man.

As the scarred-faced-man took a steady step forward, flexing his dirty toes across the frigid street pavement, the troupe exchanged quick glances and carefully began to bunch together, crushing the space between them. All appeared to be on edge, as though they knew this man very well and his deviant ways.

"Vizton Eplaville, we are never surprised by you or your vain acts of deviousness—that is why you bear your scars," said Lawrence, condescendingly.

"Come now, Lawrence, you should know better than to poke fun about my scars. They're not entirely my fault," scowled Vizton Eplaville, as he could only stick his pointy nose up at the divine leader. Vizton stood there, shifting his disturbed eyes from one creature to the other as he combed back his long and greasy brown hair with his filthy fingertips.

"This must be your third escape from Wenslue, no?" said a gallant female Seraphion, eyeing the **W** emblem and prisoner number patched against Eplaville's filthy black and white striped uniform that carelessly peeked out from under his black cloak. "Still in your asylum garb, it seems."

"And not before long will you be back in your quiet cell, Vizton," hissed Mellya. Vizton lunged forward at the gallant female member, but before he could even reach for her throat, the Seraphions expanded their long wings as a sign of caution. Vizton knew he had nearly broken one of the highest laws between him and the society.

"Hold your tongue, Mellya," said Vizton, recognizing her voice from under her mask, pointing like a cautious troll at the Seraphion. "Have you forgotten what happened to your brother when he thought his slick words could meet with mine? I'll never forget that moment with your brother because I still have his handsome head." With a snap, a small, dark swirl morphed into a wet black sack in Vizton's hand. "Feast your eyes on this!" chuckled Vizton, as he heaved the sack to Mellya's feet, coming to a thud on the street pavement.

Mellya's horrified eyes bulged through the tiny slits of her polished mask, believing the sack that rolled before her feet to be containing that of the head to her deceased brother. Instead, the morbid bag began to bounce and toss around, until the tie around it lashed open. The dozen or more hiss-giggling and nibble-eared nagglies launched out of the bag like a cannon of fiendish confetti. The slender and red golf-ball-eyed manic hare-like creatures balanced with a scuttle on their two clawed feet. The Seraphions either kicked with their thick boots or whipped with their giant wings at the hideous, tiny-mouthed creatures that scampered in circles around them. Mellya watched as a naggley dared to claw at one of her fellow members until all of the patch-haired creatures scurried into the courthouse gardens, pairs of them cartwheeling across the main lawns as they absconded.

"You're a *cruel* monster," Mellya spat.

"Thank you, I presume that after three years wrapped in pure darkness, the best of us turn out a bit monstrous," said Vizton, as he then took another step forward.

"Why this night?" said Lawrence coming close with Vizton. "What do you seek for *him*? That one you praise to be great."

Their eyes met: beaming back at each other like two wolves in the fervor of a fight.

"Like before, Lawrence, the Dark Alman wishes to learn about the manifesto of this so-called Cherished Guardian," said Vizton, rolling his eyes.

"You *still* believe in his keeping after all these years? Knowing he met his eternal imprisonment years ago, at the hands of other guardians, no less?" said Lawrence incredulously....

And at that same moment, Harvey, our extremely curious and frightened janitor, was on the ends of his nervous toes. Crouching, Harvey remembered that there was a telephone in the ticket booth. Every part of his husky body wanted to crawl to that booth and call the police, but would they believe him? Every indecisive second that followed, all Harvey wanted to do was race to the booth and seize the telephone. As Harvey found the courage in himself, all the while his late-night lunch churning in his belly, the man with a scarred face turned toward the glass doors. Harvey swore they had finally found him out...

"...Or so you believe, Lawrence," said Vizton as he turned away from where Lawrence stood, speaking with a tone of warning. "It seems as though the leader of the divine society has forgotten how much power the Dark Alman still possesses...even in his highest vulnerability." Vizton abruptly glared into the shadows that rested beyond the locked glass doors of the cinema, closely scanning the emptiness for any sneaks. He then whipped around, facing Lawrence again. "Never forget how some manifestos from our country tend to have two sides to them," said Vizton, inching closer to his opponent. "The only side of this manifesto Revlenion will know is how you and your futile mob met their end as they bowed to me and to the words of a Dark Seether...."

With another flash, Vizton snapped his fingers as eight violent black streams of electricity grew from his fingertips. The Seraphions then began to flutter their wings, readying their stances once more; Lawrence made a circuitous gesture with his hand, and his cohorts followed suit. Instantaneously: six flawless and steel infused crystal swords formed out of thin air and clasped into each of the members' tight fists. The supporting members were ready for Vizton's next move and formed into a semi-circle with Lawrence, with his own magnificent sword out at Vizton.

"I give you your last warning," forbade Lawrence, "do *not* believe our patience will weather another strike against us. Be gone, and never test the laws of Revlenion, again."

"The child that has been immortalized in manifesto will see life tonight. I have no power vested in me to stop that. Let the years go on, and your little guardian will meet the beauties of my kind, and that is when we'll happily slay your cherished filth," seethed Vizton. "The power I do, in fact, have at this moment will be enough...to put you all out of *my* misery."

As Lawrence's sword and Vizton's electricity met, the electric lashes suddenly cracked into the night sky, sending down a stronger bolt from the roiling clouds above. Lawrence kept a tight grip around the hilt of his sword, trying to repel the splintering bolts. With every blocked projectile, Lawrence could see reflected in his pristine blade his Seraphion union falling prey to the violent snake-like streams ricocheting away. The silvers that the remaining Seraphions wore began to double as a deadly conductor for Vizton's attack, transmuting their divinely robed bodies into a thin halo of ash. Vizton relished the horrific tableau he had wrought witnessing the divine creatures wither before him and as their masks melted at the very scene that left only the scarcest of traces to their ever existence.

Each stream of electricity bounced uncontrollably from the swords of the members until they, too, wilted as each Seraphion, in turn, perished. Vizton's streams continued to lash at everything in their destructive path. The street lamps grew brighter and brighter until almost every bulb exploded. The cinema's marquee lights sparked and shattered. The windshields of cars parked along the street burst into pieces.

Lawrence was now alone—so he thought—still holding strong with his sword out as his only shield.

"How dare you," Lawrence gritted through his mask, carefully inching toward Vizton who was now gleefully displaying a yellowish grin. With every carefully timed step Lawrence made, the building heat from his blade began to crawl down into its grip, leaving him to endure the searing pain that grew in his grasp.

"My friend," Vizton sighed, feeling a growing pulse between them as he adroitly focused his electric lashes into one malevolent force, hissing once more, "the Dark Alman has asked me to deliver this message: *I* am the Cherished Guardian..."

"Stop this at once!" roared Harvey, armed with only his brave sight and half of his thick body warily poking out from behind the ticket booth.

It was Vizton who fell distracted by the ordinary man that dared to break the scene. And at that very second, Harvey watched as the scarred-faced-man lashed at him, but a quick, defiant slash of Lawrence's sword rebounded the electric whip back at Vizton. Lawrence watched Vizton Eplaville toss and turn on the wet road and seethe with curses under his breath as he struggled to return to his feet. Vizton watched Lawrence's swan-like wings unravel from his robes that swayed in the chill wind and with his sword tenaciously at the ready. Harvey dove back behind the booth again, astounded at himself for bravely intervening. Without daring another peek from behind the narrow booth, Harvey's heart raced as he could now see the shadowy outlines of the two creatures that cast against the wide wall above the lobby doors and charging toward each other as a lambent light began to encompass them. After one last blinding wave of fantastic light…the two creatures disappeared.

Any common storyteller might wish to dream up such a tale for the next chapter in their never-ending story, but our Harvey had actually witnessed it all. Taking the key ring from his handy belt, not realizing, out of pure nervousness, that the window on the ticket booth had shattered away entirely, he then collected his senses and reached for the telephone that he so longed. It was useless; the cord that it once connected to in the booth had been seared to a crisp, as was the rest of the aged interior of the booth having suffered the scarred-faced-man's furor. Instead, Harvey walked across the sidewalk that had been now scattered with hundreds of tiny blue movie tickets. Harvey reached the spotted pavement in front of his cinema, little patches of fire from the electric assault dotted all along the main road. Harvey scratched the bald patch on the top of his head wondering, how was ever going to explain this scene to anyone? The marquee and its decorative lights had all shattered. Every other street lamp was burnt, broken, or blackened like the thin scorch marks on almost every building in sight. Harvey had never believed in the unnatural, until now. He couldn't stop spinning around noticing new pieces of shattered glass or the licks of fire trailing along the sidewalks. Harvey would never come to understand the happenings of that night, but could only gaze helplessly at the night sky and stars that blanketed above him. As brave-old-Harvey glanced up at the star-lit sky, hoping to catch one last glimpse of those two creatures, the courthouse clock peacefully chimed the midnight hour. The birth of the Cherished Guardian had come at last.

CHAPTER TWO

THE WONDERS OF POPLAR DRIVE

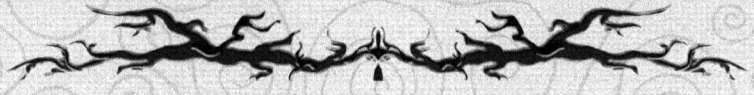

JULY 1988

There is a place, just off Islay Road, which many who know of it maintain is a hidden gem…a road, as it were. Any visitor to the seaside town of San Luis Obispo might easily miss the turn on to the secluded drive. It is true that the soaring oaks that swathe the street do obscure the road from view, but when you drive between the trees, there rests Poplar Drive, and *just* beyond its verdant gate of close-knit branches is a world of its very own. Every house on the drive has a welcoming presence, and every sight of the neighborhood looked as if not a delicate stem were permitted to go untrimmed. Each house was sprinkled with comely gardens that weaved before several wide patios and long, emerald lawns. On both sides of the street were arching rows of more tangled oaks, causing a tunnel of pleasant shade all the way down to the very end of the drive.

During the summer nights, the road fills with children lighting noisy fireworks or gathering for midnight rounds of hide-and-seek. Christmastime on Poplar Drive unquestionably called for strands of crystal lights, wrapped around every leafless branch, washing the road in festive radiance. Poplar Drive could've actually been an artist's living canvas, believe it or not.

And on top of all that comeliness about Poplar Drive that

stretched on through to its cul-de-sac, one could find the infamous silver lamppost. Unlike the rest of the stubby streetlights that sat between the arches of the towering oaks, this lamppost had quite the history. Last spring, teenagers Ian Flemm and Edith Whar shared their first kiss under the lamp's relatively romantic light, until a pack of hyena-cackling neighborhood kids ended their spectacular moment with flying water-balloons and rotten eggs. The silver lamppost was also the permanent safe spot during any street game for the neighborhood children, and it was also the lamppost that stood at the base of the most talked about house amongst the children. For years, it had been the house no child dared to stop by on Halloween or dare each other ring the doorbell and run. And even though this tale has already revealed the charming details about the homes that lined the drive, it would be remiss of this story not to mention that it was the *only* abandoned home: a forgotten house. Quite unlike the pretty details surrounding the other warm and inviting structures that sheltered full families (ones that have for some odd reason kept their curious eyes on the deserted place for nearly a decade). A mirror image to the silver lamppost, the house at 1245 Poplar Drive was known for its macabre past.

It was a quarter past eleven in the morning, and the Tuolumnes had been traveling south from Salinas, finally making their arrival to our familiar seaside town, and here their curious tale was about to begin....

Behind the wheel of a 1970 red Dodge Challenger, and in the midst of searching for Poplar Drive, Aunt Marion Tracey was humming along to *I'll Be Your Mirror* by The Velvet Underground that oozed from the car radio. While squinting through her cat-frame eyeglasses at passing street signs, her ten-year-old niece, Makari Tuolumne, began with a peculiar query:

"Tell me again, Aunt Marion," said Makari, as she folded her prized red diary in her lap, "the house we're driving to, it once belonged to our grandparents?"

"That's right, your father's parents. You might already know this, but it was your father's childhood home," said Marion, after a great yawn, noticing the paper-coffee cup in her hand was nearly empty. "He and your mother grew up in this town together."

"I remember some of the stories you once told me," said Makari.

"Which stories?" asked Aunt Marion, grinning.

"You know, like the one of how our mom and dad met," Makari giggled, as she glanced over her shoulder at her older brother, Landon, the messy hazelnut-haired boy, who had nestled his short body in the back seat and had not uttered a single word since they departed Salinas, and that was nearly three hours ago.

Our Landon and Makari were around three-years-apart, but if you placed them side-by-side, they looked *almost* identical. Makari's red hair kept brushing against her freckled nose while she stuck her head out the car window, swallowing breaths of the warm air and gazing at the new surroundings with her piercing, blue eyes. Landon eyed this new world around him through tired green eyes, shuffling his hair as he sat restlessly and yearning for this car ride to end. Landon and Makari's aunt, however, looked nothing like our curious siblings. She was a hive-haired woman, and quite stubby, like a walking pastel wedding cake, though it didn't matter to Marion Tracey what anyone thought of her. Marion was content to see her world through her purple-mascaraed black eyes. After a near howling yawn, Aunt Marion returned to her thoughts.

"Oh, those old fairy tales," said Marion, after a pensive deliberation with a risen eyebrow above her eyeglasses, "old tales, my honey, that I am too tired to recite now."

"You know I love hearing them," murmured Makari, resting her chin in her hand while she traced her sights eagerly on the passing homes.

"Well, I believe we should be coming up to the drive, right about…now," said Marion.

Turning on to the old, shrouded road, Makari fell into a trance. Marion could agree with Makari, there was gentle sense of allure in the swaying oaks. "Isn't this place wonderful, Landon?" asked Marion, eyeing the perfect houses.

"Sure," shrugged Landon, as he shoved an elbow into his aunt's oddly shaped suitcases next to him.

"Don't be such a crab. Are you still upset that you lost, yet again, at our game of rock-paper-scissors?" hummed Makari. In order to allow fair chances, Landon and Makari always found it necessary to engage in such a game, if—let's say—either wanted the center seat in the aisle of the movie theater they attended, one would have to draw the best hand in a round. Like, whoever lost on Monday nights would have to brave the trek with the *always* inconveniently torn garbage bag out to the backyard trash bin, all while fearing the idea that some kind of crude monster might giggle at them from the darkness that loomed near the garden hedges.

"Absolutely…*not*," groaned Landon, as he lunged his knee into the back of his sister's front seat. "I *love it* back here."

"Come on, Landon, have a look," cheered Makari, pointing at the Poplar Drive children riding their bicycles, "it's so pretty here."

"Pretty boring…I bet the neighbors are boring too, and uptight as well," said Landon, turning his head to view the passing houses. "It's not like back home, it wasn't so annoyingly perfect looking."

"Oh, stop, Landon. I'm sure the neighbors are very welcoming," cooed Marion.

"M," Landon continued as he freed himself from the cluster of luggage, abbreviating his sister's name as he always did when he felt it necessary, "I'm sure there's a crazy old hag that lives next door to one of these houses. I bet when a family moves in, she's quick to welcome them to the neighborhood with little pink cupcakes on a platter, and then in about a week, she starts spying on them."

"Landon, don't be so melodramatic," said Marion.

"I'm not, you know it's true," tossed Landon.

"Well then, wait until these little yokels set their sights on pretty ole' me," chuckled Aunt Marion. As Marion continued to drive down the peaceful road, there at its end was *the* house. "See that lamppost?"

said Marion, as she eyed our siblings, "we're here."

Coming to a stop just below the silver lamppost, the three unbuckled themselves and stepped outside of the car.

"Has this place ever been up for sale?" said Makari, as she swung around the stem of the silver lamppost.

"Maybe at one time or another, though I can't quite recall when. Your father at some point decided to just keep the house within the family, though" said Marion, examining the gopher holes in the dying lawn. "Good thing, too."

Pacing their steps toward the front door, Landon and Makari couldn't help but stare at the dark enormity of the house; as old as the town itself, this dilapidated, two-story country villa stood fairly slender and longed for a new coat of paint. The face of the house stood in stark contrast to the other modest abodes on Poplar Drive. Unlike its neighbors, this house welcomed them with unkempt shrubs that weaved and patched through a flowerless, pebble stone garden that snaked near the front door, and remained disturbingly hidden between the twin weeping willows that nearly blanketed the entire rooftop. Coming to the front door, Marion took from her triangular purse an old ring of keys and proceeded to unlock the door (with a bit of a fuss to wiggle the lock) precipitating a massive creak as the great cedar slab edged open. "Who wants to enter first?" said Marion, with a bouncy jaunt in her throat.

Makari grinned as she gave Landon a push on his back and then followed him through the threshold. As Makari was about to enter, she glanced over her shoulder: as many children as there were parading up and down the drive, she noticed that none seemed to venture anywhere near the house, or even acknowledge the presence of the family moving in. After a simple shrug, Makari followed after her aunt inside.

The foyer was damp, dark and had been horribly neglected for nearly a decade. As Marion pointed out, there were three branching hallways that led to separate sections on the first floor: to the immediate left was an eloquent dining room; a quick right led to the modest study room, and following the path forward, would be the family sitting room. Above them in the center, rigged by a single frail wire, was a heavy marble-glass chandelier that now housed little more than layers upon layers of abandoned cobwebs.

"Oh, many, many years it's been since I've stepped into this house," said Marion, bittersweet. "I believe the last time was when you were born, Landon."

Each of them had decided to explore the rooms on their own: Makari wheeled right, entering the study. The study room was generously apportioned: a large chesterfield sofa rested in the center of the room, facing the thick writing desk that sat just before the nook window that, in turn, surveyed the front lawn. Makari peered through the swaying vale of branchlets from the willow tree outside. Makari then spun on a heel, her eyes reeling with fascination at not only the sight of the two in-the-wall bookshelves that towered over her, but at the old grand piano that hid underneath a still dust blanket.

Makari had grown into a liking for pianos over the years; after having brief moments inside the music room at her previous school. Her mother and father took notice, of course, and surprised Makari with a baby-grand piano of her very own: turquoise with funny gold finishing around the box. Unfortunately, Makari lost her prized piano when…a certain, dark event occurred on a late November evening nearly one year ago. The very occurrence was the sort that brought Makari and her brother to the house they were in the midst of having to become familiar with or, as her brother dreaded, to call it their *new home*. Softly dancing her fingers over the treble clef keys was enough to crush Makari's hopes, as the miraculously in-tune keys unhinged Makari's carefully kept composer. Just hearing the octave come alive after a tap on the key played Makari's last memory of her parent's in her head like a never-ending horror film—and she was the star of the movie. So, Makari pulled herself away from the keyboard and instead glanced over the titles along the bookshelves across from her and the quiet piano.

"At least they enjoyed the classics," murmured Makari, praising her grandparents' collection of fine literature, as she trailed a finger across the dusty spines of the hardcover books.

Marion found her way through the main hallway, pulling off a sheet from one of the paintings that hung on the cold wall. The shroud fell away, revealing an exceptional landscape painting of a grassy valley that depicted two leafless trees, entwining their branches into a swaying yet lifeless dance, and peeking through the lock of branches were two beaming orbs, a sun and a blooming moon.

"It's beautiful, who painted it?" asked Makari, as she came beside her aunt.

"A genius did," said Marion, as she then hovered a finger just over the oil brush strokes. "I gave this painting to your grandparents as a gift after I curated it at my private studio back in New York City, years ago…and don't you dare ask how many years."

"What is it called, again, what *you do* exactly?" queried Makari.

"I am—was—an Art Curator. Though in recent times, my eyes and age have caught up to me, I unfortunately don't find the love in it anymore," said Marion, as she realigned the wooden frame. "Nowadays, I'm content in only collecting as many rare pieces of art as I can." Makari then noticed initials at the bottom right corner of the painting:

A.G.

"Was this shack this bad when it was last lived in?" said Landon, wiping away an irritating strand of cobwebs, circling around the long dining room table and then rejoining the others in the main hall.

"Oh," gasped Marion from the hallway, "of course not. When your grandmother was alive, dust never had a chance in this house. I remember a tale your grandmother once recited at a dinner party, long ago, when he was younger than you, Landon…there was this one time, and I do mean one time, your father thought it'd be funny to chase the neighbor's mud-bathed dog through the house."

"That's something Landon would surely do," laughed Makari, as the three continued to the archway at the end of the main hall.

As Landon and Makari followed after their aunt out of the art draped hallway and at times feeling bends and creaks through their shoes from the floor's wooden panels, the three now made way into the sitting room, seeing all the dormant furniture had also been concealed with dusty sheets. It was a quaint sitting room: nestled in the room's corner was a marvelous granite fireplace and just before it was what seemed to be a circular coffee table, two (hopefully comfy) long, aged leather couches, and a reading chair that had all been pushed to the center of the room.

"It's as though someone knew we would be moving in," said Landon. "You know, preserving everything in a kind of way."

"Your parents fixed everything with all these drapes after your grandparents passed on," said Marion, trekking across from the family room to the kitchen, while eyeing the tangled backyard through the pair of glass doors beside the kitchen's archway.

A tarnished chaotic twin to the common room's order, the kitchen was small and cluttered. Bronze cooking pots and pans hung from a steel rack that dangled along the ceiling directly above a square cooker's island, and just a few steps in the corner of the kitchen was a narrow flight of stairs that ascended to the second floor.

Makari then rounded the island, after begin the first to examine the tiny kitchen, as she then peered through the small window above the sink, noticing a mossy pond in the backyard that had become overrun by crawling ivy. Makari then looked down into the sink, jumping at the sight of a fat-bottomed spider crawling up out of the drain.

"Yuck. No water," said Makari, twisting the faucet knobs.

"I'm sure we can survive one night without," said Marion.

"What about...the toilets?" probed Makari.

"We shall improvise. It'll be as though we're out camping!" quipped Marion, as her niece then tossed a wry grin back at her. "The water should be running by tomorrow morning, don't worry. Well," Marion hummed, continuing, "what do you two think of your new home?"

"I love it," said Makari, clapping her hands on her sides. "I feel like we've just stepped into one of Edgar Allan Poe's dreary scenes."

"You can't be serious, Makari?" sighed Landon. "This place...this...*shack* cannot be called our home."

"Well, you better get used to it, Landon, it's going to be your home for a long time," said Marion, tapping her hand on the cooker's island.

"Whatever, it'll never be anything like back home," sneered Landon, rolling his eyes.

"Landon, there isn't anything for you back there...that house doesn't even exist anymore—this is yours now," said Marion, gripping Landon's shoulder, while circling her sights around the dingy room.

"What you have here is all that *truly* remains with us as a family."

"I just don't understand why we had to leave everything we owned behind," groaned Landon.

"Landon, listen, you and your sister were still allowed to bring a few of your most precious items along, but we *had* to let everything else go, so that the both of you could let it all fall with the past," said Marion, softly. "What you have here is everything to build a new life."

"—This place is from *your* past! It'll be easy for you." Landon then realized his voice was raised as he then took a step to the side away from his aunt.

"Landon, it's...it's for the best," pleaded Marion. Landon could only look his aunt in the eyes and shrug. Landon knew deep down inside, as he retraced his steps toward the car, there wouldn't be a way to return to what he called 'home' that once stood many, many miles away.

"Landon, Aunt Marion's right, you know," said Makari, hurrying behind her brother. "It's not entirely bad, it really isn't."

"M, I just don't know how to explain it," sighed Landon, on the verge of tears, "I had such hopes with everything." Makari eyed her brother closely as he rested against their father's old Challenger.

"I miss mom and dad, too, Lan," said Makari, as she took hold of her brother's hand and smiled.

"I just can't believe how it'll be a year in November…on my birthday, since…*that night*," said Landon.

"You don't have to speak about it, you know how it makes me feel," sighed Makari.

"I'm sorry, it's just that I can't ever stop thinking about what happened and what it has done to us. To also think of all the friends and belongings we had to leave behind. I feel as though Aunt Marion wants us to pretend our lives in Salinas and…*that night*…never happened," said Landon.

"That's not true, Landon, *I'm* still here…I was there, too. I believe Aunt Marion wants what's best, that's all," said Makari.

"You're just like mom was, always the first one with your chin up," grinned Landon, as his sister's face blossomed a smile. "You're right," sniffled Landon, "if we held together through what happened to us back at 510 Kirkwood, then I suppose we can get through this."

"Could this be the worst summer, ever?" huffed Makari, as she then joined with her brother for a lean against the car, sharing a half-sighing chuckle.

"It could be worse…it really could be worse," said Landon, as he and his sister then eyed the gloomy façade of their new home on Poplar Drive.

The Tuolumnes were starting over, and spending the next cool summer afternoons with their aunt transforming their new house into a home was their first step. Starting with downstairs: Aunt Marion and Landon were removing the thick, dust-heavy sheets off every piece of furniture as they began to rearrange the family room to their liking, while Makari was busy tiptoeing on a wobbly stool, dusting the hanging pots and pans. Ascending the stairs that rested at the corner of the kitchen, the Tuolumnes had their work cut out for them on the second floor. Aunt Marion took to the master bedroom, while Landon and Makari went on with their usual quick draw of *rock-paper-scissors* in a contest to see which of them would win the larger room of the two. Landon won the larger room at the end of the hall, nearest to the street, which turned out to be just the right size for him.

As he began to examine his new dusty room and the bookshelf, banners, and writing desk that collected along the walls, Landon could feel the sudden comforting warmth grow deep within his stomach, knowing that this was once the room his father had grown up in. Landon admired the wall-pinned collection of classic movie posters he immediately recognized: *7th Voyage of Sinbad*, *Yojimbo*, and *A Fistful of Dollars*. As Landon traced a few fingers along the aged posters, he began to remember the times his father would pick him up early from school, and together on the sly they would venture to the downtown Fox Theater, hoping to catch the matinee for either a Science-fiction, double feature or a gun-slinging afternoon marathon of old spaghetti westerns. No matter how stale the popcorn was or how many times the projector would wrap up and spark into a celluloid jam, Landon knew, even then, to cherish every moment of their cinema escapes.

Prompted by the band posters that lined either side of the room, Landon was reminded of a time he once knew: when he, his father and sister would blare old records by David Bowie or Queen long into the wee hours of the night, betting on who could sing the longest and loudest until one of them forgot the lyrics entirely. After setting aside his luggage trunk, Landon sat at the foot of the bed, not minding the popped box springs; he then noticed the white tips to a pair of shoes peeking out from under the bed. They were a classic and worn pair of Chuck Taylor Converse, size ten, and with his father's nearly faded away name, Aiden, that had been scribbled on the inside tongues of the shoes. Landon kicked off his brand new shoes and quickly laced the old pair on. *Perfect*, Landon thought, even though he could feel a fair bit of wiggle room at the tip of his big toe.

"It's funny that you'd win this room, over the other," said Aunt Marion, leaning against the bedroom's doorframe.

"Funny? Sort of, I was just thinking that, maybe," Landon turned away from his aunt and stood from the bed and peered out the window at the base of the room. "Maybe, everything *will* be alright."

"And everything will, we just have to give it time, that's all," said Marion, placing her hands on either side of her nephew's shoulders, "you're home now."

"Aunt Marion! I need your help in here!" called Makari from her room, as the sound of a dozen books came crashing down on the bedroom floor.

"Now, let me just go help your sister."

By the week's end, and now in the first, blistering days of August, our new Poplar Drive residents had now reignited their house with a soul again, for which it had been longing for many years. Our siblings and their Aunt Marion had transformed the once cobwebbed cavern into something habitable. Landon had unpacked his clothes and restored his father's old room from top to bottom and made it his own. Makari had also nestled herself in her cozy bedroom with the help from her aunt: replacing the shelves that were once nailed to the wall and stocking them with her most prized collection of literature that had passed down to her from her brother. It was a peculiar line of literature that had a special meaning to Makari; such books that included L. Frank Baum, Edward Gorey, and Diana Wynne Jones. Makari could never go without those three authors; at least one of their books traveled with her like a lung wherever she went. All her books were alphabetically aligned with surviving pictures—happy ones that allowed Makari to remember past summer vacations with her family, the one she once knew—and precious trinkets and seashells that basked in sunlight near her bedroom windowpane.

While Landon and his aunt gathered the last of the trash bags after having piled them in the foyer waiting to be tossed outside from past days of cleaning. Makari was tidying up the last details of her room, gathering a box of old pieces of paper and broken antiques that she found scattered around the room while cleaning from the day before. In spite of the fact that it was slightly heavy for her, Makari was determined to carry the box downstairs herself. After a few unbalanced steps out of her room, though, the bottom of the box collapsed, releasing an avalanche of broken china and blankets of dust in the middle of the hallway.

"Of course!" grunted Makari, carefully kneeling down to pick up the bothersome mess with a few quick sneezes when a haze of dust danced across her face. Through her watery eyes, Makari noticed the small, music jewelry box that she had decided to throw away (after a bookshelf in her room collapsed and shattered the spinning porcelain ballerina inside) had split open to reveal a thin compartment under the pink wooden box. Makari examined the long green ribbon that poked out the box, taking it out completely, until finding a small note had been clipped to it:

Because I knew you would take care of it

Makari hummed, peculiarly, as she folded up the strange note and set aside the box, and as she combed a wisp of her curly red hair behind her ear, the thought occurred to her, *why not?* Measuring the tips of the green ribbon together until it was even, she flipped her hair forward and then back again, adjusting the ribbon into a hairband until it fit perfectly. As Makari checked her work in the oval mirror of the broken jewelry box, there came a sudden thunder of movement from the ceiling, like a large chair being pushed aside on a hardwood floor. Makari quickly reeled her head back, taking notice of what seemed to be an attic trap door above her.

After a week, you'd think one of us would have seen this? Makari thought. She then realized that wasn't a sound coming from downstairs, as she first suspected; the unnerving rumble had emanated from above in the attic.

"Makari, are you going to bring down your box of trash this century?" said Landon, as he climbed the kitchen stairs. As he reached the top of the stairs, Landon found his sister with her gaze locked on the ceiling.

"Did you ever notice this door?" asked Makari, pointing up at the ceiling.

29

"No…that sure is strange though, there's no string to pull a ladder down either," observed Landon.

"I could've sworn I just heard something move up there," said Makari, still pointing. Landon tilted his head at his sister's fixation.

"I have an idea."

Taking the wooden desk chair from his bedroom, Landon placed the chair on top of the mess his sister had abandoned the task of cleaning. With a slight balancing act and a devilish grin, Landon stretched a long arm up to check if the attic pull-strand had been cut-away.

"Do you hear anything?" said Makari, eyeing the door suspiciously, as if waiting for a creature to break through the ceiling at any moment that would devour both of them whole.

"No, I don't hear anything, but who would put a lock on an attic door?" said Landon, noticing not a strand to pull, but only a small lock as he traced his index finger around the mouth of the keyhole. "Are you sure you heard something up here?"

"I'm positive I heard a noise, and I'm sure our grandparents put a lock on it, just my guess," said Makari, as she held onto her brother's legs to help keep him balanced.

"Haha, Makari, the 'noise in the attic' trick in an old house, clever one," Landon laughed, noticing his sister rolling her eyes with annoyance. "But still, I've never known any house to have a locked attic door—strange."

"Well, for good reason, I suppose. Keeping whatever might be up there locked away," said Makari pointing up at the ceiling, again, while her brother leapt from atop the chair.

"Yes, more and more useless antiques, deadly ones!" said Landon, lunging out his hands in a monster like manner.

"Trust me, Lan, I know what I heard."

"M, this is an old house…the only movement you'll hear is the sound of termites gorging away at the ceiling. Anyway, the door obviously needs a key—the house key?" said Landon, snapping his fingers.

"Possibly," said Makari, returning to the piled mess in the middle of the hallway.

"I'll have Aunt Marion take a look at it—where'd you get the string?" said Landon, tapping the ribbon in his sister's hair.

"It's not a string, it's a cute little ribbon," scoffed Makari, "I found it."

"Sure…" nodded Landon, as he helped his sister clean up the last of the box trash in the middle of the hall. Together, they took to the stairs, as Makari gave one last look up at the attic door before following her brother downstairs.

▼

In the absence of even the barest whisk of delightful ocean breeze, the summer weather that afternoon had heated up to absurdly high levels, even for late August, as the disgruntled weatherman apologetically reported. ("Phew! Ladies and gents, boys and girls— we're cookin' up a hot one today!"). Aunt Marion could barely keep herself focused while she read from a book she found in the study; she seemed trapped in a never-ending cycle of fanning herself with a lace hand fan one moment and gulping down the endlessly refilling iced tea that was ever close at hand the next, then repeating. Aunt Marion anchored herself next to the old radio she found in the garage as she ran through this cycle, gently tuning in and out of the static-bathed weather station or the one that was playing Curtis Mayfield's *Move On Up*, still hoping to hear of cooler weather on the loom. Either way, it was the clearest weather the Tuolumnes had been graced with for some time. Back in Salinas, the months of June and July were outright dismal for the Tuolumnes; their summer days had either been stifled with unusually low temperatures or encompassed with scattered thunderstorms and an oppressive blanket of the grayest clouds imaginable that kept them from journeying to the nearby beach.

As Aunt Marion gathered ideas for dinner that night, Landon and Makari collected the trashcans from the garage for tomorrow's garbage pick-up. The summer evening was finally creeping over Poplar Drive as a long overdue cool breeze licked Landon and Makari while they busily housed the two trash barrels on the street curb. Together, they noticed the stubby street lamps flickering on, one by one, like a choreographed dance, reaching its peak as their own private silver lamppost began to twinkle with a snap.

"Hello," squeaked a voice to the right of the siblings. Not at first noticing this chubby apparition on a small turquoise bike, Landon and Makari turned to the boy who smiled wide with a gap where his two-front-teeth should've been.

"Oh, hello," greeted Landon, for himself and his sister. Chewing his bubble gum with a smacking, gooey sound, the little boy tilted his baseball hat up and introduced himself.

"Derek Orror, welcome to Poplar Drive," he said, forcing a handshake out to our siblings, "oops—went down to the trench for frog catching!" Derek displayed his filthy palms proudly to the siblings as he propped his elbows on his handlebars. Makari and Landon wiped the sides of their jeans, forcing smiles.

"Nice to meet you, Derek. I'm Landon Tuolumne," he introduced, as his sister grinned in return, "and this is my sister, Makari. Do you live next door or around here?"

"Yeah," noted Derek, "I'm your next-door neighbor." Landon and Makari eyed the smallest and second-most unkempt house on the Drive.

"How old are you?" said Landon, eyeing the size of Derek's bike, compared to the size of the boy. Derek noticed.

"How old are you?" hummed Derek.

"Twelve, I'll be thirteen in November, " said Landon.

"I just turned ten, back in May," said Makari.

"Too old for me to play with…I'm only eight," grunted Derek, "oh, and three-quarters! My birthday is in October." Derek then came a bit closer, still holding onto his bike, and with a near whisper: "So, you two actually live there?" Landon eyed Derek's finger pointing up at the eerie face of the house.

"We moved in two weeks ago. It once belonged to our grandparent's; it's an inheritance," said Makari. "Why are you so shocked?"

"Inheritance? Do you two even know what happened in that house?" cringed Derek, still with his awkward whisper.

"What do you mean?" said Landon.

"I'm amazed you two are even still alive!" curdled Derek.

"Alive enough to be talking here with you!" said Landon, wondering why he was even continuing this absurd conversation with this boy.

"Wait, what do you mean by *what happened here?*" interjected Makari.

"*Awful things,*" said Derek, with a shake, "the older kids at school have teased me about it for the past two years...just because I live next door."

Landon quickly shifted his focus from just Derek to the boy's story. Landon could hear the genuine fear in the young boy's voice.

"What sort of awful things?" Landon asked.

"Nightmarish stuff! Why do you think it's so ugly?" Derek barked, jetting his eyes over at our sibling's house.

"The house has just been neglected, and has been that way since our grandparents died," said Makari, nodding her head at Derek.

"Good thing, too...being neglected, I mean," said Derek.

"Derek, nothing has happened here, trust us," said Landon, hopefully reassuring the frigid boy. Landon then noticed Derek's fellow neighborhood friends watching from a distance, swapping curious looks from behind one of the thick oaks. Realizing this boy was probably someone's poor messenger; Landon could only shake his head.

"You'll see, none of us kids ever set foot near this house and *especially* not on Halloween," warned Derek.

"I think your friends at school are just pulling your leg, a little too far," said Landon, signaling his sister to follow him back inside their house.

"No! I'm telling you," whimpered Derek, as he reached out for the siblings, allowing his bike to fall over on its side, "Who would want to live in a house where a murder happened?"

Landon and Makari stopped in their tracks and turned on their heels toward Derek one last time.

"A murder?" said Makari, with a slight sense of skepticism.

"My best-friend, Breny, *he* even told me so. He said he overheard his mom talk about it with one of her friends on the phone," said Derek.

"I think you heard the wrong story, Derek," said Landon, growing annoyed.

"Last summer, a few friends of mine decided to sleepover, hoping I'd dare one of them to walk up to your front door. We even stayed up past midnight, as the old story about the murder goes," said Derek, waving his hands in near excitement.

"Then what happened?" said Makari, still fascinated by Derek's tale.

"Well, my two friend's from summer camp had heard about the story...the wind that night was absolutely terrible as we snuck out of my bedroom window and crept across the lawn to get to your house. As we walked up on your front door, we quickly crossed your front lawn and hid behind that large tree there," Derek then gave a loud gulp, after eyeing one of the swaying willows. "And the next part—is the worst: as my friends argued about who would be the one to walk up to the front door. I noticed out of the corner of my left eye, a small light, coming from that room there," Derek was unknowingly pointing to the study room, "I thought, it had to be my imagination playing a trick on me. Thinking nothing of it, I whistled my friends to follow. As we tip-toed to the front door, we could hear a commotion inside the house, so we crept to that front window there—and together were these cloaked people—hopefully human—walking around with these odd looking flashlights...it was as though the light was beaming out of their own palms!"

"You can't be serious?" said Landon, eyeing his sister who seemed completely fascinated by Derek's ridiculous story.

"Did they notice you?" said Makari, encouraging Derek to continue his story.

"Not at first, but when my friends noticed the people walking around in that house, they went running back to my house like mice," said Derek, turning away from the siblings, reaching for his bike.

"Oh, and you mean to tell me your great bravery took over—you didn't run away too?" said Landon.

"I couldn't," Derek then swallowed his chewing gum with another loud gulp, "it was as though my feet were glued to the ground. I watched them walk around your house before they disappeared into the darkness. Three months later, the kind old couple in that house died. I've never dared to ride my bike anywhere near that house, until now, to warn you two."

"Derek, its time to come inside, hun!" a short woman from Derek's house called across the lawn.

"Ugh, that's my mother...it was nice meeting you two...be careful in that house. My story isn't as bad as the other one you might hear," said Derek, kicking his stubby leg over the bicycle seat.

"Dare I ask what the other story is?" said Landon, now making his way back to the front door.

"The story about your house being haunted...but, that's for another time—see ya'!" said Derek as he quickly peddled away.

Landon was already at the front door when he realized his sister was still standing near the silver lamppost where they had listened to Derek's quite ridiculous tale.

"You don't actually believe that kid, do you?" said Landon.

Makari gave a quick look at the menacing house, as the setting sun began to paint it with a summery orange shade.

"Didn't you?" said Makari, as her brother smirked and followed his sister back inside the house....

Later that night, Aunt Marion decided that after a full day of cleaning, that a nice order-in of pizza from a local pizzeria downtown would be the perfect accompaniment to a calm evening. The hungry family gathered around the cooker's island in the kitchen while

Landon volunteered to serve his aunt and sister each slices from the pepperoni pie. They sat together on wooden bar stools that Aunt Marion had found stacked in the garage earlier that afternoon.

"I noticed from the study room window, that you two were nice enough to introduce yourselves to one of the neighborhood children," said Marion, after taking a bite of her hot slice of pizza. Wiping the cheese and smooth basil-kissed tomato sauce off the side of her mouth, Makari began to recall the tale Derek had delighted her and Landon with. "Very interesting," Aunt Marion continued, "though you two know that your grandparents were not murdered. That was just a silly and awful assumption that this boy came up with. You two know how you're grandparents passed—"

Marion fidgeted and quickly broke eye contact as the siblings stared blankly at her, then silently went back to eyeing their food, though they seemed to have lost all interest in eating.

"Actually, neither of us know how or when our grandparents died," added Landon, after taking a sip from his glass of iced tea. "Our grandparents rarely visited us when Makari and I were much younger, and I can't remember the last time we visited them…come to think of it, our parents barely let either of us out of their sights."

"It doesn't need to be made into some nasty mystery—your grandparents were both very old and terribly sick before they passed," said Aunt Marion, "that's probably why you never had to chance to truly visit with them." Marion took a sip of her tea and then reached out to Makari's hand, trying to comfort her. "Anyway," Marion shifted her eyes back and forth from her niece and nephew, "tomorrow should be fun. Every Thursday there's a local farmer's market held downtown, and I'm sure you two would love to visit that. It'd be a splendid way to get out of this house for part of the day." Marion then reached for another slice from the pizza box.

"Sounds…fun," Landon guessed, after another sip of his iced tea.

"Aunt Marion, do you know if the house key works for the attic door?" asked Makari, quickly jumping into her question; ever since she heard the noise upstairs, and Derek's curious story—Makari felt she needed to ask.

"The attic door? I tried going up there earlier this afternoon, but the house key wouldn't budge the lock. It's the only key we have. I wouldn't dare try shifting that door open, though; there's probably mounds of fallen antiques and furniture jamming the door shut, anyway…and it all could come tumbling down and crush any one of us should we manage to pry it open," warned Marion.

"Worth trying after dinner then?" said Makari, hoping she might get to search the mysterious attic before bed.

"Why so adamant to go up there this evening?" said Aunt Marion, wiping her mouth after another bite of her slice.

"Well," Makari eyed her brother, hoping he wouldn't say aloud that she had heard something in the attic, "just to explore?"

"Makari, there'll be no exploring up there anytime soon, in fact, the last time anyone was up there was your father and *he* almost fell through the old flooring," said Marion, as she began to gather her niece's plate, as Landon insisted he would take each of their plates to the sink. "This house is dreadfully old, and I don't want either of you going up there… just like your parents, *always* with the endless need to venture."

"I know what you might like, tomorrow before we go downtown, I'll show you a little something special out back in the garden, sound fun?" insisted Marion.

That was not what Makari or Landon wanted to hear, as our Makari was desperate to see what could possibly be hiding up in the attic and if Derek's tale could prove to be true.

"I know you want to go up there, too," murmured Makari, as she carefully slid her plate into the filling sink. Landon could only glance over at his sister once before he returned his gaze to the kitchen sink window, trying his best not let worrying about the noise Makari heard upstairs or Derek's odd tale diminish his excitement at the idea of what other old belongings he could find of his father's that might be tucked away in the attic. Landon continued to ponder as hot sink water began to emanate billowing clouds that filled his face.

▼

Thursday morning had arrived: Aunt Marion kept her promise to her niece by sharing what Makari's own mother, Annette, had once shared with Marion years ago. Marion had Makari follow her through the backyard garden and beyond the little pond, once inhabited by koi fish and now home to levels of what looked like mutating emerald moss. Hiding right between the thick locks of hair-like ivy that surrounded the yard was an hourglass-shaped door, and it was here that Aunt Marion began to share a new tale: "It leads to the park on the other side of this wall," said Marion, twisting the rusted doorknob.

"And of course, it's locked," sighed Makari.

Aunt Marion shared stories of Makari's mother to her, like one tale of how, as children, Annette and Aiden would run from their chores and escape through the garden's door to enjoy a brisk afternoon on the park's sprawling lawns. As the story was happily shared, little did Aunt Marion suspect that Landon and Makari's strategic attempt to unlock the attic was already underway.

Landon stood there, barefooted in the kitchen, watching his aunt and sister explore the rest of the garden from the glass doors that led to the backyard, and with a spin on a bare heel, Landon spotted his aunt's ring of keys resting on top of pieces of mail that had the oddest looking stamps he had ever seen and a page from the local newspaper. Quickly swiping the ring from the pile on the cooker's island, he dashed up the kitchen stairs and placed a wooden stool (that his aunt had been using the day before, as he found it to be much safer than his wobbly desk chair) directly under the locked attic door.

Landon stood on the stool and stretched out an arm with the house key in his right hand: the key fit like a glove as it entered the lock's mouth. Trying first with a gentle turn...the key would not budge. Looking over his shoulder to listen for his aunt and sister entering the kitchen from the backyard, he returned to try each and every key he could possibly fit and unlock the attic door, trying to shift the lock open. Working furiously, he tried his best not to snap any of the keys in half. Like a warning, as Landon attempted to budge the lock once more, a loud rumbling sound rolled out from inside the attic. Jumping off the stool quicker than a startled fox in a forest, Landon stood there, tracing the ceiling with his eyes as a pocket of panic began to bubble in his stomach. Again, the attic shifted with a tremor, like a massive wine barrel being toyed with by some trapped giant. Landon reached for the stool and as quickly as he ascended the stairs, his thin body went diving down into the kitchen, nearly knocking over his aunt.

"What are you doing!" snapped Marion, grabbing hold of her nephew's flying body. Landon's face blossomed like a mortified cherry, the ring of keys still in his right hand. Marion then heard the faint clanking sound of keys and then finally noticed the ring of them in her nephew's right hand. "Were you trying to pry yourself up into the attic?" Makari looked up at her aunt and then tossed her eyes at her brother. "Did you know what your brother was up to this entire time?"

"No, she didn't," Landon quickly answered, "I just wanted to test the key and try to get up there myself."

"You mean, to see if you could go and get your self hurt!" flared Marion. "Landon, I specifically asked both of you *not* to worry about the attic. The flooring up there can be very dangerous and you could've fallen through it for heaven's sake!"

"None of the keys work, anyway!" barked Landon, as he then slammed the ring of keys back on the pile of newspapers and mail.

"Listen to me when I ask you to, please, Landon. I expect that from you, especially," said Marion, as she then spun on her heel, retreating to her bedroom upstairs. But before she did, Marion was sure to slip her ring of keys into a pocket under her pashmina shawl —unaware that Makari had taken notice. Landon eyed his sister, both sighing at their failed plan.

That afternoon, fortunately, went on without any other rumblings from the attic. Aunt Marion cleared her mind as she found herself reorganizing the pantry below the kitchen stairs. Now sitting in the study room's nook, in a comfortable position beside the window mantle, Makari rested and sighed as she looked out at the calm oaks swaying as the hot summer air weaved between them. Makari folded open her favorite diary in her lap and began to write, finding herself lost between her thoughts and tracing the corner of one of the annotated pages with a curly doodle that sparked her mind.

Within the family she once knew, writing was a known passion of Makari's, and it was her ultimate expression of the world around her. Here, she was able to pen her thoughts about the new house, her brother, and her favorite memories she once shared with her mother and father. Makari now had a curious feeling that there had to be a profound connection between the noise she heard in the attic and Derek's tale.

"Makari," called Landon's voice, as she quickly threw her favorite fountain pen in the center bind of the diary, closing it, "I have to tell you what happened earlier when I tried unlocking the attic door." Makari's eyes lit up as she twisted her body around and set her diary to the side.

"Tell me, tell me!" sparked Makari, as though she were about to be told the most marvelous secret.

"I think you might be right," said Landon, slightly closing the heavy study room door behind him, "there's undeniably something strange hiding up there—"

"—Did you hear the noise?"

"Not only did I hear the noise...I felt it," said Landon, sitting on the edge of the wide office desk.

"*Felt it*, how so?" asked Makari, curiously.

"As I took the key to try and budge the lock, I suddenly heard this loud, rumbling sound, as if some sort of giant was having a fit," said Landon, now walking around the office desk.

"You're kidding me, right?"

"M, when have I ever?"

"Plenty of times, Landon—and you're just trying to poke fun at the entire situation, aren't you?" said Makari, growing upset.

"M, calm down, I'm telling you the truth—do you think Aunt Marion would ever keep anything from us?" said Landon, now looking through the small crack of the study room door.

"In what way do you mean?" tested Makari.

"Like something out of the ordinary," said Landon, "maybe Aunt Marion is behind all of this...maybe she knows just what exactly is hiding in the attic?" Landon now found himself circling the room like an amateur detective with the right clue in his midst.

"Well, no," Makari insisted, "I don't believe Aunt M—"

Makari and Landon stopped, eyes wide with shock. Makari's journal had fallen to the floor, hurling with an unusually loud thud as it folded flat open. Makari's favorite pen flew just about a foot away from where she stood, and after picking up her journal and as she reached for her fountain pen, the most unexpected event happened. It was something that was worse than any most terrible noise that could come from any ole locked attic.

Makari's favorite pen began to spin, and spin before it flung into the air like a wild hummingbird looking for its nest. Landon jumped right next to Makari; both of their mouths wide open and anchored in awe. Without hesitation, Makari reached out for the flying pen. Landon quickly pulled his sister's hand back in time as the square end of the fountain pen began to poke out into the air. Makari's diary then came alive with such vehemence, as it, too, flung itself into the air and plopped back down on to the office desk, violently flipping to an empty page. This unbelievable event was quickly unfolding before our sibling's eyes. During this entire scene, neither Landon nor Makari dared to move from the scene that played out before them, astounded by the crazed wonder of whatever else might soon reveal itself. Together, the siblings watched as Makari's fountain pen and little red diary calmed until the careening objects gathered like two old friends meeting in a park.

"Are you seeing this?" whimpered Makari, trying her best to keep her voice hushed; fearing that the pen she so cared for would turn on her at the slightest move. Landon then pointed at spectral pair: the shaky pen began to write, and with some a visible show of effort, scribbled a message:

The answer is 'you'
-Helpfully Yours-

The fountain pen remained upright, as though an invisible hand continued to keep a firm grasp on it. At that very moment, though, as Aunt Marion entered the room, the fountain pen snapped like frail twig.

"*What...on earth*—you two have made a mess!" shrieked Aunt Marion, stomping over to the ink-covered faces of her niece and nephew. Aunt Marion had only missed the scene of Makari's flying pen and diary by mere seconds.

"We were—"

"—Makari, I don't want to hear it. You two better clean these ink blotches off this desk, it's an antique!" Aunt Marion turned on her heel and reached for the study's door, "Please and quickly, wash up—it's nearly time for us to make our way downtown for the market..."

Aunt Marion could only shake her head at the ink-smothered faces of our two curious siblings.

"I'm two-for-two with her today," sighed Landon, as he wiped away some of the runny black ink off his chin. Makari and Landon looked down upon the puddle of ink where the diary lay soaked. Makari groaned, as she carefully picked up her diary by the tip of her fingers. All of her finest entries were now ruined.

"What do you think it meant?" rattled Makari.

"All I can guess," said Landon, wiping away the lash of ink running down his face, "I'm afraid to admit it, but Derek might've been right."

CHAPTER THREE

THE SLEUTH FROM CAPPA

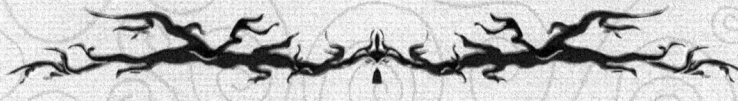

In the world where Poplar Drive resides, the bizarre, the unexpected and the *unusual* courses everywhere, happening at every moment. And terrible to think of though it is, an absurd amount of souls care not to exercise this privilege to experience the...*unusual*. But for those curious few that have dared to dance with the...*unusual*...aren't too different from our young siblings, Landon and Makari. And the wondrous appetizer the dear Tuolumnes tasted in our previous chapter was but a bitty sliver of the conundrum-plagued feast that is, one of our curious siblings might guess, without a doubt waiting to make the acquaintance.

After a quick wash up and slip out of their ink-stained clothes, the siblings (with a deep promise not to speak near their aunt about the happenings in the study room), set off on foot—to the tree-lined downtown market that was only a quarter of an hour walk from Poplar Drive.

Higuera Street was fairly busy that late afternoon; people from all over the town were perusing and weaving between the local vendor tents and crates filled to the brim with the freshest vegetables and the most tantalizing fruits the Tuolumnes had ever seen. Makari watched as the surrounding townsfolk barked and bartered over stacks of salvaged paintings and mounds of antiques. The Tuolumnes continued to interweave between the clustering shoulders until they reached a break in the traffic where they came to a halt at the most enchanting aroma that was kettle corn sweeping the summer air. It was the smell from the festival cauldron that fishhooked their noses like most of the people that anxiously waited in line for their giant cone bag of caramel glazed popcorn.

As the Tuolumnes continued through the slow pacing crowds of people enjoying smothered pork ribs or grilled artichokes, Makari quickly pointed out to her aunt a narrow entrance between two buildings, and asked if they could—together—see why so many people were hastily drawing near to it.

"Oh yes, Bubblegum Alley," said Aunt Marion, grinning with just bit of apprehension. As Landon and Makari raced to the sidewalk, they squeezed between other children who were doing the most unusual thing with their chewing gum: people were taking the gooey pieces from their mouths and pressing it like a stamp with their thumbs or forefingers against either side of the narrow alley walls. Landon and Makari watched as patrons either created art out of their gum or poked love notes against the walls.

"This is disgusting…but so incredible," said Landon, gazing up at the millions of patches of colorful gum dots that blanketed the high walls. "Aunt Marion, this is absolutely gross," groaned Makari, even though she couldn't break her smile at the scene. Makari did her best to keep to the center of the alley, trying not to bump into the filthy walls. Alas, Landon found the crude pleasure in teasing his sister by giving her few gently pushes toward the walls, sending her into a shrieking fit.

"I believe your parents made their own little patch along the alley," said Aunt Marion, as she waved her hand toward the center of the narrow passage, "this was a stop they made on one of their first dates when they were teenagers. Your mother once told me, your father made an arrow out of his piece and your mom made the first initials of each of their own names, and placed the two letters on either side of the between arrow."

"So gross, yet so like them at the same time," said Makari.

"I thought so, too, but now their art is just buried beneath the rest," smiled Aunt Marion, wistfully, as she eyed the gum-lathered alley.

"Oh, here, I found a pack of gum in that old desk drawer in my room," said Landon, as he unwrapped two pieces of Bazooka chewing gum from his pocket. Within just a few seconds and chews after popping each of their pinkish sticks of gum into their mouths, Landon and Makari quickly realized that after years of hiding in the drawer, the pack of gum had become terribly stale. "We're not gonna' enjoy it all day," said Landon, as he and sister's face pursed, "it's for the wall."

"This is so gross, but I can't help it!" laughed Makari, stretching her gum in the form of the letter **M**. "I couldn't think of anything else to make out of mine."

Landon followed suit, forming the letter **L** out of his pink gum.

"Perfect then," clapped Marion, as she then turned on her heel and made her way back to the street. "Are either of you hungry?" Aunt Marion pointed over at a woman wearing a chef's hat while she rapidly grilled steak kabobs for a growing queue that gathered under her red tent.

"We'd rather keep looking around for now," said Landon, while his sister agreed.

And so they did, until they approached the next shop corner, noticing the abundance of other buzzing children through the wide windows of a narrow shop called **Terry Taff and Creamery Co.**

Landon felt almost like he was in a cattle draw with his sister and aunt as the three poured with fellow children inside the clustered salt-water taffy and cream soda brewery. Makari steered her troupe through the zigzagging line between old and fat wine barrels that now housed nearly three-dozen varieties of bursting taffies. Landon and Makari each took a striped paper sack from the mime-suited shop member, as their eyes began the strenuous hunt for the best flavors: strawberry shortcake, black cherry, peanut butter, blueberry, dark chocolate, candy-corn, pineapple-punch, island kiwi, red licorice, watermelon-cream, lemon zest, pumpkin spice, apple-cinnamon kiss, cream soda, sardine…

"I *dare* you to eat one," tittered Makari, handing her brother the gray sardine taffy.

"I'll take that dare," Landon winked, tossing an extra one into his taffy sack. "In case I like it." While her niece and nephew forged ahead with their taffy selection like the rest of the pecking mob, Aunt Marion gave her sights to the clanking confectionery belt of caramel colored glass bottles that wrapped overhead and completely around the entire shop. The bottles' journey began from somewhere in the back of the shop until reaching two, enormous steel vats behind the register counter where two zit-faced brewery boys capped each and every soda that came into their grasp.

"Lan, my dear, be sure to toss a few black-licorice taffies in your sack for me," pointed Aunt Marion, as Landon frowned in distaste at aunt's choice, "and that honey flavored one too!"

"Two, half-pound bags today?" grinned Janet W., as it read on her shop name tag, while she measured Landon and Makari's bags on her polished red scale. "Would you three like to add our freshly bottled taffy-cream soda to your tally?"

"Yes, please do!" cheered Aunt Marion, as one of the brewery boys slid three chilled bottles toward his coworker across the front counter. After Janet gave couple more taps on her chiming register, our troupe gave a wave good-bye to their sweetshop girl as they made quick spins on their heels and while they uncapped their sodas and finally found their exit from the shop. With every bubbly gulp our troupe took from their caramel and cream swirled soda, for them it was like a quenching escape from the slithers of the summer breeze that suddenly began to crawl as they advanced through the market.

"Look, Aunt Marion, there's an art gallery there," said Makari, unwrapping a red licorice taffy, "we should see what's inside."

"That gallery will be seeping with Francis Bacons and Warhol knockoffs, I'm almost sure of it," mused Aunt Marion, as she then pulled a fist full of wrinkled dollars from her purse, "and that's in the case either of you find something you like—I'll meet you two back here in thirty minutes." Landon and Makari departed from their aunt, each still with their sacks of taffies clenched in hand, they continued on through the busy market, wondering what they'd stumble upon next.

"I think I might like living here," said Makari, as her brother eyed her, "I'm not kidding...well, I'm definitely giving our house second thoughts."

"Don't remind me," groaned Landon, trying to enjoy his gloppy taffy.

"Any ideas about what that message meant?" said Makari, as she and her brother hurried between bystanders of a live jazz band that played on the next street corner.

"Either Derek's warning was right or something strange is going on," said Landon.

"It can't be...could it?" reflected Makari.

"Well, there's no point in both of us getting worked-up over Derek's story," said Landon, as he then turned to his sister, "though, I'm not denying what we both saw this afternoon—I would think you'd be the first one wanting to solve the mystery of your flying journal."

"I'm not denying what I saw either, and the same goes for what we both heard in the attic," shivered Makari, at just the thought of the gathering clues. "Let's not talk about all of that bizarreness now, anyway."

"Fine, should we just find someplace to scuttle about?" shrugged Landon. The siblings then realized they had reached the very end of the Higuera Market, but there was still one final vendor tent they had yet to visit.

"We could try that interesting spot over there," said Makari, looking over her brother's shoulder. Across the busy foot-traffic street, Landon and Makari could see a fat and rundown yellow-circus-striped tent nestled under an over-hanging tree and beside an overflowing trashcan.

"Shall we?" Landon urged, as they dashed between the shoppers and made their way across the street toward the rotting tent.

"*Fire sale*," Makari hummed, reading the poorly chalk-written sign posted outside the tent. Makari then tossed the empty Terry Taffy bottles in the neighboring trashcan, noticing her brother's eagerness to peek inside the tent. The tattered tent drape looked like it ought to be secured with a heavy padlock, but it swept aside like a stage curtain as Landon and Makari entered the nest-like tent. The muggy interior was lit by only a massive drip-palace of old candle wax that smoldered sullenly on the center table, which was ringed by the other smaller tables that lined the tent, all of which housed such glorious piles of…

"Junk," said Landon, eyeing the mounds of salvaged fortunes.

There was everything from metal trinkets, to candelabras, leather-bound books, umbrellas, and even a set of chipped porcelain dolls that Makari privately found to be terrifying.

"Such excellent junk, though," said Makari, twirling the hanging ornament above her. "How can anyone sell such stuff? It all looks like priceless treasures."

"Can't imagine why anyone would want to pay for it," said Landon, circling a couple of wooden stools that balanced a dozen or more aged vases and goblets.

"Truly, it is only junk," croaked an Old Man, hiding in a shadowed corner in the tent, "but imagine what you could learn from all of it?"

From head to boot, the soot-washed man was old and frayed as the trinkets that surrounded him and brandished tarnished silver rings on each of his stubby, dirty fingers. He wore a brown leather overcoat that had been stitched on numerous occasions, the shoulders of which were just brushed by his greasy blond skullet. As he adjusted the ponderous layers of key-laden necklaces that he wore like a necktie, the toad-like man came closer to our siblings and unexpectedly…bowed.

"Luc Looter, at your service…I trade, sell, and even, *maybe*, buy!"

he announced, with a practiced cadence.

"Thank you, Luc," coughed Landon, as his nose snatched a wave of Luc's rancid breath.

"Say, what do you have hiding in those sacks, any goodies you'd like to trade?" said Luc, as he hovered closer.

"Salt-water-taffies, would you like one?" offered Makari.

"I love taffy!" hooted Luc. "Qui, mademoiselle, how kind of you —please let me surprise myself with a flavor." Luc Looter then slowly reached out for Landon's open taffy sack, his ringed fingers mimicking a crawling spider as he carefully chose his flavor. Like a candy-deprived creature would've done, Luc giggled and honed his sights on the single wax paper wrapped gray taffy that he quickly unrolled into his neglected mouth.

"You're welcome," said Landon, cracking a smile.

"Ah, sardine...how tarty!" glopped Luc, with a wide grin. "Monsieur, anything you see in my hut here today is for half the price!" continued Luc, talking fast, trying his best to catch a sale from our siblings. Noticing Makari rummaging through one of the side tables, Luc hurriedly licked his chapped lips and rushed over to Makari in fright. "Please, little creature...this is a one-of-a-kind and I do mean *one*—don't touch—unless of course you intend to purchase," Luc insisted, as he then grinned, and placed the nearly melted remains of what seemed to be a blue-iron mask back on its mantle.

"Well, maybe she is interested?" said Landon, nearly towering over the hunched tinker.

"Um, *well*, maybe not that item...it's very precious to me," mumbled Luc, chattering his teeth again, watching the siblings very closely.

"I hope you receive all the customers you need. Seeing all this stuff, it doesn't really seem you sell much of it," said Landon, circling around another table of trinkets.

"Only the happiest of occasions do I receive such visitors who, like you two, seem to have an interest in my items. Though, no matter where I stake this beautiful tent of mine, someone quite curious always comes along," grumbled Luc, as he noticed Landon taking an interest in a massive goblet and shuffling beside him, "and those few curious ones are whom I truly wait for." Taking the heavy goblet from Landon with a small fuss, Luc began to lecture an annoyed Landon on the significance and origin of the goblet, as Makari then found a lone table at the furthest corner of the odd tent. Makari then began to trace her eyes through a few of the dust-shrouded towers of books that leaned between an examination-worthy bed of trinkets: a scratched magnifying-glass, hordes of broken pocket watches, eyeglasses of all different frames in all sort of exotic dimensions, and useless fractured or chipped baubles and tea kettles. But what sat oh-so-perfectly between all of the flocks of lost treasures was a box, no bigger than one that might be found waiting for you on the kitchen table on your birthday—unless you were that tumultuous, bratty kid who was always showered with gifts that were two sizes too big, much like his or her head. *Our* little box was not only wrapped with Makari's lured attention, but also with an excessive amount crinkly brown parchment and a tight bow of yarn. Makari quickly looked over her shoulder, watching as Luc relentlessly explained the usefulness of his bronze goblet to her brother. Then, without the slightest hesitation, Makari reached for the brown wrapped box and held it up with ease. It wasn't very heavy for her at all, and she marveled at the idea of what could possibly be hiding inside, it was then that Makari felt an unexpected warmth rush through her palms, up her arms and straight to her beating heart. Luc then glared at what his little shopper was doing. Tossing his goblet back onto the table carelessly, Luc shrieked as he dove toward Makari, with the wrapped box still in her hands.

"My little lady, you have not the *slightest* clue as to what you have in your dainty hands," warned Luc, with a bit of fear stuck in his throat.

"Landon, I think I found what I'd like to buy," smiled Makari, as Luc squealed with laughter.

"*She* wants to buy? Ha! Ha!" cackled Luc, as he swayed closer toward Makari, "impossible—I will sell you that melted mask you had in your filthy hands, plus ten items more at a single price, but not this item—now please," growled Luc, a hand out for the box.

"No, we'll pay whatever you ask," said Makari, her nose up at Luc.

"I SAID," Luc then stopped himself, giving a few taps on his stubble chin, "I can name my price, you say?" hummed Luc, now chattering a few words to himself again, "that could definitely be my money to pay my fines and get myself a new Portler Badge *and* get back to Cappa Valley—"

"—We have a deal then?" queried Makari, trying to restore Luc's attention.

"—Eh, no! Oh, but the Cappa courts would have my head if they knew I *sold* it," Luc was fixed on selling the box, but it seemed far too complicated for him. "I mustn't get sidetracked. I cannot sell this item to you, young lady."

"Why is this box so important?" darted Landon.

"Ha! I would be probably be drained of my blood if it were found that *I* divulged that sort of delicate information to either of you…as it is, I'm already a wanted Cappamite," whimpered Luc.

"You're a thief, aren't you?" asked Landon, pointedly.

"*Moi*, un voleur?" spat Luc, in French, pressing a hand against his key covered chest. "How dare you give me such an unflattering title—I cleverly collect my items from people whom have decided to take them for granted."

"If you can't sell this, then figure out a way we can make a deal," said Makari. Landon stood confused by his sister's steadfast desire for the box.

"Figure out a way?" hummed Luc, as he turned on his booted heel, shuffling ideas under his gurgling breaths. "Well, I could win out in my situation…*the R.C.C. might even thank me in the end.*"

"The R-what-what?" puzzled Landon, never had he ever heard such words like Cappa-whats or R-hum-not.

"How much for the box, Luc?" bartered Makari, again.

"Hush girl, an idea has come to mind," burbled Luc, spinning back toward his visitors, "unfortunately, the box cannot be exchanged for money, as the magnificent properties that slumber within those wrappings would find it remarkably disrespectful. So, you want a deal —my eager little redhead—if either of you can answer my riddle, I will allow you to walk away from my tent with that box." Landon and Makari quickly eyed each other, as though they shared their own silent accord, when Luc Looter continued, "I must forewarn, neither of you are ever to come back to me with the box; that thing has brought me more trouble than fame," quivered Luc, pointing at the wrapped box.

"Deal," nodded Makari. Landon then came side by side with his sister as Luc cleared his throat and recited his riddle for our curious siblings:

"Ye stand where thine eye seeks a mere reflection, where one comes for the others collection...who am I?"

"Who am I?" repeated Landon, looking at his sister, hoping for an answer.

"I think that's how that ole' riddle goes," snorted Luc.

"Where thine eye seeks a mere reflection...a mere reflection?" Makari kept repeating the verse aloud.

"Only the ones worthy of the what's inside that box have ever solved the riddle," noted Luc, "or so I recall."

"*Mere...mere...*mirror?" Landon pondered.

"Reflection!" shouted Makari.

"Who would seek a mirror's reflection?" Landon thought, still puzzled.

Luc grinned, tapping his scruffy chin.

"'*Ye stand where thine eyes*'...another word for ye, '*You* stand where your eyes seek a mirror reflection where one comes for the others collection,'" guessed Makari. Suddenly, a coincidental idea hit Landon like a house falling out from a tornado whirled sky:

"M, I got it, I know the answer," gasped Landon, "It's a riddle within a riddle and it just may be one of the craziest flukes…"

"What's your answer then, boy?" grinned Luc.

"The answer is…*you*," answered Landon.

Makari jolted her head at Landon's answer, as Luc's mouth flew open.

"How did?" gasped Luc, "you couldn't be from…or maybe?"

"That is the answer then?" said Landon.

"Regrettably so," said Luc, as he then huddled again with the siblings, eyeing the wrapped box closely, "on second thought, I'm glad you answered correctly."

Makari still held the wrapped box in her hand as Luc then guided our siblings by their collars to his tent's exit.

"Wait, this doesn't seem right. What's so special about this box, Luc?" said Landon, as he took the ornament from his sister, frowning at Luc's sudden loathe of the box. "Here, take it back…"

"No! No! My boy, you love riddles so much, that thing in your hands will feed you riddles until you're dead," croaked Luc, as Landon tried setting it back on one of the trinket bathed tabletops. "There's more than just helpful clues inside that box I made—It has silenced more with its obstacles and games than I should've ever allowed." Makari then gasped, seeing Luc quickly reach for a blade from inside his long coat. "It now knows that you're my successor… *now leave!*" Landon grabbed his sister by the wrist and darted from the tent, not a dare to look back at Luc, his face swollen with regret.

The afternoon sun had nearly departed when Landon and Makari reached the midpoint of the market near the art gallery their aunt had gone ahead of them to visit. Gasping for air, after they ran as fast as they could from Luc Looter's tent, bumping shoulders of market patrons as they raced, Landon and Makari took a rest on a wooden bench just outside the gallery entrance.

"Landon, the diary…you thought of the message from the diary, didn't you?" said Makari, as her brother remained clutched onto the wrapped box.

"I wasn't thinking of it at all, the idea just came to me," said

Landon, eyeing the parchment box in his hands.

"The message in my diary, that riddle, and now this box?" sighed Makari.

"There *has* to be some odd connection, there just has to be, M," said Landon, "and I want to know what it is."

Quickly ripping the tight yarn that held the wrapping together, the siblings each tore from corners on the box like a Christmas present, until revealing a severely timeworn wooden box with a small, triangular latch on its top.

"Should we open it now?" wondered Landon, drawing his finger over the gold finishing on the small latch.

"I think—"

"*There* you two are—I've been scouring the market for nearly half an hour," said Marion, with a new brown tote of celery and baguettes popping out of the bag, and noticing the box in Landon's lap, "found something from the market?"

"Yes...it's a—"

Landon suddenly became tongue-tied.

"Jewelry box for me," averred Makari.

"Nothing really sparked my interest," said Landon, eyeing his sister.

"Well, that box looks quite...unique," said Marion, resting her bag on the bench between our siblings. "You two are fairly quiet."

"Just hungry," said Landon.

"Good thing I grabbed a few things here at the market," said Marion, taking a note from her coat pocket, giving it a quick glance. "Well, it's no good to sit there, that bench isn't going to feed you. Come along, I've got some great news to share, and I'll tell you two when we get home...."

The great news Aunt Marion had to share with our siblings was that she had been invited to meet the gallery proprietor to discuss the possibility of becoming the gallery's new art collector....

"That's wonderful, Aunt Marion!" said Makari, as she placed pairs of silverware around the large dining room table for dinner.

"Truly exciting, as it has been nearly a decade since I've had the opportunity to be involved in the art scene," said Marion, placing the porcelain bowl of spaghetti and meatballs on the dining table. "I figured we could celebrate with a fine dinner--a famous recipe I perfected with my old Mulberry bohemians when we were just trying to survive in New York." As Landon came from the kitchen stairs with his sister's new "jewelry box" in hand, he decided to join his family.

"There you are, Landon, and I see you haven't let go of that odd box," said Marion.

"I...have liking for weird things," laughed Landon, not knowing what else to say.

Makari shot Landon a sharp look, trying to get her brother to set aside the box. Landon quickly placed the wooden box on a side table next to the hall archway; Landon then gathered the three dinner plates and the basket of warm baguette slices from the cooker's island, then he made a second run fetching the pitcher of homemade iced lemonade that his aunt had perfectly crafted. Within seconds, each of them began to dive into their brimming bowls of delicious spaghetti, spinning their forks into the basil and tomato drenched pasta.

After a solid half-hour passed, Makari made her family roar with laughter after erupting with a booming burp.

"*Excuse* me," said Makari, bashfully, even surprised at herself for her manners.

Landon and Makari rushed through the after-dinner chores; tossing their dishes in the sink to soak while Aunt Marion prepared each of them a small cup of vanilla-whipped pecan and caramel ice cream.

Taking to the family room, Landon and Makari popped open the mahogany coffer that sat next to the fireplace, finding several decades-old board games and picture puzzles to choose from. The three of them decided on a thousand-piece jigsaw puzzle depicting the unusual yet mesmerizing Escher masterpiece *Relativity*. Makari whistled amusingly while scanning the front of the puzzle's worn box. None of them could immediately decide which section they'd choose to manage, in order to complete the mind-boggling puzzle illustrating a gravity-defying world of interconnected stairs and faceless inhabitants. And so, Aunt Marion carefully splashed the surface of the coffee table with the entire set from box, hoping that all the pieces were present. Not realizing it, almost two and a half hours had passed since the three began the nimble task of piecing the illustration together by deciding to find the puzzle's corners and to work inward from there on.

"Ack! Would you believe it, six pieces missing," tutted Aunt Marion scanning the giant puzzle wildly, and while her nephew checked for pieces that might have fallen from the table.

"M, look inside that chest for any stray pieces," Landon said, as he then spun his head around to see that his sister had already dozed off to sleep on the couch. "Sis?"

"It's been a long day," whispered Aunt Marion, "let her rest. We've come this far with the puzzle—we can come back to it tomorrow." Aunt Marion remained insistent with her nephew, not missing a beat while grabbing hers and Makari's empty ice cream cups.

"No, it's okay," urged Landon, unclasping the puzzle's box from his sister's hand, "we're missing a few pieces as it is. It's not all that worth it anymore."

"Not important? Landon, of course it is," pressed Aunt Marion.

"We may not see those most precious pieces around now, but they're worth looking for." Landon held back his hand, seconds from sliding the nearly complete puzzle back into its tattered box. Setting aside the box, instead, Landon eyed the missing patches around the sheet of jigsaw cuts when he then tilted his head back up to his Aunt Marion.

"How do I do that?" said Landon. "I don't know what truly is worth looking for anymore, because it's become more of a battle for me now...the only thing I want to go looking for is my mom and dad…and what for? I know exactly where it'll lead me and I hate it—I hate it so much, Aunt Marion, that I don't even know *my* own worth."

"You are worth *every* fiber of your being, Landon—you *and* your sister both," said Marion, "I'm here to remind you of that, I'll always be."

"I appreciate it," Landon sighed, as he then paced his way to the cooker's island. "Though, I still need to figure out this moment for myself and need to be honest with you here and now," said Landon, as he then paced his way to the cooker's island. "Having you around is new to me, it really is. Makari might resemble the openness that you're hoping for each day, as goes for me—and I can't quite explain why—just know it will take me some time getting used to you."

Landon's aunt stared at him contemplatively, and it occurred to him that his parting shot might've affected her more deeply than he'd intended.

"I know the occasional birthday and Christmas card isn't enough to expect you and your sister to feel like you know me. And I don't know how much my sister and your father spoke of me, and I know *you* only met me once before…before *that night*," said Marion, as she struggled to convey her words to Landon. "I want to help rebuild the world you and Makari lost, Landon, but it starts with you. Let Makari see you glow once again, just as bright as your handsome eyes. It is possible, Landon, with what you have here, that you and your sister have a chance to find and be yourselves again." Marion then reached for her nephew's hand. "You *will* overcome this."

"I only hope I can," said Landon, as his aunt gave him a gentle nod. Aunt Marion then woke Makari and helped her sluggish body up the stairs as the three of them then took to their own bedrooms for the night.

▼

Landon now found himself shuffling through a small suitcase in his closet that he had yet to unpack, gathering his record player and select few records that he was able to bring with him when they moved. And there, at the bottom of the case, was an old and folded up newspaper, noticeably tattered at its edges. As he paced from the closet, with the dozen or so record slipcovers under his arm, Landon suddenly spun on his heel, trying to locate the source of the faint ruffle of paper that slipped into the small space of air in his room. Now eyeing the folded newspaper that had fallen from between his pile, Landon hastily placed the records and player on his desk before picking it up from his cool, bedroom floor and allowing it to unfold with a dangle. Landon had miserably read the front page spread over a hundred times before, but still found that same, sickening hopelessness grow in his stomach as he began to glance over the column: housing a square picture of a blanketed young boy and girl holding hands while their lost faces peered from between hurrying police and firemen that surrounded them with questions....

THE NIGHTMARE STORM

City officials and investigators are baffled by isolated tornado.

Police officer Zachary Nicely was first to respond to the call when neighbors of Tuolumne residents of Kirkwood Lane reported the unbelievable scene: an isolated tornado of lighting and rain roared through the neighborhood, only destroying a few street lamps, signs, trees, cars, and finally collapsing half of the house that stood at 510 Kirkwood Lane; the house owned by Aiden and Annette Tuolumne—the only fatalities to arise out the unseasonable weather phenomena. Local officials and meteorologists reported no evidence of said tornado on their radar, reporting that nothing

more than scattered rains were expected that evening. However, eyewitnesses have gathered and pointed out that evidence of the said occurrence still remains on their street. These ill events that have unraveled on Kirkwood Lane leave the two surviving children as wards of the state until legal guardianship can be established among their surviving relatives. The Tuolumne siblings are still—

Landon then crumpled the newspaper in his hands, tossing the yellowing pages into the air, before they fell into an ugly pile on his bedroom floor. Landon's tears were heavier now, like his breathing, while he hurried his hands through his stack of vinyl records. After hastily plugging the power cord to his player behind his desk, Landon plopped himself onto the desk's chair and fastened his headphones over his ears. After a few seconds of dead noise and audio pops from the record that spun, Sonic Youth's *Starpower* began to flood Landon's ears with every striking beat and guitar cry. Landon strained his thoughts while reveling in the dark spectacle that was the clear star-filled August night that gleamed through his bedroom window. Shuffling through the hodgepodge of records before him, Landon couldn't help but recount the disturbing events of the past several days. These curious incidents that had so quickly occurred in his new home felt somehow connected to the anomalous misfortunes that had befallen him at his old home, back many, many miles away. What did a strange house with flying diaries and floating pens have to do with anything? Terrifying noises coming from the attic? Not to forget about that box from the market—Landon's scattered mind ran circles through these, bitterly unable to apprehend their meaning. Slowly, Landon's head sunk onto his arm that splayed across his desk, just beside the record player. He was sure that the answer lay somewhere among his precious memories of home: not the wretched events that had brought him here, it had to be something much earlier. The evasive truth that Landon tried to peel from his memories remained trapped in his head, gamboling impishly. The infuriating presque vu got the better of him, however, and his mind slowly gave in to exhaustion.

Landon was now in his quiet slumber and could feel his perception spilt between the cosmos that his dream was sinking him deeper through. He could somehow still feel his body squirm at his desktop while he slept. Landon opened his eyes, not revealing his moonlit room, but the sight of endlessly spinning crystal walls everywhere he looked. One spot at the edge of his attention appeared to blossom into a wavering, checkered-floored corridor, but time and again as he tried to focus his eyes and mind on it, it withered and dissipated into the revolving wall. Suddenly, the walls stopped and violently crumbled, revealing a mist lurching toward him. Landon stood there, not a moment frightened by the crawling clouds or at the next instant when the outlines of human figures began to form before the giant crystal shards that slowly appeared through the ghostly haze.

Landon kept a steady pace as he trekked through the room the fog had now created. None of the figures seemed aware of Landon, almost as if he didn't exist. Landon then came closer to the scene that was playing in front of him: recognizing his much younger self, sitting on a hospital bed along with his newly born baby sister, Makari. Landon really had no recollection of this supposed memory that his brain was displaying for him like some odd movie reel. Little Landon then kissed his sister's blue lips until her body began to glow colors like the warmest summer sun. Landon could then hear echoing voices whirl around the crystal room, darting his eyes in every direction to find where the voices were coming from:

"He's saved her, he's saved her!"

"The Guardian has saved her!"

Two more figures then appeared out of the mist, smiling softly at Landon who watched from afar. Landon instantly recognized his mother and father, who were both plainly reminiscent of their children. Landon sighed at the sight of his loving parents, hand-in-hand, and called out for them, but his cry couldn't be heard.

Seconds later, Landon's cry began to echo overhead as if through some invisible loudspeaker, growing louder and louder until the crystal scene around him shattered and sent him whirling deeper into his vortex of images. Landon then felt a gentle resistance cease his fall and was struck with an immediate sense of sickening dread as he recognized his surroundings. Landon realized he had somehow returned to his old residence on Kirkwood Lane, the very house he had grown up in until *that night* destroyed it all...

Landon now found himself slowly pacing again, down a hallway in his childhood home, seeing whirling memories of his mother and father grasped by unwilling sorrow, as they were discussing something in secret in the dinning room with Aunt Marion... Another whirl seized Landon and now he could see that he was no longer in his house, but now following behind another memory that would soon become his nightmare...

It's the night of Landon's twelfth birthday, as a jazzed Landon led his family out of a crowded cinema, still with popcorn bag in hand and thrilled by the spectacular ending of *The Princess Bride*. The Tuolumnes are on their way home, umbrellas in the air, hurrying along on foot from downtown as a lightening storm begins to seize the sky...

Landon and Makari are the first to bolt through the front door of their house, dripping wet after racing each other in the rain. The siblings then realize their parents are nowhere to be found.

A monstrous gust of wind from the billowing storm outside slams the front door shut on Landon, while the crashing sounds of thunder and heavy beads of rain echo all around...

Landon could feel his body fly toward the front door while the morbid delusion pried its way through his tumultuous dream. Suddenly, the door burst open with a deafening scream that shredded through the doorway. Landon could now see his mother and father reaching out for him and his sister through the whirls of horrifying rain and lightning.

An amorphous black mass then began to smother Landon and his sister as he desperately tried to reach out for his parents one last time before the front door violently slammed closed.

Landon suddenly flailed himself up and back into the bend of his chair, escaping the hard clutches of his nightmare, as he could feel a coat of tears beginning to flood his tired green eyes. His headphones were still clamped atop his head, and he noticed the record must have continued spinning tirelessly in his sleep. Landon stood up and began to slowly pace between his desk and bed as the moon's luminance fixed across his face, finally deciding it was now best to try return to sleep. Sliding the turntable needle back on its hub and clicking the OFF switch on his record player (ceasing the spinning sound that emitted from his player), Landon then heard the hoots, whistles and metal rowing of a distant train. And now with a spare hand against his bedroom window, following the heavy sounds that now seemed rather near, he could then see through the tired squints of his eyelids the silhouette of a slender cat, basking below in the light of the silver lamppost. As it twirled and twisted its tail in the most calculating way, Landon wondered if the cat had even cared to notice him through his second-story window.

And in the next moment, the cat then turned on its back feet and disappeared into the darkness, well beyond the gentle blue glaze of the lamplight outside. Landon then reeled himself from the dark panel of his window and instead slid between the cool sheets of his uncomfortable bed, still listening for that late-night train in the distance. Never in Landon's life had he ever experienced *such* a palpable dream before, as he thought about it now. Still trying to keep himself calm, he dug his head into his pillow as he kept a steady eye on the stars that continued to watch over him through his bedroom window until his eyes found rest once more.

It was now half-past three o'clock in the morning, and Makari found herself wide-awake with her back against her chipped headboard. Makari's eyes were fixed on the blue light that loomed from atop of the stairs near the hall's end, seeping under the crack of her bedroom door. Little do you know, that it wasn't exactly the ominous light that woke our shivering Makari—since light cannot produce such mammoth roars—it was the rumbling charge outside her bedroom window that shook Makari right out of her sleep. Only seconds after the billowing whistles of what sounded like a massive train rushing directly over the roof of her house did Makari find herself petrified by the ghostly sight that heralded her eerie scene. It was obvious to Makari that this curious light was billowing from somewhere downstairs. Half of her body wanted to jump from her bed and investigate while the other dared not move a muscle from her safe blankets—Makari went for it. As Makari crept to the end of the hall, she felt a heavy churn of bubbles in her stomach, now almost regretting the idea of following the light that roamed downstairs. When Makari reached the bottom of the kitchen stairs, an idea had time to fly through her mind: *could it all be just a dream?*

Standing in the threshold between the kitchen and the sitting room was a tall figure (tall to Makari anyway, after having lunged to the floor). Makari's heart was racing; all she wanted to do was yell out for her brother but dared not move a muscle again, fearing she would disturb the figure that stood only a few feet from her. At last, taking the tiniest breath and rolling to her side: it stood there very calmly and in the sitting room that was now being painted in the most enchanting strokes of light Makari had ever seen. The figure's back was to Makari though, as it stood slightly slouched and, every other second or so, it would twitch its head of hair, as though it were trying to solve the most difficult jigsaw puzzle imaginable. Makari was determined to know the source of this blue light.

Possibly from something in the figure's hand? Makari thought.

As Makari crawled a few inches closer to the figure, she began to hear the faintest sound. A sound that sent a grim chill down her spine: it was the sound of dozen tiny voices echoing around the figure.

"How do you open this?" whispered the Figure.

Makari froze, now noticing that it was holding on to a cane that somehow operated like a candle that was blossoming the room with its flaring tip. Her eyes widened at the sight of the figure's cane beginning to levitating beside itself in the room's frigid air; it was like something out of her favorite fairy tale.

Makari yelped and clapped her mouth shut, hoping the figure hadn't heard her tiny cry. Like Makari's fears dreaded, the figure slowly turned around and shot a glare down to her, who at the same moment, slowly stood up. Makari calculated every movement of the figure: the figure was actually a young man, not much taller or seemingly older looking than Landon; his thin face was lit up by the tip of his incredible cane, but it was not only the thick, black wayfarers the young man wore that caught the eyes of our nervous Makari, he was holding the box that she and her brother had won from Luc Looter. The young man wearing the dark wayfarers took a careful step toward Makari, but at that next second, he jolted his head in the direction of the kitchen stairs.

"—What are you doing down here, Makari?" yawned Aunt Marion, hands on her sides, and with a few, Medusa-like hair curlers atop her head. Makari curled her fists into her eyes, rubbing the burning sensation out of them after adjusting to the sudden blanket of light that had crossed the entire kitchen.

"I was—" Makari reared her head over her shoulder, surveying the room for the man in the sunglasses.

He was gone.

"On your way back up to bed, I hope?" hummed Aunt Marion, following another yawn.

"I was just—grabbing a glass of water, that's all," stumbled Makari, as she reached for a chipped glass in the cupboard.

"Fine, but go back to bed after—it's nearly four!" grumbled Aunt Marion, as she yawned once again, turned on her bare heel, and finally ascending the kitchen stairs. Makari set her glass of water on the cooker's island, not an ounce thirsty, but in need of an answer. She walked slowly to the threshold of the kitchen, giving a look down the darkened hallway to the foyer's end when Makari then bumped a bare foot into something on the floor: it was the strange box from Luc's tent. Crouching down and observing a new crack in the box's frame, she picked up the box and eyed the room around her.

If that man were truly a thief, wouldn't he have just escaped with the box in hand? Makari thought, shoving the box under her arm and quickly followed her aunt back upstairs after she flicked the kitchen lights off behind her.

▼

The next morning arrived far too quickly, Makari thought, slowly rolling out of bed as the irritating and muffled sounds of static blared out from her nearly garbage-ready alarm clock. It was a quarter past nine on that warm, Friday morning. Makari remained in her pajamas and took a peek into her brother's room: his bed had already been made. Then, as the early morning fatigue slowly began to slither off, Makari heard the sounds of Aunt Marion's radio popping a morning soundtrack and the appetizing tapping and clanking of a fork or knife on an indubitably chipped plate downstairs.

"Good morning," said Makari, after a long, tiger-like yawn at the bottom of the staircase.

"Morning, M…there's some toast and scrambled eggs for you on the stove," said Aunt Marion hurriedly, looping a button on her green wool skirt-suit. Makari gave another long yawn and then finally took a seat at the cooker's island next to her brother; he, too, still in his pajamas and with the same tired circles he always seemed to have around his marvelous, green eyes.

"Sleep well? You look like a zombie," Landon grinned, taking a sip of his orange juice, while flipping through the local newspaper comics and bouncing his head to the beat of *The Boy With The Thorn In His Side* by The Smiths.

"*You're* the one who looks like the zombie," smirked Makari, taking a sip from her brother's glass of orange juice. "Why are you in such a rush this morning, Aunt Marion?" Makari then helped herself to a bite of the cinnamon-sprinkled toast from Landon's well-worn plate.

"I have a meeting this morning with one of the directors from that art gallery downtown," said Marion, picking up her purse from the island.

"Aunt Marion, I was just curious: Is there a train station nearby?" inquired Makari, after another bite of her brother's toast. Landon felt a twinge of recollection at Makari's talk of trains.

"A train station? Why would you think that?" hummed Aunt Marion, apparently stumped by her niece's question.

"Yes, because last night it sounded like there was a full, steaming train stampeding right *over* our house," said Makari, miming the shape of a train with her hand, swooping it over her brother's head.

"My goodness, Makari," darted Marion, after rinsing her coffee mug in the sink, "you don't say! I am sure there are other matters in this world than worrying about the possibility of flying trains." Makari could hear a note in her aunt's voice, apparently unmoved by her train query. "Well, I'm ready to go: Landon and M, would you two please fix up the kitchen before you two do anything else today," Landon and Makari then stood from their chairs and followed their aunt into the garage, "please, could you two be on your best behavior —Is that how your parents usually said it?"

Landon and Makari then eyed one another, sensing an odd cringe spawn between them by how much their aunt was oddly trying to mend into her new role.

"I...I guess so," said Makari.

"And I can trust that the both of you will stay away from that attic door while I am out for the day?" Aunt Marion hoped, "I'd just like to return to the house to find that you two had a lovely day all to yourselves—and free of any broken limbs!"

"Aunt Marion, I think we'll be just fine," assured Landon.

"Absolutely, positively—no messes. Conniption, devastation

free," nodded Aunt Marion, as she then slid into the red car, allowing her nephew to close the driver's door for her. As the rumble of the car rolled on out of the humid garage, Landon and Makari swore they heard their aunt hoot, "I'll be home no later than five-thirty!" as she waved with a handkerchief in hand to our siblings as a goodbye token, for now. Aunt Marion made a right turn onto Islay Street and was gone.

"Aunt Marion told me she found you downstairs early this morning," said Landon, placing his breakfast plate into the kitchen sink.

"You'll never believe what I saw last night," whispered Makari. "Why do you think I look so dead this morning?"

"I guess neither of us had a nice sleep," said Landon.

"What happened to you?" queried Makari.

"I was having some of the most terrible nightmares," said Landon, suddenly rubbing his eyes.

"As bad as the ones you use to have back on Kirkwood?" dared Makari.

"*Worse*—One of them actually ripped me outta sleep," said Landon.

"Can you remember what happened in any of your dreams?" said Makari.

"Not," shifted Landon, "so much of them, anymore. But there was this one, odd moment in the dreams when...I kissed you."

"What?" spat Makari, poking her tongue out and cracking a grin.

"The dream had something to do when you were born," teetered Landon, confused by the dream's images, "people around us were happy about what was happening...and mom and dad were there, too."

"That's what caused you to have nightmares?" said Makari, as her brother returned to his seat at the cooker's island beside her.

"Not entirely, but don't worry about it," said Landon, feeling his stomach churn at the sudden thought of remembering what his dream had truly frightened him with.

"Well, I might've actually *lived* a nightmare last night," nodded Makari.

For the next five minutes, Makari told her story about the young man in sunglasses from the night before, as Landon suddenly stepped away from the island and seemed as though he was about to go on a search.

"Makari—Where's the box?" asked Landon.

"Upstairs, in my room," said Makari, apprehensively.

"Let's go get it…"

Landon and Makari each took to their rooms and quickly dressed for the day, before their examination of their trinket could begin. Together, Landon and Makari returned downstairs with the box in hand. Makari took the box from under her arm and gently placed it on the coffee table in front of them (never minding the incomplete picture puzzle that remained splayed there, too) as they each took a spot on the large sofa.

"I think, that man was without a doubt someone Luc probably sent to track us down," guessed Landon, eyeing the box. "Aunt Marion probably just scared him away."

"Look, the frame is badly cracked now," said Makari pointing at the triangular lock. Without hesitation, Landon then twisted the small pyramid counter-clockwise, realizing that that was the only direction the pyramid wanted to be turned. After a few more twists, Landon was unable to twist the pyramid any farther, and as he released it the shape began to slowly spin and chiming out six unusual notes. Landon and Makari quickly reeled back as the box lid then popped open, startling both of them. The Tuolumnes, for some odd reason, leaned in closer to see what was hiding inside.

"He was trying to open it, I knew it!" Makari whooped.

It was a beautiful, golden cube. There it sat, very light in weight until Landon dared to pick it up out if its wooden shell and place it next to its broken home on the coffee table.

"Feel it, it's—so cold," said Landon, marveling at the cube. Fitting perfectly in Landon's hands, he eyed every intricate detail and that had been etched into its solid design like dozens of tiny hieroglyphs.

"If this were real gold, wouldn't it be extremely heavy?" said Makari, as Landon placed the cube into his sister's hands.

"Your guess is as good as mine, M," said Landon.

"These words, they look scrambled somehow," said Makari, examining the cube, closely.

"Scrambled?" said Landon, tilting his head.

"Landon, these *are* scrambled words, almost like a puzzle—wait," said Makari, as she then bit her lip. Makari began to scan the cube a second time: She noticed the fine detail in the cube was not only just scrambled words, but axes around which the cube could be easily rearranged with a simple twist of its structure.

"What are you doing?" asked Landon, watching his sister's move more closely.

"Look!" cried Makari, as she flung the cube back on to the table, "the words!" Makari had somehow awakened the cube with her one movement of the piece, as a letter **T** began to glow a magnificent bronze.

"This is *not* any ordinary puzzle, M…we've got to put it back in its box," shied Landon, as he stood up form the sofa taking a few steps back.

"*No*, this could be the answer to all the strange occurrences," urged Makari, "let's finish it while we're here, together." Makari then tapped the sofa seat cushion next to her.

Landon took a deep breath and glared at the cube on the coffee table, their first move still glaring bronze. Wheeling around the coffee table, he kneeled down opposite his sister with his hands flat on the table.

"This is your call, sis," said Landon.

The **T** was still glowing as if waiting for their next move.

"Where on this cube would this T match another word?" said Makari, scanning the cube again. "The T must be a starting point, so…"

For the next hour, Landon and Makari each took turns at adjusting the cube, and after a few tries, the siblings realized, that if they turned the cubes pivot in the wrong order, the letters would lose their radiance and needed to treat that as a sign of an incorrect combination of words.

Landon and Makari had created three words in just over an hour of time:

"'The,' 'guardian,' and 'to'...these words by themselves don't make sense," said Landon, turning the cube around in his hands.

"Maybe it doesn't have to make sense...it could be part of another riddle? A random verse?" said Makari, with a few scraps of paper and a pen in hand (that she had fetched earlier), writing their three words out in different combinations.

"*The guardian to*..." Makari read aloud her writing on the paper.

"Find!" shouted Landon.

"Find, what?" darted Makari.

"Another word formed after I twisted the cube this way," Landon pointed. Our siblings had now four words formed in their game with the cube, still examining the trinket, even more closely now. As they continued to twist and turn the cube in every possible combination, within minutes later, they had nearly formed, what they believed to be, a sentence.

"*The guardian to find...where the guardian...*" Makari read aloud the words they had combined together. "Ugh, I think I have these final words figured out, Landon—but, the cube won't budge anymore."

Makari then placed the cube in Landon's outstretched hands with her own resting on top.

"The final words are in the center, here," said Makari.

As Landon held the top and bottom bases of the cube in his steady hands, Makari fixed her eyes on the few remaining letters. A few seconds more and Makari turned the cube's center pivot three clicks to the right:

The guardian to find, where the guardian to see.

CLICK! The combination of the cube was complete and without warning, the words that were together as one stopped glowing. The cube then spun out of Landon's hands with a heavy thud back onto the tabletop. Landon and Makari sprang to their feet and began to witness the most extraordinary scene. The cube came to life at an instant, even more than it already had, rolling onto one of its corners, aligned perfectly vertical on the table. Landon and Makari remained as calm as possible while the cube then burst into sudden movement again, spinning faster, and faster, and faster, as it began to slowly levitate into the air. The cube then abruptly stopped spinning, settling peculiarly suspended in midair.

"Wait, M," said Landon, pinning his sister back with an arm out in front of her, as she edged toward the cube.

The cube began to twist and turn, seeming to produce ephemeral sequences of words of its own volition. The golden trinket then began to rapidly fold out, spawning miniature cubes around it…and more cubes, and more and more…this scene went on for nearly ten seconds more, as the cube took on another form, entirely. The gold that was once plated around the cubes conjoined, taking the shape of something long and vaguely oval, As each gold piece locked into place, it transmuted into wood, and as the final piece fastened into place, the area enclosed by the oval wavered and solidified into a sheet of perfect glass.

It was a mirror. What was once a tiny cube that fit perfectly into Landon and Makari's hands had now morphed into a towering, wooden mirror. The bewitching gold was still in evidence, but had now become infused pieces of wood that bordered the mirror. The words that Landon and Makari had formed as the cube's combination were now stretched across a banner at the top of the mirror that was engraved with three large **V**'s.

Landon and Makari eyed each other, both bone-white, but still reluctant to quit without learning what mysteries this bizarre object could reveal. The mirror hovered effortlessly, very still and embossed with detail that was far beyond any craftsmanship either Landon or

Makari had ever seen in their young lives. Each side of the mirror had flourishing embellishments of swans in flight with their gentle wings tangled in ivy vines.

Landon and Makari then warily inched closer to their mirror—struck with the unquestionable belief that somehow the mirror was now theirs—seeing their full bodies in the giant reflection in the center of the family room.

"How the hell are we ever going to hide this?" Landon sighed, seeing his favorite bumblebee striped shirt in his reflection.

"Pfft!" Makari coughed, "hide it—are you kidding? It's levitating as it is!" panicked Makari, rolling up the sleeves of her darling turquoise shirt.

"Aunt Marion's going to think we broke into the attic if we don't hide it," said Landon, giving his head a baffled shake, "imagine her screams when she sees this."

Landon couldn't help but laugh now.

"I have an idea," said a calm voice.

Landon and Makari then darted their eyes at the reflection that stood behind them, smiling. Our siblings spun on their heels and greeted the young man in sunglasses with a few shrieks as if he were some decrepit monster.

"Who are you, what do you want?" demanded Landon, arming himself with the cube's wooden box, while the young man remained calm, leaning slightly on his sleek, white-tipped cane.

Makari darted behind her brother, "That's him..."

"Of course it's me, missy," said the Wayfarer Man, still very calm, "I mean you two absolutely *no harm*—as for that wooden box in your hands, young fellow." The young Wayfarer Man nodded, "I hear splinters can be quite nasty."

"What are you doing here?" said Landon, still nervously armed with the splintering box.

"These past months," said the Wayfarer Man, adjusting his thick black pair of wayfarers, "have been dreadful waiting to see you again," the Wayfarer Man continued, walking between our startled siblings.

The wayfarer man stepped up to the base of the mirror, admiring it, and tracing a single finger along the deep engravings.

"If only you knew how powerful this piece of art actually is," the Wayfarer Man lamented.

"We don't care how powerful—" Landon tried.

"*Oh, Landon,* but I really think that you do!" the Wayfarer Man playfully snapped, slowly twisting away from the mirror, "I know you do, because you're still standing there. It actually makes me sick that you're even detesting the thought of not wanting to know this mirror's unrivaled abilities."

"You know us—" Makari then tried.

"*Yes,* Makari, I know quite a lot about you and your brother, as I should…that's my job," said the Wayfarer Man, taking a step toward to the siblings.

"A-and your job is?" quivered Makari.

"First, may I help myself to another glass of water?" asked the Man.

"Another?" lurched Landon.

"Yes—your sister here was kind enough to leave me a glass on the counter, last night," nodded the Wayfarer Man, "and if I'm going to do all the talking, as I'm afraid I feel as though I'm going to be, I'll need to keep my tongue fresh."

Landon and Makari looked at one another, both visibly stunned by the man in wayfarers that still seemed so calm and collected. Landon then expelled the splintering box down to the floor while he and his sister watched their visitor stride toward the cupboards beside the kitchen sink.

"You're welcome to…help yourself," nodded Makari, watching the Wayfarer Man figure his own way around the tiny kitchen.

The Wayfarer Man nodded in return, and again turned on his booted heel, giving his cane a single twirl as it then somehow wondrously thinned out into the air with a snap, missing our siblings spark into a silent awe as they watched the young man glide into the kitchen while he hummed whatever might be his favorite song. The Wayfarer Man carefully selected one of the more hard-done-by glasses residing in the cupboard, then ferried it over the faucet and gave it a quick spritz.

"Now, where do I begin?" said the Wayfarer Man, after a few puckered sips, now returning to our mystified siblings whose presence he seemed to have only just remembered.

"Where…did your cane go?" puzzled Makari.

"I'll get to that later—"

"—You could begin by telling us *your* name," interrupted Landon.

"How rude of me, sneaking into your home without ever properly introducing myself…my name is Jade Cooper," he said, throwing a spare hand out at Landon. Makari shook the young man's hand quickly, still dazzled by his cane trick.

Landon remained hesitant to shake Jade Cooper's hand, as he was busy calculating the eccentric black man that stood in rouge boots, and only a few inches taller than him. Dressed in a palate of three striking and definitely solid tones, Jade Cooper embarked in his beloved and faded black pea coat that (having been noticeably stitched in a few odd places) covered the solid black vest where a red necktie rested against a white buttoned-down shirt, and all perfectly matching his solid black slacks and his unkempt jet black hair that, at times, brushed atop the frames of his wide and solid black wayfarers.

"Are you some sort of…magician?" asked Makari, eyeing the sharp man.

"No, *no*," assured Jade, as he adjusted his thin tie, "I'm a detective. That move I did with my cane was just a bad habit of mine that I like to perform in front of strangers—catches them off guard."

"What kind of detective are you, anyway?" said Landon.

"The best of my kind—well—the only one of my kind, to be honest," said Jade.

"Quite obviously not a detective from around here," added

Landon.

"Right you are," said Jade, nodding at Landon.

"Where are you from, exactly?" asked Makari. Jade Cooper then unexpectedly pointed his long arm at the mirror. "A place as curious as your own."

Landon and Makari eyed each other once again, just as you or I might have done if a man in a thin necktie told us he lived in a mirror. Our reactions, however, are only of academic interests. Our siblings, on the other hand, have a rather more immediate stake in things.

"That's funny, but where are you from, exactly?" forwarded Landon.

"I suspect, and others have agreed with me on the matter, that you two might have some difficulty in understanding, particularly you, Landon," said Jade, shaking his head.

"Others, what *others*?" Makari said, coming close to Jade.

"The R.C.C., otherwise known as the Revlenion Chamberlains Committee," emitted Jade. "They're nosey employers of mine, who, with a generous grant from the Haus of Cappa, have enlisted my expertise to handle your case."

"*Cappa*, you mean from Cappa Valley?" sounded Landon, assuming.

"Why, yes. It's the royal municipal of Revlenion," Jade was explaining, until he threw a fast stare at the siblings, "hold that last line…how are you two already aware of Cappa Valley?"

"By *chance*?" clammed Makari.

"Not a chance!" said Jade. "Careful secrecy defies that sort of chance."

"That's how we came into possession of that mirror, well, now it's a mirror," said Makari, addled by the sight of the mirror, "it was a cube before we solved the riddle that was etched onto itself, and then, it formed into…that."

"I've known about this mirror for years, that information isn't important to me, what's important is, how you two were aware of

Cappa *before* my arrival?" said Jade, as he began to circle the siblings, awaiting a quick answer.

"A man from the market downtown, who gave us the cube, spoke about that place. He seemed awfully terrified of it, and now I'm beginning to know why," recalled Makari.

"Luc was his name, and he didn't just give us the cube...we won it," noted Landon.

"Luc Looter...I *knew* it," grunted Jade. "How exactly did you win the cube?"

"He asked us to answer some odd riddle of his and I was able to answer it," said Landon.

"You answered his riddle?" asked Jade, curiously.

"Yes," said Landon.

Jade returned to his calm state, arching a curious eyebrow above the frame of his wayfarers.

"Should we be worried?" quaked Makari.

"Not when you're with me," Jade reminded, as he then came close to the siblings, "Luc is the one who should be worried; breaking nearly a dozen laws...you *two* should be more concerned about why I have come here today." Jade then paused, as though preparing for a long speech. "I have been searching for nearly two years, trying to find the perfect specimen that would not only have the answer for me, but possibly, be the principal player to a peculiar manifesto that has remained unclaimed for many, many years. I've been keen to acquire a venturer that possesses and reflects the abilities like that of a noble fellowship whom originate in my country," Jade pointed at the mirror, again, "the Elddri Mirror is a threshold to the place where anyone like either of you can display the extraordinary capabilities that I dream one of you keeps, stowed deep within those precious minds of yours. I must say again, for the past two years, and I will not lie, there *have been* a few conundrums on my expedition. While trying to guide these children to or through Revlenion, this mirror here has played its part by detecting whomever steps through its vortex, which has troubled several of my cases. As puzzling as that may sound, the Elddri Mirror can actually think—"

"What do you mean the mirror, 'thinks'?" queried Landon.

"The Elddri Mirror is a living, magnificent figure," noted Jade. "It's not all wood and glass, as it may look, but it's all part of the guise it must retain in order to protect the three-centuries-old sanctuary that now stands with the Haus of Cappa, and myself. We are the ones trying to preserve it and invite you two in."

"Can the mirror decide who can enter Revlenion?" asked Makari.

"Eh, well, it allows *everyone* in, I should say," Jade said, tapping his fingers on his chin, "the mirror is blind, not holding a single capability of judgment when it senses whatever wayfarer wishes to pass through its frame, however, it has been charmed to detect and neglect those who'd rather be dishonest in their engagement with the mirror. Tricky creation. The mirror has a clever way of guiding you through itself, too, which we'll soon demonstrate, but first," said Jade, as he then pulled a red-ribbon tied scroll out from his coat pocket, "here's your summons to further explain why I am here."

But before Jade could hand either of our siblings the scroll, he slipped a quite curious line at our siblings that would probably have anyone to wonder, "like I said before, I've been on the search for *one* curious child that could be connected to an unquestionably risky manifesto, but as interesting as the Elddri Mirror might be, it's evident to me, that with the addition of a sibling before me, makes me wonder—that the superb workings of the mirror might already be in motion." After Jade handed Landon and Makari the auburn scroll, upon unraveling it, together our siblings read aloud the curly, embossed words before them while Jade leaned in with an ear:

HAUS OF CAPPA
a Manor of Wisdom and Amenity for the State
Est. 1792

~

To Whom Queried the Ventures,

The Haus of Cappa and the Knights of Ordinheir would like to cordially invite you to Revlenion; the birthplace of marvels—*just like you*. The Haus looks forward to meeting you and wishes you the best on your future expeditions.

With all honor,

Antoine Emmanuel and Dionne Mariette Cappa.

"What sort of manifesto might we have?" asked Makari.

"The finest one of them all," nodded Jade.

"What is a manifesto, exactly?" asked Landon.

"Well, by definition, a manifesto is along the lines of a declaration, but as I've come to guess from my research, in Revlenion...a manifesto could truly mean anything," nodded Jade, adjusting his black sunglasses.

"You expect us to just run away with you to some foreign country and accept this invitation like it's for some birthday party?" said Landon, eyeing the scroll again.

"Let Jade finish, Lan," said Makari, intervening.

"Well, in that precise notion of yours, I suppose that's the gist of my plan—you could dwell in this house here forever and have a go at trying to convince your aunt that this mirror here is all part of her crazed imagination or take the dive into the eye of Elddri, where you'll no doubt find its beauty," winked Jade. Landon glanced over to his sister, seemingly inclined to Jade Cooper's agenda.

"He's right, Lan," said Makari, as her brother then came close to her.

"You're not so sure of your abilities, are you, Landon? Even though you're showing the symptoms of the others that failed," said Jade, hunching his body to get a closer look into Landon's eyes, "you just might be the greatest star a manifesto has ever bore."

Landon then gulped; the very idea of him not knowing what sort of impact a manifesto could bring was daunting. It was only an hour ago he thought nothing more of the cube that recently was could elaborate into a scene like the one he now stood. Eyeing

Makari closely, she not noticing in those fast seconds, Jade then took a few steps between the siblings while giving his right hand a quick twirl. Just as it had disappeared into the air before, Jade's black and white tipped cane reappeared into his hand as he raised the end of his cane to the top center of the mirror.

"Now, how about that little demonstration I promised?" grinned Jade, as he readied himself, as though he were retracing a mental note, deep within his mind. Landon and Makari watched closely as Jade began to trace with the end of his cane, in a counter-clockwise form, three inverted triangles against the glass of the mirror. "'Three counter V's, shall allow you to see'…a friend once told me to remember that, should I ever have to cross this mirror." Jade then took a step back as the mirror restored itself into an almost breathing state of life once more.

Instantly, the three reflections of Landon, Makari and Jade that stood in the mirror began to ripple, as the oval glass of the mirror suddenly metamorphosed into a pool of silvery liquid. Each of the trio's reflections returned as the silver mass began to still, while Makari came close with her own reflection.

"If I was you, I'd surely be convinced," said Jade, eyeing the siblings with his reflection from the silver glass.

"How is this possible?" asked Makari, as she touched the silver glass that was cool to the touch, seeing her freckled face ripple in the mirror.

"It's possible because it is what it is and was created by extraordinary people that weren't too different from you," said Jade, eyeing Makari.

"Landon, we have to listen to him," said Makari, "we both know what sort of abilities he's talking about. We've always wanted to know what they mean."

"M, *be quiet*," snapped Landon, quickly.

"Listen to her," urged Jade, "open your mind and learn to master your birthright, the abilities that have been straining to reveal themselves." Jade then pointed at Landon's chest with his cane, in the place where his heart would be. "I did."

"We'll follow you, Jade, but promise me now, that if any harm comes to follow my sister or myself, you will return us back here—agreed?" said Landon, with a hand out at Jade.

"Like I attested earlier about my previous prospects, there are always going to conundrums when you pass through this mirror, but I'll promise you this, Landon and Makari Tuolumne, I will ensure your safety to the best of my ability," bowed Jade, as he saluted, gripping the can over his heart with one hand and clasping Landon's in the other.

"Fair enough," nodded Makari, as she gripped her brother by the hand.

"Fair enough," echoed Landon, as he eyed his sister with a freeing grin.

"Perfect. Now…go grab your coats," said Jade, with a tap of his cane. The Tuolumne siblings returned to the sitting room after each of them grabbed their favorite jackets from the hallway closet upstairs and now, with their own coats donned and Jade at the ready, Makari unraveled the sleeves of her favored denim jacket, buttoning its cuffs at just the right size around her wrists. Landon, in turn, left his ragged red hoodie unzipped as he and his sister returned to the room. Jade then popped his neck and shook the stiffness out of his shoulders as he then followed with a few lines of preparation before their departure. "Remember, the Elddri Mirror ultimately decides your entry, we'll begin with this test," continued Jade, as he gave a quick turn on his booted heel and brusquely sent his hand through the silver mass. Landon and Makari watched with trepidation as Jade's hand, arm, and half of his body slid through the mirror. Makari then gave a glance behind the mirror, hoping to find some trick door, but there was none.

"All it takes is trust," said Jade, as a dozen silky blue strands began to slowly slither from the mirror's silver pool. Jade snatched one of the unraveling strands that looked like stringy arms that disentangled with awaiting hands. "Just grab one and don't let go!"

Allowing the misty hand to guide him, Jade Cooper vanished beyond the ripples of the mirror.

"Is this a terrible dream?" pondered Landon, suddenly aghast as one of the blue hands began wrapping around him and his sister's torso.

"Makari! Grab my hand!" shouted Landon, as his sister was then lifted up as high as the ceiling.

Together, Landon and Makari were being reeled into the mirror like two easy catches from a harbor. The strands were gentle, though, almost ticklish, but what Landon feared most was the thought that he and his sister were at the mercy of whatever eerie unknown rested beyond the mirror. Makari was laughing and relished every moment while the strand pulled her closer to the mirror.

"Why are you laughing?" panicked Landon, as he stretched an arm out to his sister.

"Trust it, Land—" tried Makari, before she was channeled through the silvery mass.

She was gone.

"MAKARI!" screamed Landon. Landon feared that his sister was done for, and knew he was next. Struggling to free himself from the strand, Landon could see his fear-drenched face in the mirror's rippling reflection. As he was reeled closer toward the mirror, Landon instead crossed his arms over his face and allowed himself to believe in his sister's last words. After one final breath, as though Landon were about to take a mighty dive into an icy river, he disappeared beyond the silvery threshold; just like his sister and Jade had done before....

Landon was now falling fast.

He couldn't tell what was up or what was down.

He felt light as a feather amidst the roaring sounds that whirled around him.

He didn't feel dizzy, not in the slightest, but could sense a tickling churn in his stomach, like plummeting from the highest point of his favorite roller-coaster.

The air that blasted across his face was as chill as the wind on the coldest winter day, and the silver mass that siphoned his body was as delightful as the plushest bedside blanket…

The final sight Landon caught was of a giant, black and white spiral spinning relentlessly, knowing his body was being drawn inexorably toward it.

And with a golden flash that was bright as the summer sun.

The curious Tuolumne siblings had finally arrived in Revlenion.

CAPPA VALLEY
THE ROYAL SEAT OF REVLENION

Landon opened his eyes and felt the strand that had wrapped around his torso pull him back like a stretching cord, slowing his plummet to the rocky ground below. The strand then calmed Landon's tossing body, as it carefully brought him to his feet, uniting him with his alive and well sister and Jade.

"You took forever up there, Landon," said Jade, "have a good time?"

"Is that your way of having *a good time*?" huffed Landon, pointing up at the strand that slithered back up to the clustering gray clouds above, waving its fingers in a way that almost looked as though it were trying to say, *ta-ta*!

"What was that, anyway?" asked Makari.

"That was our bodies passing through the port of the mirror, to safely arrive here at Elddri's Point," explained Jade, "and those strands—well, hands, really—they keep you from getting lost in the split from your Poplar Drive and *this* little country of ours—to let go of your guiding hand—all the luck is to you ever finding your way out."

"How comforting," said Landon, groaning.

"*And*…I'm sorry to have forgotten to mention that before we exited your living room," said Jade, curling a childish smirk as if Landon knew that Jade found a dash of chaos to be as acceptable as sugar in one's cup of tea.

"Is this place the only exit?" asked Makari, suddenly feeling a small and irritating stone rolling in the inside of one of her shoes.

"No, there are several—entrances included—but we'll get to that later; you don't want me to reveal everything to you now, do you? Follow me this way, before we get caught up in the mist," said Jade, as he signaled to the siblings. It seemed to be the late afternoon there in Cappa Valley, though the day maintained a heavy overcast that loomed overhead. Together, Landon and Makari hurriedly followed Jade out of the rocky cavern as the side of the jagged hill that they were standing on began to billow a knot of the thickest fog. The trio had made their way to the end of a narrow trail as some of the fog slowly parted with the eastern winds, when Landon and Makari could see a wide, rolling valley of pine trees and splayed through its core was: "Cappa Valley, the royal seat of Revlenion," said Jade, welcoming the siblings to his town. The pine valley stretched as far as our trios' eyes could see, and booming with an enormous square plaza that bedded in-between the embracing forest. From their daunting heights, the trio could see far below: a dozen or more villages sitting scattered around the center and the tiniest dots of movement that were the people of Cappa Valley carrying out their lives amongst the downtown streets. "A sight for sore eyes, isn't it? You two should see Cappa Square at night from this point, it's like a bowl of shining stars in a dance."

"You see, everything is fine, Lan —" tried Makari, grasping for her brother's side, as the roar of a train whooshed overhead.

Like a plane zooming in the sky, a glistening-silver locomotive pierced like a massive art-deco bullet through the grayish clouds ahead, leaving mammoth swirling cotton-like clouds of mist in its wake.

"You could've told us we're standing in the path of a train!" gasped Landon, as his darted eyes trailed after the cloud-railed train.

"I've never known for that train to ride that low over these hillsides, my deepest apologies for the scare," frowned Jade.

"A…t…a train…*a train* in the sky?" huffed Makari, trying to catch her breath, pointing at the soaring locomotive.

"Absolutely! The Egarim Express of the Cloudline Railways—one of many modes of transportation in and out of Revlenion just like I had mentioned earlier," said Jade, as he then continued their journey down the hillside, until the trio advanced onto another gravelly route.

"One of many?" asked Landon.

"Yep, anyone can catch a ride on the Egarim, that's what I took to get myself to your house late last night," noted Jade. "Oh, and I don't believe I ever apologized for frightening or nearly getting you into trouble with your aunt last night either, Makari…meeting you in that fashion wasn't exactly part of my plan."

"So that *was* you and that train I heard late last night?" grinned Makari, as she hopped over a fat boulder.

"Indeed, how else was I supposed to get to Poplar Drive?" said Jade.

"What would've happened had one of our neighbors seen that train hovering our house?" asked Landon.

"Sure it would have been a mighty dilemma, even the R.C.C. would shake at such a thought," cringed Jade, "but I gambled on the idea that nobody should be awake at such hours of the night. Come to think of it now, I hope someone on your street actually did see the Egarim, as there's no harm in witnessing something fantastic."

"Imagine if Derek saw that train through his window?" guffawed Makari, eyeing her brother over her shoulder.

"We'd never hear the last of it," said Landon, still carefully trekking beside his sister.

"As I was saying," Jade continued, "*sure* there is more than one way of getting into this country, and out. The Elddri Mirror however is one of the more complex modes that you two have managed to reopen. As for that beast of a train, it can take you anywhere your voyage desires. And just so you know, the Royal Egarim Station is just a few avenues east from the central plaza."

Makari then noticed a golden plaque that had been fixed in a large stone on their trail:

Four Nobles Place
a village of honor

"Come on, we're almost there," hurried Jade, as our siblings pressed onward.

"Where?" hummed Makari.

"Just down this trail we'll arrive to my cottage," said Jade, leading them down the now grassy road, "I'm in a dire need of a coffee break, how about you two?

"Sure?" Landon shrugged, realizing no one had ever suggested such an affair to him—not that Landon had never had his own cup of coffee, it was only Jade's phrase that he had only heard those turn of words from middle-school teachers, with a sigh or two, at the end of every class period. It was as if the cup of coffee itself were some kind of miracle elixir that could fuel the mind well enough into the next day.

"Though, I can never make my espresso as creamy and delightful as they do at my favorite café downtown," hummed Jade, then frowning, "le sigh."

"What did that placard mean by 'a village of honor'?" asked Makari, unable to contain her questions.

"'Tis' the subject of what I am going to explain to you and your brother, once we stop at my house," said Jade.

"Oh," said Makari, biting her lip.

By now, the trio had reached the road's end arriving at the few Tudor cottages that sat quietly at the foothills of Cappa Square.

Landon and Makari continued to follow Jade through the village as they went. The trio came up to a wooden house that, by the looks of it, needed a little repair. Standing out like a wart, even among the homely cottages surrounding it, Jade's gleeful abode loomed ahead. Obviously Jade didn't mind, to him, it was just home sweet home.

Landon and Makari glanced around: families were preparing for dinner or countless evening agendas. The other cottages were spotless and well apportioned with smoking chimneys. However, they too were in need of a little splash of new paint. Jade then quickly began to search for his house key in every pocket inside of his coat.

"Only a brief rest here, *I promise*, so don't get too comfy," nodded Jade, as they crossed the tall yellow grass and ascended the couple steps on the short patio. "Here, it's the red one—I always forget," huffed Jade, seemingly to himself, and with a single quick turn of his tiny bronze and red embellished house key, the trio entered the cottage.

It was a small place, but still spacious enough for Landon and Makari to feel comfortable standing in. The cottage housed numerous bookshelves; tabletops of endless stacks of unorganized files seemed almost to revel in their ubiquity, watched over by the frames of old RKO Pictures and a dozen other cinema posters Landon and Makari soon recognized.

"*King Kong...The Hidden Fortress*," hummed Landon, tracing a few curious fingers across the rare yet damaged movie posters that hung on the walls.

"*Vertigo*...I remember that one; Landon you used to watch that movie almost every morning before school," said Makari, eyeing the leaning poster frame on the cottage floor.

"I sure did," said Landon, finding himself cracking a smile, "you remember that?"

"How could I not? That scene with the floating head and the beautiful blond actress, oh, what was her name?" said Makari.

"Kim Novak," answered Jade.

"Yes, her!" Makari clapped.

"Everyone always favors that movie," said Jade, grinning, "to me, the real prize to any Hitchcock picture can be found in *Strangers on a Train*—or—most definitely in *Psycho*. Oh, never mind it, don't get me started on this. I could seriously talk about movies till I'm violet as Violet."

Jade's lounge was only big enough for a single padded down sofa and, much like his pea coat, patchwork was in evidence among Jade's furnishings. There was a small circular coffee table made from half of a tree trunk, with thick branches serving as table legs and that was placed in front of the sofa. Jade quickly made his way to the bed that was just visible among the room's clutter, resting his coat on the corner of the dusty headboard. He then turned toward Landon and Makari with another quick twirl of his cane as it vanished away.

Jade waved at the siblings to claim a spot on his holey sofa, watching them as their bodies sank into the old seat cushions that popped dust into the air around them.

"Sorry, it's a tad dusty 'round here," said Jade as both Landon and Makari each exploded into a sneezing fit. Jade seemed to be in his kitchen, found just behind the sofa, shuffling through clanking pots and pans.

"How did you come across all of these rare posters?" asked Landon.

"From the Le Emmle Palace, downtown; it's actually under renovation as we speak," said Jade, as he toppled over a stack of iron pans, "it's a gorgeously aged cinema; where else do you think your country sends old movies when they're done with them? And a few of those posters are the ones I was able to collect over the years while I worked there when I was in high school, a few years ago. I simply *love* going to the movies. However, it's only just that I've recently developed a phase of never having time to go anymore."

"I know how you feel," said Landon, as a splash of his memory that was as fast as a droplet of ink falling onto a blank yet ready page, he knew that the last time he had ventured to a cinema was not at all the most pleasant time. "I haven't been to the movies in almost a year."

"Oh…" said Jade, sensing a vibration of trouble in the air; he could somehow hear the slightest bit of sadness in Landon's voice.

Makari then eyed her brother, recognizing a hint in her brother's tone and trying her best to distract him from falling back into their shared dark past.

"Are you ever going to explain how you can produce that fantastic trick of yours?" said Makari, mimicking Jade's twirl with a hand in the air while as she watched Jade humorously tumble throughout his clunky kitchen as she did.

"I have you unquestionably hooked by that ole trick, don't I?" laughed Jade, slapping away nets of abandoned cobwebs that blanketed over a pile of his coffee mugs and then quickly dousing them with water from the kitchen faucet.

"Without a doubt, the best trick I've ever witnessed a magician pull off," simpered Landon.

"A *detective*," said Jade, humming.

"I'll call you Detective Jade Cooper after you introduce us to the manifesto you're unquestionably keen on presenting," said Landon, "until then...*magician*."

"Quite the cheeky kid," grinned Jade, "fair game, buddy." Makari shook her head at her brother who simply returned her a nod and blooming grin.

"Not too much cleaning around here, huh?" said Makari, tracing her sights around the cottage again.

"I don't do too much cooking or cleaning here—I always get so anxious and caught up with my cases, not to mention, I stay most of my nights up at the Manor," explained Jade.

"The Manor?" asked Makari, excitement coursing through her words.

"The House of Cappa, where Antoine and Dionne live, the ones who've summoned you," said Jade, returning to a maddening search for his favorite coffee press.

"Do you have any matches for the chimney? It's getting a little cold in here," said Landon, as he stood from the couch. Jade finally found his coffee press, raising it into the air with a triumphant smile.

"Yes, on top of the mantelpiece," pointed Jade, "there should be a long canister of matches. Perfect timing anyway—go ahead and light the fireplace, I'm going to need the fire to heat this kettle."

Landon took only a few clustered steps over piled books on the floor to the mantelpiece that was dusty enough for him to spell his entire name out. A tall copper canister rested on the edge of the mantel; he twisted the lid off and reached into the canister pulling out a single long wooden match, and with one strike, the match sparked a flame and he threw it into the already lumbered fireplace. Within seconds, the entire cottage had its own blanket of warmth. Jade then quickly rinsed out his coffee press and prepped another fresh batch of ground coffee beans from his dust-ridden jars. Jade then returned to the siblings, coffee press in one hand and three espresso mugs in the other and finally taking his own seat on a short ottoman, and right where he began:

"We'll let the kettle heat up for a few minutes, then we'll enjoy a delicious press of coffee, before tonight's dinner," said Jade, hooking his cast iron kettle above the crackling fire.

"Dinner, here?" said Landon, eyeing the cramped setting.

"No, ha, *no*…we'll be having dinner with the Heads of Cappa tonight, up at their manor—I'll get into all of those fancy details later," said Jade, as he handed empty mugs to our siblings.

"What time is it here, anyway?" said Makari, eyeing the darkening cottage.

"Ah, yes, *time*," Jade then slipped his bronze pocket watch out from the inside of his coat. Flicking it open, "it's a quarter-past five in the evening here in Cappa, see," Jade pointed at his clock's face that housed red and green dials depicting his time and the siblings'— "when *you* are here in this country, each event you or your brother passes through the Elddri Mirror, or by any other means of transportation in or out of Revlenion, time in your world—somehow —becomes altered. Once you exit through Elddri's Point, or by any other means of transportation into Revlenion, your time is set back into motion, at regular speed. Your Poplar Drive and my Revlenion run side-by-side through *almost* exact times; it's when the time barrier is then broken, in which you've obviously passed through, ultimately becomes altered. Fascinating, isn't it?"

"I won't ask about it again," said Makari, puzzled.

"So, who or what is Elddri, exactly?" asked Landon, as he took a seat on the sofa with Makari, again.

"More like, who *was* Elddri," said Jade, "he's key to the origin of my little trick. A rather interesting tale that results in the *why* you have been summoned to Revlenion in the first place."

Unlatching a secret compartment on the leg of the coffee table, Jade pulled from the hollow trunk an emerald-dyed and suede bound book. Makari guessed the book to be more than a hundred-years-old, telling from its tired trim. With ease, Jade peeled open the book, a pop-up book—to Landon's surprise. Cursive writing abruptly sprang to life; paper and page took their places, folding every which way until weaving between the clever cutouts that depicted an eerie forest that splayed the book's title, *The Siblings from Shelverstein*. Makari was mesmerized; a pop-up book with such astounding mechanics, it was like a book out of her wildest daydreams. To Landon, the funny workings within the book engaged in a peculiar way that reminded him of a stop-motion-animation, functioning right before his very green eyes every time Jade turned a page.

"Is this a scary story?" asked Makari, side-eyeing her brother, as if he knew the answer. Makari seemed antsy when Landon looked at his sister, and in such a way that it reminded him of a time he made the mistake inviting her to his room to watch a terrifying Boris Karloff film one, late summer's night once ago. Watching scary movies were always a protest in the Tuolumne residence, but something was now telling Landon and Makari…maybe they needed them now more than ever.

"Not yet…" warned Jade.

Jade turned to the next page, revealing a fanned illustration of four unique trees each haunted with humanesque expressions embedded in their trunks.

"Just as long as there aren't any werewolves; I hate werewolves —ask Lan," vexed Makari.

"I'll take your word," nodded Jade, readying for his story time, again, "The Four Nobles were the founders of this country, each of them creating very remarkable relics that have since paved the history for Revlenion and the creation of the first manifesto."

Jade pulled another tab within in the remarkable book, revealing hidden squares of text, furthering his sharing of this strange history lesson.

"Long before Revlenion came to be, and ages before either one of us were born, in a far land's pasture, were a dozen of these trees called, Shelversteins. They were a society of mythical trees; Saint-like, if you will. Powers so misunderstood that only a forest where these botanical creatures resided, could only, somehow, be contained. Poet, the Shelversteins' youngest, one day announced he had a strong intuition after a long meditation under an autumn sun. Poet owned a power that he wanted split into three counsels. The first one was said to be that of a single leaf to be bequeathed to the soils of the earth. Disapproval arose against Poet because a Shelverstein is never to give away any part of their body, including a leaf, for those are a source of tremendous knowledge. Still, Poet courageously neglected the words from his doubting fellowship and on that following night, Poet shed a single leaf from the tallest branch from his head and did nothing more than watch his delicate foliage bounce through the air 'til it met the moist soil below." Jade then instructed Makari where she could find the page's brilliant pull-tab that activated this portion of book into a fully animated spring, as if life was actually breathing between the folds of the paper-forest cutouts.

"As you can see, the surrounding trees watched restlessly again as, so very suddenly, their own twisted roots from under the ground began to gently constrict Poet's leaf and pull it to the earth underneath," Jade furthered, "Poet knew his fellow brothers and sisters still doubted his every movement, especially an older brother called Ulpio, who was determined to break Poet's message as only a hoax by fiendishly protesting Poet's dreams. Poet was still quietly saddened by his brother's remarks; it wasn't until the Shelversteins next full moon that anything would evolve from the young tree's first advice."

Landon was then urged by Jade to continue the tale, now kneeling down close beside the edge of the coffee table so he could examine more closely the miniature forest now working before him.

"Try this one," suggested Jade, pointing at the flat tab poking out from a corner on the page. Makari couldn't hesitate, not a second, but was taken aback momentarily when tiny flares began whizzing and snapping out from the folds of the book and in front of her face. The tiny beads froze into place, levitating just above the book in order to mimic a miniature starlit and full moon sky and floating above the Shelverstein forest.

"What else can this book do?" wondered Landon, easily waving his hand through the book's illusion, nearly dumbfounded.

"Let me finish," Jade nodded, clearing his throat again, "while the moon speared through the Shelversteins tallest branches, a sudden split in the ground startled the colony, as the earth's roots returned with a blossoming of two children. Poet then declared their names as Adlanion and Azlazion while his fellowship quickly broke into bellowing debate over the authenticity of the two, earthly creatures.

By the time of the siblings' sixteenth birthday, after years of guidance carefully kept in Poet's bind, he then decided it was time to announce the second counsel: Even though the birth of the two children had been accomplished, the time had come for them to travel north afar, near a cove to seek the Four Nobles, and bring them to the Shelverstein forest. The forest denied Poet's second theory, dismissing the idea that more *human* life could be found beyond their ring. But Poet was steadfast, reminding the siblings only to follow the northern wind and waters or other enchanted wonders they would undoubtedly find until they reached a cove of rocks and a body of water that could match the size of many forests."

Jade then turned to the page, but this time, something was different about this particular passage that both Landon and Makari felt the need to sit just a little closer. Maybe it was the purplish monster that leapt from the cutouts, or was it a depiction of a mirror that strangely resembled the one still floating about back at 1245 Poplar Drive?

"Hey, that's our mirror!" pointed Makari.

"*Sssh*, we're getting to the best part," Jade grinned, poking his tongue out in protest. "Three years passed before Poet's creations made their return, but when they did, it was beyond any expectation that the Shelversteins could have ever reason. Bloodied, beaten, and yet still accompanied with the Four Nobles, Adlanion and Azlazion made their journey back to the forest with a mission fulfilled…so they thought. The Shelversteins could not believe their eyes all while the Four Nobles gasped at the display of talking trees as they cautiously approached the towering elders. The men and women that were the Four Nobles, Adlanion and Azlazion included, recited their tales of traveling the North and their encounters with such fierce beasts—What sorts? Nobody truly knows what may have plagued the journey to-and-fro. Azlazion told Poet that the Four Nobles had joined them without hesitation, and were prepared to complete the counsel for Poet. Little did Poet know that the Four Nobles also had an impressive counsel to share with the fellowship: the nobles revealed that they would share their alchemy and all their might with the Shelversteins, but in return, the trees must spare the sap of their branches, the lumber of their trunks, and the water of their roots… to create the elixir for *the great seeing*."

"See, *I told you* it's our mirror," clapped Makari, as if she guessed the ending of the tale before Jade could finish.

"You impatient shmoo," shook Jade, incapable of holding back another laugh.

"A sh-*what?*" Landon queried, cracking a grin.

"*And so*, reluctantly," furthered Jade, ignoring Landon entirely, "the Shelversteins granted the Four Nobles their three requests. Within days, the tribe had concocted a metallic liquid from the gifted saps; they even carved and fashioned together the given splinters of timber, until each noble created a mirror of their very own. As though they had a heart of their own, the core of the mirrors began to beat, as the given properties began to course uniquely brilliant and sappy cocoons of gold, ruby, purple and emerald along the mirror borders. Nights passed, all while the Nobles' mirrors stood waiting, the Shelversteins and all their apprentices tolerantly awaited the purpose of the mirrors to illustrate. Unfortunately, Ulpio was tired of waiting and, during the nights when the mirrors were being created, the shrewd brother had been holding secret meetings of his own with a raven that nested itself on his shoulder. The raven would speak to him—telling Ulpio such frightening ideas that eventually consumed him. Against the wishes of his family, Ulpio shed a leaf of his own and, once it tumbled to the ground below, a pair of black serpents quickly slithered from the earth, constricting the leaf and pulling it underground like tortured prey.

Now with their tale in such a strange tangle, Adlanion and Azlazion were still unsure of what to expect of their mirrors. Not even the nobles could comprehend their relics' true purpose, until Ulpio announced that he had a counsel of *his* very own: Ulpio cried that the Four Nobles had unknowingly created masterpieces that would *curiously* reflect anything that stands before it, but it was one of *those very mirrors* that were truly meant to be a threshold to a haven destined for Adlanion and Azlazion. The fellowship then fell into an uproar, after Ulpio confessed of his act of baring a leaf to the earth, but their curses toward their brother came to a halt as the ground began to quake. A violet shade then broke from the ground while roars and woe eclipsed the Nobles and the fellowship. Adlanion and Azlazion could only watch in horror as a tall, emaciated humanoid began to erect itself from the ground, blooming as if the most hideous of all corpses had been given a second chance. Ulpio then demanded his words to be marked between his fellowship and Poet's creations: his dark beauty would rule beyond the nobles' threshold and claim crown as the most feared, forever. Ulpio demanded that his creature multiply and crossover through one of the mirrors. However, Poet would not allow the purity of the noble creations to be corrupted at the hands of Ulpio's insidious creature. Poet and his fellowship charged for the dark beauty, but after every slice from the claws of the violent creature, the Shelversteins began to welt with blight. The violet creature fell, cornered by Adlanion and Azlazion, when suddenly, turning towards one of the mirrors, it took hold of the golden frame and leaped through its silvery mass…"

As if it knew it was interrupting, the iron kettle dolefully began to whistle, startling our siblings. Hurrying to the disturbance, Jade gingerly wrapped the kettle handle with a small cloth and lifted it from the fireplace and poured its boiling contents over the mound of espresso waiting in the press.

"I'll let that sit for just a few more minutes, just enough time to allow me to finish the tale," nodded Jade, eyeing the whirls of steam swimming from the press.

"So, what became of the Shelversteins?" Landon advanced.

"After Ulpio's creature escaped through one of the nobles' creations," said Jade, continuing with the tale, "Poet gave one last order to his children: he revealed to the apprentices that his third and ultimate counsel solely relied on the their next choices, that *they* would need to choose between the venture that rested beyond the Elddri Mirror or remain in the safety of their relatives to dwell on the thought of what destruction Ulpio's creature might spawn, beyond. The ultimate counsel had more than one core though, and that was to create a sanctuary for Poet's progeny—to set the stage for future manifestos to mature and vanquish the dark beauty and its thralls. Poet and his fellowship perished before the eyes of his creations, falling quietly like common old trees. From that day forward, Adlanion and Azlazion sought to fulfill their creator's final precept…"

"And the Four Nobles, what became of them?" asked Makari, as Jade began to serve her and Landon mugs full of the most deliciously robust, caramel soothed espresso.

"They survived the attack of the dark beauty and soon joined the endeavor of the Shelverstein children," revealed Jade, as he took a sip from his warm mug. "The six compatriots vowed to uphold Poet's counsels, to seek light and banish darkness in the land beyond the gateway. Together, they decided to venture after the dark beauty, but not before deciding the hiding place for each of the four mirrors. The Nobles, in turn, bound themselves to the power of their respective relics, avowing that none might use their creation to the detriment of the others, instead, imbued the mirror with characteristics of their own."

"As if leaving a trace of themselves *in* the mirror?" asked Landon.

"Precisely," nodded Jade, "Noble, Winifred Worlmis, declared her mirror the master of fathom—a mirror that can show you how to solve your greatest misunderstanding. Noble, Rosalba Feomor, declared her mirror the master of vigilance—one that can show its possessor an impending danger. And Noble Amar Idolcem declared his mirror the master of eternity—granting that lucky owner a life of perpetual wishes that don't go unpaid without judgment. However, it was their youngest Noble, Ekram Elddri, who declared his the master for the untamed. His mirror would be sovereign among the four, an elemental force beyond that which Elddri's brethren wielded. Ekram Elddri *was wise*, a young philosopher that devotedly cherished his fellow Nobles and their creations, so Ekram warned that the boundary between worlds must be traversed only by his creation, for the dark beauty must not be allowed to escape the land it had invaded, the land where it was now to be vanquished. Adlanion, Azlazion, Worlmis, Feomor, and Idolcem then strode through Elddri's Mirror and began their quest to seek out the dark beauty... and *that*, my new and curious friends, is how this village came to be."

"Remarkable," said Makari, sipping her sweet espresso, "the story, I mean."

"What happened to Elddri?" asked Landon, "did he follow after the two children and the other Nobles?"

"Elddri's fate has gathered quite impressive theories over the past centuries. Historians have spent their lives trying to piece together the whereabouts of Elddri, because, according to historical facts, Elddri had only ventured beyond his creation on two separate occasions. And according to pieces of his private journals that have found their way through official channels, Elddri felt his duty was to guard the boundary between worlds, keeping the darkness that infested *this* world from spreading."

"Guard it by giving it the cubic disguise?" Makari made certain.

"Just that very idea, a disguise indeed," said Jade. "Historians learned a very significant detail from Elddri's journals...Ekram Elddri had traveled the lands beyond your Poplar Drive and even sailed its seven seas in order to find ways to protect his relic. Acquiring skills of transfiguration from several reclusive mages and clever jesters, Ekram had become a master of the skill, eventually rendering his mirror altogether unrecognizable. Elddri knew he wouldn't live forever, so he didn't stop with just transforming his creation, he applied the words of Poet to his creation's new form. If Elddri was to protect *this* growing sanctuary, even from the grave, mere obfuscation was not going to be enough. He gave the mirror the ability to test those who sought Revlenion, blocking all but those who believed in this place and allowing them to find their very own manifesto."

"The riddle on the cube," Landon nodded.

"Exactly, and if you haven't figured it out by now, Elddri is an anagram for, well—makes all the sense now, doesn't it?" revealed Jade, as he watched Landon and Makari laboriously attempt to trace the letters in the air in reverse. "Elddri's mirror and my cane, which was made from the bark of a Shelverstein and given to me by an old mentor years ago, are what truly inspire me to seek solutions to my cases beyond and within Revlenion. Though, I've never had to solve Elddri's riddle—I was born in Revlenion," continued Jade, "which reminds me, you two are in need of a badge."

"What kind of badge?" Landon asked, setting his lukewarm mug back on the coffee table.

"A Portler Badge, and it's meant for those like you two, to keep on yourself at all times. It allows your presence on your visit to be legal, by Revlenion Law—really ridiculous if you ask me."

"I don't mind getting one, do you, Lan?" nodded Makari, as she eyed her brother.

"It's just that they run entirely counter to what Revlenion originally stood for," challenged Jade, as he then gathered their chipped espresso mugs, tossing them back atop the mountain of dishes. As the approaching hour referenced by his pocket-watch indicated, it was time to continue their way to Cappa Square.

Jade peeked through the tiny window above the sink and noticed that the sun was about to set beyond the west hills. Returning to his bedside, Jade reached for his coat, but when he did, he was sour to find a new, jagged tear along the back end of his pea coat. "Oh, not again."

"What's wrong?" asked Makari.

"*Tisk*—a molk must've flown through my kitchen window and is now, unfortunately, most likely crawling around. They're nasty, winged bugs—*worse* than mice—and feed on almost anything, *especially* fine wool," said Jade, noticing Makari dart a few panicky eyes at the cottage floor, fearing one those winged critters was already inching up one of her pant legs. "No worries though, I'll just have one of the Manor-Wardrobers patch-up this ole cloak of mine." Jade the Jade slid his arms into his sleek coat, "best to keep your food sealed-tightly in a jar or box if you don't want a fat molk sniffling through your cupboards."

"I'll keep that in mind," said Makari. Jade reached for the front door knob, now allowing Makari and Landon to lead the way out of the cottage, as he gave a slight wave with his cane, sending an extinguishing swirl into the air and down into the fireplace.

"I'm trying to keep your time here the most worthwhile," said Jade, now leading the way through the quiet village.

"I'm still shaking off the shock from the fall," huffed Landon, as Jade then laughed.

"I sort of want to believe that we've always needed a place

exactly like this," declared Makari.

"Don't you two worry, you'll soon meet some extraordinary individuals that I have had the privilege to work with while I've been researching the manifesto that may be pertaining to you two, specifically," said Jade.

The trio had now made their way to the end of Four Nobles Place village, crossing the long Donosaw Bridge, as it read on another golden commemoration at the entrance of the arching, marble bridge.

"Caldera Donosaw, a genius architect; she not only designed the early structures of Cappa Square, she produced the royal manor, herself," inticed Jade, "though, decades ago while drinking her afternoon tea, a molk found it's way into her cup, and not noticing the nasty bug, she choked to death after a single gulp."

"Why all the gruesome details? That's terrible," sighed Makari.

"*I told you*—wretched little beasts," reminded Jade, as he and the siblings climbed the stretch of aged bridge.

"Where does this river run from?" asked Landon, peering over the rounded ledge.

"That's the runoff from North Vorloren Sea and runs directly through to the west of Cappa," explained Jade, tapping his cane along the ledge.

"On and *on* it goes," said Makari, as she, too, gave a glance over the short ledge and eyeing the rushing river that disappeared through the surrounding pine forest ahead. Donosaw's bridge came to an end at the base of two large pine trees, and walking between the two towering pines, Landon and Makari followed Jade at his sides as they made their quiet entrance into Cappa Square. Unlike the Four Nobles village that sat quiet and seemingly lifeless, the long promenade that stretched on through the town square was like a stampede; full of hurrying townsfolk that evening: Jade signaled at Landon and Makari to quickly follow him, but the siblings were spellbound by the sight of the eccentric structures of the town's square.

From rooftop to foundation, the shops, town apartments, and

emporiums that lined either side were twisted, twirled, and even jagged at some points in their own, perfect way. Each building seemed stacked onto one another and blossomed like an art deco world that had been soaked in a charming inkwell. Pounding through the shops and the square itself were the Cappamites, walking along or crossing the busy streets with bags full of market goods or elaborate packages from more upscale shops. Children were bedecked in largely uniform finer; shorts or skirts and summer coats, fleeing from their exasperated parents, whose hands were filled with parasols, overstuffed briefcases, and dog leashes. Makari took notice at how prim and proper many of the Cappa people dressed: most men wore sleek business suits and several topped with either a bowler or a wide-brimmed fedora. The women were equally fashionable; impeccably coiffed and laced into picturesque high-necked dresses and cloaked in luxuriant shawls.

"Don't be fooled by their lush attire, some of them can be astoundingly prissy," said Jade, as he slithered between a mother and her fat, unruly child that was stuffing its large mouth with a dollop of blue cotton candy. Jade's young followers were subsumed entirely in the sea of opulent Cappamite culture that was the town square. As our trio trekked through the crowded sidewalks, Jade began to point out some of the most fascinating shops that lined downtown, while our curious siblings found themselves pressing their faces against every shop window in sight: The Ole Seven Nebbitt, a decadent pub and restaurant—Marble of Mint, a heavily secured and prized house of ancient jewelry—Cindlers & Nooklers, the largest and most prestigious bookshop in all Revlenion packed with an overwhelming array of curling aisles with countless book spines. Skopeins, another shop that Jade pointed out: an emporium featuring a wide selection of telescopes and astronomy utensils.

"Ah, my favorite of all the shops, Dingoduns Espresso Emporium!" rejoiced Jade, bringing his face close upon the giant glass window of the bustling café. The trio stood just below the eyelash-like awning of the corner emporium; beloved not only for its signature coffee beans, but for the massive sculpture of a grinning man's head (that doubled as the emporium's emblem) that was topped with a ginormous black top-hat tipped at a rakish angle and sporting a peacock feather, and accentuating the head's grin was an exceptional mustache with a curly flourish. Landon and Makari mimicked Jade, eyeing the flock of Cappamites that waited in line for their favorite beverage. "Such a magical place with so many enchanting pastries, lattes and candies…I don't even know where to begin to explain just how *good* this place actually is. Oh, what I would do for a Butler-Ripple latte, right now," said Jade, as he turned on his booted heel.

"A Butler-Ripple?" cooed Makari, licking her lips at the sight of other children bouncing inside the emporium with their porcelain mugs and wiping away thick lashes of whipped cream from their lips. Landon and Makari were desperately trying to catch a better glimpse of what Jade was seeing, but failed as a group of tall business-suited men stood in their sight from inside the café.

"We couldn't see anything else in there," sighed Landon, "seems a bit hectic inside."

"Always is, but it's *so* worth the wait. I'd love to take you both inside but, unfortunately, we've already had our coffee fix and we're on a tight schedule," said Jade, as he signaled at the siblings to follow him again, "I promise you two, we'll make a stop there on another day."

"Another day?" hawked Landon. "How long do you expect us to stay here?"

"Manifestos can't be understood in just one day, kiddo," said Jade, "patience first, or so I've been told. But in the meantime, keep up!" Jade's recent revelation had left Landon anchored in thought in the middle of the street where his sister and wayfarer-eyed friend had already crossed.

"Ay! Watch it kid!" roared the Slender Cabbie, adjusting his ruby-framed eyeglasses and fixing his grip on the steering wheel. Jade and Makari spun on their heels as they watched Landon swiftly dart backward on a heel as a steaming carriage nearly crushed our green-eyed-boy.

Landon let out a sigh at the impudence of a world that refused to move at the pace of his thoughts, but was swiftly distracted from the train of thought by the thin man-creature that glared at him from its florid carriage. The creature of Landon's present attentions then reclined in its seat, spurring the carriage onward in its journey to the north end of the square. Landon hadn't gotten a particularly clear look at the dapper creature aboard the carriage, but, as he told Makari after rejoining her across the street, he was fairly sure that, whatever it was...it wasn't human.

As the trio came to halt at the corners of Promenade and North Square Street (catty-corner from the plaza's skyscraping-undecorated-year round Christmas tree), Landon began to notice several heads of the Cappamites turning at the sight of his and Makari's presence.

"Jade, why are people staring?" said Landon, as he began to notice their rather peculiar complexions.

"Damn, I had hoped you two would blend in, but as it seems, a Cappamite knows an outsider when they see one," said Jade, as he hurried the siblings across the street, as a man steering an engine-drawn carriage zoomed by. "Notice the dark circles around their eyes and pallid faces. Poor Cappamites, their valley isn't the sunniest of places in Revlenion. They're all still kind people and they are who they are, just don't comment on their gaunt appearance as most of them find it quite rude. And should you hear any foul-mouthed child running rampant shouting, Sculpt, take no consideration into repeating that nasty word aloud."

"Why?" asked Landon, as he followed behind Jade and his sister.

"It's an old and demeaning term the editor of Cappa Gazette branded his own people years ago, because of their sun-deprived appearance," said Jade as he came to a sudden stop.

"What's wrong?" asked Landon, as he eyed Jade quickly, who was peering up at the sight of what seemed to be an abandoned building gathering patches moss on the side of its structure. Makari looked up and read the chain linked sign swaying above her, *Alley 19*.

"I wonder if he's here?" murmured Jade, as he tapped the tip of his cane against his chin.

"Someone in particular?" Makari asked, after deciphering the words that emitted under Jade's breath.

"Oh yes," said Jade, noticing Makari was eyeing him, and as he reached for the shop's door, "since I've been away from Cappa for nearly a month, I think I need to pay just a quick visit to an old friend —I promise it'll only take a few minutes from our schedule…Little lady first." Jade let Makari lead the way into the shop.

One by one, the trio entered the moss ridden-shop. As Jade began to step inside, he noticed Landon looking off into the distance: Landon stood there peering over his shoulder at a small crowd of Cappamites that were observing him and Jade more intently now, as though up to something quite fiendish. However, as quickly as the Cappamites eyes assessed Landon's appearance, Landon shifted his eyes away from the gawking citizens, noticing the shape of what seemed to be an enormous house, creeping between the delicate twilight fog and resting high on a mountainside that overlooked the entire valley. Jade then called for Landon, "Come on inside."

With one final glance at the looming structure, Landon crossed the threshold.

▼

The front door closed with a loud *clank*. Landon followed behind Jade as they both entered the shop.

"I'm closed 'til nine, tonight," said the raspy voice of the lone man behind the bar, not even bothering to turn around and face our trio. Landon and Makari began to examine the small shop that looked as though it had been abandoned.

It wasn't a shop as they had first thought, more a tavern, and quite spacious with a dozen or more high-top wooden stools, tables with unlit center-piece candles, and a vaulted ceiling where two giant cobwebbed chandeliers made of moose antlers hung that dimly lit up the muggy tavern.

"Is that the friend?" whispered Makari, as she noticed a narrow balcony above the bar side, residing just before a back hallway from behind the bar.

"Yes," Jade side-mouthed, "good evening to you too, old man." Jade then descended a few, crackling wood steps, and having Landon and Makari follow behind.

Landon and Makari then noticed a burly, snoring man surrounded by a collection of empty beer steins at one of the lone tables, periodically giggling in his bearish slumber. The man from behind the bar abruptly whirled around, finally facing the trio: he was much taller than Jade, but his skeletal frame was so severely hunched it was hard to tell. Sporting a greasy salt and pepper receding hairline and dressed in a harlequin vest that had been obviously been left out for a molk or two, the man looked as if he hadn't left the bar in some time. The man's face was dominated by a puckered scar that zigzagged through his left eye, which winked laboriously, as the tavern master began his introduction:

"Good evening?" replied the Tavern-Man, again with his weary rasp, "I'll enjoy my evenings when the Chamberlains stop over-taxing me…dare I hold my breath?" Landon and Makari eyed one another as Jade went along conversing with the gravelly-voiced man.

"Rasp, any day can be a good day, it's just how you see it. Good luck with the R.C.C. though," said Jade as took a seat at the bar side, pulling a pair of seats out for Landon and Makari as he did so.

Rasp rolled up his dirty sleeves, "Jade, sight is a sense in which I most appreciate. However, Jade, it's the R.C.C. I do not," he thrummed, as he stuck a long and bony hand out to Jade and together they shook. Without warning, Rasp took a tight grip of Jade and pulled his arm into place, as though preparing for a game. "How 'bout a little game of arm wrestle?" Rasp cheered, winking again with his bad eye, hoping it was as gruesomely intimidating as the dark tale behind the scar. "Now, I'm all for fun n' games, but when it comes to you, Jade, someone is destined to lose an eye."

"Rasp, can you j—" Jade tried.

"—Hold on here, lemme' finish," gurgled Rasp, breaking his grin, "speaking of the pretty bunch-do-no-harm R.C.C., if any one of them was to see these kids in here, I might as well join our snoozer right there and be as dead as the spiders in this place." Landon and Makari shot looks of their own to the burly man, snoring to his empty stein as if they were the mute audience to his snuffling stupor. "You win, you and your short-talkers can join me here in this fine as wine tavern of mine—I win, well, be sure to take snoozin' Viggo there with ya'!"

"You've got yourself a game, *old man*," Jade smiled with a risen eyebrow. The tired old man had him at his mercy. Jade let go of his cane as the strain made his face look like an overripe tomato.

"And again, as I always say, if you don't know how to play...go sit at the kiddies table," rasped Rasp, grinning wide after his solid win.

"I hear you," said Jade, giving his arm a quick massage, while receiving his cane from Makari, after she retrieved the magical fitment from the pub floor. Rasp's smile then wiped away, eyeing Landon and Makari closely as he tossed a hand out at our siblings while they hoped Rasp wouldn't try some foul trick on them.

"I try to set rules, but to hell with the R.C.C., you three can stay," said Rasp, knocking his knuckles on the bar as if ordering-in his patrons. "Say, who are these two anyway?"

"*These* are the siblings, Landon and Makari," said Jade, introducing them to Rasp. "But, you'll have to excuse me for a second." Jade then nodded at our siblings as he rounded the bar corner, shouldering a pair of swinging saloon doors.

"You know where the toilet is," hummed Rasp, as he then slammed two petite glasses in front of Landon and Makari. Our siblings watched as Rasp then pulled a carved and wooden red apple shaped carafe from his wall of bottled liquors and began to pour from the wormhole spout an amount of the sallow elixir that could fit into their glass. "There's a simple rule upon your first visit to any tavern: should a barman serve you whatever he, *or she*, ever so-wishes-to serve you, you take it…as it goes, it's bad luck should you foolishly turn your cheek."

"What is it?" queried Makari, hovering a nose above her glass.

"House cider," nodded Rasp.

"Cider?" quizzed Landon, picking up his tiny glass.

"Drink it quick, so that you may enjoy its trick," smiled Rasp, as he then poured himself a tonic from a slender bottle. "Cheers!"

The bar trio gulped their glasses in one, fast motion, as Landon and Makari quickly darted eyes at one another, guessing what sort of sour and cinnamon zest was sliding down each of their throats.

"Yuck!" coughed Makari, as she gently placed her glass back on the bar counter.

"That wasn't *too* bad," puckered Landon, as he and his sister began to grin.

"*Oh-my-manifesto*," said Jade, as he returned to the barstools next to Landon and Makari. "Wormson Cider, Rasp!"

"It won't hurt 'em! Just a nice little kicker of solid good-luck," giggled Rasp, as he then reached for three steins from his topmost shelves, and served each of them a spritz of his bubbliest ginger ale from one of the large wooden barrels behind the bar counter.

"Please forgive my very *old friend here*," said Jade, swiveling his head away from Landon and Makari,

"Drink up, it'll do you good—it's a nice palette cleanser," said Rasp, as our siblings eyed their barman's pour, as he then began again with Jade, "so, you're back from your expeditions from beyond Cappa, again? Still chasing after your detective work, are you?" said Rasp, "if you haven't noticed by now, Jade is very rude. I'm Fedele Channer, and like most of the whiskey-tangos that come through here, you two can call me Rasp—it'd be most appreciated."

"Jade has brought us our summons from the Haus of Cappa," said Landon, after a gulp of his ale, feeling a burp vastly growing in his chest.

"*Oh*, ritzy-fritzy business," mocked Rasp, dancing his fingers above his head in the shape of a crown, "not much of a Manor fanatic, if I do say so myself. Especially that Antoine, hell no."

"Rasp isn't really a nice one when you bring up the subject of the Royal Manor," said Jade as he took a sip from his glass. "Neither is his choice of certain words."

"Ah, donkey lips! Doing my time in-the-name of the Manor has ended me scarred like this!" barked Rasp, pointing at his scarred cheekbone.

"How so?" asked Makari, as she and her brother leaned forward with their steins.

"BAH!" Rasp then bellowed a laugh after giving the siblings a much closer and gruesome view of his awful scar. Landon and Makari shared a startled smile at the man's twisted antics. "Works like a charm, every time! But, if I may say so, I'd allow myself to be scarred in much nastier places if meant protecting Madame Cappa. Dionne…she's *the* most breathtaking woman that has ever graced this land—a shooting star, that one. To wit, I'm sure you'll be joining the Royals and their pawns later this evening?"

"These two mean a great deal to the Royals; as such, a meeting with them is in order," said Jade, as Rasp went on with his daily chores.

"Those poor Sculpts, merely sculptures of deception. I can't believe what this once glorified capital has come to. Keeping that Antoine Cappa in full authority has nearly run this valley into the ground," said Rasp, shaking his head. Jade then jolted off of his barstool, nearly ripping his pocket watch out of his vest, "Landon—Makari, we need to be on the move, we're going to be late!"

"Late for what?" asked Landon; nearly choking on his ginger ale after Jade bumped him.

"The Cappa Solstice Gala, of course, I *completely* forgot that it's tonight! It happens every year at the end of the summer—and we still have to get you two registered for badges," hurried Jade.

"You mean the gala of gathering idiots!" cackled Rasp. "Wait, Jade," Rasp turned to a back counter of stacked steins and oddly bottled liquors that bounced light from the candles that leaned on a wooden beam above, "here, I too almost forgot, do me a favor and drop this letter off at the postbox outside the Bureau of Chamberlains, as I'm sure you'll be passing it," said Rasp, as Jade took a wax-sealed black envelope from Rasp's hand.

"Sure," said Jade, taking hold of the envelope, and after flipping a shiny coin out of his coat pocket and into Rasp's skull-shaped tip jar, "and thank you for the cider, Rasp. We'll see you again, soon." Landon and Makari gave a wave of thanks to their barman, seeing the skeletal man retort with a wink from his good eye. Our siblings then spun on their heels, hurrying after Jade out of the tavern and back out to the busy sidewalks.

Crossing the street, Landon and Makari both observed the grand Cappa fountain that was rooted in the middle of the road, spouting a long pillar of the clearest water from its center. Makari smiled at the staring Cappamites that congregated around the mantle of the monument.

"The registry closes in twentyminutes, and there's another forty minutes before the gala begins…we need to hurry," said Jade, tucking away his pocket watch again. The trio raced across the cabby-filled street, coming to a stop at the corner of Royal Gate Lane. They stood at the bottom of giant stairway, where a flurry of people were dressed in formal court robes and suits, several of them with briefcases in hand stamped with a look of bewilderment as they left the colossal marble-column temple for the evening. "Follow me," Jade continued, after tossing Rasp's sealed envelope into a post box, beckoning as Landon and Makari raced after Jade and ascended the fifty steps.

As the siblings and their escort entered through the tall wooden doors of the temple, an official cloaked in a fawn robe bowed to them, "Welcome to the Bureau of Chamberlains, how may I assist you three this evening?"

"We're just making our way to register for Portler Badges, thank you," said Jade as he hurried Landon and Makari ahead of him. Jade impassively accepted the official's rebuke that the office of registration would be closing in less than ten minutes, then led the group through the massive House Hall, trying not to attract the attention of the officials that filled the airy lobby. The dark granite lobby split into three seemingly endless halls filled with arching stone columns that propped up a high dome ceiling, across which was splayed a mural depicting some of the more illustrious past chamberlains.

"I believe the registry office is this way," said Jade, as Landon bumped shoulders with a robed temple clerk. Jade guided his troupe through the center hall, past endless rows of glass-cased priceless vases and sculptures of Revlenion's historical figures. Finally, the trio arrived to the end of the hall coming to a halt at the base of a desk that stood absurdly high mounted against the temple wall. Sitting in between a nest of books and office papers was a man devoted to his work, scribbling along in his gigantic leather logbook.

Department of Ports and Registries
Albert Gellwerg — Head Registrar

The golden banner read that was wrapped around the temple's coat of arms against the tall base of the register's desk.

"Excuse me, Mr. Gellwerg, I would like to reg—" tried Jade.

"—Terribly sorry, but my department is now closed, you can come back tomorrow, eight a.m. sharp," sighed Albert Gellwerg, not even caring to look at the trio standing below him.

"You don't seem to understand, I'm here on official business," said Jade, tilting his head up at Albert who then gently dabbed his quill in an inkwell.

"No, you don't seem to understand, I am rather busy at the moment and I am closed for the evening, so you can feel free to see your way out through the north wing," sneered Albert. Jade grinned and, with a simple flick with his cane, shot a tiny ribbon of light from the tip that stretched until it met Albert's quill, which promptly disintegrated into ash with a snap. *"Why you little sh*—Oh, Mr. Cooper!" exclaimed Albert, standing from his chair and slamming his logbook shut. Landon and Makari stepped back, somewhat perturbed by the short and stubby gargoyle-like creature as he pushed his gold-rimmed spectacles back on his crooked nose. "Why you bothersome boy, why didn't you say that it was you, Jade? How is that I can be of service to you…three?"

"I need to register these two for Portler Badges, if that's not too much," asked Jade, tapping his cane. "Oh, most certainly. Is this the same royal business the Chamberlains sent me a memo about this evening?" asked Albert, adjusting his suspenders after shuffling through a few stacks of papers that cluttered his desk. "If so, I'll waive the charges for their application."

"I…suppose? I wasn't aware of any memo," hesitated Jade.

"Here we are," said Albert, placing a few folders under his arm. Albert Gellwerg then quickly descended with a waddle down the narrow flight of stairs from the top of his nestled desk, then coming to the small podium and high stool that stood at the same level of the trio and now placing the registry files in front of himself. A sudden thought then struck Landon, as he and his sister craned their necks to get a better look at the creature that now sat before them like a fat Humpty-Dumpty caricature. Albert Gellwerg was strongly reminiscent of the gargoyles that our siblings had seen in illustrations from the fairy tale books they had checked-out from their favorite library when they were much younger, and seemed to be another of the same sort of creature that had nearly crushed him with its cab earlier that same evening. Unlike those illustrations though, it was apparent that Gellwerg had undergone some modifications; he was a wingless creature, and the horns atop of his balding head appeared to have been sawed down from some time before.

"So," said Albert, scratching his scabbing baldhead with his talon-like fingernails, "these two creatures would like to apply for a Portler's registration, correct?"

Landon and Makari nodded.

"Excellent," said Albert, as he then reached for his quill again, not realizing only moments ago, Jade destroyed it, "Mr. Cooper, I'll need my quill back, please." And with another wave of his mysterious cane, the ash that rested on the desk high above them flew into Albert's claw like left hand, fully reconstructing itself into another swan quill. "Thank you, now, please state your names, starting with you, young man—"

"Landon Aiden Tuolumne," he said. "TWO-all-M-E"

"—And you, young lady?" asked Gellwerg.

"Makari, MUH-car—with-a-K—E, Arina Tuolumne," she said.

"—Ah-ha, siblings…and your age and birth dates?"

"Ten, May twenty-third," said Makari.

"Twelve, November twenty-eighth," said Landon.

"—And a birthday on the way, how lovely," said Albert, as he swiftly scribbled into two individual booklets. Albert then retired his quill on the podium, as he took two spare red quills out from a drawer inside the podium. "Hold out your hands, please," Albert continued, as the new quills then began to levitate in the air. Before either Landon or Makari could retrieve them from their floating state, however, the quills poked their forefingers like angry wasps with a swift jab.

"Ouch!" screeched Makari.

"What was that for?" barked Landon, after he stuck his bleeding finger in his mouth.

"Collateral—we can keep tabs on you this way. With each of your quills you will sign your badge booklets, which should be sufficient for the duration of your errand. If you wish to stay beyond that, Revlenion's laws allow three ways one might obtain permanent citizenship: One, wed a current resident of Revlenion within the legal age limit of eighteen years or have written consent of a living blood relative or living legal guardian that is not presently holding a Portler Badge and not currently condemned by Revlenion law. Two, have a manifesto declared, accomplished and previously approved before this application process by more than two living High Chamberlains.

Three, be awarded Highest Honor, by either a Cappa Head of Haus or a living High Chamberlain," recited Albert, "any further questions?"

"What exactly is a 'Highest Honor'?" asked Landon, spinning his quill between his fingertips.

"An act on your own behalf that reflects the common good," said Albert.

"Is this all so necessary?" Landon asked, eyes beaming with a haze of hesitation.

"I told you from the beginning," Jade then whispered between our siblings, "trust me."

"Also, these must be worn at all times," instructed Albert, relinquishing two, white armbands that were both marked with an inverted triangle patch.

"What does the triangle mean?" asked Makari, as she buttoned the band around her left arm.

"The band signifies that you are not a resident of Cappa Valley," said Albert, clearing his throat. "Simple security measures."

"Quite outdated, if you ask me," hummed Jade.

Albert cared not to entertain Jade's enticing remark.

"Since I doubt that neither of you will be accomplishing any event that would stand for Revlenion's commonwealth, I'll be awarding each of you only three days allowance before you will need to renew your badges—and that's *if* either of you don't acquire salvage points against your badge—or simply return to where ever it is that you two came from…or face a trial and punishment from the Bureau of Chamberlains."

"Three days, that should be enough time," said Landon, as he and his sister signed the bottom line of their own Portler booklet contracts.

"For what exactly, young man?" smirked Albert.

"To prove you wrong," said Landon, with a slight tilt of his head.

"Every child, like you, *prove* one thing and one thing only,"

Albert leaned from his podium, pursuing his chapped lips, "that you *are* a child." Albert Gellwerg suddenly snatched the quills out of the siblings' hands. "Well, Mr. Cooper, you will need to sign their booklets as well, as you will be their Revler-advisor during their stay. I believe, Mr. Cooper, you know your way out... have a good evening," said Albert Gellwerg, as he handed Landon and Makari their red-leather bound badge booklets with an impatient shove, and in return made his way back up to his higher desk, not rewarding another look back at the trio.

"What's his problem?" said Landon.

"He probably didn't enjoy my quill trick all too much," said Jade as he led the siblings through the north wing.

The trio was some of the last patrons at the Bureau of Chamberlains that evening, as they exited from the north entrance of the temple, returning to the sidewalk before Royal Gate Lane. Landon and Makari pointed out the hustling packs of Cappamites securing their satchels and purses bursting with their fortunes in hand, hoping to make a deposit or pay-off a hefty debt. The Cappamites all rounded the east intersection of Crow Call Avenue, leading directly toward the tall and elaborately rune black-stone and marble bank, Grendelords Royale, that took up the entire block corner. Landon eyed the three oxidized copper dome towers that leaned in every direction a few stories above in the sky. Each gothic tower thronged with watchful guards, cloaked in black-leather trench coats, and matching black round goggles. The leather-clad guards at ground level directed traffic through designated pathways as each Cappamite entered through the maw-like threshold. The guards fulfilled their duties with an eerie precision, curtly directing each patron before smoothly locking back into position.

"I've always been creeped out by this place," said Jade, noticing Landon eyeing the dome-capped bank, "no matter what time of day. Thank goodness I only have to venture inside once a month, so that gives me...two more weeks."

"Why does that place scare you so much?" said Makari.

"Well, the guards for one, but inside, it's just *so* cold and unwelcoming," said Jade, with a shake. "The bank tellers are just as bad though; they're all practically identical and…well, it's hard to describe. As far as I know, only once in the bank's two hundred year history has anyone ever broken in and managed to get out alive. *The Great Heist of '62*, it's still called, and the security's only gotten more draconian since.

"Where are we going now?" asked Makari, looking to her left and right as they crossed from the corner of the Bureau of Chamberlains.

"To the manor," said Jade delightfully, while pointing his cane up to the pine mountainside.

The evening fog had finally begun to dissipate, and our siblings glanced at each other in amazement as the spots of gleaming light from the silhouette against the night sky revealed the gargantuan scale of the manor. The trio crossed over to Royal Gate Lane, advancing along the length of the wrought iron fence, towards the spiked gate that formed its centerpiece. All along the route, climbing jasmine entangled the ironwork, reaching to meet two, towering carved stone plinths. And atop of the tall pedestals were perched swans, both frozen in the sway of a wing dance.

Sitting on an iron stool in a silver security booth just before the entrance of the gate was a young man wearing a red formal guard suit (the sort of relentlessly itchy costume that reminded Landon of the one he had to wear during a terrible middle-school rendition of the musical *Les Misérables*). Royce the guard, as his embroidered lapel identified him, gave a slight adjusting wiggle of his tight collar around his sweaty neck as they approached, wearily rattling off a scripted set of orders. Jade, ignoring the man entirely, deliberately rapped his cane against the crest that adorned the great barrier.

"No admittance without invitation," droned the Royce the Guard. He eyed the trio closely, hand out-thrust to demand their documentation.

"Royce, I don't have time to play your silly games right now. You know who I am, now will you kindly open the gates?" said Jade, hands to his sides. Royce's face scrunched in growing consternation at Jade's refusal to comply.

"Don't blame me for doing my job, Jade. I'm supposed to keep people out who can't provide the necessary documents. It's not my fault if you can't be bothered!" said Royce, reluctantly turning to open the gate for them. Reaching into his uniform, Royce took out a key looped around a long chain around his neck and inserted it into a panel in his silver booth.

"Yes Royce, your eternal vigilance is an example to us all," said Jade, a grin spreading across his face. Landon and Makari nodded thanks to the curse-murmuring guard as they hurried to keep step with Jade. The black gate unlocked with a clunk and slowly swung open, splitting around the fancy **C** emblem upon the central crest. As the gate then swung back and locked itself, a guard posted on the other side led them to a waiting carriage.

"Oh, thank the royals for this, my feet needed the break," said Jade, as he leaned heavily on his cane. "Imagine climbing this mountain ourselves!"

"I wouldn't mind," said Makari.

The Clydesdales bound to the conveyance galloped toward them from the forest trail ahead, suddenly coming to a halt as the massive horse neighed a greeting, sending Landon and Makari into a fit of giggles. The trio swiftly stepped into the warm cab and with a snap of the cabby's whip, the carriage circled back onto the trail and up through the thick forest. Jade and Makari sat comfortably next to one with Landon seated opposite; our siblings could only gawk at just how brilliantly fashioned their chestnut carriage actually was: bedazzled with burgundy cushions and tiny egg-shaped lamps that splashed along the lavish wooden paneling.

"Just up this trail and we'll arrive to the main grounds," said Jade, resting against the back of the carriage. Leaning back in his seat, Landon thought he spotted out from the corner of his eyes a dark figure ghoulishly weaving through the thick foliage. Startled, Landon glanced at the trees again, closer this time.

"Something wrong?" asked Jade, noticing Landon's sudden interest.

"I'm fine," Landon prevaricated nervously, "just thinking."

Jade nodded hesitantly, watching as Landon then rested his head back against the soft headboard, closing his eyes with a visible effort. The carriage galloped on through the trail, high above Cappa Square, and after five minutes time, our trio arrived at their destination.

The carriage then came to a jolting halt, bringing them to the main pebbled road at the end of the forest trail, just before a perfect line of a dozen more valeted horse carriages parked along the great lawn of the manor. With a welcome from Royal Greeters (Jade tipped a nod at one of the servants, seemingly recognizing him), the trio was given a hand out of the carriage and was guided to the stone path that led them to the main doors. This time, Landon and Makari led the way, while Jade followed behind, reveling in the awe of the siblings as they first encountered the true enormity of the royal manor: the sandstone-cream manor reached high into the crescent moon sky as a lavish emerald lawn, and lavender-splashed garden spread their rich colors across the grounds. The manor was equipped with four, wide-balconied towers, each piercing high into the sky with jagged rooftops atop its wide, golden trimmed facade, studded with tiny crystal glass windows gleaming with light from deep within its halls. Leading to the main doors was an enormous fountain, a rather more exuberant one than Cappa Squares. Makari eyed the two sculpted knights, each posed with a sword in hand, as the moon reflected water spouting from the tips of their long blades. Jade hurried the siblings up the steps leading to the main entrance, giving them little time to pause and admire their surroundings. The front doors were massive and made of thick polished steel, embellished with a frieze of swans frozen in mid-flight, and standing at base of the manor doors were two heavily armored guards; Makari fidgeted at the sight of them, unsure whether they were more statuary until one nodded at Jade to continue inside the house.

Suddenly, the doors opened with a half-split, revealing a beautiful, yet urgent Cappa-woman with her hands folded in front of her icy blue dress.

"We made it," said Jade, coming closer to the woman. The pale woman spoke in a high, clear voice as she beckoned with a forefinger to our trio.

"And late, of course, even when we're expecting you, Jade," said the Royal Host, while she began to evaluate the siblings with a couple sharp glances, "I am your host for the evening, please continue on through the foyer."

Down the main hallway, light continued to blossom from the precious candelabras that, in some odd fashion, looked as though polished golden hands were hoisting them along the house's walls. As Landon and Makari advanced within the manor, they noted how much of manor's interior looked like it had been trapped in some sort of 1940's time warp. That, combined with the opulent decorations reminded the siblings of the haunted mansions ubiquitous in the Vincent Price pictures that they so admired.

Progressing down the hallway, Makari noticed a portrait of an extraordinarily enchanting young man with broad shoulders and neatly groomed long brown hair.

"Who is that man, Jade?" said Makari, pointing at the portrait.

"Oh, that's a good friend of mine, Arrison Clarence Cappa," noted Jade. "The only child of the Cappas. Arri, as I've always called him, is out of the valley with his fiancé, Audrey Honrrin, at the moment. Audrey is the youngest of three daughters of the Great Honrrin dynasty, or as I've always preferred, the Great-Stinking-Rich family."

The trio's Royal host paced behind them as they followed her direction, at one point stopping to turn toward the grand front doors and raise her hands, precipitating an eruption of sparkles from her fingertips that drew the steel doors sway to a gentle close. Hurrying to catch up in a manner that made it very clear she was in no hurry to catch up, the woman swished through the corridor so gracefully it didn't seem as though she was walking at all, ethereally gliding like an incorporeal shade.

"Now, if you would take the stairs to the right, the gala is already underway. Mr. Cooper, I'm sure you know your way from here," said the Royal Host, as she then turned away and entered another hallway beyond the lobby.

Entering the stunning globe lobby, Landon and Makari were treated to a vista of crystal perfection, where large, ionic marble columns fused with the ceiling at their intersections and, situated directly above our trio, an enormous diamond and silver chandelier dangled like a great stalactite, replete with snowy-white candles that flickered away with brilliant flames. Across the lobby were three massive hallways leading deeper within the labyrinthine manor, swathed with red velvet drapes that ran along their length.

"This is the Grand Cappa staircase, quite the feat of engineering," said Jade. The trio moved inexorably onward, climbing the long staircase that forked like the tip of a snake's tongue, embracing a giant blue vase of tiger lilies that spouted in the stair's center, and reuniting as it approached the balcony that interconnected them to the east hallways. The corridor ahead loomed with more golden hand candelabras stretching eerily out of the cold walls, looking so lifelike that Makari was attempted to poke one to see if that provoked a reaction. Landon nearly pressed his nose against one of the cool-to-the-touch hexagon windows, eyeing the bowl of lights that was Cappa Square far, far below. Finally, our trio reached the end of the hall, and to the right of them, nestled under a wide arch, was a short flight of stairs. "Shall we?" said Jade turning his head toward the children while making his way through the arch.

As the trio ascended the steps to the balcony, a disgruntled man in a fine dinner suit hastily descended from the humming gala, nearly colliding with Jade as he frantically rushed towards the exit. Nearing the top of the stairs, the background purr of a heavy crowd that had been steadily growing reached a crescendo, now interspersed with strains of an orchestra playing a staccato waltz and laughter echoing

120

through the crisp night air. Gathered together here were nearly three-dozen Cappamites and foreign dignitaries, many of them dancing and, unlike our curious siblings, all of them were opulently garbed for the posh gala. The balcony was made up of entirely glass and stone, wrapping around the entire east tower; an elevated veranda sheathed in a single stroke of continuous glass. The glass balcony was bedecked as extravagantly as its occupants; bathed in diamonds and crystals, tall plinths that housed branching candelabras, luxuriantly draped tables laden with the finest china and silverware, and massive velvet curtains that framed the nocturnal panorama. "Follow me to the House table," Jade waved, as he led the siblings around the adjacent dance floor.

Standing short and sharp with pen in hand and golden writing pad to match, a journalist in one corner of the room was in her element. Crowned with a brunette bun and gowned in a black, crocodile leather suit, she flung her razor-like questions at the gala's guests—all while shadowed by her considerably less photogenic young partner, who attention seemed to be occupied with taking pictures of the guests seated at the front of the party. "Ugh, *she's* here," Jade grimaced, looking over his shoulder. Landon and Makari noticed the two guests Jade had directed his distaste at, eyeing the short woman as she stuck her dagger-like gold pen into a slip beside her exaggerated jacket lapel. "That's Florence Mentirosa, Editor-at-Large for the Cappa Gazette. She works under her father, Editor-in-chief Octavio Mentirosa. The unkempt man that's usually seen scampering behind is her photographer and assistant, Luis O'Brice. Whatever you do, never answer her questions—she'll twist anything you say to suit whatever angle she's after."

The trio could feel darting eyes probe their backs, feeling a prickling sort of anxiety building as they made their way through the crowd. By the time they neared the head table, every guest had their retinas on them—and at that same moment, the orchestra suddenly stopped playing.

Florence Mentirosa steadied herself, already formulating a cover story headline for tomorrow's paper. The trio and the entire party then swung their heads to the front of the gala as a deep voice boomed from the head table.

"Jade! Where are you, my boy? Make your way up here," said the Head Man, seated at the head of the house table signaled, with a single flourish of the hand not clutching his goblet. Jade had only a few seconds to whisper to Landon and Makari that that man who beckoned them was none other than Antoine Cappa, the Head of Haus. The trio forged onward through the huddled party, splitting the crowd as they went. Antoine stood up: he was just as sallow as the rest of his fellow Cappamites, yet was ruddy with the delicately applied pats of red powder that dusted his round cheekbones, reminiscent of the fat kings that reside in a typical deck of playing cards. The king had the build of a man that had never quite shed his baby weight, and was crowned only with a crop of short, slicked-back black hair. The overall effect was that of an overripe tomato and was further accented by the bed of exaggerated pointy lapels that his head rested upon. Clearing his throat, Antoine Cappa began to speak again.

"I see you've made your way back—and not alone, it seems." Antoine exhaled through his wide nose, gesticulating carelessly at the siblings. Jade bowed, Landon and Makari quickly duplicated.

"I've happily returned, but please—I'd prefer we speak of lighter matters with so many distinguished guests nosing about," said Jade, stepping closer to the head table. Jade winked conspiratorially at a taciturn man in formal military garb seated alongside the royals. Before anyone else could speak, an elegant woman seated beside Taking a sip from her tall glass of milk, her flawless skin, nearly translucent with the trademark Cappa complexion, and platinum curls that swept across one side of her face would've given the impression of a ghost, if not for the warmth her cheerful face seemed to radiate. Landon and Makari seemed spellbound, so rapt with attention that they hardly noticed that the volume in the room had died down to a whisper. The tall woman that now stood reminded our curious siblings of the silver-screen starlets that on occasion had dazzled their Sunday-afternoon escapades at their favorite cinema; muses of the kind that had graced the better sort of motion pictures in the silent film era. Landon and Makari then eyed each other, but before they could voice their thoughts found their sights had once again returned to the woman that must be Dionne Cappa. There was a fierce yet sensitive grace about the woman that, though garbed in a lavender gown that matched Antoine in its extravagance, was nevertheless free of any rosy powders, the only notable color in her face the soft red lips that parted as she began to speak.

"He's right, Antoine," murmured Dionne Cappa, delicately placing a hand on her husband's shoulder, "it shall wait."

"Well Jade, please seats for yourself and our visitors. Join us all for our gala," Antoine limply flailed a hand, waving a welcome to the siblings and Jade to make their way to the head table. With a snap of Antoine's thick fingers, the orchestra resumed their playing. The guests that had begun to drift towards the edge of the dance floor glanced at one another and returned to waltz along with the orchestra once again. The trio slid through the inquisitive flock of guests, nearly all of them clamoring to suss out their origin as they reached for seats just below the Head table. Landon then helped his sister into her chair as Jade hid away his cane with a twirl. Their dinner table was round and candlelit, the tabletop as classily wreathed as the manor itself: from the crystal flower centerpieces to the dark green and burgundy tablecloth that spilled over the table's edge, every surface bristled with baroque embellishments. Even the delightful appetizers that were given to them glistened as though some wizard chef had transmuted them out of precious gems.

Waddling through the crowd was the picture-hungry Luis O'Brice, tossing his plump camera to the side as he wandered to the long table of hors-d'oeuvres. Luis's eyes squinted with anticipation as the unsettling sensation in the pit of his large stomach had him aching for a nibble of one of the hundred delectable sweets and cakes on display before him. Truly, there were scores of different sorts of crackers, each adorned with a whole array of spreads and cheeses; it all seemed like a simple dream of deliciousness. On a three-piece platter were sets of the richest chocolate dipped strawberries, the sweetest slices of oranges, kiwis, and the freshest creamy little éclairs topped with a drizzle of white chocolate. Panting at this most marvelous sight, Luis O' Brice knew this was his chance for the greatest treat....

"Luis!" A stingy, growling voice poked from behind Luis's ear, causing him to drop his tasty éclair out of fright. "Do you have any idea what this means?"

"*What* does what mean, Florence?" Luis sighed, trying to take a bite out of another éclair.

"Luis, those children are *very* peculiar, and I want to know why they're here," said Florence, blocking Luis's heavy appetite. "Just look at them—dressed like some bottom-feeding gargoylian, *sickens me*. If there's anyone at this party who has an insider's note about the Cappa's agendas, it's Oswill Lenner. He and his crooked nose are so deeply anchored in everyone's circles, it'd be Revlenion's *end* if *he* didn't know a thing or two about those kids."

"Okay, so what do you want me to do?" said Luis, aching to take a bite out of his melting treat.

"We need to work together, my dearest. If I can just snag a few quotes from those two kids and get the inside scoop from Lenner—while you take the beautiful snapshots of me, of course—it will make headlines! Tomorrow's newspapers will be flying off the stands!" cheered Florence with a deliciously harsh grin, again blocking Luis from his treat.

"Whatever, Florence, whatever will make us more money," said Luis, finally taking a bite.

"Just eat your éclair and follow me," said Florence, rolling her eyes as they continued through the guests, "thank goodness I came to this wretched party, leaving you with this task would've gotten my headlines nowhere."

As the first course of dinner began, the royal servers came through the doors at the end of the balcony, strolling along the aisles between each table. Uncorking dozens of bottles of wine, they provisioned each guest with plates for the gala feast. The guests were in a riotous mood: laughter spread across each table as other groups joked and cheered, the clanking of forks pervading the soundscape. The royal servers, some of them wingless gargoyles, then came to the Head table, serving up large silver platters laden with lovely steamed lobster. Each of the Head patrons then began to unfold their silk napkins and placed them gently on each of their laps. Landon then noticed a Head table patron, a man much like whatever species Albert Gellwerg was dressed in a fine suit and bowtie, shoo-away one of its fellow gargoyle creatures that stood too close to him.

"Wonderful meals every year, but it sometimes gets a little overbearing—go on, dig in, you two look starved," said Jade as Landon and Makari lifted the dome covers off their silver plates. Jade then snagged the freshest lemon for his lobster tail from a small basin on n the center of the table.

As Jade began to slice the lemon, an older gentleman dressed in an excellent scarlet uniform with rows of distinguished badges on his lapel, suddenly pulled himself an extra seat next to Jade.

"How are things, Jade?" said Hugh Cathaway, clearing his tired throat, "great for you to join us tonight—Dionne wasn't sure if you were going to make it." Jade smiled and shook the officer's warm hand.

"Chief Hugh Cathaway, all is well, my good sir. How has your time been away from Arkgothin City?" asked Jade, after taking a sip of his champagne.

"Quite pleasant, still keeping the city crime and illegal gargoylian gambling at bay," said Cathaway, as he served himself a glass of champagne. "Dionne tells me that you're working on a new Abandoned Manifesto case for the R.C.C.?"

"Sure 'am," said Jade, slicing into his plate. "These two are Landon and Makari Tuolumne, the latest developments in my case."

Jade then introduced Cathaway to our siblings, who returned the welcome with a simple nod.

"Lovely to meet you, children," smiled Chief Cathaway, bouncing a finger, "don't let this Cooper boy get you two into any deep trouble; I've known our fellow here since was just a youngster—sneaking off with fellow bad kids into the West Royal Pines, nearly giving us all heart-attacks!"

"My sister and I are happy to take part in Jade's case," said Landon.

"As I'm sure you are…Jade," said Cathaway, clearing his voice as he shifted in his seat, "solving old riddles and chasing after grim ole tales doesn't seem like hefty detective work at all—more like simple child's play, really. You should reconsider my offer in joining the Royal Academy, and take your place as a worthy Revlenion Officer."

Jade simply smiled with ease.

"I don't believe what I do is simple, but I've come to realize my place as an aspiring detective for the manor is true ambition," said Jade, taking another sip of his champagne.

"Think over my offer once more, I believe you'll soon realize that better fortunes can be found with the academy rather than dead manifestos," said Cathaway, as he slipped an envelope out from his coat pocket, "read my letter and learn about what you can truly accomplish by setting your personal standards higher."

Cathaway then slid the brown envelope to Jade as a gargoyle server then approached their table, tapping on Cathaway's shoulder and following with a whispering of notes into the old Chief's ear.

"I'll give it another gander," said Jade, staring at the envelope on the table, sensing not single ounce of guilt for not picking it up. Landon peeked to his right as he noticed Jade wasn't too fond of Cathaway's offer.

Cathaway nodded at Landon and Makari as he then excused himself and made his way to the Head table. Landon watched as Cathaway stepped up to the Head table to find his reserved seat. Before sitting, he generously nodded to both the Cappa Heads and after that, took his seat alongside Antoine Cappa.

"Someone that you're not happy to see?" said Makari, after taking a sip of her cold glass of seltzer water.

"Seeing Cathaway is always a pleasure, but sometimes he can cause quite the irritating ring in my ear," said Jade, shuffling in his chair.

"Who is he anyway?" asked Landon.

"Cathaway's a well respected man of Revlenion, as Chief of the Arkgothin Bureau of Revlenion Officers," nodded Jade, "And as unequivocally celebrated as he might be, he does test my patience sometimes."

As half of the guests returned on to the dance floor, while others remained in their seats sipping on either delicious wines or cups of espresso, out of nowhere, an ill faced man swathed in a fine gray suit and donning black-round sunglasses, suddenly approach the Head table behind Antoine Cappa. Makari was first to notice the odd man, alerting her brother to take part in the gander. Landon twisted his head around, eyeing the gaunt man from the corner of his eye, watching him whisper something quick into Antoine's ear. Landon suddenly looked away, as the gaunt man detected Landon was trying to eavesdrop on the nearly silent conversation. Landon gave another swift look from the corner of his eye:

"Who is that man, Jade?" said Landon, looking up at the Head table, "he looks awfully pale, worse than most of the Cappamites."

"Hovering over Antoine like a mosquito, right there, that's his executive assistant, Benjamin Varick. He's a bit on the tight-lipped side. You'll only see him around when it means royal business, and since we are on the subject."

Jade began to point out every patron of the Head table, from left to right, for our siblings to recognize. "Very important to become familiar with these faces, as I'm sure you'll be meeting each and every one of them soon or sometime again."

Landon and Makari began to picture the patron's names written and underlined in chalk as though they were being written on some invisible blackboard, trying to tie faces to the names:

Timothy Savini

Benjamin Varick — Chief Hugh Cathaway

Antoine Emmanuel Cappa

Dionne Mariette Cappa

Lewa Qwara — Loward Schmaltz

"Qwara and Schmaltz are?" asked Makari.

"Oh, Qwara is the Vice-Manor Head, under the Cappas, and longtime friend of Dionne…and that gangly man with an exceptional mustache is Schmaltz," addressed Jade, "owner of Dingoduns Espresso Emporium—no doubt the leading sponsor behind tonight's gala."

Antoine then stood from his seat again. With his champagne glass in hand, he softly tapped his silver fork against his glass, chiming the gala's attention. The orchestra calmed as Antoine prepared a simple speech:

"Ladies and gentlemen," he said, looking amongst the crowd, "my dear wife Dionne and I, wish to thank you all for attending our Eighty-Sixth Annual Cappa Solstice Gala, as part of our partnership and charity for the loving students at St. Madeline's Academy for Sacred Children—" as the entire party clapped in honor. "Tonight we are gifted with many treats: the attendance of members of our renowned R.C.C.," applauded Antoine, showing a hand out to the select table of the three members, and Savini, sitting cheerfully with a glass of champagne in his manicured paw, "in addition, the acclaimed Grams-Ellenstein Symphony Orchestra, is delighting us this evening with their magnificent company of strings—and of course the newly invited," nodding to both Landon and Makari, "both whom are most warmly welcomed this evening to our home of royalty and wisdom." The party returned to another wave of applause before Antoine spoke again:

"And lastly, I've been keen on silencing the rumors, that I've had the pleasure of reading in the Cappa Gazette," as he then chuckled, sardonically, "as I am pleased to announce, that beginning this October, I will begin the empowering event for the renewing of my signature and stand as the Head of Cappa Valley for next year's running elections, and crowning my twenty years of keeping the peace," said Antoine, triumphantly, and toasting his glass in the air as he eyed his busy patrons. Makari smiled and added to the cheer, while wheeling her head around, noticing a few collections of sunken faces in the crowd, free of any grin or merriment, but only rather disgusted by the vain announcement. "For nobility and courage, those wise and full of heart—we salute you and the peace of our fine Cappa Valley!" Antoine cheered as the party raised their glasses at their Head's word.

The guests returned to their stacked meals and began spitting comments like hornets in a heckled hive. Landon then turned to Jade, who was slowly sipping on his glass of champagne.

"Jade, what does Antoine mean by, renewing of his signature?" said Landon eagerly.

"You see," wiping his mouth, "every six years, the Head of Royalty must reclaim his or her throne by a leading vote from their citizens and the High Chamberlains. Each running member for the throne has opponents who are selected by the people of the supporting valley, Cappa being one such. Only can a person run for the throne that has been voted for by their natives and has a hand in marriage. In Antoine Cappa's case, he balanced the line to succeed by marrying Madame Dionne Cappa, who grew up in the Vales family. He won his first run for the throne since he was the sole heir for his father, Sir Almerine Cappa, but only by that. Since then, he has successfully reclaimed it by full vote," Jade continued again, with much more of a whisper, "because every six years for his signing, the persistent old 'Cappa Curse,' arises."

"A curse?" asked Makari, with a chill running down her back. "Every single one of Antoine's opponents have dropped out of the elections or become unavailable, one way or another," said Jade.

"One way or another?" said Landon.

129

"Let's just say, unhappy accidents have been the major culprit. Whether it is from drowning while taking a dip upon the Vorloren Beaches, falling down a spiraling staircase, or sometimes, even more peculiar, the opponent vanishes entirely," uttered Jade. "Don't mistake my words, Antoine, clever though he might be, is a gentle man; he's not the one to blame."

"Will his son, Arrison—inherit the position after him?" said Landon, hunching.

"That's if he," Jade shifted his eyes on the unnoticing Antoine, "decides to gift it over to him, and that's something of an *if.*"

"Why wouldn't he? He's engaged, isn't he?" said Makari.

"To take the throne calls for major responsibility—not saying Arrison or Audrey aren't capable of pledging to such a grand opportunity. True, Arrison is engaged—it's just the idea of the harsh history behind the throne. Antoine has proven his people worthy over the years, family included, however, some might take issue with Arrison's political leanings. I suppose the citizens of Cappa Valley have come to place a great deal of trust in Antoine, and that can't be gifted," said Jade, taking a bite of his buttermilk biscuit. "Or maybe, just maybe, Antoine doesn't want his son to end up like the rest of his challengers. I do recall—there was this one man, I remember, just one—who managed the stick the election out. Didn't do him a lick of good, mind you; he still lost. With all that said, though it is possible, that if Arrison is not suited to take the seat, it will be left open to the next of kin, on the Cappa bloodline, or Lewa Qwara would have to accept—that's if the R.C.C. hold a vote…but I don't foresee any Cappa family tragedies in the future. I don't doubt for a second, though, that Ms. Qwara would be a fine leader for this country."

There was a long pause before Landon could barely return to eating his steamed lobster, knowing what possible troubles that sat so near at the Head table. Makari then noticed that horrid Florence Mentirosa, standing before the Head table, scribbling possible quotes from Cathaway and the Royals. Florence was smiling wide as flitted from table to table, posing just long enough for Louis to capture the tableau, then darting to the next. From her cheery disposition, Makari guessed Mentirosa had an unflattering headline for tomorrow's paper brewing in her mind as she and her odious partner swept past the head table.

As Antoine and Dionne Cappa finished their meals, they stood from their seats and made their way to the dance floor, where the other guests joined them in a formal dance. Antoine spun his wife skillfully, her gorgeous gown swaying across the stone floor as she whirled. The ivory moon broke from the clouds, joining the star-lit sky in illuminating the scene. The quartet burst into a blistering arpeggio, somehow reminiscent of a song Landon swore he had heard once before on the radio back home: *Hong Kong Garden?* Landon thought.

Jade then stood from his chair and offered a hand to Makari, who stared blankly for a moment, surprised by the invitation. Landon smiled and nodded, encouraging his sister to brisk along the dance floor with their new friend, and was surprised himself when, not long after, he felt a gentle tap on his shoulder. A rosy-cheeked girl in a belle-tutu dress stood with a gentle hand out Landon, smiling.

"Me?" said Landon, trembling at the thought of having to dance, as the girl's outthrust hand insistently indicated.

"Of course, *silly boy,*" said the Curly Haired Girl, as Landon then took her lace-gloved hand.

The curly girl, who seemed to be around the same age as Landon, led him onto the dance floor despite Landon's feeble protestations, nearly crashing into several cavorting couples. Landon then noticed a clan of young girls covering their mouths and cackling like witches around a roiling cauldron, watching our boy struggle to keep up with the massive party that waltzed in near-perfect unison. Landon could feel himself breaking out in a cold sweat as he tried not to look at his feet, though the girl was undoubtedly leading their dance.

As the quartet finished their song with clash from a pair of cymbals, the girl smiled at Landon and wordlessly turned on her heel and sped off back to her gang of giggling nymphs. Jade, Makari in tow, then appeared next to Landon, laughing, "Don't look so embarrassed, Landon! You did fine."

"Yeah, yeah," Landon grumbled, feeling very put upon.

The floor cleared as everyone returned to their seats, as the diminutive orchestra conductor bowed to the party, "Ladies and gentlemen, please be seated as I introduce our final piece for the evening—*Summer*, as performed by the Frió Ballet!" announced the conductor as he turned toward his ensemble once more.

With an adjustment of his monocle and a gentle tap of his baton, the performance began. The front row of strings commenced as the hammer from the percussionists thrummed through the entire party. Suddenly, two slithering beings ascended over the party, trailing great swathes of sparks as they zoomed overhead. The music swelled to an impossible pace, building until it resonated deep within the audience's chests. These zooming apparitions transformed and intertwined as troupe of a dozen ballet dancers congregated in the center of the dance floor: their gray hair coiffed into gravity-defying whirls and curls, lips blue as the stars, and eyes shining as brightly as the moon above. The troupe's silky blue bodies radiated grace as their movements perfectly reflected the tone of the music, dazzling the spectators as one blew a kiss that ballooned into a swarm of luminous fireworks.

Landon and Makari watched with amazement sparkling from their eyes as each of the performers danced, flipping and twirling in perfect synchronicity with the roaring quartet. The audience had fallen silent, transfixed at each wonderful move. The aerial performers again shed a veil of sparks upon the audience, timed to a burst of exuberance from the orchestra, while their terrestrial counterparts spun in formation, ending with a bow in the center of the balcony dance floor as the row of violinists fiddled their final string. The entire gala clapped and whistled as the troupe continued to bow.

And then chaos erupted.

The entire Head table flew back from their chairs and onto the cold, hard balcony floor. Other guests were blown into the night sky with debris from the shattered balcony dance floor, bursting through segments of the glass veranda. The orchestra fell from their seats and ducked for cover. Thick pieces of the stone floor came smashing down on the elegant party tables, guests dodging—and failing to dodge—falling stone left and right. The ballet members were thrown everywhere from the center of the dance floor by the sudden eruption. One after the other, Cappamites in the square below began to gather and point with shock at the sight of the billowing mayhem high above. Thick smoke continued to rise from the hole in the balcony as a dozen Manor guards quickly trampled onto the scene:

"Makari, are you okay?" coughed Landon, hovering over his sister who lay splayed on her side with a small gash on her cheek. Landon frantically tore a piece of tablecloth and dabbed at her face, oblivious to the blood that was even now trickling into his eyes from his forehead. He was vaguely aware of Benjamin Varick in his periphery, who seemed to be struggling to overcome his panic as he grabbed hold of one of the house guards.

"KEEP STEADY AROUND THE BLAST!" Varick ordered. When no one appeared to be doing so, he repeated the order, glaring at the sudden void that had so abruptly disrupted the evening's festivities.

"*Ouch*—J-Jade are you okay?" said Landon while crawling over to Jade, shaking him. Landon then noticed Dionne roll over to her husband; both of them were fine. The Cappa Heads and Cathaway helped up Landon and miraculously unharmed Jade…Dionne snapped at nearby guards to send medical attention as she huddled next to Jade and the siblings, taking Makari in her lap, who seemed to have been rendered unconscious by the blast.

"Are you two alright?" Dionne panted, gripping Landon's shoulders as she scanned them for injuries. Landon and Jade looked around at the remaining guests, holding out hands to bring others to their feet. The room was swiftly flooding with guards, and the injured Cappamites found themselves carted out to the lawn, where medical care was waiting. Dionne, however remained focused on Makari, growing more and more agitated with each moment the girl failed to wake. Suddenly, a high-pitched laugh echoed from the void in the balcony. Jade recognized that laugh, a laugh he remembered hearing years ago.

Everyone that still remained at the party-turned-disaster spun to watch the smoke billowing ominously from the dark hole in the veranda, frozen with fear of what might emerge. Out of sheer habit, Luis was still frenetically snap photos of the disaster as something began to take shape from the within the smoke. A few of the more prudent guests backed away as far as they could manage, gasping at the sight of the figure moving out of the debris: Its hunched form straightened to reveal its slit-scarred face framed with long, ratty black hair that flowed down over a tattered, black-green double-breasted leather jacket. Luis clicked another shot from his camera as the camera bulb finally popped with a flash. Florence shrieked and attempted her partner as a human shield as the Intruder drew close to them, smirking. After a moment's consideration, it turned away from the petrified couple and lazily extended a finger from its long, skeletal hand at Jade.

"Men, seize the Intruder!" ordered Antoine. Four manor guards charged with their long, ruby scepters drawn toward the Intruder. The hand the Intruder had pointing at Jade swatted aimlessly in the general direction of the rushing guards, and with a screeching snap, the scarred faced man conjured a single bolt of lighting, violently displacing the guards through the air and out the shattered segments of window that remained along the veranda. Turning back towards Jade, the Intruder then began to curl a wide, devilish grin at the mayhem his arrival had precipitated.

"I hope that I didn't harm anyone on my way in," giggled the Intruder, kicking aside broken decorations, "I suppose one might call this entrance a *terrible* overreaction, but you know, it was an awful strain on my good will to throw such a lovely soiree without inviting me." The Intruder cautiously edged out of its crater. "And instead, you invite...them." The Intruder was now pointing at our siblings, leading the spectators to fix their attention upon these most curious guests. Jade, two Manor Guards, and Cathaway surrounded our siblings in an apparent hope to shield them from an expected attack. At this point, the room was buzzing with whispered speculation from the surrounding Cappamites:

"That's him...*Vizton*—"

"—It can't be him..."

"The lonely Eplaville Boy?"

"Look at his face—"

"—Look at those *scars*..."

"You have no purpose here, you sad beast," said Dionne, still clamped on to Makari, noticing Jade's gritting face. The Intruder gave an annoyed chuckle, somehow managing to swagger as he tiptoed across an unconscious waiter that still held a tight grip on a platter full of desserts.

"Myy dearrrest Diiiionne," sighed the Intruder, stressing each word as he helped himself to a debris-ridden éclair with his dirty fingers. "My purpose is as pure as yours...the Dark Alman and *his* manifesto still linger, you must not forget that." The Intruder then took a bite of the pastry, chewing for a moment before bulging his eyes and spitting out the bite at Jade's feet. "Just like the Cappas, fat-headed and devoid of substance."

"If anything lack's substance," said Jade, now pointing his cane at the Intruder, who seemed to have discovered a sudden fascination with the patterns on the wallpaper.

"You can put your little toy away, Mr. Cooper, I won't be dragged into whatever melodrama you've imagined for yourself now," smirked The Intruder.

"You have less than thirty-seconds to rid yourself from this house!" warned Mr. Varick.

"Plenty of time for me to relay a few kind words. Now...though

I'm not quite the orator that our fat Antoine seems to be, I, too, have an announcement." The fidgeting Intruder began to retreat steadily back to the hole through which it had entered, "the voices of my long-suffering master have request I relay that, all of you," he pointed to the surrounding guests, "all of you will be laid low from your seats of power and made to taste the imprisonment you've so graciously blessed him with. Mark these words, Cappamites; nothing will or can prevent his return to freedom. It is inevitable," as he then pointed at Landon and Makari again. "The Dark Alman will ring a death knell on this chapter in Revlenion's history!" The Intruder declared, locking eyes with Landon and shooting off a final rejoinder as he dove into the hole once more, "your move, my Cherished Guardian."

A few brave Cappamites and Manor Guards edged forward to peer into the blasted ruin that was once the balcony floor, scanning the darkness below as an echo of seething laughter emitted from the void. Jade set his cane at his side, now calm as he looked over to see a pale-faced Landon.

"You promised," Landon frowned, quivering a fright.

"Who...who was that, sir?" asked a Manor Guard, coming beside with Chief Cathaway.

"A bad man, a *very* bad man," said Cathaway, noticing Makari jolt awake with a sputter. Makari rubbed her eyes, taking in the smoking debris that had so recently been a party.

Less than one hour later, the last of the guests had been hurriedly escorted out of the manor in loose clumps by cadres of Manor Guards. Not, however, before Chief Cathaway had ordered an impromptu investigation on the gala attack that evening, subjecting nearly half of the manor staff and attending Cappamites to interrogation and leaving the Cappas with a warning to be as tight-lipped as possible with the public, especially with regards to the Cappa Gazette. As for Landon and Makari, the manor walls that had seemed so safe now appeared markedly less so, now that the full enormity of their task had begun to make itself clear. With the possibility of Vizton Eplaville lurking around the grounds casting a pall of fear and apprehension over the manor, Jade, the Cappas, and the Revlenion Chamberlain Committee were rushing a slew of precautions into place, sending guards on patrol across every inch of the property. Shoulders heavy with the feeling that they should be doing more, Dionne and Antoine reluctantly made their way to their private courters near the north end of the manor to rest for the night, too wrapped up in the events of the night to even spare a farewell for Jade or our siblings. As for Landon, Makari and Jade, two large guards promptly escorted them to a spare bedroom for the evening, winding through a labyrinth of hallways that the siblings did their level best to commit to memory.

"Is there a library in this house?" asked Makari, wishing she could cuddle with a book to calm her mind. Instead the stern guard escorting the trio through the manor simply replied with an exasperated stare. "Ah," Makari recoiled, realizing the guard's job very likely entailed keeping her from wandering off to find such a place, if it existed. After a short jaunt up the west tower elevator, reaching the ninth floor, Landon and Makari found themselves being introduced to Lewa Qwara.

Ms. Qwara welcomed our siblings, offering each a gentle handshake and thanking them for their visit to the manor and hoping very much that they were still enjoying their visit to Cappa Valley, recent events excluded of course. She was a relatively unremarkable in appearance, a stout black woman perhaps forty years old, clad in a purple beret that tilted to one side of her short and wavy hair and a matching necklace to fit. Ms. Qwara was the Vice-Manor Head, and known to be the most approachable member of the Manor High Executives, though her time was so tightly scheduled few ever found out first-hand without an appointment.

"Hello Tuolumnes, this will be the room you two will be occupying during your inaugural visit with us in Cappa. Remember, you two are more than welcome to ask me any questions about the house, or anything else that I'm able to answer." Landon and Makari's marble-tiled bedroom was quite spacious, an intricately furnished space with two four-poster beds, a massive wooden wardrobe to match and plenty of shelves that housed such an array of antiques, books, and assorted oddities that they made the room look more like a museum than anywhere people actually might live. Jade turned a dial on the room's wall, and the light radiating from the bedside table lamps brightened up a corresponding degree. "Also, there are fresh pajamas in the wardrobe there for the two of you; you really shouldn't sleep in those tattered clothes—leave them by the wardrobe, there, a Manor Wardrober will attend to any stitching or cleaning your clothes might need," Ms. Qwara took a moment to clear her throat, "we're all set for the night then? I believe it would be best, Jade, that they receive a good night's rest—for you two will be meeting with the royals for an early breakfast tomorrow."

"Alright then," nodded Jade, as Ms. Qwara smiled and waved a good night to the siblings and exited the room, closing the rosewood door behind her.

Jade looked away from the bedroom door, darting a look of relief at Landon and Makari who were sitting at the foot ends on each of their beds.

"So...when were you going to tell us that someone hates us here?" inquired Landon, a note of stress in his voice.

"I can't believe that that actually happened; he came out of nowhere!" sighed Jade, tracing a sight of uneasiness that clung to Makari's face. "I'll say this, I gave you my word that I'd keep you two safe to the best of my ability, and I will keep that promise. That promise, though, comes with a few caveats. One; for me to keep you safe, you must *always* stay on the same path as me while I guide you through this curious case of ours—where I go, you go, simple as that. Two, an old friend of mine who once found himself in a similar situation failed to account for the fact that when making a promise to keep another safe, one should not take it to imply that the future will be safe or predictable—neither Revlenion, nor any other world I'm aware of for that matter, is ever so accommodating."

"We understand," said Landon, as he and his sister exchanged a knowing nod, sharing something that went beyond the circumstances of the evening. "We'll keep close."

"Good," sparked Jade, tapping his cane a few times, "so then, like Ms. Qwara said, you two will be meeting with the Cappas in the morning to further elaborate on your summons. And, as I see it, the best course of action at this point would be for you two to end this frenzied day by going to bed."

"Yeah," nodded Landon, again.

"Before I forget, I believe I happened to overhear your aunt saying something about keeping yourself out of any attic-related trouble today, correct?" said Jade.

"*Oh*, our Aunt Marion, yes?" said Landon.

"In the interest of doing right by her, I feel impelled to remind you two not get into any unnecessary trouble, especially not while both of you are settling in the manor. Given the events of the past few hours, I expect the guards that trek the manor halls are going to be on high alert, so now would be an exceptionally bad time to get it into your heads that you ought to go exploring. If you should be so foolish, don't be surprised if the guards aren't terribly kind. *Trust me*, I've been on the wrong end of those conflicts more often than I'd like, and I'd like to spare you the trouble," warned Jade.

Landon and Makari nodded.

"If you need me for anything, I'll be in my room four doors down, g'night you two," said Jade, turning to the rosewood door.

A few minutes after Jade slid out from the room, Landon and Makari took turns stepping into the bathroom across from their beds and slipping into their checkered pajamas. The siblings tried to relax in their own beds for some time: Makari rested on her side, gazing at the sky through the tall, half-draped windows beside the balcony doors. The night sky was striking, filled with pearly stars that set the night aglow, shining brighter than any she had ever seen before.

"Makari, are you falling asleep?" asked Landon, tossing on his side.

"I can't. I can't help but think of that man's…hideous face again, over and over," sighed Makari, turning over on her stomach.

"Ugh, I can't sleep either," said Landon, as he turned over on his side, again, and turned up the dim on his oddly shaped bedside lamp.

Landon then reached for the art deco radio on the shelf of eccentric vases and globes across from his bed.

"Turn it down!" shook Makari, as a roar of static filled the bedroom. Hoping that a bit of noise from radio might help them fall asleep, Landon spun the stiff dials until the radio waves cleared, catching the ending of some song when a cool, mellifluously smooth feminine voice sparked through the speaker.

"*Alright now kiddos,* that was The Grass Roots' *Midnight Confessions,* and nearing the midnight hour it surely is. If you're just tuning in, this is R.E.V.—FM 1, and I'm your everyday host, Lately Lynne," she said, as Landon and Makari listened on. "I'm coming at you loud and clear, all the way from Arkgothin City; can you hear me kiddos? Good. Before I sign off, some ugly rumors are circling the airwaves on this cool, summer night: someone with absolute miserable manners has taken upon himself to shake things up over in Cappa Valley, Vizton Eplaville, the heir to that near-forgotten cabal of Dark Seether nonsense that was makin' headlines in The Arkgothin Times before their fiend of a boss was apprehended and the rest were routed and run outta town by the Ordinheirs some time ago," Lately Lynne then gave a derisive hum through her microphone, as our curious siblings then gathered closer to catch any details the midnight host might unveil, "…And all of you Revlers know just what an absolute cad *that* fellow was, lifted straight out of the more unpleasant sort of fairy tale, if you ask me. He was the king of darkness, the king of many fiends, claimed to be the king of a lot of things, now that I think of it. Elliott Creshion, or the Dark Alman, as his lackeys called him: Evercanezer, the hideous little punk got his in the end, locked up for the rest of his days after being found guilty of just about everything they lock people up for. Good riddance, I say. Revlenion's a far nicer place without him. As it seems, that fidgety Eplaville seems to have decided that he's not hated enough 'round these parts; not only did he ruin a perfectly good shindig up at the manor, injuring several partygoers—word has it, at least—this party was attended by a couple of guests from beyond Revlenion's borders. Another go for a magnificent manifesto? Is Eplaville trying to get the band back together? Let's see how this new tale of ours pans out—anyone care to place a bet? My money is on the curious kids from outta town. And on that note, here's a classic tune that reminds of the bad old days and of one, particular kiddo that took part in the manifesto that silenced that miserable Creshion fellow. Here's *Nature Boy* by the legendary Nat King Cole. Good-luck kiddos, if you can hear me—this is Lately Lynne, signing off at this midnight hour, nighty night...."

Lately Lynne's show then faded out to tomorrow's depressingly predictable gloomy weather forecast and some sprightly commercial about a new brand of toothpaste.

"That's Eplaville's plan, then? He's gathering new Seethers, or whoever they are," noted Makari, as she returned to her bedside.

"And a new manifesto, it seems," said Landon. "It's beginning to seem a lot clearer. But I'm tired of being given a tour, we need to find some answers on our own."

"*Ouch!*" frowned Makari, clamping her head where it had met her pillow when she'd tossed her head back against it.

"What's wrong?" leaned Landon.

"This day is just getting more and more interesting," said Makari, as she revealed a tattered leather book that had been placed under her pillow. "I was wondering why my pillow was so uncomfortable."

"Who could've left it?" said Landon.

"There's a note too," said Makari, untying the piece of parchment from the cover.

"What does it say?" said Landon, racing across the cold marble floor to Makari's bedside.

"You'll never believe who it's from," panted Makari, as she and her brother read the scratchy words on the taped parchment:

I found my answers on the third floor.
Look Amongst the place
where there are aisles and spines.
-Helpfully Yours -

"Not him...*or* her, again," marveled Landon. "I think we might have a stalker."

"It couldn't be Jade; he's specifically told us *not* to leave the room," said Makari. "Where there are aisles and spines?" Makari thought, "A library? That's easy enough." Her brother, in the meantime, flipped through the pages of the leather book. Landon jumped from Makari's bed and reached for the bedroom door, giving a small peek out to the hallway, empty.

"Wait, we can't! Didn't you hear Jade? The manor is like a maze at night," huffed Makari.

"Oh, come on, we'll manage. M, both of us need answers, and I'm not going to sleep until we get them," urged Landon.

"We promised Jade, Lan," darted Makari.

"And?"

"*And* we can't go against his wishes, obviously," crossed Makari.

"So, you'd rather sit in here and wait?" hummed Landon.

"I...*no*, but I'd rather do our searching the *right way*, with Jade!" said Makari.

"How about this, one round of rock-paper-scissors—You win, we stay in here to ponder, and if I win, I'll lead the way—deal?" said Landon, leaning nonchalantly against the door.

"Deal," sighed Makari, her china-blue eyes glaring daggers at her brother.

Landon drew scissors—Makari, paper. Landon then gave a quick winning jig as Makari spun on her heel.

"Ugh, you just want us to get maimed, don't you?" said Makari, shaking her head, as she grabbed her green ribbon-headband from the wardrobe, along with their shoes from the bottom drawer. Landon cracked opened the rosewood door again; both of them shivered as a cold drift whirled past them. After a shiver, Landon and Makari made their way into the dimly lit marble hallway. Landon closed their bedroom door, all while trying his best to not make any noise.

CLANK!

"Let the entire manor know we're out here, why don't you?" cringed Makari, as she tied her hair back with her green ribbon. Landon grinned as he then retraced their steps along the candelabras fixed in the walls until they reached an elevator at the end of the long hall.

"Our helpful friend says they found their answers on the third floor," said Landon, as he pushed the silver down-arrow button. "Let's go have a look."

Landon and Makari could hear the humming within the elevator shaft as they awaited the opening of the ornate silver doors.

"Where's the guard?" shivered Makari, eyeing either end of the long and eerily still corridor. With a faint chime, the elevator doors slid open, and, quickly stepping in, Makari clicked the third-floor button, and the doors sliding shut with another chime.

TING!

The elevator doors slowly slid open and the Tuolumnes found themselves standing at the top of a short flight of steps, gingerly taking a few nervous footsteps out of the elevator cabin. Makari dragged her feet at the idea of venturing deeper into the manor by themselves, but her hopes of turning back diminished as the elevator doors shut behind them. Our siblings continued down the stairs, keeping to the patches of light cast by the moon beaming through the row of oval windows along the hall. Reaching the end of the moonlit hall, they came to another short flight of steps, leading up to a stone balcony that overlooked a vast library.

"Aisles and spines, oh my..." said Makari, ecstatically.

"The Almerine Memorial Library," Landon read over the cursive script that had been engraved into the mosaic floor at the entrance to the library. "I'm really beginning to like this 'helpfully yours' fellow."

The room was massive, and like the hall that preceded it, was brought to life by the moonlight that streamed in through the wide skylights above. The bulk of the space was occupied by rows of circular tables arranged along the edges of countless winding bookshelves that overflowed with books, many of which seemed to have been left to collect dust for quite some time. Even though Makari was an absolute lover of books, the absolute scale of the collection was intimidating; she was struck with the sudden realization that, even if she started right this moment, she would likely die of old age before working her way through a fraction of the knowledge contained here.

"Where do we even begin to search for answers?" groaned Makari, as she began their descent into the sea of tomes. "Look!"

Two lamps were lit and placed side by side, as if prepared for the two of them, at the giant mouth of the unlit fireplace that gaped just under the side-curling staircase.

"Landon, I think someone is *really* intent on guiding us here," said Makari, peering into the dark spaces of the room that surrounded them.

"Or maybe, these belong to someone who's still roaming around in here," gulped Landon.

"Oh, don't say that!" gasped Makari, eyeing a web-draped aisle ahead of her.

"This isn't going to be easy and as scary as it may sound and much as I'm afraid to, let's split up—"

"*Are you serious*, Landon?" Makari screeched.

"M, it'll allow us to comb through the library faster," said Landon, shaking away a chill.

"Ugh," wailed Makari, giving a shivered look down another darkened aisle, "if we have too."

"I'll take the right side of the library, if you'd like the left," said Landon, as he then pointed at one of the study tables in front of them, "meet back at that table in ten minutes, and try to bring back as many books with the best information you can find about manifestos or Revlenion and M, if anything bad happens, just shout for me," said Landon, as he then spun on his heel.

Makari nodded, as the silhouette of her brother slipped between two towering shelves and was gone. Makari trudged off into the darkness, shining her lamp at an opening between two looming shelves as she tiptoed on through the aisle.

DEATH RECORDS—SECTION: E

Noticing the sign, Makari worried what she might find—or meet—down the aisle. Walking through the dusty passage, she trailed a finger over the spines of a few books, her finger quickly collecting a patina of dust. After wiping the crusted debris on her pajama pants, Makari nervously glanced over her shoulder, noticing how far she'd already managed to stray from the entrance of the aisle and hoping the small, oil-lit lamp in her hand wouldn't burn out. As Makari turned to continue her search, a ghostly chill lashed across her face, causing her to wheel around with the lamp, flaring it as bright as it would go. She immediately regretted doing so, as flying wearily above her between the tops of the shelves was a lazily drifting swarm of what appeared to be ghosts, absolutely terrifying ghosts, at that, many appearing mutilated or partially decomposed. Makari was anchored to the spot with terror, confronted with as direct a reminder of one's own mortality as ever one might encounter, leaving aside entirely her fear that she had lost her mind or was about to be gruesomely murdered by a swarm of specters. Nevertheless, Makari took a deep breath, forcing herself to look up at the grim figures hovering above and between the long and winding shelves. Struck by a sudden urge, stupid though she feared it might be, Makari looked up at one of the ghosts and waved:

"Excuse me," Makari shook her head, "oh, what am I saying?"

To her chagrin (and no small amount of relief), none of the moldering spirits reacted in the slightest. Shivering, Makari took in another deep breath, hunched her shoulders and walked further into the aisle. Moving at a glacial pace now, she eyed the thousands of old book spines, trying to somehow both ignore the ghosts and keep an eye on them in case they turned hostile. Coming to a turn in the aisle, she ventured deeper and deeper into the gloom until a little voice cackled between the cramped books.

"*Ask, ask, ask* them a question!" said a petite voice. Makari froze, barely managing to sputter a response.

"Ask whom a question?" trembled Makari, shifting her eyes up and down the high shelves.

"The ghosts, you strange girl, ask the *ghosts!*" hissed another little voice.

"*Ask, ask, ask* them a question!" said a gentle voice across from Makari. Snatching the book from the shelf and peeking through the emptiness, she then looked at the dusty hardback book in her hand.

"Not me, silly girl, the ghosts!" said the leathery face that plated the incunable's cover. Makari shrieked and shoved the heavy book back in its place.

Suddenly, all the books began to roar with laughter at Makari.

"What do you want me to ask?" cringed Makari, for the first time understanding why someone might want to burn a book.

"Oh! What a senseless little redhead, lost in a library," said another cackling voice.

"We'll teach her a lesson," chimed a pair of tiny voices.

At that very moment, Makari's eyes darted along the towering shelves ahead as the thousand or more of the books that rested above began to rattle, causing a torrent of tattered pages and some of the more precarious volumes to tumble to the aisle floor. Makari leaped back in shock, backpedaling frantically to dodge the heavy books that crashed to the ground all around her:

"I bet she doesn't even know how to read!"

146

"I wonder if she even knows what a paperback is?"

"Pathetic, *little child*—" said another voice giggling.

"And *lost, lost, lost!*" echoed all the books at once, cackling loudly. Makari pulled right at the next corner, leaving the cackling aisle behind and, in a moment of respite, looked up at the slow traffic of ghosts that lingered above her.

"Please, which one of you ghosts can help me?" said Makari. As the horrid books had indicated, Makari's question finally prompted a response from one of the specters. Swooping down to Makari, a translucent old woman, gentle looking despite the unnatural angle at which her head was cocked, nodded at Makari, smiling.

"We can't help you, little girl," moaned the ghost, as her left arm began to drift in a different direction from the rest of her. Glancing at the offending limb, the woman frowned and it snapped back into place. "All we can do is clog these dusty aisles... haunting the books where our death certificates have been improperly recorded."

"Can you at least tell me where I could find any books about the history of Revlenion?" asked Makari, leaping aside as the woman's floating path carried her through the spot where Makari had just been standing.

"I recall a time in my past life when I was studying—I aspired to become a historian for the royal manor, seems rather pointless now. At any rate, there was this boy at the end of this aisle who would incessantly distract me with his childish tricks and fantastic tales, I tried to pay him no mind, but he was rather insistent. It's almost comical now, I don't think he cares much for the dead, yet now I'd love to actually hear one of his stories," lamented the ghost, lapsing into introspection as her misty body was pulled inexorably back up to the river of ghosts. Makari opened her mouth to ask the shade to come back, but it had already melded into the roiling hodgepodge of apparitions above. Following the ghost's few enigmatic words as best as she was able, Makari trekked further down the aisle until it opened to a large circle in the center of more twisted shelves.

CHAPTER THREE

ADOLESCENT TALES—SECTION: Q

Makari entered the circle, noticing a few dusty chairs and a bronze statue of a young boy posing, as if he were reaching for one of the bookshelves that encompassed him. Makari drew the flame of the lamp closer, reading a few spines from the shelves:

"Backstabbing Qyollerbaux, The Black Fox's Grin, The Hunch of Willow Creed."

"—It is pronounced 'K-ALL-ER-BOW,' the 'Q' is pronounced like a 'K,'" said a sprightly voice from behind Makari. Startled, Makari twisted around to face the voice, shocked to see that it emanated from the bronze statue. For some reason, Makari found the idea of a sapient statue far more disturbing than she had the ghosts. "Oh, that book is one of my favorites, I've read it about three hundred and seventy times—*or was it seventy-two?* Either way, you should read it sometime!"

Makari screamed.

Landon, still browsing the other side of the stacks, broke into a cold sweat at the sound, dashing off through the twisting shelves towards the speck of light that peeked over a distant shelf, heedless of the cobwebs that snagged at his limbs.

"I hear you, sis!" shouted Landon, racing toward Makari's lamplight. Rounding the corner, Landon saw his sister, interspersed between himself and the bronze boy. Taking hold of a large book and readying to strike the statue, Landon advanced. To his surprise, however, Makari seized her brother's bludgeon and turned to introduce him to the startled statue.

"Landon, this is Martin Winter," said Makari, stepping aside from the statue. The lamplight glazed across Martin's face as the bronze boy stepped out of his shadowy alcove, a nervous grin plastered across his face.

"Hello," Martin gulped, as Landon offered to shake the nervous boy's bronze hand. "I wish that I could, but your genuine smile is all the welcome I need."

"Nice to…meet you," said Landon, curling a smile. He could see a genuine sadness trace over the bronze boy's face, seeing his idle hands proved a regrettable clasp instead.

"The pleasure is mine," Martin smiled, "I'm very sorry for the fright; a rather unfortunate side-effect of my condition is that it makes introductions maddeningly easy to botch. Not that I meet many people, of course. I suppose it could just be lack of practice, now that I think of it. At least the two of you have the decency to hear me out. It's quite depressing how rare that sort of courtesy seems to be."

"I don't know what's going on, but if Makari says you're worth hearing out, I'm not about to argue," said Landon, resting his lamp on a chair next to his sister.

"I appreciate it," nodded Martin.

"Landon, Martin says he can help us with a few of our questions," said Makari, as Martin nodded.

"Do you know of any books that might answer a few questions about the first great manifesto?" asked Landon.

"So, you two know the tragedy of the Shelversteins? Interesting," hummed Martin.

"I wouldn't say we know much about it,we've only just heard the tale from a friend of ours," said Makari.

"Recently? I would've thought there's not a school in Revlenion so imprudent as to leave that out of the curriculum. How is it that the two of you managed to preserve your ignorance so long?" asked Martin.

"We didn't exactly go to a school nearby," said Makari.

"Then where are you two from?" hummed Martin.

"From a place beyond Elddri's Point, if that helps," said Landon.

"*Beyond* Elddri's Point? That means…No, it can't be true?" gasped Martin. "Two children from the beyond, in my presence? I feel like I'm living in one of these fairy tales!" Martin danced around Landon and Makari before settling himself, "I've read dozens of stories and articles about the places beyond Elddri's Point. *Oh*, how I have fantasized about venturing to it." Makari almost found it amusing, for only seconds, that a creature like Martin was far more pleased to meet her than she was at first for him.

Landon showed Martin his Portler Badge, pulling it out from his hoodie pocket.

"That's what they look like? Oh, how fortunate you are," said Martin, flipping through the Portler booklet.

"Why is that?" asked Makari.

"Goodness girl, didn't you read the fine print when you signed your name to have one of those?" chuckled Martin, handing back Landon his badge.

"We did have help with them—Why, should we not have done so?" Landon asked.

"*Somebody* wants you here, is what I mean. Portler Badges cost a fortune, regardless of that, they can grant you unlimited access in and out of this country. Oh, to explore the worlds," Martin sighed, smiling, "lucky ones."

"You appear to know a great deal about our home, well, *the other places*," said Landon.

"These—*places*, can you tell us about yours?" asked Makari. "Revlenion, I mean."

"Why yes, of course," said Martin, "when you have unlimited time like me, all the better to read about the world that's around you. How did you find Revlenion anyway?"

It only took Landon and Makari a few minutes to recite the story of how they found and ventured into Revlenion, and as their tale came to a close Martin burst into applause, his metal hands sounding like someone had dropped an armful of pipes down a staircase.

"Hmmpf—a summons?" Martin pondered. "From what I've read, it can only mean two things, either you've been exposed smuggling norsescabs, wingcrokers, vicious yolquers, or…"

"Norsescabs?" asked Landon.

"They're nasty, little four-eyed rodents with one ugly overbite, but clearly, that's not the reason why you've been summoned by the royals or the House Chambers. If we're being precise, it's not the royals who truly summon you," Martin shifted his beady eyes, "I have an inkling, follow me."

Martin led the way through one of the aisles in the adolescent tales section.

"May I hold your lamp? I haven't held fire this close in many years, and it would bring me some comfort, I think. Not very many people have occasion to go so long without such a simple luxury. As someone who has gone a great while without a great many such things, I wouldn't recommend it," said Martin, eyeing the flame of Makari's lamp.

"Martin, if you don't mind me asking," said Makari, as she followed behind Martin, as he took a sharp turn around a bookshelf.

"Go on," encouraged Martin.

"Are you a ghost haunting a statue or something else?" asked Makari.

"Ha Ha! *Something else*," Martin giggled, "no, ghosts are lost creatures; I, on the other hand, am not. I am merely a byproduct of the fantasy that permeates and ultimately constitutes Revlenion," said Martin, as he winked at Makari over his shoulder.

"A byproduct, huh?" Landon figured, "are there more like you?"

"Not *exactly* like me, but Revlenion is home to a great many creatures, many as strange or stranger than me. Some individuals, through chance or artifice, become loci for the forces that call Revlenion home. The effects range from benign to ruinous, but blessings and curses are largely a matter of perspective, no?" Martin then twisted one of his hands out front of him, examining it as though it were the core of his misfortune. "I've come to love the magic that looms, but that is not a tale for tonight."

"You do seem rather amicable about your curse," nodded Landon.

"Indeed," said Martin.

"When you say that fantasy forms Revlenion, do you mean that the fantasy makes it real, or that the reality inspires the fantasy?"

asked Makari.

"Yes. The fantasy *is* the reality," pointed Martin, while Makari fluttered her eyes, calculating her next thought.

"And this applies to all fiction, does it? Surely you don't mean to say that we might run into a unicorn out there!" huffed Landon.

"Well, that depends entirely on what you mean by 'out there,' I suppose. Semantics aside, though, I mean precisely that." Martin then spun on his metal heel, stopping his new friends in their trek, "I wonder, though… it's interesting that you'd ask about unicorns, in particular. Do you have any inkling of what a unicorn is, beyond just a horse with a horn?"

Landon and Makari shook their heads.

"There do seem to be an awful lot of unicorns in our stories, I suppose. Every tale seems to describe them a bit differently, I guess," said Makari.

"You guess? It might be more accurate to say that an awful lot of stories form around unicorns. They are the most powerful and freest of creatures…one shouldn't be surprised when they produce stories worth telling," said Martin, leaning heavily against a bookshelf.

"They *are* real?" gasped Makari.

"Absolutely. As far as I know, there have only been five encounters with them in all of recorded history, but each accompanied events on a truly legendary scale," said Martin.

"But only in Revlenion, right?" asked Landon.

"Oh no, unicorns go wherever they please. Their reasons for doing so are known only to them, but—or so it's said—unicorns seek to inspire. Historically, they've appeared to people on the precipice of despair, those who, in their moment of greatest need, lost sight of the hopes they had nurtured," informed Martin, "More than that, though, a unicorn is the *freedom* inherent to fiction…they are the *truth* in the inspiration that ties fantasy to reality and makes the potential actual," Martin waved a hand through the air, gesturing at the shelves above, "and the *heart* of this country."

Martin halted mid-step, turning to return Makari's lamp; he

began to rifle through the wall of books that towered overhead, overcome with a sudden frenzied mania.

"What's wrong, Martin?" asked Makari.

"What sort of book are we looking for?" asked Landon, nearly tripping over a stack of books.

"An anthology of children's novellas; it holds a short passage that I read years ago. I thought of it almost immediately after you two told me about how you found Revlenion. Its contents are, if I recall correctly, oddly reminiscent to your story," said Martin, eyeing the dozens of books that had been thrown on the library floor. "...And someone seems to have thought the same. I know this section like the back of my hand, and whoever was here last seems to have been searching for the same tome that seemed to have matched your tale."

"How peculiar," mused Makari, as she picked up one of the heavy books up off the floor while Martin crouched down, reading several of the spines on the haphazardly stacked piles of books that were strewn across the wooden floor.

"We're looking for one that delves into the peculiar properties of manifestos. And, as it turns out, several of the best books on the subject are now *missing*—but did our Goldilocks find just the right one, I wonder?" said Martin, shuffling through several floored stacks. "Ah, excellent! *It's still here.*"

Landon, Makari, and the bronze boy returned to the circle at the entrance of the adolescent tales section, putting two chairs together to set the sturdily bound anthology upon them.

"*The Children of Our Own* by Gilinora DeMortles," Martin read aloud. "There's a segment in the book that questions the boundaries of manifestos and the upbringing of Revlenion."

"Upbringing?" asked Makari.

"Yes, Revlenion of Adlanion and Azlazion, they named this country after their first born. According to historians though, the child was killed before its sixteenth birthday. That is why there's a statue of a faceless knight at the front of the manor, a tribute to the lost child," said Martin.

"How was Revlenion killed?" asked Landon.

"It's not particularly clear, mind you—there wasn't exactly a historical tradition at the time—but I believe it was a bud from the initial dark beauty that infected this land pursuing its manifesto by slaughtering the child," said Martin, his voice marred by a harsh undertone. Landon and Makari eyed one another as Martin unlatched the triangular shaped locket on the front cover of the book.

The cover's latch popped open with a soft *click* as Martin lifted the books cover, revealing a line of red letters neatly spread over the first page. Landon and Makari leaned forward to read the calligraphic words:

One that asks for hidden lore—I will find the story for

"How is a book supposed to answer questions?" asked Makari.

"Give me the tale about the manifesto of Revlenion," ordered Martin, nodding.

The words had hardly left his lips when a brilliant light began to emerge from the frayed pages, flickering as the book shuddered as if alive. The tattered pages whipped frantically about as if blown by a great wind, flipping through uncountable stories until, suddenly, the movement stopped. Craning over the book, Landon and Makari read the title that splayed across the displayed page:

Chapter Fifty-Two | The Champion's Paradox

The rest of the page appeared blank, but no sooner had they registered this when a calligraphic passage began to appear in rows of purplish ink that seeped through the pages from within the book:

~

Their first child was meant for the task, as its manifesto declared. There the final task of Revlenion is where it would be; yet the demise of its object leads it no closer to completion. Unfortunate in death as any ever were in life, Revlenion the lone knight proves wanting, unable to seal its dialectic. Revlenion died alone as it was born, and freedom from that embrace remains out of its reach.

As the last miracle of Revlenion destroyed itself, so must its new paradigm construct itself upon the Krinzen Staircase: the champion's well of trial. In this double effect will the manifesto find in itself strength matched to its challenge, and only in finding this strength will it be divided within the Hallways of Quinn: the champion's hollow of truth.

As death is found ever in life, so must life be found in death. Though the aggregate was unbound, its telos cannot be buried and must reach through time and space until the circle can be closed.

~

"Any ideas what that means?" grunted Landon, massaging his head as if a barrel was being bounced around between his eyes.

"It sounds like we're some sort of successors to the child Revlenion's mission," said Makari, eyeing her brother.

"Successors?" Landon gaped. Martin moved to speak, but was cut short at the sound of heavy footsteps descending the library stairs began to echo between the bookshelves.

"Oh no! You two cannot be found in here!" cried Martin, as he slammed the novella shut. "It must be the manor guards, they're as likely to eviscerate you as ask your name." Landon and Makari looked over their shoulders towards the source of the fast-approaching sound.

"Martin, when can we see you again—?" it was too late, Martin Winter had already returned to his immobile posture, a lifeless statue once again.

"Leave the book, come on, M!" tugged Landon.

"No! Lan, we can't!" cried Makari.

Landon grabbed his sister by the hand and raced her through the aisle he had first appeared from.

FLORRISH!

One of the manor guards cannoned a fiery arrow from the tip

of his golden scepter, sending it smashing into the novella resting on the two chairs, shredding the thick book into charred pieces.

FLORRISH!

Another guard cannoned another bolt, clipping the corner of a tall bookshelf as the siblings raced around it.

"THE INTRUDER IS OVER HERE!" roared one of the Manor Guards. Landon was sure it wasn't the guard's intention to harm him or his sister, but he wasn't feeling particularly optimistic about that goodwill winning out over the prudent option of shooting first, given the nervous state the scar-faced man had left everyone in.

"Run forward along this aisle and don't stop until you reach the end, I'll meet you there—GO!" Landon commanded Makari, as she nodded and raced to the aisle's end.

Landon ripped the heaviest book he could find in those few, panicked seconds out of the towering shelves above him, and with all his might, he spun around like a discus player, heaving the metal bound book into the air. The book flew through the air, spinning for a few seconds.

Hitting the top corner of a leaning bookshelf, the impact of the metal bound rocked the bookcase on its casters, teetering until, like a giant set of collapsing dominos, the tower leaned too far and fell, bringing every other crowded bookshelf that was in the struck shelf's way crashing down. Clouds of dust exploded into the air, obscuring the alarmed guards that directed their arrows blindly at the falling shelves. The horde of charging guards raced toward the fallen shelves like a pack of bloodhounds on the hunt, stumbling in their efforts to apprehend the intruders. Makari gasped at the sight of the hundreds of bookcases collapsing, relieved to see Landon wheel safely around the corner of the twisted aisle, still apparently whole and unharmed. Landon took her hand again; racing across the library foyer and back up the steps to the corridor, then back down the moonlit hall until they returned to the doors of the elevator. Landon and Makari threw themselves into the elevator cabin and quickly clicked the ninth floor button.

The doors to the ninth floor chimed opened, allowing Landon to pop his head out and toss a quick glance down the two corridors to the left and right of the elevator doors. Turning to give his sister the signal to run ahead, Landon followed Makari as she slid down the hallway and through the crack of their bedroom door and, as quietly as possible, shut the door behind him, slumping to the cold marble floor.

"M, that was close," panted Landon.

"Almost too close," said Makari, as she tossed her winded self onto her bed.

"Who trains their guards to just shoot at will?"

"It wasn't us they were actually after, M."

Makari rolled over on her side, pulling the thick blanket over her, "Well, we're lucky we didn't get blasted away, Landon. I guess that's what we get for wandering around the manor at night. Too bad though, I think one of the guards destroyed the book Martin found for us."

"Not exactly," said Landon, standing up, "I ripped that page out before we ran off." Makari took the enigmatic page from Landon's hand, re-reading the passage.

"You are fantastic," said Makari, "such a shame though."

"What?" asked Landon, as Makari handed Landon back the torn page.

"How can we share this with Jade without him knowing we're to blame for that mess in the library?" said Makari.

Landon grinned.

"It's not funny, Landon, we could've been seriously hurt," sighed Makari.

"Don't worry. I'm sure there'll be a time and place to discuss the passage with Jade."

CHAPTER FOUR

THE GUARDIAN MANIFESTO

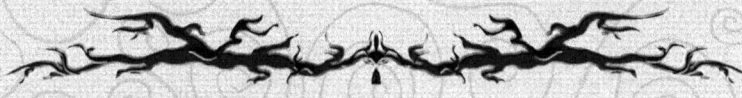

As Cappa Valley's crescent moon fell beyond the serrated hills, the newspaper printers at the Cappa Gazette were racing against the rising sun to get out the morning headlines. Peter Nerly, one of the Gazette's early morning paperboys, raced through one of his paper routes in the Northern Cappa and East Gargoylian villages, still holding out hope that he'd be able to outpace the early-morning rush of Cappamites that was bound to swarm Dingoduns. His fears proved unnecessary, though; arriving at the famous coffee shop, he found it mostly deserted. Locking his bike up beside a tall streetlamp, Peter marched with practiced steps into the aromatic miasma that filled the cafe and secured a medium-sized Split-Pepper latte and a generously glazed honey croissant—for only five solbecks. Peter allowed himself a few precious minutes to savor his delicious beverage in the warm embrace of the café's comforting aromas. His stay was necessarily brief, however, as Peter's favorite route of the early morning deliveries, the one that took him up the hill and through the grounds of the royal manor, was next. Though the climb was a steep one to pedal up, if Peter timed it correctly he was treated to a view only he and perhaps a dozen other Cappamites had the pleasure of witnessing each day; the sun bursting over the distant horizon, blazing for a few glorious moments before being swallowed by the dense fog that invariably followed it. Reaching the summit,

Peter Nerly sprang off his delivery bike and tossed the bound stack of newspapers at the base of the manor doors. One of the guards shot him a grateful nod, passively observing as Peter Nerly jumped back on his bike and disappeared through the royal pine.

Landon rolled onto his side, trying to evade the beam of sunlight that lanced across his sleep-lined face. As he fought for a few more moments of sleep, Landon tried to hold on to the still-fresh memory of the dream he'd been having: walking through a mirror, a huge mansion of some sort, a balcony, and a talking statue? These flickers of disjointed images seemed far too real, disconnected though they were from everything else. Stretching, Landon was struck by how remarkably comfortable his bed seemed.

It hadn't been this soft before, had it? Where was that peeving box spring that would somehow find its way to poke Landon's back? With a start, Landon opened his eyes as he felt two sudden pokes on his shoulder:

"Ah!" Landon gasped, pressing his head back into his massive pillow.

It seemed as though the ancient, gray-haired gargoylian that worked as the manor's Wardrober had been hovering over him for a few minutes, as she'd already prepared Landon's neatly pressed black jeans, bumblebee-striped shirt, and stitched-where-need-be red hoodie, all waiting for him hanging from a wooden hanger.

"Good morning to you, too," croaked Pattie McDaniel. Pushing her gold, hexagonal eyeglasses further back along her crooked nose: Pattie, as per her usual, was clad in her long Manor Staff coat, but, far from the impersonal uniform it might've been, every inch of hers was covered in embellishments of one kind or another; hundreds of pins in a variety of sizes were stuck through both of her lapels; her pockets overflowed with a wealth of thimbles and just-in-case rolls of thread, and it seemed that several additional pockets had been tacked-on to accommodate them. Her hair completed the look, neatly pinned back into a bun that was very nearly thimble-shaped itself.

"Th-thank you, but you didn't have to do that," said Landon, as he sat up against the headboard.

"Better to let you run around Cappa with holes in the knees of your pants, hmm?" scoffed Pattie, as she tossed the hanger of clothes on top of Landon's head. "Just like that Cooper boy, my goodness, parading about in that tattered old coat. No sense putting on airs if you don't even have the decency to treat your clothes right." Landon wheeled out of bed, keeping a watchful eye on the woman as she meandered towards the door. "Quite the scare last night, wasn't it?"

"What scare?" hummed Landon, hoping McDaniel hadn't figured out he and his sister were the root to last night's fiasco in the library.

"Huh, and they said you were bright—the gala attack, boy," shook Pattie, as she turned to face Landon again, "I'm sure you've been pestered with all sorts of excuses and apologies, but, if you'll forgive me saying, this manor is no stranger to such hullabaloo, much like the one you and your sister caused late last night in the library," McDaniel then began to whisper, not before tossing a side-eye toward the bedroom threshold, "but if it was in the name of sacking that hideous Eplaville, well then, not only is your late night excursion kept secret with me, but you have my blessing."

Landon scanned Pattie's demeanor for anything that might indicate that she couldn't be trusted, but was met only with a knowing wink.

"That…was only our intention, but how do you kn—" said Landon, as he reached for his clothes.

"Never mind that now, hurry it up! You're not getting dressed for some ball—You needed to be up and dressed about five minutes ago if you want to be on time for breakfast downstairs with the Cappas, your sister and Mr. Cooper," sparked Pattie, after a sudden clap, as her usual fast-paced mood returned.

"I'm hurrying, I'm hurrying," rushed Landon, as he nearly toppled-over after sliding both legs into one side of his pressed jeans.

"For goodness sake, I'll meet you at the end of the hall," groaned Pattie, as she then picked with her callus, talon-like fingers a square candy-cane mint from a pocket on the front of her long coat and popped it into her jagged mouth.

Remembering to keep it close, Landon surreptitiously slipped the torn page (that had been kept under his pillow) the night before into one of his shoes, his stomach churning at the realization that he didn't really know any of the people who surrounded him.

Dispelling the discomfiting thought, Landon gave the marble room one more scan before he exited, noticing his sister's bed had already been neatly turned over for the day. Landon closed the bedroom door behind him and squinted his eyes ahead, taking notice of the broad shouldered guard chatting with the Wardrober at the end of the hall as they waited for the elevator.

"Please take this handsome yet tardy boy down to the Platter Room, the Cappas are expecting him," ordered Pattie, as she gave Landon a gentle push into the elevator cabin. The Manor Guard replied with only a simple nod to her command. "Until next time, Landon."

Landon smiled and tried to return a wave of farewell to the insistent woman, but was left waving to his own polished reflection as the smooth cabin doors slid shut. The guard didn't appear to pay much attention to the small boy behind him, remaining rigidly at attention as the elevator descended.

Not ten seconds later, the elevator doors opened to reveal a long hall, much like the one from the night before that had led our siblings to the Almerine Library. Landon looked up at the guard, who silently pointed down towards the end of the hall. Following the drapes that lined the corridor as the guard had indicated, Landon heard the growing sound of a song playing on a radio intermingled with the tapping of silverware. Rounding a final corner, he found himself in the Platter Room, a huge dining court walled off by a couple of towering glass cabinets (that looked as though they had a slight lean in their stance) crowded with an astounding variety of fine china and porcelain plates. From the ceiling dangled yet another magnificent chandelier, much like the one in main foyer, and the walls were flanked with a series of portraits depicting elegant dining halls and the dinner parties that had once filled them, interspersed with suits of polished armor that, to Landon, were far too reminiscent of the ghoulish one he recalled from a favorite episode of Scooby-Doo.

"I absolutely cannot stand anything that Mentirosa writes!" scoffed Antoine Cappa, tossing aside the front page of the morning edition of the Cappa Gazette. Antoine's two powdering and pampering Manor Wardrobers quiver midst their application of Anotine's peculiar morning visage ritual. Half of Antoine's round face is being painstakingly covered up, aside from the few scratches on his face obtained by fly debris at the gala attack. Antoine tried to calm himself, sitting with a slight squirm in his customary burgundy and long lapel Manor suit.

"Sir, you're going to need to sit still," squeaked Farinda, a bead of sweat rolls down her forehead caked with an alabaster powder.

"Don't you shudder an inch, my heavenly friend," quipped Hillard, Farinda's gangly twin as he tried to carefully pin a carnation to Antoine's lapel; he smiles through his crooked teeth with a skittish cringe. Taking a sip from her tall glass of milk, Makari glanced at the headline atop the half folded newspaper that Antoine had unintentionally flung in front of her:

ROYAL DANGER

Is the Royal Manor Hiding a Dangerous Secret?
~ By Florence Mentirosa | Editor-at-Large ~

Despite our present Royal family's long history of spectacular blunders, the Cappas managed to make all previous efforts pale in comparison last night, when a negligent breach in security led to dozens of their guests being severely injured at the estate's annual summer gala. It all began back in April, when the Haus of Cappa and Executive R.C.C. Board put into effect their latest initiative trying to stoke the dormant flames of our country's illustrious 'manifesto' tradition....

Makari sat back in her cushioned dining chair, startled by Antoine's thick fist snatching the fallen scrap, crumpling it into a small lump. The circular table party went quiet for a few seconds, allowing only the radio on the fancy silver breakfast trolley to be heard.

"It's freedom of the press, Antoine, you'll have to thank your Great, Great Grandfather for that, my dearest," said Dionne, taking a sip of her coffee from one of the fanciest porcelain cups Makari had ever seen.

Dionne then tossed a quick look at Makari and Jade, both gingerly nursing their own morning drinks. Farinda, tense, hands Antoine a hand-mirror to check her work. Makari presses a finger over her lips after noticing Antoine's fleshy-orange face and rosy cheeks that appear ridiculous today, and he knows it.

"Did you wake up blind or are you as dumb as yesterday?" Antoine pricked, glaring back at Farinda. "My cheeks are uneven. The flower is off. Fix. Them. Now."

However it must feel like to be pinned like a carnation, the wardrobe-twins' nerves could tell you just that. Antoine then regained his attention to the table, "my dearest, slander was not part of the deal. Tell me the purpose of slapping Eplaville's horrifying face on the front page like some kind of bogeyman?" The Farinda and Hillard desperately weaved to do their grooming on the fat man while he flagrantly chewed on his breakfast, allowing Makari to catch a gross sight of the morning meal dancing in mushy chunks while the Head Cappa yammered, "Need I remind you that the elections are approaching us—this is not at all what *I* need at the moment jeopardizing my precious Cappamite votes."

Hillard attempts to apply lipstick upon Antoine's charcoal-cold lips when he suddenly jerks his head at the slightest chuckle come from Makari; she can barely contain herself. Farinda is agape, witnessing her brother's misfortunate work; a messy line of red lipstick is coursed across Antoine's face. Jade and Dionne see the messy line of lipstick, too.

"*Anty*, sir, y-you mustn't move so much—" shivered Hillard.

Antoine rips the hand-mirror from Farinda's hands again, furiously this time.

"What, you think this is funny?" snarled Antoine, darting at Makari and Jade.

"Darling, don't be so," Dionne tries to hold back a bout of laughter, "ridiculous."

"You, too, then? So my disease is this morning's joke?" huffed Antoine, wiping away most of his makeup with his napkin. Antoine's real, silvery face was now free again.

"Antoine Emmanuel—You stop it now," ordered Dionne. "You've been fidgeting in your chair all morning and now it serves you right. Antoine felt it not necessary to joust, rather, he instead took another careful bite of his crispy waffles.

"Good morning, Landon. Please, darling take a seat here," said Dionne, noticing Landon approaching the table. Landon watched as the hauntingly beautiful woman gestured in her gray day gown at the empty bronze chair next to her. After a second's deliberation, Landon hesitantly moved to take a seat at the table; not knowing if doing so might precipitate another outburst from the choleric Antoine.

"How...how is everyone this morning?" said Landon, as a royal server appeared out of nowhere next to him, placing a silver tray that showcased a cupped poached egg, slices of zesty orange and wheat toast, surrounded by polished silverware, all perfectly at-the-ready. Inspecting the toast further, Landon was astounded to see that the face of his bread had been branded with the manor's crest: an elaborate hexagon that housed a bold C in its center, flanked on either side by muses.

"All is well. Did you find yourself a good nights rest?" asked Dionne. Landon began to answer, but was distracted by a flicker of movement in his peripheral vision, in the direction of the suits of armor.

"Y-yes, thank you," Landon murmured, eyeing the armor suspiciously. Dionne, noticing his focus, laughed lightly.

"Don't be alarmed, they're as old as the Manor," said Dionne, "most of the ones you might see throughout our home are merely serving their place as either messengers or ushers for the Cappa Manor Network…poor souls that haunt the suits, they still find it necessary to serve the Manor, even in their afterlife."

"If you say so," hummed Makari, as she twisted her head around, throwing another curious eye at one of the empty suits.

"As I was saying, I was hoping you and your sister had found a decent night's rest, even after last night's episode," Dionne continued. Landon nodded in thanks, readying his utensils for the challenge they were about to be subjected to, then reaching for the honey in the honeycomb-shaped ewer and drizzling it over his fancy toast in a crosshatch pattern.

"So, Landon, is there anything you'd like to share with Dionne and I about yourself?" Antoine asked thickly, choking the words out around mouthfuls of his own breakfast. Landon froze before taking another bite of his poached egg; firing Antoine was referring to the incident in the library last night. Antoine began shooing away the twins (now finished with their work) gave Landon a few seconds to come up with some far fetching excuse. Instead, Landon had no choice but to stare blankly back at the unevenly made-up face waiting for a narrative to unfold.

"Your sister tells us that you have a heart for exploring…where does Cappa Valley rank on your previous trekking?" asked Dionne.

"It's definitely top of my list. I'm sure there's nothing quite like it, not even where I come from," said Landon.

"And that is the truth, boy," said Antoine, a self-satisfied grin plastered across his face. "There is no other place like Cappa—you've a lot to learn from it."

"Landon and Makari's hometown does seem it could be the happiest of places," vouched Jade, eyeing the Cappas, "a small yet big-at-heart village along a shore. The, um, street that they live, Pop

—Oh, what's it called again?—Yes, Poplar Drive is absolutely a bloom!"

"Sounds like you're trying to sell me some subordinate piece of property in this, what'cha call it, happiest place," gibed Antoine, "Cappa has a shore, too. Registered Revlenion voters have not only deemed it the happiest of places, but the only city in the country they can truly count on."

"W-well, just be glad to know that they are here to learn about us," said Jade, tapping a finger on the elaborate table.

"I'm more than willing to learn, just as much as my sister is," said Landon. "And we'd be happy to tell you anything you'd like to know about our home."

"Nobody is doubting your will to learn," Dionne interjected. Antoine flipped over to a column in the morning newspaper and showed Landon the bold headline:

STRANGE VISITORS UPON THE MANOR
Are they to blame for this summer's "annual disaster"?

"I already know quite enough, thank you," vexed Antoine, tossing the paper aside. "Not to sound rude, but I'm sort of hoping your stay is not an overlong one."

Lately Lynne's sprightly smooth voice then occupied the breakfast scene, as if the radio host was a late guest to the meal.

"Good morning, kiddos!" popped Lately Lynne, "more offbeat news involving the two cool new beats over in Cappa this morning. Is the Manor gonna' fess up or clam up about last night's baaaaad-baaaad blunder? As some of you rebel Revlers out there might already know, when things get a little too spooky for the Royals, we're bound to see the king with no crown turtle himself away like a cowardly-lion in a burgundy suit, the spotlight of truth is ready for you, Cappa!"

The entire party, excluding the eye-rolling Antoine, had their eyes on the rectangular radio that popped with a few brave lines about the Manor. Even the Manor Server that was at-the-ready abandoned his own duties, as he stood still to hear his favorite radio host's fearless remarks. "In the meantime, kiddos, here's a classic hit from the legendary Buddy Holly with his rockin' That'll Be The Day," hooted Lately Lynne, as her tune began to play.

"Would someone please turn that ear sore of a woman off," hissed Antoine, as he side-eyed his handy server. Realizing he'd become the latest object of his employer's scrutiny, the server rounded the breakfast table to complete his Head's order. Before he could reach the radio, however, Benjamin Varick materialized, and with a simple twist on a dial, Lately Lynne's morning show was no more.

"Enough of that, wouldn't you agree?" said Varick in his characteristically nasal tone, his head cocked at an odd angle. The gaunt man appeared not to have changed out of his gala attire, still wearing his darkened half-moon sunglasses and buttoned up in a sleek gray suit. Benjamin Varick then gathered the attention of the entire table. "Cappa, young comrades! I'm truly sorry if I've interrupted your breakfast, but today's meeting with the R.C.C. has been pushed ahead against all of our arranged appointments."

"Dionne, we must be off…Jade, would you kindly escort the Toomblees to wherever you see fit," said Antoine, rising from the head of the table. Their ears still ringing from how badly their surname had been botched, Landon and Makari stood from their seats simultaneously.

"Actually, I would like for Jade to join us for this morning's meeting. It seems appropriate, given the subject of our gathering," affirmed Dionne.

Antoine shot Jade a vitriolic look, choking back whatever he'd been about to say.

"Eh, the children can join me for my afternoon trip downtown. We can even become well acquainted," interjected Varick, eyeing the siblings through his dark sunspecs.

"That sounds lovely. Would you two like to join Mr. Varick

today?" said Dionne, as Landon and Makari gave each other uncertain looks.

"We're really appreciative for what you're all doing for us, but I really think we ought to be at this meeting as well. If you're discussing us or the man who attacked you on our account, it seems we might want to be there," said Landon, as the Royals and Varick exchanged quick looks.

Antoine's heavy body spun on a heel.

"Young boy...you and your sister's presence in my home has caused quite the stir and, if I might add, put an unnecessary spotlight on this venerable institution. Jade will be your liaison and explain to you what is truly necessary," said Antoine, as he came close to Landon and flaring his wide nose, "I'm afraid I'm quite unwilling to be subjected to any more interrogation, if that's all right with you."

Jade quickly came around the dining table.

"D-don't worry, I'll take it from here," said Jade, as he put his hands on Landon's shoulders.

"Perfect," said Antoine, his lips pursed again, as he then turned away and nodded at Dionne to follow him. As Antoine reached the archway near the room's corner, Landon noticed a male gargoylian Manor Executive awaiting Antoine's departure. Within seconds, the two men disappeared beyond the archway.

"Please do forgive my husband," Dionne spoke apologetically, reaching out a sincere hand to Landon and Makari, "The duties of his office weigh heavily on him, and recent events haven't made his work any easier."

"I guess we'll be off then?" suggested Jade.

"Yes, Jade—Mr. Varick, we'll leave the children in your possession now. I hope you two enjoy your afternoon down in the 'Square. Be sure to stop by and try Dingoduns, it truly is quite the charming experience," said Dionne, as she nodded to the siblings, "I'll meet you in the Chamber's Board, Jade...do hurry." Dionne followed in her husband's course, but not before giving our siblings a single gesture of what they thought was the most genuine a nod of good luck. And after that, Dionne vanished beyond the thick archway.

"Again, sorry about Antoine...as long as I've known him, he can be worse, but his snickering is truly uncalled for. It's not your fault that his security is under par," said Jade, as he collected a vibrant orange from a large bowl of fruit.

"Now Jade, you know as well as I do, it's not the security to blame," said Varick.

"Let's not get into that right now," said Jade, as he tossed the orange between his hands. "Well, I'll meet back with you two after the meeting. Mr. Varick, do you have your Trans-Oidar handy?"

"Always at the ready," said Varick, adjusting the hexagon-shaped pin on his wide lapel.

"What is that, exactly?" asked Makari.

"It's a two-way transmitter, every Manor executive has one. It's part of the Manor Network and a way to keep all of us in instant contact," said Varick.

"Clever," said Makari, as Varick halfheartedly grinned.

"I'll sound you from mine if I end up exiting the meeting early, Mr. Varick," said Jade. "Could you give me a few minutes with Landon and Makari?"

"Certainly, I'll meet you two in the main foyer in five minutes," said Mr. Varick, as he made his way to the elevator beyond the dining room.

"Jade, I'm not so sure about that man," said Landon, tracing his eyes in Varick's exit. "He seems somewhat—"

"Unsettling?" Jade added.

"Yeah. I don't know if that's the best way to describe it, but I just get this sinking feeling in my stomach whenever he is around," said Landon.

"So do I," said Makari. "And we just met him hours ago."

"I guess I'm not the only one—he doesn't seem at all like himself, particularly these past few weeks. I thought I noticed something a bit off a few days before my expedition beyond the

Elddri Point," said Jade, as he then reached into his coat pocket, "but this is much more pronounced."

"And you mean to leave us with him?" sighed Makari.

"He won't harm you, if that's what you're implying. Besides, the entire staff has been on edge since last night's incident. I'm sure this is just the stress," said Jade. "But my trust in people hasn't always been rewarded. Here, take this," Jade pulled a red-enameled Oidar pin out from his inner coat and handed it to Makari.

"How do you work it?" Makari asked as she took a hold of the small transmitter.

"Just press its center and talk into it here, and swivel the volume dial there," Jade demonstrated.

"Like a walkie-talkie," said Landon.

"A what?" Jade asked.

"Never mind—"

"Hide it in your pocket and keep it ready at all times," ordered Jade, "sound off immediately if you feel awkward in any sorts—And here," Jade then pulled a few worn dollars from his coat pocket, "ask Mr. Varick to escort you two inside Dingoduns—that favorite café of mine—treat yourselves to something nice. He should know where to find it."

"What are these?" asked Makari, accepting her share of purple dollars that housed a small oval portrait of Dionne Cappa.

"Revlenion money," said Jade, "you each now have five solbecks. Anyway, please be aware of your surroundings and keep close to Mr. Varick." Jade, watched to make sure that Makari slid the transmitting pin safely into the front pocket of her denim jacket.

"Okay, but Jade, meet back with us as soon as you can. So far, you're the only one around here who really seems trustworthy," said Makari.

"You can trust everyone on the Manor staff—and trust me, I'll share with you everything I can from what I learn at the meeting if it at all concerns either of you," said Jade, as he put both his hands on each of the sibling's shoulders. "Alright, I've got to get going," continued Jade, "remember to keep close with Mr. Varick—I was your ages once," said Jade, as he tossed his orange in mid-air, catching it, then turning on his heel and exited the dining court in wake of the Cappas. Landon and Makari exchanged curious looks and followed in the direction of Mr. Varick.

Landon and Makari had led their own way through the Manor doors and taking notice of Benjamin Varick, awaiting their arrival like a strange mannequin and standing beside a motorized cabby on the peddled trail for the troupe's voyage.

"Hello again, children," said Varick, after the cabby door propped itself open, "hop in." It was a wooden cabby infused with bronze fixtures and was similar to the cabby Landon and Makari had traveled in the evening before, all except for the fact that there was no driver present. "Brilliant machinery, isn't it?" Varick continued, as he settled into his seat. Landon and Makari quickly took their seats next to one another on the opposite side of Mr. Varick, as he then called out, "To the Cappa Gazette, Cappa Square, please!"

However the bronze cabby was able to understand, it then suddenly clanked into gear and began its drive on through the trail between the royal pines. Makari sat back in her seat with an anxious hand over her right pant pocket and exactly where the small radio badge hid.

"Everything all right?" hummed Varick, as he scanned Landon with his blackened sunspecs.

"I'm fine," Landon bit his lip, "just...just a bumpy ride, that's all."

"Is this a sun-powered cabby?" asked Makari, quickly breaking Varick's attention from Landon.

"Indeed," said Varick, as he then reached for a twistable compartment above the center of the cabby, "powered by elsol stars."

Landon and Makari squinted at the sight of the radiant, tumor-like cluster of stones floating in the center of a clear cylinder that was slowly absorbing its useful energy.

"Elsol stars?" asked Makari, as she began to reach out two

fingers to feel for heat.

"Beautiful in sight," said Varick, as he then quickly slid the power cylinder back up into its compartment, "harmful if touched by bare hands. Every quarter or so, our sun prepares for a new layer of its vibrant façade and sheds its old layer, and as it sheds, the layers fall into our atmosphere and break into clusters, plunging into our East Vorloren Sea, where marine laborers probe the ocean floor and collect the fallen rock. It's a fascinating show when the layers fly across our sky, in constant spectacle of shooting stars. So very resourceful and are used all throughout Revlenion."

"Fascinating," gazed Makari.

"They are, indeed, and what started the exchange of currency: Gold to elsol star. Transfusing elsols into our money. Their worth is as much as Revlenion's might. Oh, there's so much more than this for you two to learn," said Varick, humming.

The cabby journeyed for a few more rounds of minutes, passing through the Royal Gates, and quickly arrived to Varick's commanded location. Coming to a smooth halt, the cabby doors propped open as Makari took the first step out on the busy sidewalk from the cabby. Varick and Landon followed as the bronze doors closed behind them.

"We're going to pay a visit to the editor of the Cappa Gazette this morning. I'm delivering a 'cease of subjective print' order on behalf of the Manor," said Varick, as he led the way through the busy afternoon crowd.

"On what sort of subject?" said Makari.

"Any more negative remarks about—" Varick nodded a heavy brow at our siblings.

"Oh—"

The siblings followed along with Mr. Varick as he guided our siblings through the late-morning crowd. Makari held onto her brother by the arm of his pushed up hoodie sleeve until she tugged at him, pointing at the row of black and white "Beware" bills of a mad face that had been slapped against a brownstone wall. It was

Vizton Eplaville's scarred face that beamed from his ugly portrait and where our siblings stood along the busy shoulders of Cappamites. Even though it was a poster, Makari felt that the bill would find some harsh way of springing to life and reach out with a giant hand to pull either her or Landon into the mean portrait.

"The look on his face," stirred Makari, as Landon urged her to follow after him. Mr. Varick then reached the corner of the giant brownstone, our siblings now at his side, and standing before three tall glass doors to enter from either side of the soaring building. The face of the structure was made mostly of glass windows that had been fixed to make the shape of a V and a bowing marque that displayed massive, wrought iron letters that spelled out: CAPPA GAZETTE. Matching its enormous marque was a globe-shaped clock, positioned high above the shaped windows, ticking away the day's minutes.

"I have an idea," said Mr. Varick, as he suddenly stopped in front of the east entrance, "since the origin of this decree is solely due to your presence at the Manor, I would suggest you two not accompany me inside. Entering this establishment as Royal personnel with either of you would only rally up even more unwanted press."

Makari eyed her brother.

"Jade instructed us not to leave from your side," said Makari.

"Oh, did he?" snickered Mr. Varick. "A naïve boy like him to give such direction after the Chamberlains instructed him not to go looking for you two in the first place—Oh, dear me, I've said too much," Landon's veins were beginning to rush with irritated heat. "Again, it would be best for you two wait for me…over there," said Mr. Varick, pointing at the swamped entrance of Dingoduns Espresso Emporium across the street.

Landon and Makari quickly glanced over their shoulders.

"I shouldn't be more than half-an-hour inside the Gazette. Here, take a few solbecks and wait inside Dingoduns until I fetch the both of you," spat Mr. Varick, taking his wallet from his inner jacket pocket and trying to shove a crumpled solbeck note at Landon, noticing our boy and his sister taking a step backward. "And do yourselves a favor and try not to attract more pathetic attention."

"No thank you," said Landon, "but I think my sister and I came well prepared." Makari then followed after her brother, after leaving Mr. Varick (whose lips were in a tangle) with only a sharp grin as they sped off across the street with the morning crowd.

A few hurried reporters bumped into the still Mr. Varick, who was standing in the way of the glass entrance. Before Mr. Varick followed the hurrying staff into the Cappa Gazette, he watched our siblings cross the busy street, curling his lip as if a horrible idea had crossed his mind.

Meanwhile.

"Mr. Cooper, please come forth to the podium," said Andler Moltair, his face resembled a dry prune. Jade stood from an uncomfortable wooden bench and calmly made his way to the podium in the center of the courtroom. Before any of the Chamberlains or Manor Heads could ask another question, Jade scanned the cold, wooden and stone infused courtroom that made him feel as though he were standing in the palm of beast's five-fingered claw. Each of the cagily perceptive Chamberlains had a tiny balcony, which sat aligned and perched like a nestled desk more for a watchful crow than an executive. All were a few feet above, suspended before the center podium and side-by-side and some between the irises that were shaped into windows. Jade had only ever entered this exclusive room only thrice before, knowing from where he was in the manor, he could see the west edge of Cappa Valley from one of the windows that scaled just behind that uncomfortable bench. Dionne then tossed a nod of good-luck at Jade, as it seemed to Antoine who sat beside his wife at the Head thrones that conjoined just across from the center podium and below the calculating nests of the Chamberlains.

"Please state your name for the record," asked Rellen Carigen, nodding.

"Jade Alexander Cooper," he announced, resting his hands on the podium, gazing at the sight of the man who always looked as though he had only acquired an hour worth of sleep from the night before.

"Mr. Cooper, two weeks ago, the R.C.C. approved an expedition of yours, could you state, for the record, what exactly the expedition entailed?" asked Cassidy Noma, fixing her eyes closely on Jade, a red fountain-pen at-the-ready.

"I was to investigate and locate a possible missing acquaintance to an abandoned manifesto," said Jade.

"Exactly so, and where in your previous statement and under our prior agreement, was there ever mention of acquiring two fauxrevler acquaintances?" hummed Noma, with a risen eyebrow.

"To call either of my acquaintances fauxrevles is quite the harsh statement," said Jade, adjusting his wayfarers, "and to add, both Landon and Makari are far from that belittling label."

The board members exchanged rapid murmurs as Antoine and Dionne kept their attention on Jade.

"In this case, Mr. Cooper," Noma heightened her voice over her murmuring peers, "in the eye of Revlenion law, the Tuolumne siblings will remain to be deemed—what you seem to find oddly belittling—fauxrevles, until their stance as absolute residence in Revlenion is found to be genuine. We are an institution of grace and tradition, we must uphold all accounts."

"Ms. Noma, if may continue my last statement, in accordance to Revlenion law, had I allowed the secrecy and security of our country to be left with the non-accompanying child, tell me then, what would've have been your scrutiny then?" said Jade.

"Jade, I believe you should reveal to the R.C.C. just how necessary it was to bring both of the children here to Revlenion," said Dionne, halting Noma before she could spit out another word.

"Yes, Mr. Cooper, tell us why you found it necessary?" said Noma, as she swiveled a pair of churlish eyes from Dionne and back down to the wayfarer-eyed detective.

"Having witnessed the siblings unravel the Elddri Cube was

enough evidence for me to bring them both through the mirror port. If I may add to our growing statements, according to the mythos of Revlenion and its manifestos, one who can unravel the Cube, is an acquaintance of Revlenion," said Jade.

"Yet mythos can often be so misleading," sparked Moltair.

Jade took a deep breath.

"Jade, the R.C.C. appreciates that you're joining this meeting today, but unfortunately you will be bound with corrective action and new instruction," said Antoine.

"Corrective action, on what grounds?" said Jade, gripping the podium with force.

"You were never instructed to," Moltair opened up a long, purple folder in front of him, "establish a Portler Badge for either of the Tuolumne children, without prior consent, thus jeopardizing our treasured secrecy."

"I believe that the time to break the barrier is imminent. Revlenion law for what you call," said Jade, nearly biting his lip, finding himself having to utter a despised term, "all fauxrevles must acquire a badge upon arrival to this country. I was merely keeping to protocol...I witnessed Landon and Makari handle and conquer a trinket of our country, knowing just how difficult some of those may be. I highly doubt a common Cappamite could figure out Elddri's damn riddle."

The Chamberlains then tossed a few calculating eyes back and forth at one another, until aiming their arrow-like sights again to our young detective.

"There are ways of proving your words, Mr. Cooper," said Moltair.

"And for the record, I would be thrilled by any means to prove them," said Jade. "Not only do I believe the Tuolumne siblings are truly part of our country, but that their manifesto is beyond the worries of abandonment."

"What do you mean by that?" said Antoine.

"At least one of them might be a Cherished Guardian of their manifesto," nodded Jade.

"Mr. Cooper," coughed Donald Wollerheid, after a damper in his gulp of water from his desk glass, "that is a preposterous belief." Jade then eyed the broaden shoulder man, now pouring himself another glass.

"Jade, if either of those children had an ounce of cherished abilities, then their duty should've been to apprehend Vizton Eplaville last night, without difficulty," said Antoine.

"Landon and Makari's current abilities cannot be placed on some testing podium," said Jade, "your securities should've been at the better-ready for any foul play last night. The Tuolumnes, somehow, lack of Revlenion exposure is their only difficulty…their right to learn about their manifesto should be the Tuolumnes only duty."

The courtroom fell silent.

"We're all pleased to see your amateurish skills as a detective grow," croaked Mr. Savini, as Jade matched a sight on the aged gargoylian executive, "and we do appreciate what you're doing for this Revlenion cause, as we all know, what sort of legendary history and horrific impressions that other manifesto adventures have left on our dear country. We simply do not wish to awaken those past abnormalities that obviously dare linger, but like Ms. Noma aforementioned, we are a country of tradition, and we must adhere to the Tuolumne manifesto. But allow me to offer a slice of advice," the gargoylian Chamberlain then cleared his throat, "we are all forms of beings that have united for the reputation of this municipal, and for what rests beyond this here valley, but as a country, we all have a place in it. You and I are creations of Revlenion, and the Tuolumne siblings are fauxrevles—I know you might not like that label our law has bestowed upon them, but the Tuolumnes must own that title. Now, if you're going to chaperon the siblings into our beliefs as relatives of Revlenion, it will without a doubt come with a price— every being, just like my very own gargoylian race once did—must adhere to the ways of Revlenion."

"What sort of price?" Jade asked.

"Whatever you or the very siblings themselves allow to woe your way, just know now," Mr. Savini then dabbed one of his talon-like fingers into the air, "that is the price. In these circumstances though there lies a dilemma—without what I'm about to advance our abrupt meeting with this morning, would defy my theme about price," Savini continued, "have you ever heard of the Ordinheir Alliance?" asked Mr. Savini, as his fellow peers broke into whispers.

"Of course I have, their name has always been on the Manor summons that you've all signed away for me, and I've come across many essays about their time of power," said Jade.

"Very good, it does look like you've done your research," nodded Savini.

"Mr. Savini, the Ordinheir must not be brought into this meeting, as it truly has no beneficial claim to Mr. Cooper's investigations or his corrective actions," said Moltair.

"Incorrect, the Ordinheir has everything to do with Mr. Cooper's investigation. The Ordinheir Alliance should be willing to hear your theories, but they will only interact with the one who comes to them with a true query," said Savini, thrusting another finger in the air.

"True query?" asked Jade.

"A purpose to awaken them," said Dionne. "They aren't exactly part of the living world anymore."

"Where would I find them?" asked Jade.

"Here in—" said Dionne, when Moltair impertinently halted her.

"Let's not get distracted with these messy theories. We are gathered here today to shed light on the R.C.C.'s expectations of Mr. Cooper," Moltair stood from his chair, "and that the integrity behind the magical intelligence of our fair country is to be upheld. We have every recorded native and relative born from the vein of Revlenion, and the Tuolumne children are nowhere to be found in our, nearly, two thousand-year-old registry. However, we understand that our world can be rather...mysterious. In that light, it has been decided that, if you are to continue with your investigation of these siblings, any unlawful act that they are found to be at fault of it will be you that shall be held responsible. In addition, if any foul occurrences that are linked to the Tuolumne siblings, like that of last night's attack, the R.C.C. will have to see to it that the children's Portler Badges be revoked—the two children will then be banished from Revlenion—and all of your future investigations will be suspended until further notice."

"The choice is yours, Jade, if you wish to continue with your investigation of this abandoned manifesto, but realize that there are severe consequences should you lose control of your work. My valley, nor its people, need not to suffer because of your careless actions," said Antoine, as he too stood from his throne. "There are without a doubt reasons why certain manifestos are left abandoned."

"Chamberlains," said Jade, as he stepped from podium and came toward the panel, "I have nothing to prove to any of you who doubt my case, but for the record, I will prove that those children will accomplish more for our country than any of you have ever done for it, combined," Jade nodded, kindly excusing himself from the courtroom.

"And he'll prove it too," said Dionne, as she too stood from her throne, curling a grin at a few irritated Chamberlains.

▼

And together, with a great push on the espresso emporium's revolving golden and glass door, Landon and Makari entered the bustling coffeehouse. At that same rewarding moment, dozens of different blends of coffee bean aromas instantly overcame them. Our siblings could only recount two, or maybe three different times they had ever stepped into a coffee shop in their spare time, but none before could match the enormity or the charmed sophistication of this bewildering emporium. The coffeehouse was odd in shape, but wide enough to house the near shoulder bumping patrons, in what looked like inverted bowl that had tall windows on either side of its circular stance. From the polished red tiled floor to the emerald draped ceilings, a mixture of metal and wooden shelves nearly encompassed the entire shop, housing perfect rows of clamped-shut jars with all sorts of colored coffee beans that neither Landon nor Makari ever thought existed. And on an opposite wall, paper-bagged and ribbon sealed selections of the emporium's more exquisite and rich house coffees were at the ready for purchase. Makari watched tiny Cappamite children run from their parents who waited in the zigzagging order lines; every child, and sometimes an adult or two, became enraptured with their sights on the alluring inner-workings of the emporium, pressing their faces and hands against the giant glass wall and sometimes scrambling with one another to render themselves the best view. The coffee roasting and dairy room were like the mechanics of a pocket watch, but with a few extra screams of steam, vats of churning beans and clouds of ground cocoa slithering about. Dozens of copper tubes that lined from the backroom and shot fresh batches of milk and coffee beans to the main espresso island. Emporium workers were safely planted in all specific bases around the workshop, some of them either separating or hauling the morning deliveries that arrived in giant green trucks that dropped massive burlap sacks of imported coffee beans and gallons of glass bottles of pearly milk.

While Nancy Sinatra's Sugar Town spun and caroled from the gigantic, ruby horn on the gramophone from across the emporium, Landon and Makari found themselves inching along in one of the tall ordering lines that made way to the center espresso counter. Makari traced her sights on the coffee island: each barista worked their unique magic on every latte, soothing hot tea, and most simple yet not very simple cup of the house coffee. The top-hatted and emerald vested baristas moved around their espresso island from counter to espresso machine seamlessly, never spilling a drink, or sloshing precious steamed milk, or forgetting to swirl the top of every beverage with their world renowned Cappa Cloud Cream. It was like a circus of organized chaos.

While Landon tried to differentiate between what a Butler-Ripple latte or a Midnight Honey Creamer was, he noticed his sister twist her head at the moment a tall, gangly man with the most exceptional curly mustache, suddenly surrendered the siblings' attention.

"What a dreamy thrill it truly is," cooed Loward Schmaltz, tossing a bony hand out at our siblings. Landon and Makari quickly tossed each other a quick stare, and back up at the grinning man in the fine espresso tinted suit donning a nearly outrageous emerald bowtie.

"Nice to meet you, Mr. Schmaltz," nodded Landon, noticing Schmaltz's espresso stained grin.

"Oh, no need to be so reserved, call me Loward, I wasn't expecting to see you two here this morning, if had known the Manor was going to delight my deliciously infectious emporium with your presence, I would've rolled out our emerald carpet," said Schmaltz, giggling. "Are the Cappas here, too?"

"No, we joined that odd man, Mr. Varick, on some errand of his for the Manor," noted Makari. "He sent us over here to wait for him."

"He's more of a cold man, really—he just needs a gulp of my Moch-York, it'd do him some good," winked Schmaltz. "And as it seems, I know you two have been deprived of my emporium your entire lives."

"Y-you know about us—and our summons?" hinted Landon.

"Who doesn't?" snorted Schmaltz, "I've heard some petty murmurs here and there, and with this morning's obnoxious Gazette headlines, and especially after from last night—and I must say, that was quite the unexpected scene that ole rebel displayed, and I hope your outlook of our country, as I believe, truly is our country, hasn't been tarnished."

That was the first time, other than Jade's constant belief, that a single Cappamite had shown a hailing relation of acceptance for Landon and Makari in Revlenion.

"So, you believe in our summons?" forwarded Makari.

"Absolutely, but none of that heroic, fantasy talk right now," swatted Schmaltz, "it's almost time for you two to order your first, and definitely not your last, Dingodun latte!"

The emporium master led our siblings to the coffee counter, and along its leaning walls, Landon began to notice the rows of emporium-made dark, milk, spiced or caramel whirled and wrapped chocolate bars, biscotti squares, and peculiar shaped boxes of Schmaltz Malted Chocolate Spheres and Buzzing-Honey-B Drops; the latter were little candies in the shape of tiny bumblebees meant to either sweeten your coffee or delight your tongue for after. And not to mention the tantalizing pastries that filled up every delectable, perfectly displayed double-decker glass case that towered beside each ruby register.

Loward Schmaltz then introduced one of his baristas named Yula (operating one of the registers with a peacock feather poking out from the side of her uniformed top hat) to our curious siblings, and gleefully noted that this was Landon and Makari's first foray into their impeccable emporium. Landon and Makari gave their sights to the top-hatted barista, as she began to suggest her beloved lunchtime lattes that lined the chalk-written menu board that had somehow been enchanted to levitate itself and write which selections of beverages or coffee beans that were available for brewing, directly above the island:

DINGODUNS ESPRESSO EMPORIUM

~

-Dingo' House Originals-
Cappa Cappuccino (Single, Double) 2.25 GR
Cappa Cloud Creamer (No Espresso) 2.75 GR
The Butler-Ripple (Single, Double, Triple) 4.00 GR
Dingo Revleniano (Single, Double, Triple) 4.25 GR
Dingo Mallow Macchiato (Single, Double) 4.50 GR
Manor Moch-York (Double, Triple, Quad) 4.75 GR
-Emporium Full Leaf Teas-
Cappa Crescent Leaf 1.50 GR

Dingo Yawn Leaf 2.00 GR
Empress Leaf 2.25 GR
Honey Wink Leaf 2.25 GR
Midnight Shade Leaf 3.00 GR
Masala Dream Leaf 3.00 GR
-Delectable Additions-
Emporium Espresso Shot: Add .50 GR
Extra Cloud Cream: Add .50 GR
Emerald Soy Bean Cream: Add .50 GR

~

"Moch-York, a minty, dark chocolate latte, that's quite famous and yet another signature of ours," said Yula, after Landon's query.

"How about that one, Honey Wink?" Makari pointed.

"Ah, a tea drinker? That one is known to vanquish the worst sore throats, if you feel that you have one," nodded Yula.

"Cappa Cloud Cream?" asked Makari.

"Ever wonder what the fluffiest cloud in sky tastes like? Well, 'cloud cream is about as close as you'll ever get to actually tasting one —a whipped cloud with dash of milk," said Yula.

"A long time family-secret-recipe of mine," nodded Schmaltz. "Try the Mallow Macchiato, one of my finest creations!"

"Mallow?" tilted Landon.

"A hint of marshmallow and a whole lot of Cappa Cloud Cream with your shot of espresso hiding just under the swirl of 'Cloud Cream," said Yula, using her hands in the same motion as though she were actually creating the beverage right in front of the siblings.

"Have we decided?" hummed Schmaltz, noticing Makari beginning to eye the flaky row of golden-brown butter croissants.

"I-I'll take…a—single, Butler-Ripple, please," Landon ordered.

"A Honey Wink for me, with Emerald Soy, please," Makari ordered, after she placed the honeycomb-shaped box of Buzzing-Honey-B Drops on the counter, "and one box of these, thank you."

"Wonderful selections," cheered Yula, tapping the keys on the register like an old typewriter.

"That'll be six solbecks and seventy-five grendels," said Yula, as our siblings' grand total popped up on the face of the register with a faint chime.

"Don't you mind it," Schmaltz reached, "you save those solbecks for another day; let these treats act as a tiny celebration of your entry into Revlenion."

Instead, Landon slid all four of the crumpled solbecks that Jade had so generously given to him and his sister into the emerald tip jar beside the register, as Yula grinned with a fine nod and thanks. While Schmaltz led our siblings around the espresso counter to await their hand-crafted beverages, Landon and Makari set their sights on the transparent tubes that scaled from the backroom, shooting the famous Cappa Cloud Cream down into tiny hoses where a spare barista topped every beverage that came their way or where the other tubes cannonballed beans to every humming espresso machine, replenishing each of the hoppers atop of the three steaming and purring machines when needed.

"Goodness me, is it already the afternoon?" sighed Schmaltz, peeking at his silver wristwatch. "My dear youngsters, I must bid you farewell for now."

"Wait, Mr. Schmaltz, one last thing," Makari grabbed the emporium master's elbow. "The murmurs you heard about us—did you hear anything about—"

"—Manifestos," whispered Landon.

"There's no need to whisper, as it goes, we really shouldn't discuss such delicate intelligence like the 'Big M' here, as I like to call 'em," said Schmaltz, eyeing a few of his prying eyed and ear-muttering guests. "These Cappamites know a celebrity when they see one, obviously from your public attire and the fact you two made the front page of the morning edition."

"We've been through a lot in just a round of a few hours while being here, gathering our own info about this place and…the Big M," said Landon.

"Nearly mutilated doing so," Makari nudged.

"Strolling the Manor at night?" hummed Schmaltz, noticing his young guests quickly biting their lips. "As I imagined. You two aren't the first ones who've entered this country, not knowing who you are or why such curious occurrences are suddenly taking form, but know this; I've saluted each and every single brilliant being that has believed in finding their rightful home and at the same time accepting this curious country for what it is. However, be wise on your trip, the Big M is no laughing matter, and like I said before, the previous ones that have set foot into Revlenion, have indeed come into this very emporium, even my Great-Great-Grandfather Sir Dario Dingodun had the privilege of meeting each of them, like I am now, and those marvelous minds were no different and just as curious as you two."

"Can you name one of them, someone who's also taken part of a manife…a Big M?" furthered Landon.

"I thought you two were meddling 'round the Manor for answers? My mind is short at the moment of Big M tales," said Schmaltz, as he then handed Landon and Makari each of their frothed porcelain mugs, "and as much as I'd love to sit and sip on a sublime cup of Midnight Shade, I must digress, my emporium calls for me."

"So, its safe to say, that you believe in them?" asked Landon.

"Oh, why of course I do, as I believe that every Cappamite, Gargoylian, and the next being in this entire universe has a Big M out there, but far too many rather stray from its grueling expenses. Alas, Big M's have without a doubt, arduously shaped Revlenion in such glorious ways, and as it seems," Schmaltz then bent his tall body closer to our siblings and whispered, "I think we're all in for one more dabble of their magnificence." Schmaltz then erected to his usual welcoming stance, giving his bowtie a tightened fix and single twirl of his curly mustache. "Tah-tah!"

And like that, Loward Schmaltz departed from our heartened siblings, as they watched the gangly man weave between the ordering lines, greeting as many of his delighted Cappamite guests as he could.

Makari then let out an almost relieved sounding sigh, as her brother simply tilted his head.

"Everyone has a Manifesto?" wooed Makari, as she eyed her brother.

"That was unexpected," said Landon, as then he took a careful sip from his mug of hot and chocolaty Butler-Ripple.

"I wonder just how much he actually knows about Manifestos, or what he's actually witnessed others do with them?" Makari questioned, placing her nose over her steaming, honey whipped tea.

Landon and Makari then began to rally about just how scrumptiously crafted each of their beverages were, and at times leaving a mustache-like streak of cream on their upper lips.

"Did Schmaltz say that we made the front page of this morning's newspaper?" asked Landon, with bit of awe in his throat.

"Yes, and our frightening picture was followed by some nasty headline about us," said Makari.

"No kidding?" said Landon, flattered.

Even if they couldn't garner focal information about their manifesto—or Big M's—from Schmaltz, Landon and Makari insisted between those few moments when they sipped from their heavy coffee and tea mugs, that in some fortuitous fashion their manifesto would soon reveal itself. Then, a piercing whistle from someone's lips triggered from somewhere behind our siblings: sitting in an open curtained booth toward the back of the emporium were a pair of red-headed boys; one of them signaled (what seemed like it, anyway) at Landon and Makari to join them.

"I think that boy just whistled at us," said Makari, pointing with an obscured finger against her chest, as her brother traced his sights on to the wary boys.

"Are you sure?" Landon eyed around at possible friends the boy might've been calling for, as the older of the two boys then pointed at him, "I guess it really is us that he wants."

Maneuvering through the crowd, Landon and Makari

approached the booth occupied by the two reticent boys, and as it seemed, they were around the same age as our Tuolumnes. The two boys were in matching rouge neckties and hunter green coated uniforms from the St. Madeline's Academy for Children, as Makari figured from the school's crest: a knight's helmet bathed between rings of fire while twin lions reached for a floating heart that had been patched on one of the boy's blazers that was hanging from the booth coat hook. Neither of the red-headed boys greeted our siblings with a welcoming handshake, but only with sparse, calculating eyes.

Before Makari could take her seat, casting her eyes on an occupant on the other side of the boy's tall booth, she watched as a red-hooded figure sat hunched, murmuring with hiss whispers into what Makari thought was an oddly shaped hand mirror.

"Are you going to sit with us or what?" The older of the two boys snapped Makari out of her daze upon the hooded figure, noticing her brother had already taken a seat in the booth.

"Sit, M," said Landon, placing his mug on the wooden table.

"It's not every day we share this booth, but today I'll make the exception." The older of the two boys spoke again, after a sip from his thick coffee mug.

"Grateful," Makari smirked.

"As you should." The younger of the two boys then spoke, picking at the raspberry muffin in front of him.

"My brother doesn't ever know when it's his turn to speak, but when he does, he always sounds stupendously ignorant. Don't mind this little brat—we're the Holbrook brothers."

The Holbrooks were hoping for a round of applause, as it seemed to Landon and Makari as they instead sat still for a near three-seconds, when an unfamiliar jazzy tune began to blanket over the entire emporium from the gramophone, diagonally across their booth.

"Quiet bunch of outsiders, aren't they? I'm Collin, and this pudgy one is Gavin," Collin introduced, as his younger half gave a partial smile with a quick eye roll and instead returned to devouring his emporium muffin. "So, what'd that ole bag of gangly bones have to say?" asked Collin, haughtily.

"You mean, Loward Schmaltz?" retorted Makari.

"Calm down, not here to upset…yet," giggled Collin.

"Why'd you call us over here?" said Landon.

"To meet the outsiders, obviously," hooted Collin, after a sip of his black coffee, "that mustache parade is a celebrity seeking fiend, and just like you two fools, he's a fame heathen at best."

"Not even close, he's an absolutely brilliant fellow," nodded Makari.

"Bag of boorish bones, 'smore like it," grinned Collin. "It's good to have us around, Landon—Makree."

"It's Muh-Kar-E," cited Makari, before gently popping in her seat, "wait, how do you know our names?" Makari sat up, uncrossing her arms, now with a lean in her seat. Collin then ruffled out a newspaper that had been hiding on his side and slammed the front page down on the table.

"You think I don't read, please," jeered Collin, "I've got a reputation to uphold."

"Our problems will just keep getting bigger, won't they," said Landon, as he then sat back in the cushioned booth.

"Problems? Witless celebrities like you two in Cappa won't have any problems," said Collin.

"We're not celebrities, just because we get a snapshot on the front cover doesn't mean we're necessarily branded a celebrity," said Makari.

Collin then threw himself back in his seat, making Gavin nudge nervously.

"But where this picture was taken and assuming the miserable headline is about you—you really don't get it, do you?" Collin scanned the page with a finger.

"What exactly is there to get?" challenged Landon.

"To be included in this photo is a streamline for a dozen of reasons. However, to be included in this party, there are reasons underneath that I'm sure you're not even aware," said Collin.

"We…were invited," noted Makari.

"Wait, M," said Landon, as he leaned forward in his seat, eyeing Collin closely, "what do you care?"

"Just simply making conversation—simply helping you shmoos understand what you're really getting yourselves into," said Collin.

Makari mouthed the word *shmoo* under her breath; she swore she heard someone say the same word once before.

"Yeah, what you're really getting into," Gavin added.

"Hush it, Gavin," snapped Collin.

Maybe he knows what Makari and I truly need to know? Landon thought. Makari then gave Landon a quick glance.

"So, you say you two were invited?" reiterated Collin.

"Yes," Landon allowed Makari to continue, "not just by the Cappas, but from—"

"Jade Cooper," said a gentle voice from the booth behind the Holbrook boys.

A rosy-cheeked, goldilocks-like haired girl then stood up over the booth wall, tossing back the red hood. Dressed in the same uniform as the Holbrooks, combing back part of her curly blond hair behind one of her ears. Landon quickly recognized the young girl from the gala. "Hello there, Landy boy."

"H-hello," said Landon, feeling his warm blood fill into his face.

"How do you know this kid, Britta? " said Collin.

"Because, you pimple, I too was invited to the gala last night, with Samantha Sworg and her family," said Britta. "Not to mention I was almost killed at the party, but at least we shared a dance, right Landon?"

"Why wasn't I invited?" groaned Collin.

"Yeah! Why weren't we?" Gavin imitated.

"Ugh, the Manor doesn't invite orphans to posh parties, they just like to pretend they actually care," groaned Britta, rolling her eyes at Gavin. Landon and Makari then tossed each other a despaired glance. "I hear you two are in some rowdy mess—true?"

"What do you mean?" said Makari.

"For that to happen," Britta pointed at the photograph of Vizton Eplaville during his raid of the gala, "you two definitely mean something to that scarred-face man, I was there, and I know what he said…but what's the real reason?"

"Private matters," assured Makari.

"Could it have something to do with," Britta gave a quick glance out the window and over her shoulders, and then finally shooting a cynical glare at Makari, "manifestos?"

Makari's face then went pale.

"Figured it to be true, the Sworgs know everything—they never know when to shut up, just like these two train wrecks," said Britta, as she tugged on the Holbrook's heads of stringy hair. "If that's why Jade came crawling to you, you might as well drown yourselves."

"Why would you say that?" said Landon.

"I keep forgetting you two aren't from around here, but idiots that have spent their lives chasing after their manifesto, soon find out it's either a dried up myth or a giant bowl of death," said Britta.

Landon could feel his heart sinking into his stomach.

"As far as we've come to learn of these manifestos, only good things have come our way," said Makari.

"Are you sure about that?" said Britta, eyeing the newspaper.

"Remember that story about those twin sisters Jade went searching for, Collin?" Britta knocked on Collin's head as if she were knocking on a door.

"Ouch, stop messing with me! And yes, I sort of remember," said Collin.

"I know that story," grinned Gavin, as both booths then darted eyes at the thick boy, "I heard that those twins were murdered in the manor, because of Jade."

"You really need to keep your mouth shut, you know that?" snapped Collin, rolling his eyes. "You never know what you're saying, I swear."

"That does sound familiar though, Jade always gets over his

head, and then someone loses their own," said Britta. Makari then set aside her warm teacup, quickly losing her love for the honey-winked tea. "Enough of that dreariness, are you two returning to afternoon classes?" asked Britta, as she swung around the booth divider to the Holbrook booth.

"We never even made it to the morning classes!" laughed Collin.

"I wanna go to class," yelped Gavin.

"Quiet," Collin growled.

"Well then, what's your plan?" asked Britta. "You know as well as I do since it's the first week of term, the professors will be prowling the plaza for clueless runaways, like you two." Makari had never shared time with such students before. A part of her admired their confidence of skipping afternoon classes, but Makari had a feeling they were synonymous with being terribly vicious. "You're not gonna' go rat us out now, are you?" said Britta, eyeing Makari.

"I-I…no," juggled Makari.

"Good. Well then, welcome to the Holbrook Club—" Britta nodded.

"—Excuse Britta's sudden generosity, but that invitation goes out, unofficially," said Collin. Landon's stomach churned, at the same time of being ultimately annoyed by Collin, he actually, somehow, felt like he could or should, trust him.

"Why should I care about some bogus club?" said Landon.

"We're bad kids," Collin gritted his teeth, forcing himself over the table, pushing his nose into Landon's face, "and there's a lot you need to know about being a kid in this town. Take the rare, and I do mean rare invitation if you're ever going to make it in Cappa." Landon didn't budge, he kept a hard stare on Collin as the rest of the table watched on. "Bwah! Ha! Ha! I'm only jokin'!" Collin then shook Landon's hand. "Relax, Landy, don't be such a stiff. But that part about being 'bad kids,' is true, and we've got to get a move on before the bloodhound professors start looking for their prey."

"What's the catch?" said Landon. "Are you serious about what you're offering?"

"He is, actually there's a lot we'd like to share with you and your *little girlfriend* about those messy Cappas, and your insecure detective friend, Jade," bragged Britta.

"Landon's my brother," scoffed Makari.

"Whatever," Britta sighed, rolling her eyes as she did, and lastly grabbing her book bag from her booth.

"But before we can share anything with you, we're going to have to make a deal," said Collin.

"What sort of deal?" Makari snorted, shaking her head.

"A venturous one," grinned Britta.

▼

Landon and Makari now found themselves chasing after the rebellious Holbrook clan. The fickle trio ahead of them walked briskly between charging horse-drawn cabs and steaming taxis with not a fraction of fear of being smashed by the afternoon traffic that lined through Cappa Square.

"Hurry up!" Collin shouted at Gavin, still nibbling away at his Dingodun raspberry muffin.

Landon and Makari kept at a few, steady paces behind to ensure none of their new capricious friends would hear their exchanged reasons. Makari then noticed a Chamberlain garbed woman pinning some sort of MISSING CHILD bill onto the already layered board of forgotten faces. The latest one, as Makari tossed her sights on the fresh sepia poster, was of a black Gargoylian boy, thirteen years old, and had last been seen entering his dormitory at St. Madeline's Academy, six nights ago. Makari kept an eye on the photo for as long as she could while trying to keep up with her forwarding brother, suddenly becoming haunted by the beleaguered boy's photo after she began to recite his name under her breath: Damien Blatty.

"Oh, Landon what are we thinking? Mr. Varick told us he would meet us back at Dingoduns, what if he returns and we—"

"—M, right now, with all my love for you, just stop—please. Let's just see what these kids have to share about this place. For once,

I honestly believe someone around here—OUCH!" Landon suddenly flung his away from his provoked sister.

Makari had pinched Landon on the arm like a fuming bumblebee.

"—You've really let him get inside your head," Makari pointed.

"—What was that for? And no, I want decent answers for…just for once. Take it as if we're getting a second opinion on this place," said Landon, massaging his arm. "Ugh, that really hurt, M."

"Good, especially for an answer like that—a second opinion, from them! We'd be better off getting help from the Grim Reaper," fumed Makari.

"Listen," Landon tugged on his sister's jacket, stopping them both in the middle of the crowded sidewalk, "accounting for last night, we need all the answers possible; I just want a different perspective of the Cappas, Jade, and these—" Landon eyed the passing Cappamites that looked far too occupied to care, but still found himself whispering— "…manifestos."

"Fine, I get your plan, but why does help have to come from them?" Makari sighed.

"I feel like he's telling somehow, after I shook his hand. I could literally feel that he was going to hold his word," said Landon.

"If you say so," said Makari, shaking her head while she and her brother paced after the Holbrook trio ahead.

Collin continued to direct his young troupe's path; a relatively questionable direction neither Landon nor Makari had been on, cutting in and out garbage-trailed alleyways behind many of the plaza's shops.

"Hurry up now, this way," said Collin, as he led the way now over a browned knoll.

As the troupe stomped through the thick blades of sun-dried grass along the pine border, Landon then finally realized that they were far from the sights and sounds of Cappa Square, especially when they reached an unnerving tree stump entrance.

"*Los Fronteros Muerto*," said Britta, reading from between the shape of a large skull and a broken heart that both had been deeply engraved in the side of an aged tree. "How fitting."

"Why here?" said Landon.

"You asked for answers, well, only in here can we show you," said Collin.

"This is unbelievably frightening," shook Makari.

"Oh, don't be such a whiny shmoo!" laughed Collin.

For the first time, Britta looked as though Collin's idea of entering the West Royal Pine was astoundingly absurd, after she eyed our siblings and then finally followed behind Collin and all while Landon and Makari trailed behind. Makari took hold of her brother's arm as they followed along while little Gavin trailed behind making ghoulish noises and giggling. As they crossed the border of the West Royal Pine, none of our troupe heads cared to take notice of the ominous shape that could be seen, but you would've had to be standing in just the right place when crossing the border to see the macabre face that took shape between the old and twisted trees along the border. Little did our troupe know, that they were walking directly into the darkly shape's mouth.

Collin had already led his troupe for more than ten minutes, through fallen trees and the rolling terrains of tall pines as all of them took notice of the inkwell-like scenery that had ceased life in the towers of pines that encompassed. The busy sounds from the plaza could not be heard; not a single melodious chirp of any bird from any of the treetops peeped, but only the slow, swaying sounds of the forest around them. It sounded as if it were actually breathing. Luckily for the troupe, the early and gloomy afternoon sun was still able to pierce through most of the treetops, to help guide them on their trail.

With her hand still tightly gripped around the honeycomb box of Buzzing-Honey-B Drops, Makari believed that the only way she could calm her nerved mood was by instead elating her senses with a dash of sweetness.

"Would anyone like a piece?" asked Makari, as she tore the top of the candy box open.

"I would," hummed Britta, tossing out a hand from under her

red cloak.

"Do you even know how to eat these?" darted Collin, after Britta handed him the honeycomb box.

"They're just candy, right?" Makari figured, as she handed her brother his own tiny wax paper sealed candy. And just like Makari thought it would be, easily unwrapping any other candy she adored, however, something different happened the moment Makari tore apart the wax wrapper between her forefingers. The yellow, marble-sized candy that was once carefully wrapped instantly flew from its cage-like wrapper and began to buzz in wild circles with its sugary wings above of the troupe. Unfortunately for Gavin, who instead found the monstrous pleasure in making howling noises and faces like an enraged troll, was unaware of the buzzing candy that was darting directly toward his cackling mouth.

"Hmpf!" Gavin choked after the bumblebee-candy flew directly to the back of his throat. With a slight strain, a wince and heavy gulp Gavin could feel the flying candy buzz all the down to his belly. "I'd like another one, please."

"You don't unwrap it in your hands," mocked Collin, "you simply place the entire wrapper inside your mouth and…voilà! Allow the candy to do the rest."

Landon and Makari watched as the others placed the wrappers on their tongues; closing their mouths the next, suddenly, the rest of the troupe began to twinge and giggle. Landon's eyes popped, puckering his lips the next as he could feel the tiny candy-bee's sugar stinger poke the inside of his mouth.

"It tickles!" laughed Makari, clamping a hand over mouth, as her candy began to sting a variety of sweetness inside her mouth.

"Nowf break thef bee," said Collin, trying to speak with the candy buzzing inside of his mouth. "Bite on it."

And so they did. With a hard crunch, the tiny bee's core began to ooze the richest layer of honey that slowly began to soothe the tickles that once ensued.

"I'll take another," chimed Britta, as Collin shuffled the boxed candy in his hand.

"What's a shmoo?" asked Makari.

"Ha!" spat Britta.

"Oh, c'mon," gazed Gavin, "geez, you freaks really aren't from around here."

"Only shmoos wear those armbands," said Collin, shaking his head and biting his lip, hoping not to laugh.

Makari quickly shot her brother an odd look behind her.

"What's so bad about these?" said Landon, embarrassingly adjusting his armband.

"They're the mark of the slums – the bureau invented them in order to keep track of those wanderers that we lucky enough to find an entry into Revlenion," revealed Collin.

"It's amazing to me that *you* know this," spat Britta.

"It helps to read, Britta," said Collin, then humming a curse word under his breath, mocking his cynical friend.

"So, those like us – we found the Elddri—" tried Makari.

"YOU found Elddri's Cube!?" choked Britta, halting the troop.

Landon and Makari locked their legs right in place, as though they had just let out the most repulsive burp the way Britta darted her wide eyes at the both of them.

"Eldd, what-who?" said Gavin, completely aloof.

"Since Collin is *sooo* uppity today about his Revlenion history, maybe he can tell you just how dangerous Elddri's trinkets are," cooed Britta, sticking her tongue out at Collin as she paced beside him. Collin then signaled again, having his club follow him and right where he began:

"I'll tell you about Elddri, near a *cozy* spot along the west river, and how he's linked to a story I'm about to tell," teased Collin, as he eyed his followers over his shoulder with another grin, "a few years ago," he continued, "Jade's former mentor was once at the center of a case that summoned two children—much like you two—to take part in a supreme legacy. The two children agreed with the mentor's terms and shadowed them a trail here to Cappa Valley, but unfortunately for those kids, they were driven to *madness*."

"What was it that drove them insane?" asked Landon.

"A musical jewelry box of some kind," remembered Collin.

"An insidious invention of Elddri, s'more like it," pointed Britta.

"A jewelry box, really?" pardoned Landon.

"I'm not just making this up," reminded Collin, continuing, "somewhere along that pair's venture, one of them happened to have been gifted a by an impostor that was claiming to be an admirer and friend to the Cappas. Little did the siblings or their mentor all know, that the Dark Alman had bewitched the box himself. Hypnotizing the children, the feared one's knew his magic was powerful enough to force the children to rebel and wander off deep within this forest, hoping to stay hidden from the Cappas' greedy grasps. That act sparked an enormous hunt, however, the unlucky cloud that had always shaded the children had already led them to their graves. Even though their bodies were never found, it is said by the brave souls who dare explore these pines say, if you reach the lone boulder before the west river, you can evoke the ghosts of the two lost children… with one, simple conjure."

"And the conjure is?" Landon asked.

"Clever you should ask, as it seems you're finally starting to believe me and as it so happens, I know the chant," nodded Collin, as he and the troupe climbed over a thick, fallen tree. "It has been passed on from one brave kid to the other for quite some time. You simply say, and in the form of three counts: in these woods you sleep, near the river where you wish to keep, I call you."

"And then what happens?" Makari daunted.

"The ghosts are said to appear and will utter only the truth, if you're brave enough to hear it," said Collin.

"You're full of it—" Landon spat.

"—Ah, never deny a grim tale, or else you could end up being one," warned Collin.

"How much further until we reach this lone boulder?" groaned

Britta, swatting at the humid air. "I'm sick of walking into spider webs!"

"That means we're almost there," rejoiced Collin, "once we reach the Eight Fallen Limbs, we'll be able to see the lone boulder from there."

"Eight-fall-what?" asked Makari.

"It's an old trail between eight fallen trees," said Gavin.

"*Correcto*, Gavin! And for once you are," hooted Collin.

Once again, Collin was spearheading his troupe through the forest, either by the trails between tangled shrubs or jumping into a single-file line and tiptoeing across small creeks on top dozens of fallen tree trunks.

"Stop—listen," whispered Gavin, causing the train of bodies ahead to bump as they balanced atop a giant tumbled tree.

Off in the distance, a faint rustling could be heard—though not in the brush below, but in the trees above.

"What do you suppose it is?" said Landon.

"Pinecones…Most definitely," guessed Britta.

"I hope those are big pinecones falling," sighed Makari.

Crack…

Snap…

Crack….

"Colly," Gavin panicked, "you don't think we're too close to any firethorn patches, do you?"

"How many times have I told you, not to call me *Colly*?" Collin leered, "and no, we're far off from any patches; we would've seen or smelled them by now, so hush it."

Collin, however, did pick up their pace and hastened his troupe away from the rustling that persisted off in the distance.

"What's Gavin worrying about?" said Landon, as he came shoulder to shoulder with Collin along the giant tree trunk.

"He's worried we're getting too close to the forbidden gardens, he's right though," Collin quickly eyed the rest of his pack behind, "we gotta' get away from them, but don't pay my brother any attention, he's just a paranoid little flea."

For a change, Landon and Makari took the lead of the troupe, as Collin announced that just up ahead at the approaching row of eight fallen trees, was the entrance to their main course.

"You're absolutely certain that there's no other trail?" gulped Landon.

"Not a one," said Collin.

"Better be a fast trail, Collin, or else," growled Britta.

The troupe walked on through the row of eight trees, which in some strange way created a sort of tunnel. A tunnel that allowed their gazing sights upon all the giant spider webs blanketing above (and steering clear of all the reachable ones at the forest ground) and along the broken tree limbs.

Makari groaned at the sight of the clusters of what seemed like hundreds of abandoned curtains of web, feeling almost dreadfully uneasy at the thought of some tiny brown arachnids that could be watching her and her fearless troupe quickly pacing through their webbed territory. Landon then began to tell a story of his own, with Makari taking over in parts, speaking about Martin Winter, the copper statue boy, and the first hand experience within the Manor.

"You'd think I'd believe anything about this place, I mean, we were talking to a statue—"

Landon stopped in his tracks.

Our siblings spun around, calling out for the rest of the troupe, scaling their tall and dreary surroundings. Landon and Makari had been wildly deserted. As quick as they might've realized what a harsh mistake it had been made following the Holbrooks, Landon recognized one truth Collin had spoken of was only a few steps ahead.

"Makari, look—"

The lone boulder rested on the edge of a rushing river, awaiting those who knew its ultimate purpose.

"Landon, no—we've got to get out of here—Landon, come on," Makari begged.

Ideas of knowing the truth swirled in Landon's mind; they had come this far into the clutches of this forbidden pine and was determined to recite the conjure.

"I told you we shouldn't have followed Collin, I begged you," said Makari.

"But we're here, M, we can't not try the summons, try to remember it…."

Already far and away from our lone siblings, the Holbrook boys were jetting through the pine like a scurried pair of callous foxes.

"Were they not the best pair of idiots? Easiest prank, ever!" laughed Collin, as he, Gavin, and Britta dashed between dozens of fallen pine.

"Ah! A bitter plan, Britta, I couldn't have planned it better myself," huffed Gavin, giving her a look over his shoulder. "Wait, wait, Collin!"

"What—where's Britta?" Collin shook, as Gavin darted looks around the deserted pine. Suddenly, a heavy thud to the forest floor echoed from off in the distance. It was like out of some horrid dream, a shrill scream rang from somewhere deep within the ribcage-like walls of the blackened forest.

"Do you think that was Britta?" clamped Gavin.

"Forget her," Collin shivered, tossing Makari's honeycomb box on to the forest floor, "she's on her own." Collin grabbed Gavin by the shirt and they raced against the ghastly lure of the forest.

And there, our unfortunately tricked Landon and Makari, were still standing only a few steps from the boulder and shuffled their thoughts trying to remember the conjurer's rhyme.

"It had something to do with sleeping in the river," recalled Landon.

"And it ended with keeping it and adding, I call you—Oh, Landon! Why, why did we have to follow them—I can't think in this place," Makari shook, as she glanced at the eerie tunnel behind her.

"Stop, M—Help me try and remember the chant, if we do this, we'll be at the advantage," said Landon. "Try to remember."

"Together the conjuring had to be recited in three chants...in these...in these woods...you sleep," said Makari, fearful of commencing the scene.

"Good, good, and—nearest? No. Near this river..." added Landon.

"No, it was...near the river where you—"

"—Where you wish to keep?" guessed Landon.

"Yes, yes, it was a rhyme, 'in these woods you sleep'," said Makari.

"'Near the river where you wish to keep'," recited Landon. "'I call you'—or something like that, right?"

"Okay, that does sound right, but it was in three chants, so together now," said Makari, as she and Landon began to recite those bedeviling words in three long chants.

Nothing. The lone boulder didn't budge or break into two parts that would magically open a portal to unveil a pair of ghosts, only the echoing gushes of the rushing riverbed below remained.

"I told you, Collin is a fraud," sighed Makari. Landon hoped, for a split second, to be presented with valuable answers from the dead, but instead he got what only the West Royal Pine provides to those who enter its horrifying cage. Landon and Makari jerked their heads to the sound emitting from the resting boulder: falling rock from behind the slanted stone began to boom, as if heavy pieces were splashing into the river below.

"Landon..." gasped Makari, as her brave brother took a steady step toward the boulder.

"Ugh, what's that smell?" huffed Landon, as a malodorous wave of rotted fish suddenly fumed. At the same moment, a giant, filthy claw began to slowly reach over the boulder. Landon and Makari felt almost motionless as a cold arrow of fear pierced through both of them.

"Run..."

Grabbing Makari by the arm, Landon and his quivering sister spun on their heels faster as they had ever done in their entire lives to escape from having to meet what owned that deadly claw. More and more ferocious claws began to slowly appear from behind the surrounding thick trees while Landon and Makari were bound to make their getaway. This time, the more terrifying sight was now set on the webbed trail where a pack of tarantulas had now returned and were calmly waiting for their human prey to enter. However, these giant tarantulas weren't like the ones Makari loathed from that Leo G. Carroll science-fiction horror film her brother had once gleefully subjected her to when she was much younger. These red-rump beasts were far more disturbing. The collection of eight humanoid arachnids had all crawled down from their nests that hid high in the trees or out from fetid burrows below the forest. Landon and Makari had never met such monsters, as some of their humanly fusions looked as though they were incontrovertibly decaying. The human-arachnids were lurching closer, nearly lunging their giant bristle limbs at our siblings. The arachnids simply awaited their lingering prey to reenter their web haven. There was no other option: Landon clutched a hand with his sister, right before breaking off the thickest tree branch he could find, holding it close like a sword, and leading the way back through the spiders' path. Landon swung hard and as fast as he could at the fang lunging spiders:

"I need f-feassst!" growled an Arachnoid as it lunged an arm at Landon.

"Let me bite you so that I may be freed from this hell!" cried another Arachnoid.

The arachnid beasts weren't interested in being swatted at but instead jumped from one fallen trunk to the other, hastily spinning webbed barricades in their prey's hopeful escape.

Landon kept swatting at the spiders that began to flood the forest floor, knocking their furry legs into the air as some of them hissed and flared their venom dripping fangs. As Landon slashed and slain the thickening walls of webs, Makari began to feel the fat spiders poking at her shoe heels with their long limbs. The spiders were now at the advantage to strike. With one more powerful swing to go, the largest of the hybrid-spiders stood in our siblings' way. Landon and Makari watched in horror as it arched itself on its hind legs. With his mightiest swing yet, Landon whacked the livid spider across its hideous eight-eyed head and sent it flying through its own trap, snapping Landon's branch into splinters. The repulsive spider went numb and curled before it slammed onto the forest floor. The rest of the furry hybrid colony of spiders dared not to follow the two fleeing humans, but retreated at the sight of what was truly after their lost prey, clearing the treetops high above.

"The spiders aren't following us," panted Landon, trudging to a halt.

"Are we going the right way?" sighed Makari, as she eyed the dark forest around the two of them.

"I-I don't know," said Landon, peeling off strands of fresh spider webs from his shoulders.

"Those trees over there look familiar," said Makari, pointing at a crisscrossing row of fallen tree trunks ahead.

"Collin led us through here, I can't remember, but keep moving, we're bound to find our way out," Landon urged. "I don't think it's the spiders we've got to worry about anymore, whatever was hiding behind that boulder, with a claw that size—I don't want to wait around here to meet it."

"Hold on," suddenly remembering it, Makari then pulled the Trans-Oidar badge out from her coat pocket. "Let me give this thing a try," Makari spoke into the radio badge, only to hear scratches of static at her reply.

"No signal," Landon sighed.

Makari gave her brother a look over her shoulder, not taking notice of the exposed tree roots ahead of her next step.

"Makari!" Landon cried, instinctively reaching out for her. He was too late; Makari yelped and had already fallen fast with a roll down a steep and leaf-covered hill, losing a grip of the oidar badge.

Makari had rolled all the way down the hill until she found herself on her back, wincing with a fresh gash on her knee in a dry creek bed before a patch of red plants that fortunately broke her fall.

"Makari! Makari! Are you all right?" called Landon, as he slid down the hill until he reached his sister.

"I'm okay, but I," coughed Makari, shaking off the dirt and leaves out from her hair, "lost the oidar."

Landon helped his sister up, pulling her up by her hands.

"That radio thing was useless out here anyway—wait, are you bleeding?" said Landon, eyeing his blood-like stained hands.

"No, I don't feel any cuts on me," said Makari, eyeing her blood red stained hands and arms, "I fell into this red berry patch and it broke my fall."

"M…these must be the plants," said Landon, as he began to eye more and more patches of red berries. "Gavin was incredibly terrified about being close to these plants, you even heard him."

"Gavin called them firethorns," said Makari, as she then noticed how abundant these berry patches were in the creek bed.

"Come on, let's get out of—" Landon hushed himself.

Standing only a few steps away from the both of them, Landon and Makari could not take their eyes off of the beastly creature ahead. It stood very tall, almost three heights more than Landon with muck-ridden fur from its curling, chipped horns atop of its head and all the way down to his filthy, fat toes. The pop-belly beast remained calm and hunched as it began to eye our siblings with its sunken eyes. The beast reeked of rotten fish and looked badly beaten and freshly clawed.

Landon and Makari didn't know what to do. Landon had lost his handy tree-branch-sword, yet our siblings couldn't take their eyes off this beast that vulnerably loomed with such a human presence. So unexpectedly, the beast's mouth then cracked a smile, exposing a few jagged teeth, and then frowned at the sight of Makari's red berry stained hands. The beast darted its wide black eyes around the patch, and then pointed with his large claw, one that looked much like the other that had appeared from behind the lone boulder. Landon eyed the beast's massive claws, guessing that the creature was trying to point them in a direction to leave the patch, immediately, and insisting as it did with a few, gurgling grunts.

Running across the street from a garbage clustered alley, Collin and Gavin were hoping to rejoice at having done their parts in the devious prank as they raced back to Dingoduns through the busy afternoon traffic.

"How could you be so stupid to leave your book-bag at Dingoduns? You know that if it's turned-in we're bound to be caught for skippin' classes," growled Collin, beaming a stern eye at his brother and unaware of the collision that was to be his next step.

"Speaking of," said Jade, tossing a stare through his thick wayfarer lenses at the Holbrooks. Collin ran his pointed nose directly into Jade Cooper's chest and then suddenly bounced a step backward.

Collin and Gavin went pale and both could feel their stomachs turnover as if they hadn't eaten in weeks when they set gawking sights on Jade. An unfamiliar face, to the Holbrooks anyway, at that point collected a spot alongside Jade. It was Mr. Varick, both of his hands clasped behind his back.

"What do you want?" Collin snorted at Jade, trying his best to reclaim his infamous impoliteness.

"Mr. Schmaltz tells me, that you two were last seen leaving his coffee shop earlier with three other children. Now tell me, where are they?" Jade interrogated, now eyeing Mr. Varick, noticing that he was stiff as his risen eyebrows.

Gavin quickly eyed his older brother.

"We've seen with all sorts of kids...we're popular. But we never set foot inside Dingoduns today," huffed Collin, rolling his eyes.

"Are you so sure about that?" Mr. Varick hummed, suddenly revealing a black suede book-bag, as it dangled from one of his gloved fingers while trying to read the poorly stitched name on the front of the satchel. "Which one of you is named, Gavin?"

Gavin anxiously shook, not knowing just how his brother was

ever going to salvage the lie.

"Er...Oh, you found my brother's bag!" Collin hurried, "We've been looking for—"

"Stop lying," Mr. Varick snapped, "you know damn well that you two made off with three other children today."

"Okay, now I remember," Collin coughed, dancing his eyes for a thought, "they said that they had important business to attend to a- and had to return to the Manor. They said it was really, really urgent."

"Quit lying, you little—Aren't you two supposed to be in your afternoon classes?" snapped Mr. Varick. "Let's just see what else you might be up to. Damn orphans, can't trust one, let alone two."

"Now, wait a second," said Jade, watching Mr. Varick unbuckle the book-bags lip to examine the contents inside. Collin and Gavin watched as Mr. Varick snooped with nearly his entire face pressed inside the bag.

"Books, pens, and...well, what do we have here?" hummed Mr. Varick, suddenly gasping. "What have you two been plotting?"

Jade then took hold of the small vellum scroll that Mr. Varick found inside the satchel, falling suspicious when he immediately recognized the blood red stamp that illustrated the face of a pig atop of the harsh note:

I know the plan.
I will fulfill this promise that I have made with you.
Make friends with the swine. Rid you of the enemy.
I promise,
Gavin Holbrook, Dark Seether to-be-Crowned.

"How?" Jade panicked, showing the brothers the scroll. "Gavin, who made you write this?"

"T-that's not his!" shouted Collin, as Jade suddenly eyed the boys again, noticing a small twig on the lapel of Gavin's school jacket.

"It isn't mine, I promise, I swear!" Gavin trembled, as he watched Jade roll the scroll up and slide it inside his coat. "I've never seen that in my life." Jade picked at the twig and then examined it closely, recognizing the single red berry at the end of its thorny stem.

"WHERE ARE THEY?" gritted Jade, identifying the firethorn berry, as he then snatched the Holbrook brothers by their collars.

"They asked for our help, so we did—" Collin grunted.

Jade eyed Mr. Varick with a sheer face of fear, tossing the two conniving brothers aside. Jade couldn't hesitate; instead he raced through the crowded sidewalks to the west, giving a twirl of his right hand that incredibly brandished his magnificent cane once again.

▼

Landon and Makari were still standing a few paces back from the disgruntled, horned beast.

"I think it wants us to go that way," Landon gulped.

The beast grunted again, pointing to the trail that lingered behind Landon and Makari.

"We should—" Makari tried to speak, but instead flinched at the....

RRRAWWWWRRR!

The petrifying roar boomed from the horde of four rancid beasts, stampeding toward our siblings through the barren pine. At that same moment, somewhere deep in the forest, Jade dug his boot heels into the soil, coming to sharp halt after hearing the same monstrous roar that echoed ahead of him.

One of the older beasts suddenly thrashed to the helm of its pack: it had graying patches all over its umber coat; horns fixed atop its massive head. All the creatures that joined in the garden were positively relatives of sorts, but each unique in their hunched heights or by the wideness of their awful jaws. One of the monsters then pressed its giant nostrils into the patch of firethorns where Makari had landed. The friendly beast tried its best to communicate with our siblings, hastily waving its claws at them and whimpering as if it were trying to tell them to run. The friendly beast nervously watched its elder vigorously sniffing the damaged patch, and then abruptly jerked its head at the two humans that dared to damage its garden, so it thought. Landon and Makari had taken the hint and carefully they backed away on to the new trail until the elder beast began to tremble with rage, squinting its wrath-fueled eyes. The siblings ran for it, daring to make their only escape. With another mighty roar, the leader's fellow beasts charged after our siblings like enormous cannon balls fired from a pirate ship. Fortunately for Landon and Makari, for the quickest second that they could see over their shoulders was the massive collision of beasts behind. The creature that had kindly shown Landon and Makari a way out of the firethorn garden was now bludgeoning its fuming kin with his chipped horns through their chests: claws swung and the deadliest fangs were splayed. Landon and Makari's beast picked-up and tossed its brothers in order to keep them away from his young humans, but with a charge from the eldest, the devoted creature was hurled and slammed against a fallen tree.

Landon and Makari never stopped running—they knew it wasn't an option. Landon ran after Makari, keeping watch of their trail behind. Hearing familiar snarls and snaps from the trees above, Landon could now see one of the beasts hunting them. The beast was as fast as our siblings were; scaling the treetops and calculating the right moment to fall upon them on the forest floor.

The humid air of the forest rushed against Makari's face, still running, and then very suddenly, she could see a dark figure sweeping towards her. Jade was running so fast that it looked as though he was actually flying; nearly colliding into Makari as she grabbed hold of him when Jade readily pointed his cane at the beast swinging down from the trees.

Landon then grasped his sister in arms and all while being whirled with exhilaration to see Jade, and at that exact moment,

Jade's cane began to brilliantly display its immense power. However, sharing that exact moment with Jade, Makari absentmindedly seized her brother's hand, and stepped in the elder beast's deadly path. For those next daring seconds for Makari, she and the entire forest felt like one marvelous aura as she fell into a slow-motioned trance.

Landon eyed his sister's hand in his.

Makari kept her eyes focused on the deadly beast coming towards her.

Believing in what indeed felt like an incredible reverie, Makari could draw only one more breath when she began to protect her brother and Jade herself from the charging beast.

Makari felt her left-hand fling into the air as Landon could feel an electrifying force bond in their clasped hands when.

A near blinding wall of light unexpectedly emerged from Makari's spare palm.

The elder beast couldn't turn away from the wall of light it was now about to dive directly into. Makari calmly closed her eyes. When she opened them next, Makari could see the fat beast on the forest floor, quietly slumped over on one of its singed sides.

"I-I didn't mean to harm it—" Makari slowly fell to her knees, exhausted by whatever she had conjured, sensing the euphoric bond with the forest fleetly slip away from her shoulders like a dreamy shawl. Landon crouched beside his teary-eyed sister and tried to understand what he had just witnessed. Jade and Landon exchanged flummoxed stares once the three of them returned to the outlet trail again. Jade then lent only one more cautious eye at the motionless beast that would forever rot there between the mounds of dead leaves and the rest of the forest.

Unknown to the trio, perched high above in the trees, a scarred-face man had managed to experience the phenomenal scene only moments ago, himself. With his enraged eyes carefully targeted on our trio as they crossed beyond the forest border, Vizton Eplaville hissed, and in one hand crushed an opened box of Buzzing-Honey-B Drops he found within the desolate forest.

▼

The entire journey by elsol-cab back to the Manor was highly sought by our curious siblings and yet ever so awkward. Landon and Makari sat opposite from one another and Jade and Mr. Varick the same, all tolerating the bump and sway of the old cab as they ascended the royal hill.

"Mr. Cooper," whined Mr. Varick, "you know this incident will have to be reported to the Heads, and dare I say, the R.C.C. Entering the West Pines, let alone disturbing an aviken's treasured firethorn garden, fractures countless laws between our territory and theirs—"

"—Thank you, Mr. Varick, I'll be sure to relay that report for you. Oh, and I'll be sure to mention in my report about how you managed to lose sight of Landon and Makari on your own endeavor." Jade didn't give the curling lipped Mr. Varick another look, sharing a few rattled words with our siblings, "you two are incredibly lucky that none of those brundle-arachs got a chance to have their venomous ways with you, let alone that pack of wild avikens. And had one of those spiders bitten you—the thought of it alone grosses me out—within a few agonizing minutes, you would've been sprouting eight thorny limbs, yourselves!" Landon and Makari remained quiet as possible until one moment when they caught Mr. Varick calculating them. Makari noticed it first and in return, stuck out her tongue at the belittling man when he wasn't looking. Jade was calm now and instead locked his wayfarer sights out the cab window on the passing Manor pines for the rest of the ride.

That late afternoon sun barely had a chance to crawl through the thick rain clouds that regularly arrived like an unwelcome flu to Cappa Valley at the end of every summer, but for some odd reason, the ashen clouds had arrived much earlier that year. Sun or no sun, wonderful weather or none, the Cappa Manor correspondents were still busily exchanging trade scrolls, executive books and talk as they hurried along the long hallways and back to their orderly offices on the fifth floor. Amongst these manor correspondents and daily house staff, our curious trio hurried beside them and that was right after

Jade sent our brave siblings to see Pattie McDaniel in her infirmary court; where she was tut-tutting their escapades as she treated Makari's scrapes from her tumble in the forest and bandaging the few cuts on Landon's knuckles.

"Jade, we're truly, truly sorry about going off in—"

"Don't worry about that now, Makari," Jade alleviated.

"I really hope that there's an explanation for what I did to that creature," said Makari, following behind Jade. "I don't know if I killed the poor thing or…I was just scared."

Landon remained strolling closely behind with an ear on the rest of the party and eyes on the new corridor that was fluent with more wall-mounted candelabras between peculiar glass-cased ornaments that chronicled Revlenion's art renaissance.

"Of course there's an explanation: you protected yourself and so remarkably the rest of us from that charging aviken," said Jade.

"So that's what those beasts are called?" marveled Landon, as Jade nodded a reply.

"I understand. Wait, do I? Ugh, what's going on with me?" sighed Makari, observing her hands.

"Either way, M—it was beyond spectacular," said Landon.

"What Makari did wasn't spectacular, it was genius," said Jade, noticing a pair of unduly inquisitive manor executives watching them from one end of the hall. "Just hold your thoughts for just a few moments, I want to take you two somewhere we can discuss that incident in private."

Landon and Makari kept a steady pace after Jade; around one corner and to another room they went. The trio had now entered the "manor vestibule," as Jade conveyed, where Landon and Makari eyed several more correspondents ascending or descending through wide thresholds to stairwells leading deeper into the manor. Jade nodded to our siblings to keep following after him as they rounded the massive fountain's pool below the colossal, fire-breathing sculpture of a hand holding a torch. Landon and Makari were transfixed by the massive art piece as they paced; on either side of the torch's stem were dual tragicomedy faces that spewed waterfalls from their gaping mouths that bounced glistening light from the consistently thriving flame above.

"If you wanted to get anywhere in the manor, other than taking the elevator, those stairwells would be your easiest and quickest way," said Jade, still leading the troupe's way through the vestibule when he suddenly took a right turn away from the torch.

"What was that sculpture back there?" Makari asked, eyeing one of the torch's intimidating faces.

"The Bartholde Torch; it's one of the manor's finest trademarks. When I was your age, I was always spooked by those two faces…looking at them now still gives me shivers. To the rest of the manor, they're deemed the 'faces of victory' because that torch is the only surviving piece of the original Statue of Solace that was conceived by the late Bartholde Occü," said Jade.

"What happened to the rest of the statue?" Landon asked.

"The statue was lost in the Seraphion War, over a century ago," Jade revealed.

"Revlenion has had a war?" said Makari, awing.

"Only one—Unfortunately it took a war and a couple crown-heavy leaders to make Revlenion civil, but civil we are far from," said Jade. "Where the original statue stood in the once rich bay of Arkgothin City, it found itself blown-up in the massive crossfires. The first manor heirs found it necessary to restore what was left of the statue, and plant it within the manor. However, the brilliant Occü was able to create a new statue altogether, before he died, one that has been said to be greatly enchanted with defenses should it ever find itself in harms way again."

"Where's the new statue now?" said Landon.

"The vast statue lives just off the eastern shores of Cappa, where supposedly, it stands to serve those in need; to see the torch's burning light, no matter where that person stands in the entire universe," Jade inspired, "you'll always be able to find Revlenion."

The trio was now halfway through a wide hall made completely out of windows, quite tunnel-like, and it came to an end before a charming pair of wrought-iron doors.

"The Magnolia House," announced Jade, leading our siblings into the sky lit garden.

The Magnolia House, like Jade had previously delivered, was an expansive and absolutely elegant greenhouse. The gardens within spanned along the dome glass walls that encompassed; the glass house even had enough space to splay a small pond bordered with groomed knolls and topiary figures that were peppered throughout. Landon and Makari gestured and awed at the sight of the sprawling vegetable gardens and caught glimpses of some orange species of birds that zoomed from the tops of the ivy shrubs that crawled along parts of the airy garden. Walking up the spiraling pebbled trail that lined the rumped hill in the center of the garden, it was then did our trio finally take notice the pair of familiar faces that were indulged in a pampered lunch while sitting under a giant magnolia tree.

"Not what I was expecting, but just follow my lead for now," whispered Jade, as Landon and Makari nodded quickly.

"Jade, Landon, and Makari—our enthralling trio—what a delightful surprise!" said Dionne, slicing up two roasted chicken and pesto paninis on a silver trolley while Ms. Qwara served chalices of sparkling water. "Lewa and I just finished up our meeting and are about to have ourselves lunch." Dionne took her seat at the tiny wrought iron table with Qwara. "Care to join?"

"Please, have a seat there," said Qwara, pointing at the wooden bench under the tall magnolia, "don't be afraid to join us."

The trio each took a seat on the long bench; succumbing to Qwara's offerings of Dingoduns extraordinarily warm and lovingly fresh Butler-Ripple inspired cookies and chilled goblets of sparkling lemonade from the fancy trolley.

"So, tell me, Landon and Makari, what did you think of the 'Square?'" said Dionne, after a small bite of her steaming panini. Landon and Jade hesitated for a second, tossing looks at one another and then dipped their mouths into their sparkling beverages. Makari however, was far too honest:

"We met an aviken today," she said, quite frank, "five of them, actually."

Jade choked on a gulp from his glass-goblet, darting an astonished look at Makari.

"To say you that you met an aviken, isn't exactly the right word I'd use," said Qwara, alarmingly impressed.

"Oh, I know that look," said Dionne, eyeing Jade with a wink, "even through those thick sunglasses of yours, I can see that same, child-like twinkle of trouble in your eyes."

"I can explain what happened, even though my young friends showed just how undoubtedly careless they can be…their brave acts might have actually returned with a bit of a reward," said Jade. Landon and Makari then quickly glanced at one another, pleasantly astonished by Jade's cheer.

"Well, I would love to hear the explanation from them, Jade," said Dionne, nodding to Landon and Makari when their eyes quickly danced around the garden party. "Landon—Makari, what's the story?"

After another large gulp of his sparkling lemonade, Landon began his side of their expedition within and beyond Cappa Square. Dionne and Qwara continued to take small bites from each of their paninis, eyeing the trio, and simply nodded at every detail Landon— and at times—Makari's daring side of the story when Dionne politely asked her to express a portion of their trials.

"I hope Jade didn't scold the two of you, for he too has wild tales to share that aren't so different than the both of yours," said Dionne. Landon and Makari gave Jade a look of query at Dionne's addition. "But I must say, that your day has been beyond question very brave yet very curious."

"How curious, exactly?" said Landon.

"Everything we've hoped for," furthered Dionne.

"There is something that has also happened, but I'm unsure if I should share it here—I don't want it to frighten you two," said Jade, eyeing Landon and Makari very carefully.

"Share what, exactly?" Dionne asked.

"After what happened in that forest," Landon shook, "I could be up for anything, honestly."

"No, it's worse than that, I'm afraid," Jade sighed.

"Well, go on, you can tell us," said Landon.

"You promised you would be honest with us," Makari noted. Dionne and Qwara exchanged uncertain looks.

"Jade, if it's something you'd like to share with the both us," Dionne gestured to Qwara, "in private...This can wait."

"No, I made a promise to Landon and Makari last night," said Jade, as he slipped a hand inside his coat pocket. "The part I forgot to mention was how I was able to find you both."

"Those mean boys," shook Makari.

"Yes, but when I found them, something truly didn't seem right —One of them had this," Jade then revealed the ugly scroll to the garden party, "Mr. Varick was the one who found it inside one of their school bags." Jade showed Landon and Makari the dreadful note as they carefully scanned its frightful words.

"I told you we shouldn't have followed them," moaned Makari, eyeing her brother as she sat back against the old bench. "Our time here is becoming worse, isn't it?"

"No, no, don't say that—Don't let the cruelty of others scare you that quick, you haven't shown them just how fearless you truly are," said Dionne, pointing at Makari, allaying.

"We can't deny that something terrible is assembling outside these manor walls. The three of us must advance with this summons sooner than later," said Jade, nodding at our siblings and after calculating Ms. Qwara's uncertainty.

"I'll take the scroll for now and secure it as future evidence," said Qwara, rolling the scroll within a table napkin; Jade agreed.

"Dark...A Dark Seether; that's what that man with the scars on his face called himself," Landon recalled. "He said more would come —"

"—If, I may, say this to you, Landon dear," Dionne coolly interrupted, "as well to you, Makari, that neither of you should allow yourselves to be worried by that man."

"Of course we should, we—" Landon tried, raising his voice until noticing how composed the Head Lady remained gently smiling at him the next. "Sorry…"

"I understand, first hand myself what it's like to face this country," said Dionne.

"You do, how?" asked Makari.

"I am a leader for this valley; I passionately guide each and every one of my fellow Cappamites, every day," said Dionne, placing a hand over her heart, "and I do so without fear because I know that I am not alone. You two are not alone. However, you must both remember," said Dionne, leaning forward on her metal stool, "people that choose to be like that scarred-fellow—you know—all that they know is how to scare people. That is all they know. Figures like him, they don't know guidance, honesty or compassion. I know what unfeeling sort he wishes to encompass himself with and in result, a person like Eplaville becomes severely limited. You two, I am certain," Dionne assured, nodding, "are unlimited."

"I don't know what makes me unlimited," blabbed Landon.

"Neither do I," said Makari.

"You don't have to know now, it may take time, but know that you are," smiled Dionne, "because we believe that you are."

Landon and Makari looked up at the rest of the party; sensing their hearts gasp as a suffocating grip of denial began to wither back into its cold abyss.

"At this level of significance, further exploration in the possibility of a manifesto is extraordinary. I could testify before the entire R.C.C., to get them to fully admit Landon and Makari into Revlenion and fund the expedition in me guiding their right—" said Jade.

"—I understand your determination, Jade, but you know as well as I, that the Chamberlains will want substantial proof of Landon and Makari's tale," said Dionne.

"Makari could singe some of the R.C.C.'s faces right off, maybe that could pay as proof?" said Jade, bitterly, tossing his back into the bench.

"What other options are there?" said Landon.

"There is another, but the R.C.C. would shake at the idea, especially, at any of their words," said Qwara, eyeing Dionne.

"Ah, of course—Jade, you still need to visit with the Ordinheirs," said Dionne. "I believe an introduction with them should be in order."

"Is that even...Possible? Well, I mean, they ordered me to be their liaison for the summons, but I've never actually met them," said Jade.

"Only if they wish to oblige to Landon and Makari's tale," said Dionne.

"Dionne, come to think of it though, that is quite the mighty step for these three," said Qwara.

"It must be done," said Dionne.

"Dionne, if you could, tell us who or what the Ordinheir are?" said Makari.

"Where does one begin to try and explain who were the Ordinheirs? It's funny really, when you're a person of Revlenion your entire life, you've already heard the myths and endless epic tales of the Knights of Ordinheir...and then you two charms come along," said Dionne, with a wink at Landon and Makari.

"Knights?" gasped Makari, joyously.

"Not exactly the ones in shining armor," said Dionne, with a small hand wave.

"If they were knights, then how are they going to help us?" said Makari.

"The knights have their ways," nodded Qwara, mirthfully.

"I think the last time I ever told anyone the tale of the Ordinheirs, Jade I believe you and Arri were both just little boys—it was that one Hallows' Eve when Arri and I came to visit you at St.

Madeline's; I believe, was it when you were sick with a case of appendicitis?" said Dionne.

"I remember now, it wasn't exactly a favorite time of mine, come to think of it," said Jade, recounting those two agonizing weeks in bed.

"Once more at this famous tale shouldn't hurt," Dionne then took a sip from her cool chalice and then began, "the Knights of the Ordinheir Alliance were once supreme protectors of all Revlenion and its people.

At the same time of being guardians to their people, they were strict contacts to the Divine Seraphion Society. Now, the Seraphions, during the guardian reign of the Ordinheir, always found themselves in differences with the Ordinheirs on how justice and guardianship of Revlenion should be upheld. Each leader from the two magnificent fellowships was steadfast with their own philosophies, but ever so suddenly…a bitter divorce between the societies was unfortunately made. Following the untimely separation, vicious creatures and movers of evil gatherings soon ascended. These bitter beings saw the movement between the two ultimate forces as a sign of weakness, and darker realms became the cause of a monstrous movement against the Ordinheir and their mortal followers. The Knights beckoned their divine partners for help, but it did not come and that followed in the demise to Ordinheir.

However, even in death, the Ordinheir's forces grew in the most interesting of ways by either in the number of followers or the curious abilities at grasp. Before their deaths, the Knights immortalized themselves into something much more clever than anyone had ever expected," said Dionne.

"What did they do to themselves?" said Landon, eagerly.

"Oh, usually I would reveal exactly at this point of the story what the Knights made of themselves," Dionne hummed, "but since they're here in the Manor, I'll let you see for yourself."

"Will we need full approval from the R.C.C. to enter Ordinheir's court?" said Jade.

"Approval?" giggled Dionne, "You need only mine, and that's all you'll ever need."

"Well, they'll need a Manor Executive to access the sixth floor. I'm more than happy to escort you three," offered Ms. Qwara, and exactly when a Blackburnian Warbler suddenly landed with a flutter beside Makari on end of the bench.

"Don't mind it, Makari," insisted Dionne, noticing the entire party had their eyes on the peeping, orange bird. "Tiny romp, isn't he?" Makari desperately wanted to welcome the zany bird by allowing it leap onto her forefinger.

"There's something in its beak," Landon noticed.

"Oh, Makari," Qwara awed, "has that warbler brought you a gift?" The party watched as the hurried bird carefully bounced itself along the back of the bench, when Makari intuitively displayed an open palm to the curious bird. Dropping two magnolia petals in Makari's palm, Dionne airily crooned.

"Well, well, not only did that bird bring you a magnolia petal, it respectfully brought two," lauded Dionne, after the giddy bird flew back into its nest somewhere in the mass garden.

"I've never seen a bird act like that before," gleamed Makari, "I can't even feed a flock birds in a park without them fluttering away, let alone receive gifts from one."

"No," chuckled Jade.

"Yes, I'm serious," frowned Makari, "all of them are afraid of my big, red head of hair, I guess."

"Why did that bird do that?" asked Landon, sitting dazzled by the tricky bird.

"That was no trick, I can assure you," said Dionne.

"This tree was planted by one of the original occupants of this manor," said Jade, "a very superstitious man by the name of Lockwood Pardee."

"Superstitious from what?" Makari asked, confused.

"Everything, I assume. His own shadow on the thirteenth day of every month or bewildered with anxiety by his Manor Staff who had forgotten not to wear green on Tuesdays; even after he famously abolished the color of clothing," said Dionne, "because he believed that the hue consumed the oxygen from his very lungs, if he stood too close to it."

"Green. You're kidding?" grinned Makari.

"Mental, s'more like it," nodded Qwara.

"Pardee was on the brink of self-destruction when his mother suggested planting a magnolia tree here in the garden," said Dionne.

"Why, are magnolias supposed to ward off bad luck?" Makari guessed.

"That's exactly what they've been known for," marveled Dionne, "and precisely what Pardee's mother told him, hoping it would instill a crux of good-luck," Dionne pointed at the serene tree, "unknown to Lockwood, a warbler nest was hiding within the blossomed tree. Everyday, Pardee would sit there at that very bench when he felt nearly consumed by his fears, until one day, and for no apparent reason, a warbler swooped to his lap and presented him with a petal from that tree."

"Did that cure him?" said Landon.

"Nobody knows, however, how does your petal make you feel?" said Dionne, nodding.

"I-I don't know, lucky, I guess?" said Landon. "The bird though, how does it know—?"

"—My guess? They just know," Jade believed, stretching his neck around to survey the rest of the garden, until ultimately hearing the crescendoing spell of fanciful chirps swirl the garden.

"Listen to them sing for you," leaned Qwara, as the whistle-like trills circled.

"Excellent," clapped Dionne, "Lucky, indeed, and it seems as though you three are at the edge."

"What edge, exactly?" said Landon.

"Of finding your manifesto," said Dionne, nodding at our curious trio, as she then raised her chalice in the air. "Cheers."

Landon and Makari also raised their cups and then eyed each

other, both sharing the exact thought: what would they learn in the Ordinheir's Court? After the party finished their picnic, Dionne insisted that she give the Tuolumnes a guided tour of the entire garden, as it would soothe their minds and senses before meeting with the Ordinheirs later that afternoon. Makari was more than thrilled with Dionne's tour, as Landon and Jade surrendered to Makari's wishes and admired the house's floral allure.

▼

Motionless and both breathing ever so easily, a pair of cerulean suited guards stood at the end of the short, stained glass hall where they posted before a red curtained archway. The guards, each with their fists clasped behind their backs, immediately twitched their sights on a row of eleven yellow sequentially blinking numbers fixed above the elevator doors at the opposite end of the hall.

TING!

"The sixth floor, follow me," said Ms. Qwara, unhinging her Manor Executive key from a hole in the elevator's button panel. The hallway itself was terribly silent with only the slightest hint of the late afternoon's wind bouncing whistles and creaks against the windows outside. Landon and Makari were a motley whirl of excitement; eyeing with a tiptoe over the guiding shoulders of Ms. Qwara and Jade at the sight of the coming archway. It was an exhilarating emotion shared between our siblings the closer they approached the curtain; certainly one that was reminiscent of the stage curtain that hung within their favorite cinema that they used to sneak into afterschool—when they could—to capture an escape to other worlds of fantasies, galaxies, space and time.

Funny to Landon now, whispering the thought of the curtain to his sister; Makari agreed, today they were not going to find a joyous silver screen that could appease their imaginations, instead it had to be something else. Landon and Makari deliberated for those few seconds, but ultimately they believed: behind that curtain, something special was indeed waiting for them.

"I don't know if I should be afraid or delighted to meet these Ordinheirs," muttered Makari, eyeing Jade.

"Good afternoon, gentlemen," Qwara approached the two guards first, "here on royal representation; these three will be speaking with the Ordinheirs this afternoon. That is, if you would please allow access."

The two guards slowly eyed one another; kindly nodding at Ms. Qwara's order and her troupe, both of the guards took a firm grip with one hand on the thick curtain until splitting an opening for the curious entrants.

"This is where I leave you three," said Qwara. "Use your time wisely with them."

Our brave trio then gave a thankful nod to Ms. Qwara and the calm guards that waited for them to enter the court behind the curtain. Makari was last to enter, noticing Ms. Qwara giving her a nod that looked as if it meant good luck before she and the hallway disappeared behind the curtain.

The trio was now alone.

In a room that spanned, wide and bare than anyone would've guessed was once a great dining hall of sorts and where ashen sunlight that blanketed Cappa Valley poured against the massive, stained-glass window ahead. The glistening window was so vast, that had a fortunate Cappamite entered that room on any other day— without a doubt—would've rendered their tale about it into a luminous wall rather than a glorious window that it actually was. Depicted in the window though, was a spectacular emblem—Jade guessed—well-fashioned and fused with ivory, sable and emerald glass that showed a swan in the midst of spanning its ravishing wings and its body centered in the virescent outline of an inverted triangle. The trio followed along the red carpet, lined with golden crests and odd floral embroidery that led our three to a simple wooden podium near the end of the hall. The closer our trio approached the podium, however, fire from the two oiled pool basins that situated near the wide window began to grow. The swaying licks of fire steadied, as their orangey glaze swept the room and upon the three and very unique marble busts that crept in the shadows before the swan window.

"Look at these," said Makari, as she took a few steps closer toward the busts, "they seem, almost, fleshy-like."

Our trio examined the three marble heads, carefully though by not stepping beyond the podium as each fell into deep fascination over the commanding poise of the Elizabethan head that took center and all while her colonial-attired comrades were fixed in jubilant poses on either side of her plinth, staring aimlessly into space.

"Look," Landon pointed, "the statues are named."

Indeed, each statue had a named platted in gold that was in the shape of a wavy banner, and affixed upon the brim to their corresponding plinth:

"Warner Hullen," Makari read aloud the left-sided statue's name.

"Ingrid Ordinheir," said Landon, eyeing the center statue.

"Alanto Georger," Jade hummed, hoping that he properly recited the name that displayed on the right-sided statue.

"Alright, where are they?" said Landon, dancing his sights around the room.

"It's funny now, but come to think of it, back in middle school, I remember there being a lecture on the Ordinheirs. Not specifically on these three…statues, however I do recall something about a standing at that podium, there," said Jade, pointing with his cane. "Still, Mrs. Fuller never mentioned anything about three giant heads."

"Who goes first?" said Landon.

"After what happened today, I'd say Makari should, displaying that kind of talent might be some sort of importance," said Jade. "I could go if it makes—"

Makari took a step back, second-guessing.

"—I'll go first. I put you in that mess earlier, allow me," said Landon, stepping in front of his sister and Jade. Jade then instinctively reached at Landon, watching his friend ascended the few square steps onto the podium. "Only great query should ever disturb dreams," said Landon, reading the silver line of embossed words on the wooden podium.

Landon then thought it was that random buzzing noise that you may sometimes hear deep inside your eardrum, but it wasn't the odd hiss that he somewhat hoped for, it was a purr of whispers from the busts only a few paces out in front of him. Landon kept his eyes on the three heads as each plinth suddenly began to stretch their stone necks with a twist and yawn like they were rolling out of some beloved slumber.

"We have guests," rejoiced Ingrid, calmly, eyeing her neighboring plinths. Landon couldn't take his eyes off the three talking heads, watching them as they suddenly began to arch their eyebrows at him and at times tossed such odd looks of excitement and marvel at one another.

"Ah...and he hasn't come alone, of course—Mr. Cooper!" Alanto cheered, noticing our wayfarer-boy freeze at the call of his own name; he had never met the marble statue before.

"It seems as though this one, just might—oh remember when I say this—just might be the right one," Ingrid said, as her company fell silent.

"What might I be?" shivered Landon.

"Landon Tuolumne," said Ingrid, tracing her thoughts into the air, "am I wrong?"

Landon shook his head.

"Well then, introductions, please," elated Ingrid.

"Warner Hullen, General of the knights," he said, from the left.

"Alanto Georger, Second in command and fellow knight, a pleasure to meet you," he said, smiling from the right.

"Joan-Ingrid Ordinheir, but you may call me Ingrid," she nodded, from the center, "I am the Head of the Alliance and Master Knight. We've certainly anticipated this moment—to look upon you, even in our fragile conditions, it is such a pleasure."

"I don't know if I should be thanking you just yet and as much as you've been anticipating me, I've been anticipating the truth," said Landon.

"The truth?" said Ordinheir.

"We're knowledgeable of many truths to speak, Landon, but which one do you prefer?" said Hullen.

"I need to know what my manifesto is," said Landon.

The three busts quickly darted each other with their intrigued eyes.

"You want to know what your manifesto is? The ingredients to your manifesto were given to you at birth," said Georger. "You're a child of Revlenion, you must know that by now."

"No, until yesterday, I didn't know a bit about Revlenion," said Landon, shaking his head. Ordinheir remained silent for a few seconds more, and then eyed the thin boy that stood before her at the podium who looked starved for answers: a boy who remained intent yet so timorous.

"There have been many before you, young guardians who were born knowing their own manifesto and aspired to fulfill its one-special-factor. However, there has only been one other time, and I do mean one time, a young guardian approached us and didn't know their own manifesto," said Ordinheir.

"His desires, however, weren't for the keepings of peace, Ordinheir," reminded Hullen.

"We can't forget our own common policy, only a true guardian can hold place at our platform—" said Georger, eyeing the podium.

"—So can a genuine descendant of a guardian," said Ordinheir.

"I was told that you three might be able to help," said Landon.

"Told to you by the Manor, of course, and by our associate Mr. Cooper, who was kind enough to bring you your summons, correct?" said Ordinheir.

"Yes, yes, but it was through a tale about your past, that's how I learned about you three," said Landon.

"Ah, that tale…" said Hullen, enthused.

"Tale or no tale, I need to know exactly why my sister and I were summoned here. We've been searching in circles for answers and were nearly killed, twice. Please, what exactly do you know—or—what can you tell me?" said Landon.

"Odd, oh very odd. I can hear the determination of a true guardian, but do I see standing before me, a true guardian?" said Ordinheir.

"I'll do what I can, but until then, please, right now...help me," said Landon, leaning helplessly on the podium.

"Very well," said Ordinheir.

Landon felt as though he was about to be stricken by a force so phenomenal, he could feel the tiniest hairs on the back of his neck rising as Ordinheir gave him such a foreboding stare.

"You say you've heard of our tale? But whoever told you that mangled tale, more than likely forgot to mention one important factor," said Georger.

"What's that?" said Landon.

"When you stand before us, on that very platform, your soul makes an oath with the Ordinheirs," said Hullen.

"An oath?" said Landon.

"An oath of fulfilling your duty as a Cherished Guardian," said Ordinheir.

"Though as fascinating as it is, for you Landon, at birth that oath was already decided for you," said Ordinheir.

"Who decided that?" said Landon.

"You did," nodded Ordinheir, insistently.

"I...how—why?" befuddled Landon.

"I'll never know why your star wanted to be a Cherished Guardian, but the fact is, it's obvious that it wanted you here," said Ordinheir. "However, your birth as a guardian could not be fulfilled without the help and genius of the Divine Seraphion Society, and in return, they were obliged to your birthday wish."

"But why?" said Landon.

"That's a question that leads you searching in circles, in this case, you should follow what is brought onto you," said Hullen.

"The reasons are known, but this is where it gets tricky—along with that oath, there's a subtle strike in your stance; there's something a little off about your presence at our platform," said Georger.

"That strike is eerily similar to a guardian who once stood at that very podium, just like you are now," said Ordinheir. "And that curious strike we sense in you reeks of doubt."

"If there's any proof to deny your doubts, I have evidence to offer you, my sister can even tell you," said Landon, turning to his sister. Makari jolted at her brother's call.

"A…Sister?" said Hullen. Makari took the few short steps up the podium, now standing alongside her brother.

"Hello young lady, your name?" said Ordinheir.

"—Makari Arina," Hullen announced.

"Hullen can detect the names of descendants of fellow guardians," said Ordinheir, seeing the young girl perch one of her ears. "Don't be alarmed."

Makari stood by her brother closely and looked just as bemused.

"Lovely to make the acquaintance," said Makari, and out of nervousness she curtsied, then realizing it wasn't necessary.

"An elegant young lady who knows such manners," said Ordinheir. "Impressive."

"Go on," said Landon. "Tell them what happened in the forest."

Landon and Makari were honest and spoke of every detail upon entering the West Royal Pine, just like they did with Dionne and Qwara. Jade allowed our siblings to explain themselves and kept silent and waited for the right moment to speak. The Ordinheirs slated forward at times and took in deep breaths at significant points in our siblings' recital, and at that right moment

"There has to be a great significance of what Makari conjured, I witnessed it," said Jade.

The Ordinheirs tossed complex looks a one another.

"A curious case this has become, oh so very curious, don't you agree?" said Georger, eyeing his fellow plinths.

"Why would you say that?" asked Makari, puzzled.

"The oath of a Cherished Guardian only ever beckons for one soul…and interestingly enough, there are two of you," hummed Ordinheir.

"Landon, when is your birthday?" said Hullen.

"—November twenty-eighth," said Landon.

"And yours, Makari?" asked Hullen, again.

"—May twenty-third," replied Makari.

The Ordinheirs exchanged even more beguiled looks with one another and our trio.

"The Sagittarius and the Gemini—how beautiful, and in the realm of our stars, together, they can be legendary," said Ordinheir.

"Yes, but legendary for the good, the bad, and the unfortunate ugly," reminded Ordinheir.

"I can only imagine what the bad and the ugly entail," said Jade.

"Landon, you were born in a window of time that is both wildly surprising and follows a lineage of guardians. As it seems, you were born a guardian," said Ordinheir.

"Obviously though, being oddly neglected from Revlenion for all these years has taken its course on you, and quite possibly for your sister, too. However, for you Landon, you haven't had the divine and very, very rare opportunity to grow as a true guardian—you can be an even more phenomenal guardian than you already are," said Georger.

"I'm…phenomenal?" shook Landon, unsure if he had ever been told that his entire life.

"Oh yes," nodded Ordinheir. "You and your sister both."

"That is the beauty in your curious case, Landon. You've had the privilege to explore another country in this curious universe of ours, unbeknownst to your extraordinary abilities, and still you've made your way to us," said Hullen. "Not only is your sister's illustration in the forest a sign of further capabilities, but it is more beauty and bravery than any other guardian that have queried us in many, many years."

"These other guardians that've attempted to query you, were they from my country as well?" said Landon.

"Oh yes, but previous queries were simply descendants from

Revlenion and never a true guardian," said Hullen.

"But my sister is the one who's shown any sign of potential that you're seeking. I'm not saying I wouldn't stand to your wishes, but as far as we've come—we can't be mislead," said Landon.

"You opened the cube though," said Makari.

"The...cube?" pardoned Ordinheir.

"Elddri's Cube," said Jade.

"The...Elddri Cube? Elddri. Well, now that's a name I haven't uttered in ages. Oh, Mr. Cooper, you've found yourself quite the pair," giggled Georger, nodding at our siblings, very alertly.

"Is that the bad that was mentioned?" said Makari.

"Not necessarily, but having mentioned Elddri—well—his trinkets always put the workings of guardians in an entirely new direction...and perspective," said Hullen.

"Be fair with them, Hullen. If Elddri's cube found its way into your path—if what your sister claims is true," said Ordinheir, eyeing Landon.

"It is true," said Makari.

"There's no other way for you, Landon, you must follow the legacy of becoming the Cherished Guardian," said Ordinheir.

"Tell me the purpose of the Cherished Guardian," said Landon.

"As you might've already learned, the country of Revlenion was created to be a place of absolute serenity; a sanctuary to those who detested all prejudices and judgments. A country that could create brave hearts that sought to protect its beauty of equivalence and the divine nature in understanding the acceptance of the star that had so willingly brought them to this realm," said Ordinheir, as she continued, "regrettably, like any ole tale, there came a wave of vile resentment within the kingdom we wholeheartedly admired and so deeply loved. In return, to protect the remnants of our torn home, we sought for the fabled creatures that had already once cured the lands—the Seraphions were without question as passionate as us to rebuild the beauty of Revlenion. So, we collaborated our intelligences, founded the alliance, and pursued the most beautiful minds possible. For nearly two centuries we reigned, suppressing all devious acts against nature, thus forming our ultimate plan—"

"The Cherished Guardian?" said Landon.

"Exactly—but we found that the guardians and their manifestos that we had already conquered could not brave the astronomical demand of being a Cherished Guardian that it so entitled," said Hullen.

"Why not?" Landon forwarded.

"As you see, we three knights are all that's truly left of our original state, as such, with the creation of the Cherished plan, we knew we needed to find the ultimate mind, the ultimate successor, and thusly the crucial individual that could eternally free Revlenion from the ultimate villainy," said Ordinheir.

"It has taken us years, even in our unique afterlife, to find the most precious heart, but of course, the wicked ones had plans of their own that would have us leading ourselves into these marble states," sighed Georger.

"And then, you arrived, just like a knight in some of my absolute favorite tales. What Georger mentioned about the wicked ones, now brings us to the truth in the purpose of the Cherished plan," Ordinheir then cleared her marble throat, "Hullen mentioned before, of a guardian who once stood, right where you stand now, appeared before us—he was no doubt just as charming, wonderfully brave, and yet so uneasy…much like you. But unlike you, his sights were not for the preservation of Revlenion, but instead for its sure downfall."

"What does that guardian have to do with Landon?" Makari rattled.

"That guardian was at the helm of such feared deeds, I care not to recite them in this sacred chamber, but to reveal to you, that he—as I've sensed and dreaded—is on a new, heinous frontier," said Ordinheir.

"Vizton Eplaville?" said Landon, shocked.

"Oh no…Eplaville is only a sad pawn for the feared one that I speak of…and you need not to mention his despicable cipher here," said Ordinheir.

"Are you all aware of Eplaville's recent attack on the Manor?" Jade asked.

"We are, Jade, as it is, we have been continuously trying to track and understand his peculiar motives—they're unlike anything we've seen in his previous trekking. This Eplaville creature may have gained momentum, but he has not a clue in his hollow skull that you three gallant hearts have decided to show," said Ordinheir.

"What's our next move?" said Makari.

"Since your detective friend here has matured a sacred element of his own, we knew Mr. Cooper would be your best suit," said Georger, as Jade then tossed a perplexed stare with his lensed sights at his cane that was clamped in his right hand.

"With his assistance, you must try to elucidate the long equation of you two. Like Georger said, what makes this case so curious is that the Cherished plan in which we speak of, has only ever identified with one person—one guardian—and mysteriously, there are two of you," said Ordinheir. "Because of these unprecedented circumstances, the two of you will have to solve the manifesto, together. Now, it brings me to the point of this meeting where I must speak of something, colossal. What I'll speak of must be upheld at the highest honor—and remember—my fellowships and I will do our best to help you, Landon and Makari, but only if you're truly willing to own your manifesto," said Ordinheir, observing Landon closely. Makari eyed her brother as Landon was overcome with a chill, as though his subconscious was trying to warn him. Makari took Landon by the hand.

"Absolutely," said Landon.

"Since your arrival to Revlenion, has anyone mentioned, the Guardian Manifesto?" said Ordinheir. Makari mouthed those three profound last words under her breath.

"No, please, go on," said Landon.

"It's a declaration for those—like you—must come to exist by. The manifesto is an alignment of six necessary and quite certainly life altering ventures. To our fellowship, it's simply known as the necessity, but to guardian apprentices, it is their manifesto—their guiding principle," said Ordinheir.

"These six ventures, what will they consist?" said Landon.

"They could consist of many concepts, but that's all up to you," continued Ordinheir, "with you, your manifesto began ever so simply with finding its entry with Elddri. First, every maturing manifesto has its allying comrades and first, you will need your Guide: a force who's knowledgeable of Revlenion, and it's many vicinities—"

"—Jade, that has to be you, there's nobody else we can turn to," said Makari.

"—Second," Ordinheir continued, "Landon, a manifesto calls for you to have a Courier; a vigorous being who you must confide all your teachings with as they will assist you throughout your ventures," said Ordinheir.

"M," said Landon, as he quickly eyed his bravely eager sister.

"I'll take that post," nodded Makari.

"As it seems, you three have come well prepared, and as easy as that was, regrettably your six ventures will not. From this day forward, you three must make the promise, the promise to the manifesto, the guardianship, and most of all—Landon, make the promise to yourself," said Ordinheir.

"The feared kind will no doubt make their awful appearances on the path of your manifesto, they have their ways, but your passion is above all the ultimate," said Georger.

"It's been a long, long time since we've spoken of the manifesto to a hopeful apprentice," said Hullen.

"I'm no doubt honored by that," said Landon. "I'll make the promise."

"In the beginning, you asked the inevitable question, 'why,' remember one thing, you brought yourself here Landon, including your sister. From within, you have that guardian-like stem of instinct and that is what brought you here. You opened the Elddri Cube, only true believers of Revlenion's fantasies can accomplish such a task," said Ordinheir.

"Where will his ventures begin?" said Jade.

"Oh, it's quite possible that it began when he and his sister interacted with the cube," said Hullen.

"The question is, where will the ventures lead next?" said Georger.

"Jade, are you familiar with the Realm of the Feuer?" Hullen asked.

"Do you know what he's referring to, Jade?" Landon asked.

"The Feuer?" reminisced Jade, eyeing the plinths. "I actually collected a couple of scrolls about them from the library, right before I went to find you two." Jade then eyed our siblings, "A lot of the same information about their realm kept repeating itself since nobody quite knows where to locate them, but those who have shared their delicate tale, it is said to be the place where manifestos, supposedly, begin."

"Well then, this really will be a test of your comrade's wits, though in your defense Mr. Cooper, true, only a select few know where to find the locale of the Feuer's sentry," said Georger.

"Couldn't you tell us where to find it?" said Landon.

"As much as any one of us would love to, we can not. We're simply vessels for the manifesto and the guardianship—not detective work," said Ordinheir.

"Then, what's the point of even mentioning the Realm?" said Landon.

"I only mentioned it because most guardians before you have ventured into that realm. According to my knowledge, an exquisite item is in the realm and is key in continuing your ventures. However, if you're seeking engrossing information on the realm, you can find that in the aisles of this Manor's library, I'm quite sure you've been there," said Ordinheir.

"Yes, actually," said Landon, tipping his head at Makari.

"I leave you with one last thing, Landon," said Ordinheir, as her fellowship began to slowly solidify, "you see the swan emblem behind me, don't you?"

"Yes," nodded Landon.

"Like I've told every enchanting apprentice that once stood where you stand, I told them to remember that our emblem, no matter how you wear it," hearted Ingrid, as she watched Landon cast a quick gaze over his symbolic armlet, "though it may be the crest of our alliance, ultimately, it's yours to keep. However, with you, my phenomenal guardian, I want you to never forget it. Georger and Hullen might believe in you, but I still sense that oddly curious doubt that resonates inside you. If you believe in yourself through in your manifesto, and hold that image of our symbol in your mind, it will allow you to vanquish the reluctant barrier you hold inside yourself. Remember, no matter how dangerous, no matter how much you might struggle, if you believe in what you accomplish with your manifesto, it will forever heal your hardships. Don't lose sight of your sister or Mr. Cooper, as they are the forces to your light and ventures. There's no turning back Landon, for the rotten creature that's bound, as I've said sensed, he knows…He knows that you're here in Revlenion. I fear that he will stop at nothing to silence your manifesto, but if you believe in what you see right, then you've already won. An absolute honor to speak with you three and should you need us, for whatever reason fit—all you have to do is query."

Ingrid fell silent, along with her fellowship and with only a soft smile on her marble face as a final note to our trio.

Jade and Makari eyed Landon, as he stood at the podium, just as silent as the three marble busts. Suddenly, Landon made a crack in his stance, not giving Jade or his sister another look, but nodding at the sight of the sacred plinths, as they too eyed him on. Landon turned on his heel and led his own way out of the chamber.

▼

The Manor was unusually quiet later that evening and sharing that near silence was our siblings' spare room that our trio had returned to after their meeting with the Ordinheirs. The Manor chef and his gargoylian staff had prepared a dinner for the trio in the room, allowing our three to find a fine table with chairs awaiting them. Makari picked at the few leftovers of red potatoes and sautéed salmon; still clanking the tip of her fork on her dinner plate, contemplating if she should even finish her meal. Jade sat across from Makari, sitting cross-legged, sipping on a glass of white wine, and eyeing Landon's untouched plate.

"Go talk to him," whispered Makari, urging Jade. Landon had skipped dinner entirely. Instead, he retreated to the room's balcony while his sister watched him with his back to her.

"I almost want to leave him alone, allow him to think," Jade whispered back, as he leaned forward in his chair, "we all feel the same. What was said between us and the Ordinheirs was a lot to hear —look at us, we barely touched dinner."

"Please," whispered Makari.

Jade gave a look to Landon, seeing him through the open balcony doors, resting with his elbows on the thick ledge.

"Okay, okay," Jade stood up, leaving his wine glass behind and instead gathered a stem of green grapes in a square cloth and joined Landon on the balcony.

Landon eyed downtown Cappa Valley, ruminating his previous encounter with the Ordinheir, as he scanned the smoking rooftops and the city square that was a bloom like a bucket of stars. Landon never minded the windy chills from the north that swooped his hair and face, except when could then hear Jade's boot heels clapping the stone balcony from behind.

"Whoa," coughed Jade, noticing Landon's sights on the valley below, "a little cold tonight, isn't it?" Landon didn't reply. "Here," Jade placed the wrapped grapes between them on the ledge, "just in case you were hungry." Landon then gave a steady side-eye at the wrapped grapes. "Isn't that a spectacular sight? The entire valley is at our view and so rarely do I take a moment to enjoy the scenery," Jade went on, adjusting his wayfarers, pointing at the splitting clouds that were slowly revealing the beaches that were east of the manor, "see that light there, just beyond the coast, that's the Bartholde statue I told you about. The torch burns all through the night, just incase a fellow reveler loses sight of their way home."

"Are you saying that I'm losing focus for all of this?" said Landon, keeping his eyes on the evening scenery.

"Only if you're choosing to," said Jade.

"I'm…contemplating," said Landon.

"I too did the same…I was so uncertain about circumstances that fell into my path as a youth, but ultimately I realized how much good there was in the unexpected tasks that found me," said Jade.

"Luckily for you, though, you grew up here. You understand its oddities," said Landon.

"That makes not a single difference; you've had the privilege of not only experiencing this country, but also the one you originally come from, Landon, tell me that that's not a gift in its own way," said Jade.

"Ordinheir seemed unsure about me. And as much as I keep asking myself, why are we meant for these expectations?" said Landon.

"Ingrid was harsh with her doubt, I'll agree with you on that, but I am your best witness to the potential you and Makari share. Querying the Ordinheirs is not a game, they provided their best knowledge and when they can sense guardianship, even if Ingrid announced doubt, the three of them still conveyed that you have a manifesto to keep," nodded Jade, "and not just any ole manifesto, but a Cherished Guardian manifesto, at best!" Landon sighed and then finally plucked with his fingers at one of the grapes in the satin cloth. "The time will come, Landon, when you realize you have to stop dwelling in unanswered questions and take the fine risks in exploring the unknown…allow the manifesto and its six ventures to be your start," said Jade.

"I want so much to commit to these ventures, but the idea of allowing Makari to fall into harm's way…I cannot let that happen," sighed Landon, shaking his head. "We're all that's left for each other."

"The greater harm would be turning your back on the manifesto," said Jade, as then tilted, "what do you mean by 'all that's left'?" said Jade.

"It'll be a year on my birthday, since Makari and I lost our parents…we were on our way home from the cinema, after watching a movie that I so insisted that we see that night," Landon then gulped a deep breath, "we lived only a few blocks away from downtown, and while we walked our way home from the theater, we suddenly got caught in a storm that mercilessly swept through the town in just minutes. My mom and dad suddenly became urgent and told Makari and me to race back to our house without them. The next moment, I could hear screams while the most horrifying…and I mean horrifying storm abruptly swept our street while our parents fell trapped outside…I did my best to save them, I really did…I tried opening our front door, but the billowing storm wouldn't allow me. It was as though something was keeping me from opening it. The moment the storm subsided was when I thought I could rescue my mom and dad…but it was too late…they were…" Landon stopped for a second, swallowing another gulp of thick air again, not caring to wipe away the heavy beads of tears that began to line the sides of his face. "How could something like that happen to us, why couldn't I let them back in?"

Makari then suddenly appeared beside her brother (who had been listening to the entire conversation from behind the balcony wall) taking hold of his hand that had been grasping the balcony ledge.

"I'm…very sorry…I…can't even imagine losing someone you love, so very dearly, and you both are so young," Jade sighed, "I never had parents of my own, and I grew up wondering, where in this universe did I come from?"

"Questioning the unknown in Revlenion awakens the same questions I have for the unknown that stole our parents," said Landon.

"The unknown, I agree, must be treated with caution, but there is one thing that is certain, we must face it, as there will always be truth at the end of the road," said Jade.

"You're just like us," said Makari.

"I guess so," said Jade, "I struggled to find the guidance I needed, but I found it in the Cappa family and friends who were gracious enough to take me in as one of their own and teach me necessities when I was very young, but when you're an abandoned kid like me, your soul seems almost...unbound."

"Free, you mean?" said Landon.

"Exactly, because I've never known where I came from, I was just a bad kid in the wind," nodded Jade. "You two, however, know where you come from, and you need only to remember that. My unknown left me stirring for answers, much like you two are now—I get it. However, you have guidance once again, I'll be here for the both of you."

"I knew there was something different about you and them, well, the Cappas," said Makari.

"What do you mean?" asked Jade.

"This manor, the austerity that comes with it...it really doesn't seem like you at all," said Makari.

"True, but the manor and I have a complicated history together," smiled Jade, "it's some of the people that thrive within it that are very much like me. It's the role that I've had to take on for the R.C.C. that makes me so formal. And I hate it, to be honest. I can't break the tiring etiquette that doesn't allow me to be, well, me...the detective that I am trying to be.

"The Cappas have that much control over you?" asked Landon.

"No, it's the R.C.C.," said Jade, "but never mind them, as it seems, we're on to greater things and I believe that this manifesto is sure to be promising...whatever its solution might be."

"Let's face whatever force the Ordinheirs say wants to come after us, we'll fight it together, right Landon?" cheered Makari, poking a smile out of her brother.

Jade then led Landon and Makari back into the bedroom, closing the balcony doors behind them.

"There's really no turning back?" said Landon, eyeing Jade.

"You can't turn away from your own manifesto. The Ordinheirs have said it to be and then that is the way," said Jade, as he quickly spun around at the sound of the bedroom door bursting open.

"Jade, I—" Ms. Qwara noticed she had either startled or interrupted the trio's conversation.

"—What's wrong?" insisted Jade.

"I," Qwara realized she was still grasping the bedroom door, "I must speak with you three in confidence."

Ms. Qwara closed the door behind her and then took a seat at the dinner table in the middle of the room; Landon and Makari quickly noticed how extremely alarmed she looked.

"Lewa, please tell us what's wrong," said Jade, again.

"Something very—no—absolutely dreadful has happened—a St. Madeline's student has been found—" said Qwara, trying.

"—Found how, exactly?" Jade worried.

"Slain in the West Royal Pine…beheaded," panted Qwara. "Three R.C.C. members arrived with the news, just minutes ago. I was with the Cappas when they broke the news, but I knew I had to meet with you three as soon as possible and to ask you two," said Qwara, darting looks at Landon and Makari.

"Us—what do you want to know?" Landon shook, as his sister took hold of his hand.

"Did you meet a young girl by the name of Britta Terry, today?" said Qwara.

"Yes, she—she was with the Holbrook brothers when they tricked us into entering the West Pines, but they ditched us once we entered the forest," said Landon. "We never saw her again."

"That's odd, she wasn't joined with the Holbrooks when I bumped into them in front of Dingoduns this afternoon," said Jade. "What does this have to do with Landon and Makari?"

"A very cautious note was left with her body, signed…by Vizton Eplaville," said Qwara. "The note said, that because of Landon and Makari, the girl could no longer live."

"We did nothing to her," said Makari, slowly clamping a hand over her mouth. "Could that scroll you found on one of the Holbrooks be connected to this?"

"It certainly might," shivered Jade.

"The R.C.C. doesn't care, Jade. They're threatening to cease this case, all together," said Qwara. "To them, everything is getting out of control—"

"—Ms. Qwara! Ms. Qwara! Can you hear me?" Antoine's voice popped out from a tiny speaker in Lewa's chrome wristwatch, startling the group.

"Y-yes Antoine, I hear you loud and clear. I've come to the ninth floor to collect Jade," replied Qwara, while pressing a tiny button on her watch.

Landon and Makari knew her watch had to be some unique version of a Trans-Oidar.

"After you retrieve Jade, please come to the R.C.C. courtroom and leave the Tuolumnes to their room; a guard should be at the ready nearby should they need any assistance. And please, hold off sharing any news on the recent happenings with Jade or the children," Antoine's tenacious voice popped again through the tiny speaker on the watch.

Our trio quickly eyed one another.

"Yes sir, of course, I will be seeing Jade shortly," said Qwara, speaking into her watch again.

"Thank you, please hurry—over!" Antoine's crackling voice disappeared.

"So much for keeping that a secret," said Makari.

"It couldn't be kept from either of you, especially after the circumstances of your recent meeting with the Ordinheirs—I know how important the manifesto is to you three and this foul Eplaville must be stopped," darted Qwara.

"What do we do?" said Landon.

"Well, you heard Antoine, Jade and I have to return to the R.C.C. courtroom, a guard is at the ready near the end of the hall," said Qwara.

"You expect us to stay here, alone?" exclaimed Landon.

"This room is one of the safest in the Manor. No foul-intending being can make entry into this room unless you invite it in," Qwara pointed at the bedroom door, "that door is made of rosewood and its magnificent properties is a shield against all uninvited entities."

"Perfect then, you two remain here," said Jade, with a forwarded nod. "Let me meet with the Cappas and I'll return as soon as possible, I promise."

"Okay," said Landon.

"You've got a manifesto to fulfill and I'm not going to allow the R.C.C. or Eplaville to stop it," said Jade, as he pulled his coat over his shoulders and exited the room behind Qwara. Landon and Makari could hear the fast heels of Jade and Qwara clapping down to the end of the hall, until only the stillness of the air began to ring in their ears. Our brave siblings then turned to one another, realizing how quiet their room had suddenly become.

It was nearing nine o'clock that same evening, and Jade had already been gone for over one hour. Makari found herself periodically reading the face of the noticeably loud clock that left her somewhat anxious, ticking loudly above the wardrobe. In the meantime, she flipped through useless pages of an oversized book she had seized from the bookshelf beside her bed. Landon was fairly quiet from across the room, lying back on the bed while humming the chorus to David Bowie's Starman a few times over. And as he did, he reread and twirled the torn page (having kept it safe in his right shoe all day) from the metal book Martin Winter had shown them from the night before and still hoped that it would somehow reveal a new clue.

"I wonder what would happen if I just folded this into a paper plane, and let it zoom right off the balcony...maybe then someone else could figure out what this damn passage means," said Landon.

"Don't you dare," said Makari, darting a stern look at her brother. "As many times as you keep twirling that page, it's not going to change for you."

244

"Well, here's hoping," said Landon, eyeing the page closely.

"It might've lost its enchantments after you tore it out of that book," said Makari, slamming her oversized book shut. "Ugh, these books are dreadful and completely useless, there's nothing about the Manor or Revlenion in any one of them…just poems and sonnets about sad lovers—what's wrong, Lan?"

Makari eyed her alert brother after he suddenly sat up.

"Did you hear that?" said Landon, as he eyed the bare marble wall behind him.

"No—Oh, Landon please don't play any of your scary games, now," begged Makari, sighing.

"I'm not kidding," darted Landon, continuing to eye the wall behind him as a crackling sound emanated from within the thick wall. Another unsettling, crackly sound happened again. "There, just then, did you hear that?"

"I—I did…I'm going to get the guard," panted Makari, nearly springing from her bed.

"No…wait, M," gasped Landon, as he then stood on his bed, pressing his left ear against the cold wall.

"Do you hear anything again?" whispered Makari.

The wall along the bedroom door suddenly began to rattle and roll with the sound of a dozen loud and unsettling cracks.

The wall stopped rumbling and instead the bedroom door rattled with two heavy raps. Landon and Makari then darted their startled eyes at the rosewood door.

"You answer it," said Makari, cringing.

Landon, steady, jumped from his bed and slowly made his way to the door, noticing that his sister had armed herself with the oversized book above her head. Landon reached for a silver vase on a small table next to the door before opening it.

"On three, M," whispered Landon, as he reached for the doorknob, bracing himself.

One…two.

The bedroom door swung open…nothing. Landon then darted

two quick looks down either end of the hallway, noticing the elevator guard standing with a drowsy fidget.

"Look, look!" said Makari, pointing at a wrapped object that had been plopped before the door's threshold. Landon quickly picked up the heavy parcel that had only a small note pinned to it:

"There's a note, with initials for...L and M," said Landon, as he closed the bedroom door softly.

Landon then unpinned the note and pulled back the leather cloth that wrapped it while Makari took hold of the note that had been written in charcoal:

I did my best to save it.
My favorite childhood
tale is on page 472.
-Helpfully Yours-

Landon and Makari quickly realized what possession Helpfully Yours had managed to save.

"It's the book Martin found for us, or at least what's left of it," sparked Makari, as her brother began to slowly turn through its shredded and burned pages.

"And again, this Helpfully Yours, person...why keep helping us?" said Landon.

"Be gentle with it," said Makari, as she helped Landon hold the heavy book by its broken spine. "Still, look at us though, we keep taking the help."

"Page four hundred and seventy-two, please?" said Landon, asking the book to summon the page.

The book's pages flipped slowly, as if its magnificent workings knew it had been sorely beaten. The book still did its mystic job though, pitifully this time around for our siblings. Finally whipping to the page, four hundred and seventy-two, and there, with a red-charcoaled circle around the chapter title The Carousel Torch.

Most of the chapter could not be read, but only a sliver of

words seemed to matter, anyway. Another red circle had been drawn on the page in the book around a few spared lines of the chapter:

...the fire protects.
It guards and guides the beginnings of all ventures...

"The fire protects?" said Landon, reading the sentence again.

"Landon, the chapter title says it all...Bartholde's Torch, what other torch could it be?" noted Makari.

"You're right, but that statue...is just a statue," said Landon. "If it were anything else, I'm sure Jade would've said something about it."

"He must not know exactly what it is," said Makari.

"It could be a doorway of some sorts, but even if it is," said Landon.

"Has to be where the realm is and whatever key the Ordinheirs spoke of. The connection is there, read that last line again," said Makari, pointing at the burned sentences.

"Beginnings of all ventures," recited Landon.

"Well—we can wait here or find the proof for our manifesto. This is our chance to show Ordinheir that we can stand for ourselves in Revlenion," said Makari.

"This is our venture, obviously someone wants to help us solve it," said Landon, "and I'm ready."

After a few minutes of exchanging strategizes of how they would get to the Manor Vestibule where the torch stood, Landon and Makari had two choices: escape the bedroom by climbing over the balcony ledge and scale the exterior of the Manor walls—or— somehow convince the guard at the end of the hall to escort themselves to the torch.

"I like our second choice better, Landon," said Makari, as she peered over their ninth-floor balcony after tightening back her hair with her green ribbon.

"Come on," said Landon, as he heaved the metal book under his arm and led the way to the bedroom door.

Landon cracked open the bedroom door; the fidgety guard was still settled beside the elevator doors and slowly nodding off to sleep. Landon led the way down the hall as Makari crept behind her brother, keeping eye on their trail as they approached the guard.

"Excuse me," said Landon, startling the guard awake.

"I-I-Ah…you two," mumbled the Guard, "return to your room at once!"

"Please, sir, if you could do us a favor," Landon asked.

"Young man," the Guard pounded his golden scepter against the floor, "there are no favors to be attended to, other than me guarding this floor."

"We're very grateful, but you see, we need to get to the Manor Vestibule and—" Landon tried.

"—Young man, again, you need not get to anywhere now, please, return to your room," ordered the Guard, again.

"What's your name?" asked Makari, softly.

"I said—Uh…Jimmy," said Jimmy the Guard.

"How about this, Jimmy, you could escort my brother Landon and me to the Manor Vestibule yourself, and you would still be adhering to your duties," said Makari.

"I…Ah—Herrmmf," Jimmy actually thought it over, carefully, before boasting into another order, while Landon and Makari inched their way closer to the elevator door.

"Sound like a decent plan?" bartered Makari, as Landon then backed up against the elevator buttons. The metal edge of the heavy book under Landon's arm poked the down arrow, sending the doors to slide open.

"I SAID!" Jimmy grabbed hold of Landon by the hair, managing to slide halfway into the elevator cab, and so very quickly did everything else happen next

Makari shrieked at the sight of Jimmy howling at Landon for trying to escape into the elevator and with a simple thought of stopping Jimmy from attacking her brother anymore, Makari slapped Jimmy across the face. A burst of a quick blue light rendered Jimmy in a semi-conscious state, sending Jimmy's thick body to collapse outside of the elevator while Landon stood anchored with awe and his hair in upright twists.

"Oh…no," sighed Makari, as Jimmy moaned and giggled on floor.

"You're unbelievable, M," Landon gaped.

"Is he…dead? What's wrong with me?" said Makari, as she eyed her hands. "I didn't want to kill him."

"Calm down, you didn't kill 'em" said Landon, as he stood over Jimmy.

"H-h-helllllooo!" giggled Jimmy, startling our siblings with his sudden spring. "H-h-helllllooo!"

"I think you just made Jimmy outright clueless," said Landon.

"D-d-dooo-a-dooo-dooo! Do you know where I can—? Ha ha!" laughed Jimmy, still tossing on the floor.

"We need to hurry before his screaming gets us stopped. Here, help me drag him into the elevator," said Landon, as he tossed the metal book inside the elevator cab.

"Ah! Ah! The vicious lagoon beasts have me by my boots! Help! Ha ha ha!" roared Jimmy, as Landon and Makari dragged the thick guard into the elevator with them.

"He's lost his mind," said Landon, as he clicked a silver button to the Manor Vestibule.

"Yeeeeee! I love circus rides! Aaaaah!" screamed Jimmy, with glee, as the elevator doors shut and the shaft began to descend.

"What are we going to do with him?" said Makari, turning to Jimmy, slugged against the elevator cab wall. "No! Jimmy, let go!"

Jimmy was ripping pages out of the metal book like a giant toddler; laughing and screaming at every rip he made on the valuable book.

"No! It's mine I say, mine!" screamed Jimmy, as Landon tried to pry the metal book from Jimmy's hands.

"Let go!" screeched Makari, as she again struck Jimmy across the face with her palm.

"I think you really did him in this time," worried Landon, as Jimmy fell limp.

"Ugh, Jimmy," sighed Makari, eyeing the elevator floor that was covered with torn pages. "He's made the book worse, Landon, look at it."

"We're lucky for the second time now," said Landon, checking Jimmy closely for any sign of life. "He's not dead."

TING!

Our brave siblings and the absent-minded Jimmy had now arrived to the Manor Vestibule. The Bartholde Torch was their first sight as the elevator doors then slid open. Makari gathered and stuffed the torn pages back into the metal book as Landon took a few steps out of the elevator.

"What are we going to do with the man-baby?" said Makari, eyeing the bear-snoring Jimmy.

"Leave him," said Landon, "if and when someone finds him, we'll be honest and explain—there's no turning back now." Landon then eyed the colossal statue again, still ominously burning as it did when he and Makari had first approached it earlier that day. The elevator doors slowly slid shut and hummed as it ascended somewhere within the Manor.

Landon and Makari then walked toward the burning sculpture and as they did, a pack of footsteps began to echo from the upper stairwell behind them. The siblings spun swiftly on their heels and dived to the ground behind the sculpture when Mr. Varick, a Manor Guard and a short gargoylian Manor Executive marched closely near. Landon anxiously waited for the three men to disappear beyond an archway before directing the next move.

"Are they gone?" whispered Makari, tossing a look around the vestibule.

"Yes—all right, M, what's the next step?" said Landon, as Makari then splashed the thick metal book onto the ledge of the sculpture's pool.

"Hopefully this book will still answer us," Makari frowned, as she tried to piece together the numberless pages.

"Ask it about the Realm of the Feuer," insisted Landon, keeping watch of the surrounding archways.

"Please give me a tale about the Realm of the Feuer," ordered Makari, eyeing the metal book.

The stack of torn pages then began to perturbed shuffle into the air like a deck of playing cards and swirled around our siblings until the pages suddenly slammed back into its metal case on the ledge.

At the bottom of the following page from the tale of The Carousel Torch, another red circle had been drawn around a new collection of words:

...the faces of victory answer only to
the calling of the Architect of Venture Keys, Monte Nicollet...

"Our helpful fellow has already planned our next move," said Makari, pointing at the circled passage.

"The 'faces of victory' and 'Monte Nicollet' have been circled," said Landon, then tossing a gaze up at the towering sculpture. Landon then walked away from his sister, eyeing one of the open-mouthed face fountains. Landon gazed ever so calculatingly into one of the faces on the giant sculpture, almost waiting for an idea to burn into his mind. "The faces of victory...I remember Jade used that exact phrase earlier today."

Makari stood, snatching up the metal book as she did and rounded the sculpture's ledge until she stood facing the twin face on the opposite side of the pool.

"These are the faces," said Makari. "I got it, the Architect's name is a code—it has to be."

Landon and Makari then simultaneously jumped onto the ledge and put their clues to the test, staring up at the portentous faces.

"Monte..." said Landon, hoping.

"...Nicollet," said Makari, gasping.

The stem of the torch suddenly began to drone; sputtering and jolting into full motion like a giant car motor being ignited for the first time in decades. Spinning slowly like an old circus carousel, the torch began to rise further into the air and still burning ever so magnificently. Landon and Makari walked along the ledge of the pool until they met, watching the two giant faces reach higher into the air and that still incessantly spouted their heavy streams of water. The torch then came to a halt, revealing a small door in its stem. A trail of bubbles leading to the center stem then began to pop on the surface of the pool, cueing Landon and Makari to brace for whatever was about to reveal itself from the dark waters. It wasn't a monster or some other water creature that had risen from the pool, instead, it was an ascending row of three pewter hands that erected from out of the water. Landon and Makari eyed the large trio of curled palms, knowing that there was no other way of crossing the dark pool.

"Those look...terrifying," said Makari, eyeing the eroded hands.

"Come on, we need to move fast," said Landon, about to make the first step. Landon gave a brisk jump from the ledge onto the first pewter hand, another steady leap higher to the second, and finally to the final hand before the secret door. "Hurry, but be careful, M."

Makari was still holding onto the metal book and then placed it under her arm as she then gave a quick jump. To the second hand, Makari jumped, she kept steady once more, and then to the last hand-step. Makari had made it, standing next to her brother on the final step.

"That wasn't so bad," said Landon, as the first hand-step then suddenly began to sink back into the pool.

Landon eyed for a doorknob or handle to open the door in the stem. Landon then found a small crevasse in the door and pulled it until the metal door rotated open.

"What do you see in there?" said Makari.

"There's a narrow staircase," said Landon, hearing echoes of dripping water deep within the stem. "No telling how far it goes down—Hurry, jump in!" Landon and Makari gave each other grave looks and made their way through the door as the hand-steps slowly continued to sink back into their blackened pool.

Our brave siblings held tight on to the metal railings of the spiraling metal staircase that followed fast, as they continued to descend further and further into the underground core of the Manor. Only the massive bowl of fire from the torch above our siblings was able to torrent light down the long channel of wet stairs. The further Landon and Makari descended the narrow staircase they could both feel thin streams of cold run-off from the fountain above trickle and splash on and around them. Finally, the staircase ceased and led to an archway that opened like a giant mouth full of jagged rock.

Landon and Makari entered the vast, granite cave following their long stone path between the two darkly ocean blue streams rushing somewhere deeper into the cave over beds of fallen rock. The siblings eyed the cave closely, surrounded by the mixture of fashioned stone and the mining lamps that hung throughout; the room seemed like it was some sort of incomplete shrine. It was all a marvel that had been found between mounds of fallen stone, but the true spectacle of the rocky hollow was at the end of the siblings' path amongst a bed of rock where something gleamed against the mossy green light above it.

"What is that?" Makari hummed, as she followed her brother to the center of the cave. Our siblings kept at a measured pace as they approached two slanted sheets of polished rock forked amongst a circular bed of crackling embers. Makari brushed her cheeks, feeling a slithering draft of heat bounce across her freckled face. As Landon and Makari adjusted their eyes on the polished slabs of granite, our siblings quickly realized what sort of place they had actually barged. "I believe we're in somebody's tomb," cringed Makari.

Monte Nicollet
The maker of marvels
October 1, 1766 — February 22, 1788

~

Olanna Nicollet
Forever marveled and bound to eternity of peace

CHAPTER FOUR

November 23, 1737 — February 22, 1788

Landon and Makari then fixed their eyes on the gleaming green sea-glass key resting in the granite basin anchored between the two slanted headstones.

"A key, of course, Ordinheir was actually helping us," said Landon, as he eyed the lone glass key in the stone basin. "Ingrid knew exactly what we would find down here." Landon then made a steady move, preparing to seize the grave's ornament.

"Wait, Lan, we can't just take it," said Makari, halting her brother's move.

"After all that?" detested Landon, gesturing back at their trail. "You're going to second guess the entire plan?"

"It's just too simple and cruel to take something that's not ours to begin with, let alone steal it from a grave," Makari cringed. "What if that key was the last treasure these two people ever had to cherish?"

"M, it hasn't been simple, not once. Ordinheir tossed us a hint of what we would find in here—sure she might've left out the odd specifics, but ultimately that key must have some sort of significance," said Landon.

"I just hope you're right," said Makari, taking hold of her brother's hand. Landon then positioned himself at just the right angle as he then reached over the radiant embers and drove his hand at the glass key.

It was at that exact moment, when a charcoaled hand that was nearly exposed to the bone exploded out from the hot embers and gripped the lip of the basin with all its might.

Landon lugged his hand back just at the right second, and with doing so, he sent himself toppling backward to the stone floor along with his sister. Our siblings were no longer engulfed with the odd radiance of the grave, but fell overcome with dread as a horribly burned and disfigured man pulled himself out of his ember pool. Our siblings felt more helpless than ever, as two more badly charred

254

figures crawled out from the grim embers. The three men stood barefoot in their burning pool; suited in vests and mixed suits that were as badly torched and charred like most of their bodies. It was an absolute ghastly sight: Makari noticed that all of the men were so badly burned that patches of their faces exposed layers of muscle and for two of them, half their charcoal stained skulls could be seen. The three ashy, burned suited men twisted and snapped their backs back into shape and popping out knots of hot coal as they did. Landon and Makari fixed their sights on the three beings, just as they did onto them with their sunken and scorched eyes.

"Ve could smell your fresh flesh zat dares to come so near our ember nest," one of the fiery creatures spoke, with a heavy German accent, as Landon knew it to be. "I am Pyron, eldest guardian and ze brother of ze Feuer, anz you must be some obtrusive follower of ze Ordinheir…did I guess right?"

One of Pyron's brothers then hurdled from the burning pool, clapping his bony toes against the granite floor, and creepily hunched toward Landon and Makari. Our siblings quickly jumped to their feet; Makari held close to her brother as both kept a steady eye on the fat and taunting creature that began to slowly circle them.

"Schön euch zu treffen," trembled Landon, in German, as he then returned close sights on the three fiery men with a nod. Just as Makari was blithely astounded by her brother's sudden familiarity of another language, the three German brothers were taken aback by Landon's introductory retort for only a few seconds more. However, unknown to Makari and the Feuer brothers, Landon had quite the catalog of jumbled German words and phrases that had been forever engraved, deep within his memory.

In his mind, playing out like some bad home movie, Landon could see his scrawny, eight-year-old self, sitting patiently for class to begin (unlike his hilariously obnoxious friend, Troy Fox, whom always found it necessary to slingshot thumbtacks with a rubber band at the back of one of the Kaprielian twins) in the second row, and sixth desk to left of his irritable, third-grade teacher, Mrs. Bennett. Every day, before the regular schedules of History, Math, or Geography lessons began, the gravelly voiced teacher would find the time for her class to memorize and recite together words or phrases that were said around the world.

"And how do we say, nice to meet you, in German?" croaked Mrs. Bennett.

"Schön euch zu treffen," Landon and his class echoed, stuttering on the accent halfway through the sentence. Mrs. Bennett could never get her fidgety students to say it together, perfectly.

However, Landon sure got it right.

"BOY!" barked Pyron, "should I allow you to return to your vonderable dreamscape or are you going to anzwer my question?"

"What?" Landon asked, spacey.

"Did a sveet teacher of yourz show you how to say zhat little line of German?" Pyron giggled.

"I bet she did," hissed Klork, the fattest brother of the three men, "did she ever teach you zis one, wir hassen kindern!"

Landon hadn't a clue what the creature hissed at him in German, but from watching the three men then toss rounds of chuckles, he knew it couldn't be pleasant.

"Nov, vhere vere ve?" grinned Pyron.

"Zhey are Ordinheir cveatures, they vere trying to steal father's prize," urged Erne, the thinnest brother of the three. "Must be, or else zhey wouldn't have ever found us."

"Oh yes…are you two nasty cveatures followers of ze Ordinheir?" Pyron barked.

"What if I said yes?" challenged Landon, eyeing Pyron again.

"Dass vould make you nothing more than ze thief," said Pyron.

"Ve don't like thieves in our father's tomb, no sirree!" Erne hooted. The other torched brother, Klork, standing next to Pyron then joined his fat brother, hissing and ogling at our petrified siblings.

"Move out of ze vay, Erne, let me get a good look a zhese thieves," said Klork.

"Vhy are you here?" growled Erne, snatching Landon by the

collar. Landon couldn't be spared the moment Erne poked his nearly incinerated nose close to his, having to smell creature's burned flesh. "Answer uz!" Erne clamped his bare bone fingers around Landon's face. Landon couldn't help it; slowly rolling his eyes from the mad creature to the gleaming glass key in the basin only a few paces away.

"Ah, ze thief indeed," chimed Pyron. "Ze Ordinheirs seem to be heightening zheir odds zhese days. Ve've met dozens of brave young men and vomen in our lives, but never…children, and vhat a brilliant addition to zhe deathly repertoire," grinned Pyron.

"We're not thieves!" Landon shouted.

"Then tell us vhy you have entered our realm!" ordered Pyron.

"We're simply on an operation," panted Landon, after Erne loosened his grip around his neck so he could speak more clearly, "to find a k-key of sorts that could lead us to our next phase in—"

"—Your manifesto?" Pyron chimed.

"Y-yes…" said Landon, surprised.

"Vhat traitor did you have to come by to obtain zhe location of our vonderful abode?" said Pyron.

Landon hesitated.

"My brother asked you a qvestion," snarled Erne, reinforcing his boney grip on Landon.

"Vho told you?" asked Pyron, again.

"We didn't go to anybody—we found it all on our own and the clues of where to find you and the token of the realm," said Makari.

"He vasn't asking you—you little, red headed mutt!" snapped Klork, snatching Makari by her hair.

"Leave her alone!" hollered Landon, trying to barge Erne's tight hold.

"Now, now, little thief—you mustn't tryz to budge," cackled Erne.

"You two found us on your own?" Pyron chuckled, as his brother Klork then closely whispered into his singed ear.

"*Look at the mark on their arms…*" warned Klork.

Pyron squinted through the boiled haze across his dead eyes until he fumed with tiny embers sprouting out from his nose in a show of distaste.

"Children with not a clue of vhat they wear, why am I not surprised? Say what you will, but I don't believez you did it all on your own. My brothers and I vere born in this realm, hovever ve know vhat a great deal it must be in finding uz, and it seems as though you have succeeded up until zhis point. You should really investigate your *clues* more closely next time, there's no telling vhere your little hints might send you."

"Gim'me!" Klork tried to yank the metal book out from Makari's tight grip as he held a firm lock on her head of hair.

"OW! NO!" cried Makari, constricted around the book.

"Meine liebe," Pyron cleared his throat, after speaking in German again, "my brother Klork simply vanted to see the book you seem to be holding onto ever so tightly...as if the book depended on you for life. Does zit?" Teary-eyed Makari glared at Pyron, hoping he wouldn't ask any more about the book. "Vould that book have anything to do vith your hunt for our realm here?" asked Pyron, pointing with a singed finger at Makari. Klork then shoved Makari to the ground, finally ripping the book out of her hands. The mad creature then flipped viciously through the metal bound pages, growing incensed over the amount of blank pages.

"Vhat kind of book is this?" barked Klork, frustrated and then tossed the heavy novel back at Makari on the ground and showering her with the shredded pages from before.

"Stop, please—I'll make a deal with you," pleaded Landon. Pyron then darted his eyes closely at Landon.

"A deal? Shpeak," hummed Pyron.

"I'll tell you exactly how we managed to find your realm and the true purpose of that book," bargained Landon.

"In exchange for vhat?" glared Pyron.

"You let me and my sister go free, unharmed, and I promise that we'll never return to your realm only if you first tell us the importance of that key," bartered Landon. "I can tell you this much, there's extraordinary magic within that book. There's more to that book than the words that can come from it, and if you know how to use it, you'll be able to forever prevent any more thieves from invading your precious realm." The three brothers then exchanged quick looks, and then each agreed with a nod.

"Ve'd be free of ever having to vorry again about thieves stealing father's key, Pyron," urged Erne.

"The book will tell how to prevent that exactly—it'll make you three kings above all other guards," said Landon, nodding amiably at the three men. Makari caught a sense of a small connection of thought and emotion from Landon as he quickly darted a look at her. Makari kept to the floor, hoping not to anger Klork and instead gathered the tossed pages off the cave floor.

"Kings… Ich mag die idee," said Pyron, finishing in German, again.

"Do we have a deal?" said Landon, as Erne kept a close eye on him.

"Never have ve shpoken of our master to any other living soul," said Pyron.

"I'm listening," said Landon.

"There have been countless myths that have shrouded our father's vork, but only ve know the truth," said Pyron, as he began to pace around his ember nest, and noticeably, not one ounce of pain was shed. "Monte Nicollet vas a young, aspiring inventor and the originator of the Venture Keys; known to be a direct link and the first, true stride in all of zhe Ordinheir manifestos. Dis key will allow you to access and set forth zhe Hallvays of Quinn, vhere vithin those halls, it is said that a follower of a manifesto will meet zhe true purpose of their own manifesto—and since our father vas the originator of the keys…he vas the sole maker of zem. Through zhe years, apprenticing guardians have tried and failed at seeking our father's last key, and those very few vretched guardians dared to make counterfeits. Little did zhe guardians know, that by presenting a counterfeit to the keeper of the Hallvays of Quinn, vould forever ban that guardian, even if they one day returned vith the authentic one, thus ceasing their manifesto with the Ordinheirs for eternity.

Here our father rests, alongside his very last key. I remember vhen that basin shined full vith our father's most cherished creations, but unfortunately, they vere stolen from our realm, and to be never seen again."

"That's the very last one..." sighed Landon.

"Zhe very last...and shpeaking of...I hope this will be zhe last time I ever see you two down here," warned Pyron.

"However could ve be so sure about that, if ve just let them go?" giggled Erne.

"There's no telling if you'll return vith more filthy guardians, like yourselves," said Klork. "More othervorldly treasures sleep within our realm...treasures no man haz ever dreamed existed!"

"My brothers have a point, I might have just made the mistake of telling you the truth of zhe Venture Key...looks like ve're going to have to let you vatch each other burn below zhe embers after all," cackled Pyron, tapping his bony fingertips together, darting his scorched sights on our siblings.

"Wait, the deal was to let us go, I'll keep my word—my sister and I will never return. You need to keep your word," said Landon.

"I almost vant to believe that you'll never return, but I can smell zhe atrocious manifesto all over you. Even for a child, you're not like the other guardians that I've had the pleasure of disfiguring," said Pyron. "There's something strange that lingers about you... something zhat tells me zhat you wont ever stop."

"Oh, let me scorch that handsome face—RIGHT OFF!" laughed Erne, pinching Landon's face.

"You'll have your fun, Erne, but I vant to know the mechanisms of our new book first, as goes the deal," said Pyron.

"Makari, tell them, tell them how the book works," said Landon, with a small hum in his voice.

"Awe, yes, little mutt-Makari, please tell us hov ze book vorks," giggled Klork, as Makari then followed along with the deal.

"As phenomenal as your father was, this book will be just that," sniffled Makari, wiping away angry tears as she flipped the book open on the cave floor.

"I'll be the judge of zhat," said Pyron.

"All you have to do is place the book in front of you and ask it a question, but remember to ask it only the best, for it will give you the answer," said Makari.

"Wunderbar! Go on, Klork, ask it a question, and please use the best side of vhat's left of your boiled mind," cackled Pyron.

"Give me," snapped Klork, snatching the book into his charred hands. "A book that gives you the answer?" Klork mocked Makari once more, before sensing the pressure of his brothers to ask the book a question. Pyron stood anxiously awaiting his brother to summon a question from the marvelous book. "Ugh, fine," Klork eyed his audience as a question simply popped into his skull. Klork gazed into the blank pages in front of him and asked, "How do you kill a guardian?"

Like clockwork, the metal book sprang to life flipping a few pages ahead, abiding by the fiery creature's morbid question. Pyron and Erne could hardly believe their scorched eyes, "Vell, vhat does it say?" Pyron cried with vicious awe, as Landon and Makari yearned for the book's answer. Unlike his brothers, Klork was unimpressed, and seemingly confused, as he then read aloud what the book had conjured for him.

"'My vords arc for only ze Cherished Guardian…not beasts," Klork recited, eyeing his audience again, "Who ze hell is ze Cherished Guardian?"

"I am," said Landon, cracking a smile across his face. At the exact moment the three Feuer Guards darted Landon with bitter sights, our brave boy then simply replied, "Auf Wiedersehen…"

And then so unexpectedly the next.

BANG!

The metal book exploded a misty, turquoise ball of force from its core, jetting Klork's skeletal body through the air. The metal book flew into Makari's hands, quickly jumping to her feet. Klork contorted and squealed so inhumanly as he thrashed amongst the jagged rocks, feeling his body extinguish as the fountain's run-off streamed over him.

Pyron and Erne watched in horror as their brother disintegrated before them, losing their closely guarded sights on our siblings. Landon acted fast, slamming his shoe heel onto Erne's foot and shattering his bony toe ends to pieces. Erne lost his skeletal grip of Landon and tumbled over, whirling on the ground completely unable to stand. Landon dashed toward the ember nest, diving a hand at the glass key in the basin. Suddenly, Landon felt an invisible cold string rush up his left arm when he finally held onto the Venture Key for the very first time.

Pyron then gripped Landon's left arm with such terrible force. Landon held onto the key as tightly as he could, even baring the monstrous burning pain that Pyron slowly laced around his arm.

"I must admit, your deal vas rather clever, but I've grown tired of this post my father bore me into, and previously, I had already made a deal with another being, a rather darkly creature like myself, and in that deal, it vas promised to me that I vould no longer have to live in a vorld vhere appalling childkren like you can valk so freely," gritted Pyron, tightening his singeing grip on Landon. Landon roared with agony, as he actually could smell his own flesh slowly burning. "Down vith the manifesto and long live ze Dark Alman!"

Landon then suddenly felt sick to his stomach and then ever so quickly, the pain that was once grasped around his arm miraculously ceased. Landon suddenly succumbed to his thoughts and began to conjure a magnificent idea somewhere deep within his mind. Landon darted his eyes at Pyron and then back to the two rushing streams, apprehending the idea that the rushing streams could lift out of their rocky beds and fall upon Pyron.

The next moment, Landon kept a strong focus, not on the laughing Pyron, but on the two towering streams that began to lift off of the jagged rocks. Makari had no idea what was going on as she kept her distance from Erne who crawled toward her, cursing at her. Pyron then followed Landon's focused eyes on the wall of water that was aimed at them.

"Landon!" screamed Makari, as the two streams collided in midair and came plunging down upon the ember bed. Pyron howled at the watery sight, letting go of Landon as he darted toward his sister. The ember grave ignited into a globe of ashy steam as Pyron and Erne disappeared into their watery graves. Landon and Makari's hands met, and together they charged back toward the staircase as they made their escape. Landon had lost focus of his own lethal wall of water in the immediate escape and in return, the wall of water was now in pursuit of him and his sister.

Our siblings lost their footing midway up the staircase as the water suddenly engulfed them. Landon was still hand in hand with Makari and the last Venture Key, as the raging stream of water rushed them up the stem of the torch. Landon and Makari's bodies twisted and twirled in the watery current, and so unfortunate as it could be, Makari realized she was no longer holding onto the metal book. Landon then felt a sudden tug around his neck that ceased his grip with his sister through the charging current of the water. Landon realized that the hood of his jacket was caught around a severed bar along the stairs below the torch. He had no choice, but to regrettably abandon the precious coat, and peddle with all his might out of the torch.

The torch then exploded like a geyser in all directions with overflowing water: through the mouths of the giant faces and even extinguished the top of the burning torch until all the water completely dispersed. Landon and Makari rode the wave of water all the way down to the vestibule's once freshly polished floor. Landon and Makari gasped and choked for air as the room splashed and flooded with the cave water, sending the streams run-off down the lower level staircases.

"We...did it," coughed Landon, as he then began to grin at Makari, her hair tangled around her face and both of them still clamped hand-in-hand. Our siblings could then hear a pack of rushing footsteps against the water down one of the surrounding halls.

"Goodness me," gasped Dionne, clasping a hand against her chest. Dionne wasn't alone, being fully accompanied with her husband, Mr. Savini, Cassidy Noma, Ms. Qwara, Mr. Varick, and Jade. The entire party stood wide-eyed at the sight of chaos the vestibule had become, especially seeing Landon and Makari sitting on the wet floor, both looking oddly triumphant. Makari gave a guilt-ridden "Hello" wave with her hand at the approaching Cappas, Chamberlains, Manor Executives, and Jade. Landon continued to smile on, completely enraptured, as he could only gaze at the glassy marvel that he still held openly in his left hand.

CHAPTER FIVE

THE MAN IN THE MIRROR

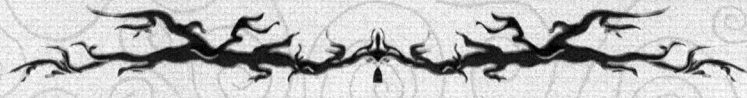

"These mischievous ventures have absolutely gone far enough, Jade!" growled Antoine, as his silvery cheekbones bloomed through slaps of fleshy-powder meant to hide his Sculpt-born skin. The Cappas had accompanied Jade to escort our brave siblings back to their spared room that same evening. Landon sat at the foot of his bed while Dionne took the liberty of administering to him wonderful ointments and soothing oils over the severe hand-shaped burn on his forearm. Between the wincing, Landon and his sister caught a few disappointed glares from McDaniel, while she stood by the Head Lady's side awaiting direction.

"You poor things, I apologize for this place; it must be hard not knowing what sort of menaces our inglorious Revlenion houses," Dionne sighed, as she began to gently wrap Landon's arm with gauze. "I'm sure back where you come from, there aren't any wretched creatures out there that can do such harm onto you like this."

Jade and Makari sat together at the foot end of her bed (while McDaniel dabbed layers of minty ointments over a cut on the side Makari's freckled face) both seemingly quiet, allowing Antoine to unfold his harsh monologue.

"R.C.C. Members, Moltair and Savini, were both present in the Manor tonight, and together their censorious eyes witnessed the chaos you two unnecessarily inflicted down in the vestibule," Antoine reeled, marching around the bedroom and at a few times jabbed a finger into the air, "how am I supposed to explain to the rest of the Chamberlains tomorrow morning, the necessity behind two fauxrevles managing to break into Nicollet's sacred grave? Hear me when I tell you this, Jade, you're continuing to allow the R.C.C. to have negative sights on the lot of you."

"You call that grave sacred? Makari and I were nearly seared and made into charcoal in that place you call, sacred, and not to mention almost drowned, " said Landon, grimacing at his pain when Dionne applied the last wrap around his arm.

"Hundred-year-old securities are what could've killed you and your sister, securities to protect priceless artifacts that are undoubtedly down there. Moreover, you allowed yourself and your sister into harms reach because you wanted to parade your ignorance and your fauxrevler manner," pointed Antoine.

"That is not true!" snapped Landon. "M and I had shared information and we had to act."

"Act on what, exactly?" sneered Antoine.

"Our manifesto," spat Landon. Antoine then made a few swift steps toward Landon, arching his boiling face into Landon's.

"Manifestos are nothing more than forgotten bedside tales. Is that what you want to be, forgotten?" Antoine said, harshly calculating Landon again, much like a caged lion would've done; hoping that our boy would've naively stuck his hand into the beast's iron cage. "Because that's all you'll ever be if it's a manifesto you desire to chase—"

"—Antoine." Dionne said, softly. As Dionne stood from Landon's bedside, sliding between her husband and Landon, he noticed a circumspect glare cross Antoine 's face; it was if he knew his wife needed not to utter another word.

"I hope I've made my point," said Antoine, fixing his thick necktie then pressing a few wrinkles out on the front of his burgundy suit. Antoine only allowed himself one more look at the company in the spare room before making his exit. Mr. Varick had been unnoticeably lingering just outside the bedroom's threshold, until Jade noticed him when Antoine signaled to the thin man to follow. Dionne followed in her husband's path, not before giving a quick word to our trio:

"Yet another surprise from you two," Dionne glanced at both Landon and Makari.

"Dionne, let me please speak with you," asked Jade.

"Not now, the best thing to do would be to rejoice the efforts you three have somehow managed to apprehend—in the morning, we'll discuss." With a gentle and slightly grinned nod at Landon and Makari, Dionne made her exit from the room.

"Hmph!" McDaniel then hummed, "you three together are worse than firemen trying to put out a flare with gasoline."

The trio eyed one another, sighing at the departure of the Cappas and the sudden escalation of strife they had now brought onto themselves.

▼

That next morning, Landon found himself a quiet spot in the Manor, sitting halfway up on the Grand Cappa Staircase, twisting and twirling the Nicollet key between his fingers. He eyed his mossy green key closely, noticing three numbers that had been embossed on each of the square teeth of the key: 6-0-1. While Landon appreciated the precision of the glass that Nicollet had created, the event of finding this key nearly matched the fate of the maker with himself and his sister.

"There you are," said Makari, at the top of the staircase. "Why didn't you come to breakfast?"

"I didn't want to. I woke up really early this morning and wasn't hungry—still not," said Landon.

"You mean you never slept. Lan, you can't keep doing this to yourself, you look exhausted," said Makari, after sitting next to her brother with a cloth-wrapped plate and a pair of silver utensils. "Here, eat something."

"Fine—" Landon pulled away the cloth to find a full plate of eggs benedict, two pieces of sausage links and half slices of the sweetest strawberries.

"See," said Makari, "I know you feel better already."

"Not really," sighed Landon, after gulping his bite of egg. "I lost dad's jacket in that tomb last night. Thinking about it makes me…" Landon shook, trying to deter the subject.

"Here, Ms. Qwara wanted me to give this to you, too," said Makari, handing her brother a spare Portler armlet.

"Sick of this thing already. Where's Jade?" asked Landon, fastening the armlet back on.

"After breakfast he said he was going to try and speak with the Ordinheirs once more before we're supposed to meet with Dionne before noon," said Makari.

"I feel like time is no longer on our side," said Landon, after a bite of a strawberry.

"What do you mean?" said Makari.

"The moment I held this key, everything about exploring our plans with the manifesto felt…limited," said Landon. "We've got to act soon."

Landon and Makari could then hear the familiar echo of boot heels against the marble floor approaching from the west hall that was at the top of the staircase.

"Hello, hello—and I see you've found the other half," said Jade, nodding at Landon.

"Any good news?" said Landon, setting aside his breakfast plate.

"I presume Makari has brought you up to speed on the current plans?" said Jade, as he plotted himself a space on the staircase next to Makari.

"Sort of," said Makari.

"What did the Ordinheirs have to say?" said Landon, after a gloppy bite of his eggs.

"Those three are very, very strict bundles of stone, but I did get a few words out of them," said Jade.

"What did you ask them?" said Landon.

"The obvious: how's your day, how's the afterlife, can you help?" bantered Jade, sighing, "but of course, I asked, what would one have to do if they did find Nicollet's key? My hypothetical question sounded far too odd and Ingrid replied, 'only the Cherished Guardian who held the key first knows how to find the Quinn'—"

"Fantastic! Because I obviously know where to go or whatever that means," griped Landon.

"My point exactly," said Jade, "but we're feeling deeper daggers in our plans, since your epic shtick last night left the R.C.C. with their jaws to the floor. However, I am still proud of you two, I really am... I know that I would've done the same—"

"Good morning," said a familiar, nasally voice from atop of the staircase.

"Hello, Mr. Varick, is Dionne ready to see us?" asked Jade, quickly standing. Landon then hurriedly concealed his emerald key, carefully swathing it with the navy cloth from his plate and tucked it away in his pant pocket. "Indeed," said Mr. Varick, in his customary gray manor suit, and still wearing his half-moon sunglasses. "Follow me—"

Our siblings eyed each other with uncertainty and stood at Jade's signal and began their trek in Mr. Varick's path.

Mr. Varick led the way, deep into the manor where neither of our siblings had visited before. Taking a short flight up a stairwell to the fifth floor first, around a mezzanine the hurried pack went, and through the west corridors until Jade immediately realized where they would be meeting Dionne.

"Makari, you're going to absolutely love where we're headed," said Jade, as the group walked between odd collections of interestingly platted battle armor and antique weaponry.

"I will?" said Makari.

"No doubt in mind," said Jade.

After rounding the hall's furthest corner, Mr. Varick instead followed after our trio into the oddly L shaped office that was suddenly found ahead. A gray tint bathed the entire room with a foggy sunlight that bounced from the morning rain clouds that wholly engulfed the manor outside. Booming from the wide window that clearly swept one side of the spacious room that not only housed hovering flocks of raven taxidermies, the window splashed its ghostly hue over the room's overstocked shelves of leather and canvas-bound books and the interspersed paired suits of armor that were fixed into poses that made them all look as if they were fighting some invisible creature. Standing beside the giant globe near the window, Landon and Makari could see Dionne and Ms. Qwara, patiently watching the fog creep past as they, presumably, tried to catch a glimpse of the valley that hid somewhere between the clouds. It was until the two women heard Makari's nervous hiccup did the two women heed the new company that entered the airy office.

"Hello you three, please, let us all have a seat at the table," said Dionne, pointing at the square reading table in the center of the room.

"Good morning, Dionne, I know you want to speak with us, but would you mind if I explore this room for a bit? I love everything in here—I promise that I'll be listening," said Makari.

"Absolutely, explore away," said Dionne, as she and the rest of the company took seats at the table.

"So, what sort of punishment should I be expecting from last night's wonderful event?" Jade exhaled. "I'm sure the R.C.C. is having a picnic full of laughs right about now."

"I'm sorry to say that you're correct," said Dionne, "However, don't defy your recent accomplishments as a negative," dancing a finger in front of herself. "The R.C.C. have always pulled for the negative in people and disregard the brilliance and the bravery in them —the very two characteristics that some of the Chamberlains lack." Landon and Makari both quickly eyed each other from across the room after Dionne's last collection of words. "As for the punishments, I'm afraid I must deliver the obvious bad news— Antoine has sent word from Arkgothin City that the R.C.C. has placed a termination bill on your case that will fall into effect at midnight, tonight. In that bill, it also states that by tomorrow at noon, you," Dionne eyed Landon, "and your sister must withdraw from Revlenion entirely until further notice."

"They're so conniving," snarled Jade.

"Are we not allowed to defend ourselves?" said Makari, after giving a light spin at the large globe of Revlenion.

"As a matter of fact, you are," said Qwara.

"I'll testify for Landon and Makari, Dionne. I'll prove to the R.C.C. they had every right to enter Nicollet's tomb," said Jade, gesturing at our siblings.

"You won't have to testify, if you can prove the purpose of barging the tomb was indeed necessary," said Dionne. "That's all you need."

"Well, we don't even know where to go or do next," said Landon.

"I spoke with the Ordinheir's earlier this morning, and all they would confide to me was some enigmatic line about how Landon should know where to go next," said Jade.

"Any ideas come to mind?" said Qwara, as she eyed Landon.

"None—" Landon shook.

"There has to something we can use, some fly-by information. You see, manifestos are like bowls of collected knowledge and shared with fellow or apprenticing guardians, in a way, that knowledge leaves a trail for others," said Dionne.

"That actually has happened already," said Makari. "Twice."

"How so?" asked Jade, darting querying eyes at our siblings.

"I knew a time to confess would happen, but we managed to help ourselves into the Almerine Library, two nights ago," said Landon, as the rest of the company eyed him and his sister with surprise. "M and I were desperate for answers, so we—"

Dionne then raised a gentle hand, stopping Landon in mid-sentence as he tried to find a sort of reprieve.

"I understand," said Dionne. "The information you two came by, it must've been truly useful, since you conquered the riddles of the realm."

"We had unexpected help though," said Makari, "and it wasn't from Jade, as you might think."

"Unexpected help?" said Dionne.

"Before we met Jade, someone had already been contacting us by some sort of magical means," said Landon.

"The first time, we thought it was Jade because the following day he suddenly arrived to our house," Makari added.

"Just how magical, what do you mean?" asked Dionne.

Makari then recited their tale about her flying diary and the mysterious message that was scribbled inside of it.

"…Only to sign every note since then with Helpfully Yours, each time he—or she—wishes to help us," said Makari, as the rest of the room quietly shuffled theories in their heads as just who could be the shadowy aide.

"Odd help, more than anything," said Landon, "every clue Helpfully Yours drops it nearly kills us."

"But you've been more than willing to take the stranger's help," said Varick.

"Sure, the first time Helpfully Yours was a stranger, but they contacted us in such a way that…was just so unreal. We had to take their help. We continued to take 'Helpfully's' clues because after each obstacle."

Landon suddenly stopped.

"What's wrong?" asked Jade, seeing Landon's face pop with excitement.

"They're not just clues, are they?" Landon said to himself, loud enough for the entire meeting to fix a tighter ear.

"What?" Makari hummed, noticing the careful stares upon her brother.

"Do you remember, Makari, what that tinker-man said to us before we ran from his tent?" said Landon, ecstatically.

"Tinker, what tinker-man?" Qwara probed.

"Luc Looter, a rogue Reveler…That's how Landon and Makari came to find Elddri's cube in the first place," said Jade.

"Go on, Landon, what did he tell you?" said Dionne.

"He said, and oh I can hear his old voice in my head now just thinking about it: 'there's more than just helpful clues inside that box I made…It has silenced more…More with its obstacles and games than I should've ever allowed'," Landon shook, recalling Luc Looter's lament "that's what he said…what I can remember anyway."

"Are you saying that?" tried Jade.

"Yes, Luc Looter and Helpfully Yours are the same person… they are Ekram Elddri," said Landon, as he watched the natives slowly sit back in their seats, astonished. "It has to be him, it just has to be."

"Elddri has been dead for centuries," said Varick, "Revelers have been known to have a lifespan beyond a century, but that would have to make him—"

"Three hundred years old," Makari gasped. "I remember it now, after the Seraphion tale, Jade, you even said yourself that nobody truly knows Elddri's whereabouts," said Makari, gathering closer to the table, "but that his abandoned journals could be proof to a life of immortality…"

"Allow me to interject," said Dionne, "I can see how the mysteries of this country might shake your direction of proceeding with the manifesto. Now, I am not denying the possibilities of Elddri's involvement; not only have his fables proven him to be as great as the upbringing of this country, but synonymous with toying with beautiful minds like yourselves."

"Why would he—?" Makari tried.

"That's unknown to many, including myself," said Dionne, "know this though, in the countless stories that have been shared about him, one thing has always been clear…Elddri has only ever surfaced for those who've believed in Revlenion as much as he did. His enigmatic tactics in helping those like you and your sister—sure

—might be as tough as nails."

"He, even if it was Elddri that Landon and I encountered, why would he want to remain in hiding?" said Makari.

"Or know how to keep track of our moves, so precisely?" said Landon.

"Like I told you," Jade reminded, "Elddri's mirror knows who crosses either side of its portal. Maybe the puzzling enchantments inside the cube have some sort of a watchful mark on you?"

"That sounds spooky," said Qwara.

"Could be true," nodded Dionne. "Your time in Revlenion hasn't exactly been the most sequestered from voices with the power to exploit your ventures. The Cappa Gazette has proven that." Landon for a second darted a look at his sister, as she finally took a seat at the table with the rest of the company. "Nonetheless, should it truly be Elddri that is on your side, it can only be a sign of good spirit in your wake."

"And about the strange help that has come your way, did this person ever leave you with anything tangible?" Mr. Varick asked.

"A metal bound book we thought to have been destroyed by the guards that attacked us in the library," revealed Landon, tossing a quick look at his sister, "somehow found its way back in our hands last night, but this time, somebody altered and added handwritten notes within the book, guiding us in our favor to discover the cave hidden under the torch," said Landon. The rest of the company exchanged curious glances at one another before Dionne continued again.

"I'm still deciding if it was all really in our favor," said Makari.

"Since we're on the subject of the realm—did any of the Feuer Guards speak to you?" said Dionne.

"They did, we got their leader to talk to us after we made a deal with him," said Landon.

"What sort of deal?" Jade asked.

"After we climbed down into the realm, we had DeMortle's book in hand and managed to convince the leader into immediately wanting it; allowing him to believe it to be more than special. All in exchange for the book, he told us the purpose of the key, but not how to bind the link between the key and the manifesto," said Landon.

"Clever," said Qwara.

"Key, what key?" asked Mr. Varick.

"This one," said Landon, leaning forward in his seat, "and we barely managed to escape with it and our lives."

The rest of the table watched Landon pull something out from his pant pocket. Having so ingeniously reused the napkin from his breakfast plate from earlier, Landon delicately placed the cloth wrapped Venture Key only to his arm's length out front of him and peeled back the four corners of the navy napkin until it revealed the sea-glass key to the pairs of eyes that had yet to observe its marvel. Landon then began to exhibit the green key to the entire room ever so carefully by the tips of a forefinger and thumb, as if he were some young auctioneer charily exhibiting a wondrous treasure. Succumbing to Jade's wish for a closer examination, Landon tried to place the key into his comrade's hand and instead gasped with the entire room. It was when a holographic security suddenly animated like a protective cocoon over the ancient key, allowing it to miraculously slip completely through Jade's own flesh and bone. Landon couldn't hesitate, not the slightest, instead he thrust out an open palm just as fast as any of those nameless heroes from the annals of spaghetti-westerns that he so admired. Catching the key in mid-air in the palm of an open hand, a sudden and unnerving shake quickly crawled up Landon's back.

"Phew, that was a close one there, Ringo," panted Jade.

"Too close," Landon sighed, returning the key to its napkin haven in the center of the table. "Hold on. Makari, you try."

Careful this time, Landon placed the Venture Key into his sister's palm.

"Never have I witnessed such securities over what I'd believe to be an ordinary key," said Qwara.

"That's the trick…It wants you to believe that it's ordinary," said Makari.

"Because it isn't ordinary, is it? None of this is," said Landon, as he watched his sister gaze into the ornament's shine.

"Did the creature say what you could do with the key or where it would lead you?" said Mr. Varick, leaning forward in his chair.

"Their leader had more harsh words to share with me than telling me what this key could actually do, but it did speak of a place I could've sworn Makari and I have heard of before," said Landon.

"Heard of before? Landon, this is your first time within Revlenion, how could you possibly know of such a place?" said Qwara.

"I remember now," said Makari, as the table heads spun their sights at her. "Landon, you didn't hear about it before, we read about it."

"What?" darted Landon.

"When we first came across DeMortles's book in the library with Martin—"

"You two have met Martin?" hooted Jade.

"He was really helpful," insisted Makari. "Lan, in the book there was that single passage about the Hallways of—"

"—Quinn," said Dionne, as the rest of the company then turned their eyes on the Head Lady.

"You know about the tale?" said Makari.

"You say that you've read about this tale from a metal bound book? Well, there is only one metal book I know of that would hold such a tremendous and curious tale about Quinn," said Dionne. "Most tales are regarded as false testaments. However, the Hallways of Quinn are very much real."

"The next step is finding the Hallways of Quinn, it just has to be," said Landon. "Take a look at this." Landon then fetched the torn page from DeMortles's book out from the inside of his shoe. After flattening out the damp page the best he could, Landon shared with Dionne the cryptic passage from DeMortles's consuming story. "Just like it says there, it is a real place."

Dionne sat back in her amber chair, a look of bewilderment flounced across her gentle face.

"I forget what sort of memories manifestos can bring back to the air," said Dionne, perplexed, "but it must be done. And as I'm sure it has been said before, you can't turn away from the manifesto."

"Dionne, what do you know about Quinn?" said Jade.

"The Hallways of Quinn has been said to be where all apprenticing guardians go to continue their ventures—Unfortunately, I don't know what exactly you'll find there now," said Dionne.

"But you can tell us how to find it, right?" said Landon.

"Of course, that is why I am here—only to help. The Hallways aren't very far from here either, if that's what you were quietly fearing, they're actually here in the manor," said Dionne, very matter-of-factly.

"You're kidding," choked Jade, eyeing Dionne, "how haven't I known about this place? I practically grew up in this house."

"The reason you haven't heard of the Hallways is because of the legendary danger that stands before it," said Dionne.

"What sort of danger?" trembled Makari.

"Come to think of it, it would definitely have to be something colossal," said Jade. "A few weeks ago, while I was completing research in the Almerine Library on an open case for the R.C.C., a Manor Executive and I bumped into each other and the tired man dropped all of these long scrolls to our feet. As I helped the old fellow gather his work off the floor, in the midst of helping him, I caught a glimpse of a scroll that had rolled entirely open to reveal an ancient blueprint. I wasn't absolutely sure at first what the blueprint was for, however in the time I was able to gather, I knew that it had to be for something big and depicted a mine-like maze made entirely out of stairs."

"Did you try asking the executive exactly what the blueprint was for?" asked Qwara.

"Of course, but the bourbon on his breath had already got the best of him," said Jade, "only to tell me that, I had no business asking about such confidential matters and he kept muttering something about the R.C.C. outsourcing fauxrevles. The strangest thing was, amongst the mess of papers that the man dropped, I kept seeing the same name circled or boldly underlined: M.C. Escher. Maybe it's the architect? I thought. I tried asking him whose name that was, but he warily darted his eyes in every which way and sped off deep into the library."

Dionne then eyed her Manor Executives, wisely calculating their postures.

"I wish I knew what exactly rests at the entrance to Quinn, even if it may be whatever you perceived was on that blueprint, but I've only ever heard that it is a severe security protecting whatever may be hidden within Quinn's hallways," said Dionne.

"So, we have to face whatever is standing in our way of entering the Hallways then?" said Makari.

"That is your only way, I'm sorry," said Dionne, as she eyed the quietly ticking grandfather-clock that towered beside her party, "and with less than twenty-four hours to go before the R.C.C. makes their terminating move, you three will have to gather close and make yours first."

"If I may," Varick intervened, "I have been part of this institution for many years; exercising my mind of the many levels, corners, and corridors this manor houses, and luckily for you three, I know just where to find the entrance that inevitably leads to the Hallways of Quinn." The trio darted odd looks at each other again, as if questioning the choice of their guide. "If youl allow me, I will do my very best to get you three to Quinn—I know of a route that succeeds the mighty security that rests before the Hallways. I apologize for my previous force of policy, but I believe in what you three seek."

"Since the manor floors will be on heightened alert later this evening, due to Eplaville's taunts, Mr. Varick would be your best guise getting past the house guards, as they will only answer to Manor

High-Executives. Ms. Qwara and I will remain on the manor floor to keep watch for Eplaville, in case he dares to strike the manor again," said Dionne.

"We have ourselves a plan, don't we?" grinned Jade.

"A plan that should all go accordingly," said Qwara.

"I believe it will, however before we disperse I have one remaining question about last night," said Dionne, seeing our trio lean in their seats, "tell me, Landon or Makari, where did all of the water come from?"

"Landon caused it," touted Makari, eyeing her brother.

"Caused?" Dionne hummed.

"Out of a thought, really," said Landon, sensing a reminiscent shock from the scene on the night before, "we were being attacked and I was so scared. The monster that had subdued me wouldn't let go, so I had to do something. At the next moment, an idea simply slipped into my mind—thinking about it now—being that I was scared at first, but once I believed that I could conjure that wall of water to act as my only protection, everything after that seemed oddly clearer and I suddenly became...much calmer."

"That's exactly how I felt in the forest," whelmed Makari, "it was as though my conjure took over all of my feelings."

Dionne and Jade then shared such a wondrous stare, as Makari noticed Dionne's sudden straightening in her seated posture, as though a triumphant idea of her own began to twinkle in her mind.

"I know first hand what sort of obstacles ventures can bring into light; sometimes they are good ones, sometimes they are bad," said Dionne, as she began to pace her steps toward our trio at the other end of the table, "its not always the obstacles that are the most challenging, its remembering to believe that you can overcome whatever it is that your manifesto asks of you. Keep the strength you have, keep believing."

"I'll remember," Landon nodded, as he and the entire room then eyed the Nicollet key still resting on the table, "I'll remember."

▼

Cappa Manor had nothing better to do than stand as the royal behemoth that it knew it was plopped atop the town's steepest hillside on that crawling, late summer evening, and just as it did for over one-hundred and fifty years. The manor could only eye its whimsical plaza below, however, unknown to the marble manor was that the Cappamites were quirky enough to know that something curious was looming behind those silver doors and crystal windows.

The morbid force that was Vizton Eplaville was a foul vigor horrifying enough to implement Cappa Valley into a lockdown. Cappa patrols doubled within the 'Square and its surrounding villages within a few hours after the Cappa Gazette published the countrywide image of the darkly crafted artwork Vizton had created downtown. Thousands of newspaper clippings featuring images of Landon and Makari from the annual gala earlier that week had been taped and together glued against an exposed brick wall near the front entrance to the Gazette lobby.

To go along with the dozens of red etched X marks over our siblings' faces, a vicious message had been spray-painted in violet along Eplaville's wall of art:

X MARKS THE LIE
-VIZTON EPLAVILLE-

The Cappa Patrols pushed back and urged their fellow citizens to refrain from taking photographs and to return to their homes. Crowds instead flocked to stand before their newspaper house with a mix of fury and astounding protest.

"Why haven't the Cappas captured this Eplaville monster?" shouted a redheaded Cappamite.

"Exile those children!" shouted a short gargoylian woman.

"Are our own children safe anymore?" shouted another gentleman Cappamite.

"We want answers!" shouted another woman.

"Please! Ladies and gentlemen, please, this area must be cleared!

The R.C.C. and the Cappa Patrol Investigation League are examining this entire area," hollered Officer Tollew over the growing crowd, as his fellow officers ordered more Cappamites to withdraw from the front of the Cappa Gazette. Camera bulbs continued to pop and spark as both crowd photographers, and investigators gathered in front of the Gazette.

"Everyone, please return to your homes!" Tollew ordered, again.

Leaning in one of the manor's many windows within its tapestry lined east corridors was our boy, Landon, squinting at the sight of a crowd deforming down below in Cappa Square. Landon sighed, insecurely slipping his hands into the pockets of the black corduroy coat given to him by McDaniel before the excursion. Landon stretched and twisted his neck, feeling an irritating itch from the old coat around his neck and felt downright out-of-place without his father's red hoodie.

"What's going on down there?" exhaled Makari, as she and Jade joined her brother at the window.

"The town is scared," said Jade. "You saw what was in the papers. The generations of Cappamites down there have forgotten what gruesome beings lurk within their very own country."

"Shall we?" called Mr. Varick, behind our trio, equipped with only a black leather bag. "A few supplies that I know we'll surely need, let us hurry on then, we're not too far from the entrance."

"Ready?" said Jade, as he eyed our siblings.

"After you," said Landon, as he and his sister followed after Jade. Mr. Varick led the way, taking our trio up a wide-mouthed flight of steps that led to another long hallway filled with timeless portraits.

"Such fine and forgotten artwork," said Mr. Varick, "nobody ever comes to this side of the manor anymore."

Our trio eyed as many of the scattered and enormous landscaped portraits while they paced through the cold corridor. It wasn't necessarily a messy hallway; the mass collection of artwork seemed perfectly positioned in every way and almost as if the corridor had become a giant storage room of countless frames.

There were so many paintings that some of them found home on the floor or leaning against other piles of overlooked portraits between unique knights armors that were still connected to the Manor Network.

"Here we are," continued Mr. Varick, as he and our trio arrived to a dead end that was accompanied with an exceptionally strange portrait. Hanging there, almost as though it was exactly eyeing them, Landon and Makari began to examine the tall portrait of an Edwardian mother that was hand in hand with a small and eerie boy whose face was quite cherub-like with a piercing stare that was more emotionless than any other portrait our trio had a chance to gaze upon.

"Alright, where is the entrance?" said Jade, eyeing the towering portrait.

"You see, that's the problem, you were never supposed to know where it is," said Mr. Varick, now reaching into his bag, and still with his back to our trio, "it makes me sick knowing you had to join us, Jade, and not let me have the children for my father's own. It makes me sick, it makes me sick, it makes…me…sick of what I've become." Mr. Varick's voice had been deepening and gurgling with every word he spoke. After a fast spin on his heel and ripping the dark sunglasses off his head, Mr. Varick was now face to face with our trio once again. Landon and Makari had no idea what dark armament Varick had now suited over his left hand, but it left Jade to gasp at the evolving scene. Landon and Makari jumped back as the violet-eyed Mr. Varick then lunged like a rabid wolf at Jade and knocking his magnificent cane aside. Grabbing Jade by his coat, Varick ripped his trans-oidar off from his lapel and smashed it as hard as he could against the corridor floor. Landon and Makari stood gasped and stunned as Varick then tossed Jade into the set of silver network suits across from them as the beast-like Varick then charged at our siblings.

"Jade!" cried Makari, witnessing her friend being tossed through the air.

"Oh dear, are you in need of urgent directions within the Haus of Cappa?" asked the Manor Armor, bewildered by Jade's impact.

"You have the key! Give it to me! Give it to me! I want to be the one who awakens father!" gurgled Mr. Varick, as he then snatched Landon by the collar on his coat.

"Let me go!" shouted Landon, as Varick lifted Landon into the air, taunting him with the glowing silver arrow on his armed black gauntlet.

Makari was hesitating while the horrifying scene that had become unraveled before her.

"Makari...quick!" moaned Jade, trying to lift the heavy armor off his chest, "grab the torch above you—use it!"

The burning hand-labra above Makari had to be the best idea. Makari jumped to her feet, unhinged the torch from the wall and hoped that Jade's plan would work. For those last alarming seconds, while Landon found himself gazing into Varick's terrifying eyes, Makari jabbed the gaunt man across the side of his face, forcing him to drop her brother to the carpeted marble floor beside her. Seconds later, Varick's body began to contort and lift into the air as his screams echoed with inhuman ability. Landon and Makari watched from the floor as Varick's mouth opened wider than his jaw actually should've allowed, guardedly observing the black mass that slithered out of his mouth like a giant ribbon. The trio watched as the violent tendril poured onto the corridor floor and desperately tried to shape itself into a fully-defined human skeleton, but instead tossed Mr. Varick's body away like a rag doll through the motherly portrait at the end of the hall. The entity screeched and cried at the sight of Makari's candelabra until it hurled itself through one of the few windows across from our siblings in the hall.

Landon stood up and ran to the shattered window, hoping to catch a glimpse of the cowardly creature. Landon then dove beside Jade on the floor grunting against the clanking and chiming suit that had broken to a few heavy pieces upon impact.

"Are you alright?" Makari gasped, as she and her brother helped lift the overwhelmed suit off Jade.

"I am, but look at that," Jade wheezed, coughing up some of the armor's dust and sweeping up his cane off the floor the next.

Our siblings then followed after Jade as he gathered them near the torn hole in the middle of the tall portrait. Jade gave a twist of his cane, as its tip began to glow such a ghostly shade of gold. Jade forwarded, driving his cane like a wooden machete around the hole in the portrait, until he and our siblings could see Mr. Varick's still body. The trio then climbed into the secret tunnel behind the canvas that Varcik's thrown body had inadvertently exposed.

"Was he…possessed?" said Makari, as she warily crouched beside Varick.

"I'm afraid he was," said Jade, pressing a finger against Varick's neck. "He's still alive though, in case you were worried."

"What…what was that that flew out of him?" said Landon.

"That was an evelisk, they're malicious creatures that I haven't seen in many, many years," Jade sighed, adjusting his wayfarers, "they occupy human hosts to complete foul tasks and as it seems, that one was obviously on a mission."

"Do they always look like that?" said Landon.

"No—They're even more ghastly when in their neutral form, but what you saw is known as their malopied shape," said Jade. "Evelisks are sometimes easy to spot in unsuspecting hosts; their host's eyes will reveal a violet tinge in sunlight or against the nearest open flame, triggering the internal beast with fright, that's why I told you to arm yourself with that candelabra," Jade furthered, as our siblings then began to eye Mr. Varick's suddenly emaciated body in Jade's cane light. "Unfortunately, the after effects are much like this…or even death."

"And fire is their weakness?" said Landon.

"It's their only weakness," Jade sighed, "their bodies warp at the slightest touch of a single flame. Poor Mr. Varick, I knew something was different about him in these past weeks, but didn't expect it to be this."

"That was a close call, Jade, a really close call," said Landon.

"Well, we can't stop here," said Jade.

"Why, is that thing going to come back?" yearned Makari.

"No, they never occupy a single host twice," said Jade, as he then tried to reach for his transoidar, finally seeing its shattered remains upon the corridor floor.

"What about that suit?" Makari asked, pointing at the toppled armor. Jade then snapped his fingers, struck by Makari's quick idea, and strode to the fallen Manor Network suit. After the disgruntled armor dispatched Jade with a guard-at-the-ready, Jade pointed at Makari to retrieve the hand-labra across from them.

"Guards will be here soon to recover Varick," said Jade, after Makari returned with the hand-shaped torch and holding it out in front of her. Jade then relaxed for a second, giving a quick shake of his shoulders, and then finally he focused on the end of his glowing cane, upon the torch.

"What are you doing?" whispered Landon.

"Just watch," said Jade as he then slowly met the end of his glowing cane with Makari's torch. Our siblings continued to watch as Jade's cane began to bloom like the color of the flame that once was by absorbing the flare until it died out and leaving only a dance of smoke to fill the air.

"Your cane can actually do that?" said Landon, eyeing Makari's torch.

"It takes a lot of concentration, but it is possible," said Jade, handing Makari his torch. "I told you it shares the magnificence that stems from Shelversteins. It's more than just magic. Okay, now, let me show you something else it can do." Again, Jade shook his shoulders and allowed his eyes to focus—piercing—as he stared through his thick sunglasses on the dark tunnel ahead. The end of Jade's marvelous cane suddenly burst into vibrant sparks like an entrancing firework until it finally belched an orbed flare down the dark passage ahead of our trio. The three watched as the hasty sphere splashed tiny orange embers throughout its flight upon the tunnel's floor and screeched in the air until it found an end. "Not too long of a hall.

Alright, watch your step and let's follow the cinders."

Leaving Mr. Varick to be found by the manor guards near the lone tunnel's opening, the trio trekked onward and in full pursuit of the tiny embers that guided them through the narrowing path. Makari, twisting her head back a few times, could see the helpful cinders expiring their light behind them the further they advanced. Arriving just in time to the end of the tunnel, the trio watched the flare sizzle until it was dead and remained stuck alongside the wall like a dried-out piece of gum.

"Look," Makari gasped, pointing at the mute figure that stood with its back facing them. Jade and Landon both stepped in front of Makari, eyeing the shape where it took a place along the short platform that followed beyond the tunnel's threshold.

"H-hello?" Jade gulped, cautiously approaching the figure that was fixed to point to an inciting direction ahead. As Jade began to round the tall shape, his fixation upon the lone figure abruptly broke and found himself just as flabbergasted as our siblings were while they quickly tailed behind. Landon, Makari and Jade didn't have to share not one word in those few magnetic seconds after they entered the gargantuan hollow that was entirely overrun with interconnected staircases. The trio didn't know where to begin as they eyed what looked like an architect's worst nightmare; a vast crypt of decrepit stairs ascending, descending and crisscrossing in every which direction.

"Huh, it's all stone." Jade gave a few ensuring taps atop the bulb-headed figure with his cane only to accept that it was nothing more than an expressionless mannequin.

Landon and Makari were on either side of Jade, both relatively uncertain about the daunting statue.

"Remember what Dionne said?" reminded Makari, tracing from the mannequin's finger that aimed to a descending flight of stairs.

Makari and her company followed to the drop from the platform where the mannequin stood and could see that it descended upon an interconnecting platform to the rest of the labyrinth-like well of staircases.

"Yeah, this place has to be the security she spoke about, but where is the entrance to the Hallways of Quinn?" said Landon, eyeing the hundreds of chained sphere-shaped lamps that dangled at dozens of unequal lengths throughout the center of the stairwell.

"It has to be somewhere in here," said Jade, tiptoeing to the edge of the first platform. Jade set the first steady step onto the descending flight, clapping the bottom of his boot against the stone stairs in order to test its sturdiness. The trio, together, each placed a hand on either side of the banister and carefully guided themselves all the way down the dilapidated staircase.

"Don't look down," sighed Makari, after she caught a near vertigo inducing shake when she dared herself to peek over the banister to see a bottomless chamber of more entangled stairs.

"I knew this place had to exist, but never did I expect it's been hiding under the floors of the manor all this time," said Jade, estimating the size the well while he tried counting the number of platforms that hovered above.

"Obviously for a long time and probably even before the house was built, you think?" said Makari, descending between Landon and Jade on the staircase.

"You might be right," said Jade, mystified.

"Should we go up?" suggested Makari, eyeing the colossal mess of stairs when they reached the second platform.

"Look, there it is!" Jade pointed while squinting his eyes behind his wayfarers. "That has to be the entrance to Quinn." Landon and Makari joined closer with Jade, seeing the wooden door that was perched high up above in a wall within stairwell. "It looks like we're going up."

"And look, look right there," Landon pointed, after catching a silhouette in his peripherals, "it's another one of those mannequins; is it pointing up?"

"Indeed it is," said Jade.

"But which one do we choose?" Makari wondered.

CHAPTER FIVE

There were two choices that our trio could make that rested beyond their platform: either ascend or descend somewhere upon the Krinzen Staircase. They agreed not to split up; however, they needed to make a unanimous choice on how to begin their trek along the stairs.

"It is a game," said Landon, hesitantly pushing his foot toward one of the stairs. "That's all this has ever been...a game."

"What?" shook Makari, following alongside Landon.

"Why does it have to be this way, Jade, what does all of this have to prove?" Landon shook, stepping closer to the two flights of stairs, again.

"As it seems, someone or something that has led us here wants to prove one thing and that is that you *can*...That Makari can...That *we* can conquer," said Jade, tapping his cane on the platform under his boots. "No matter the choice, simple or not, you'll never go at it alone."

"No you won't," said Makari, clasping a hand over her brother's hand.

"So, what'll it be?" asked Jade, pointing at the two stairs ahead.

"Up," said Landon, gutsily eyeing his sister.

"After you," said Jade.

Landon was now at the wheel of the trio, guiding them further up and through the mighty stairwell and seeing behind, Jade was and still with his cane at-the-ready out in front of him.

"This is insane, Jade," said Landon, eyeing the stairs around them, as a bulb of sweat trickled down his forehead.

"Just keep close and stay in a single line," said Jade. The trio, over the course of several minutes, began to find themselves at several dead ends and upon stairs that were leading them away from their possible exit. "We need to get to that flight of stairs," continued Jade, tracing a probable line with his cane to the door amongst the stairs.

"Those stairs are descending though," said Makari.

"My guess is that we should reach that mannequin and see where it points us to next," said Jade. Jade was now at the helm and kept to the solution that he kept drawing in his head; follow only stairs that were leading to the stairwell's silent guides. "Careful here, there's a hole in these next steps."

Platform after platform they carefully climbed and mannequin after mannequin they obeyed, the trio was scaling the dizzying staircase faster with meticulous ease, never veering from the stairs that led them closer to the promising exit that still remained patiently waiting above them.

"Wait, what is that?" said Jade, baffled.

Landon and Makari peered over Jade's shoulders to see that the forthcoming mannequin had something placed over its positioned hand.

"Is…is that my jacket?" Landon gasped, leaping ahead on the stairs. The closer Landon inched toward the headless mannequin it became clear to him that what was indeed hanging in front was his father's old jacket.

"I thought it was lost forever," said Makari, watching her brother warily pluck the red hoodie from the wrecked statue and impulsively zip it on. "How did it get down here?"

Makari then quickly helped her brother button his Portler armlet back on.

"I found it down in that tomb you two nearly destroyed," said Vizton Eplaville, rounding in front from behind another headless statue. The trio spun on their heels, heeding the harsh voice that called from up above on a higher platform. "That manor garb you were wearing never suited you anyway—you're welcome."

"Get back," Jade whispered to Landon and Makari, returning his sights and cane back up at Vizton, who had playfully wrapped an arm around the statue next to him.

"Yes, darlings, get back," hissed Vizton, giggling the next.

"So, you're the one who preyed that evelisk on Mr. Varcik," said Jade, keeping a steady view on the scarred-face man.

"Oh, goodness no," chuckled Vizton, "maybe, Mr. Varick

wanted to play host for the Dark Alman, himself. Not to mention, Benjamin was kind enough to let me into the Manor on the night of that heinous party on the balcony. However, I am on my own operation."

"Varick would've never helped you," said Jade.

"You must not know Benjamin all that well then," grinned Vizton, "Or, at least whatever is left of him. Which one of you figured out Varick anyway—was it you?" Vizton pointed at Makari, reveling with his dagger yielded hand. Makari eyed her brother and Jade with sudden qualm. "I figured it'd be you," snorted Vizton, jabbing his dagger into the air in the direction of Makari.

"Yeah, they've figured out a lot alright, great things that you'll never stand for," said Jade, "because you hurt people to get ahead... that's all you've ever done."

"Only to those who stand in my way," gritted Vizton, nodding at our siblings. "In time, they'll understand—to get anything you want you must behead those who want more than you...those that want to conquer you. Come on, Jade, you know it's true, the entire manifesto hubbub is that very philosophy."

"I would never act the way you have," spat Landon.

"I act this way because it is the only way that I can separate myself from the pigs like you," said Vizton, scraping his dull blade across the shoulder of his mannequin. "And for the record, I don't mind that you three famous pigs are trying to make me out to be the big bad wolf in this tale of ours, it's just that I'm disposing of the swine that are trying to control Revlenion."

"You're going to fail miserably," said Jade. "Dare to try all you want."

"Hush-hush, my old friend," said Vizton, "I have only a few things to say before I share with you lovely refurbishments I've made to my operation. You're probably wondering why I keep calling you three, swine. It's quite simple really; pigs are stupid creatures that feast on the droppings of their own kind, and you three manage to fit the same characteristics oh-so-well. Still, you've got to give the horrible pink oinkers recognition—they do their best to use their beady minds and tiny snouts to sniff out the next meal, and maybe even their last. In this case," Vizton eyed our trio closely, "you three have certainly sniffed your way out of your safe little kennel back upstairs. Tell me, Makari, when a little piggy leaves the kennel, where does that little piggy go?"

"Home?" groaned Makari, fearing she answered the scarred face man incorrectly.

"Unfortunately, my little red-headed piggy, they pay a visit to a very, very happy wolf," hissed Vizton, eyeing his shining blade in his fist, "and this wolf is starved."

"But you'd be the sorry wolf that would cut himself with his own blade. And from the looks of it, you might've already done so just a few too many times," said Jade.

Vizton's hideous grin suddenly withered as he then caught his scarred reflection that bounced from his polished blade.

"These are my war scars, I make no mistakes," growled Vizton, as he then jarred his dagger out at our siblings. "Well then my little pigs, little pigs…I'll let you three go in exchange for something that I'm aware that one of you so happens to be hiding in your…pocket."

"Not a chance, Eplaville," shook Jade.

"Not by a hair on your chinny-chin-chin?" Vizton sighed, grinning devilishly again.

"Not a one," Makari intruded, as Jade then lined his cane in front our brave girl.

"*Tut-tut*, then I must huff and puff and," Vizton Eplaville simply replied, grinning again at our trio while they kept their steady eyes on the scarred-face man above them. After taking a step back, Vizton then met the pointed end of his blade against the back of the stone mannequin beside him and heaved.

Our trio had only seconds to react when they realized that the old statue was plummeting toward them. Vizton raced to a flight of stairs across from our trio, seizing one of the swaying lamps above him in the stairwell. In the same time, the trio darted away from the tall mannequin that shattered into hundreds of jagged pieces and smashed away half of the platform.

Missing the chance to escape from the crumbling platform by mere seconds, Jade and our siblings made the daring race up another set crisscrossing stairs.

"Are you two alright?" said Jade, winded. Joining close with the siblings on the next platform, together the trio set their sights on Vizton who was roaring with laughter at them from across the room.

"Fast little piggies! Here I come," Vizton hissed, as he carefully jumped down onto a platform that led directly toward our trio.

"Hurry! Hurry, Jade!" cried Makari, as she and her brother raced up the stairwell. Jade kept our siblings ahead of him, meanwhile keeping watch of Vizton who was hastily in pursuit of them by ascending their staircase and aware of the broken lamp that he was carrying in one hand.

"Come, come here my little piggies!" roared Vizton, after meeting the edge of his blade with the dying elsol ember that hid within the round lamp. Jade watched as Eplaville steadied his reddening dagger into the air and tossed away the remains of the lamp and could hear it shatter somewhere upon the thousands of stairs below.

As the stairs began to narrow on our trio's escape, Vizton began to strike at the stairways ahead. With every slash of his blade, electrical whips with a fiery flourish began to lash from the tip of Eplaville's dagger, thrashing against the stone stairs and exploding heavy fragments all throughout the stairwell. Landon tugged at his sister's jacket, ripping her back into his arms before she could make her next step into one of Vizton's electrical lashings. Vizton never stopped laughing, but before he could lash another deadly bolt at our trio Jade spun on his heel, swung his cane through the air in front of him and recoiled Vizton's vicious electrical attack back at him. The crackling bolt of fire splintered along the surrounding stairs and tore apart Vizton's own path ahead of him.

Landon held onto his sister tightly as they continued to scale the

Krinzen Staircase, seeing that the door to the Hallways of Quinn was only a few more flights up.

"Keep going! Don't worry about me, stay ahead!" shouted Jade, as he kept his glowing cane at-the-ready. Jade then wheeled back toward Vizton, noticing the scarred-faced man was nowhere in sight. Without notice, Vizton then pounced in front of Jade, leaping from the stairs above.

"I'm giving you piggies a head start," snared Vizton, glaring up at Landon and Makari, "better move fast."

"Landon, Makari—don't stop for me, just go!" ordered Jade.

"Jade!" shouted Landon.

"GO—!"

Vizton slashed at Jade once again, and like a proper duel, the two men blocked one another's attacks; each of them calculating and almost knowing how the other was going to rebound. Landon and Makari dared to watch the attack intensify, tossing quick glances over their shoulders as they continued to climb the stairs and seeing the two forces each shielding and tossing magnificent conjures at one another as they ascended the stairs.

Jade whipped and swung his cane at Vizton's next stroke, sending the scarred man on his back, plummeting upon an elevated platform between a set of connecting stairs, and as unexpected as it was, Vizton rolled his thin body off the platform.

Jade dove his eyes after the falling man until he saw the awful, grinning man throw another violent slither of electricity up. Jade ran as fast as he could and hoped he'd make the jump before the flight of stairs he was on plunged and boomed through the thousands of stairs below. Jade jumped.

Fiercely clamping onto a new flight of stairs, seeing Landon and Makari on a flight of stairs above him, Jade managed to pull himself up and readied for Eplaville once again along a new flight.

"I know you have it," hissed Vizton, suddenly pouncing on Jade's back on the stairs, falling out of nowhere, "look at me, I know you have Nicollet's key—hand it over!"

"It scares you so much not having it, doesn't it?" said Jade, very calmly, seeing Landon and Makari keeping witness. Jade could now see the rage and the reminiscent lost darkness in Vizton's black eyes.

"You're a tainted soul, Jade, just like your brave boy up there," gritted Vizton.

"At least he still has his soul, you—" Jade spat, as Vizton then urged his dagger closer to the side of Jade's face to sense the pulsating heat emitting from his blade.

"—Say that one more time," Vizton dared. "SAY IT!"

"Let them go, Vizton, please," said Jade, still trying to wrangle his cane into arming.

"Such a silly plea. I knew you hadn't changed, not one ugly bit. You want to be like them, you really want to live like a guardian? It takes pain. If it's pain you want," said Vizton, as he flaunted his scorching dagger at Jade, "then it's pain you'll get!"

Jade struggled to flourish a move with his cane as Vizton readied his dagger, but it was Landon and Makari's first two heavy strikes that made the first move, raining down debris from the sibling's hands. Vizton stood off Jade, taking a few careful steps down the stairs, moaning and screaming as he held the side of his head, feeling more flying debris gash against his back. Landon and Makari were holding more pieces of rocky debris, much like the one that had bounced off Vizton's head. Jade smiled at our brave siblings and then quickly sprang to his feet and escaped from Vizton at the right moment. As Jade reunited with Landon and Makari at the top of the stairs, they realized that they were standing on the final flight of steps that guided directly to the wooden door for their escape.

As our trio made their daring race toward the door, giant bolts of electricity swiftly began to explode apart their last flight of steps. Jade and our siblings could see Vizton ascending the steps behind; he was seething at the sight of our trio making their escape; lines of blood were streaming down his scarred face. Vizton now turned his monstrous lurch upon the room and began to destroy all that was around them: gigantic staircase pieces blasted into the air, the chain-linked lamps began to pop as the electricity slithered by and the most massive debris fell all the way down the crumbling stairwell. Jade had to take the chance at that very moment; to cast a spell that could mark their fateful escape

"Hold onto me!" said Jade, after catching one of Vizton's deadly electric lashes with his bewitching cane. With one immense spin and tap of his cane against the crumbling staircase where our siblings stood: Jade held out his cane once more, behind himself this time, and watched as its end exploded into sparks and flame. The trio shot into the air like a human firework, sending them screeching through the air as they flew between and dodged gigantic pieces of the crumbling staircase that began to quake the entire chamber.

The wooden door burst open as our trio skidded and rolled across the floor within another room. Landon, dazed, still managed to jump to his feet and charged for the room's only open door. He watched in awe as most of the stairwell collapsed; the thundering roars that bounced from the ruin almost sounded as if the entire room was actually ailing from the devastation and its belly happened to be the well of stairs. Landon could now see Vizton between the billowing clouds that were quickly engulfing the hollow. Screaming at the very sight of Landon, Vizton began scaling the walls and the remaining staircases with his electric strands, enchanting his whips by some other dark means and shaped them into giant claws that were able to remarkably drive him through the air. Landon gave Vizton one more glance until he heaved the wooden door shut with a lasting slam. With a loud clank, the aged door locked itself on Landon's side, allowing a calm silence to fall upon the trio in the new and frigid yet windowless room.

"Ugh, my leg," grunted Jade, as Makari helped him sit up. "I think it's broken."

"Don't touch it," said Makari, as she then held back Jade's hand.

"Is the key still safe with you?" said Jade, eyeing Landon.

"Of course it is," said Landon, as he pulled the cloth wrapped key out from a pocket inside his red jacket. "Why do you think Vizton thought you had the key?"

"He would've never believed that a brave boy like you to be protecting it," said Jade.

"How can we go on without you?" said Makari, scanning the room that was solely lit with a sole bowl-shaped lamp that drooped from the ceiling in the center of the room.

"You're gonna' have to...and you will...*Ooow*, ugh!" moaned Jade, trying to touch his leg again.

"You were phenomenal back there," said Makari, eyeing Jade.

"Meh, that was nothing, but you two were braver than I could've ever imagined," grinned Jade, as he then winced at the pain now growing from his left ankle. "Where's my cane?"

Makari found the magnificent cane next to her and handed it over to Jade as he then tapped its end against the Venture Key's cloth. Landon and Makari watched as the cane was able to remarkably spout three thin red cloths and all while one that gently wrapped itself around Jade's leg. Jade then handed the two remaining cloths to Landon and Makari, appeasing them, allowing them to clean the small cuts that the flying debris had made on each of their chin and forehead.

"Your cane can clone things?" asked Landon, astounded.

"Yes, but only small, inanimate objects...*Oow!*" Jade winced, eyeing his wrapped leg. "My concentration is slightly obscured though, but at least the pain is...*Ahh...Ooow!* Slowly receding."

"Look at that," said Landon, gazing upon the pearly curtain that swayed in an archway across from them. The way it gently danced in the air made the long veil look more like a rolling surface to an open ocean than the pristine drape that it actually was. Landon then stood and cautiously approached the archway, sensing another bead of sweat roll down his face. After three steps, he could see a glowing pale figure gradually peel from the curtain: a silhouette of a petite woman began to take shape as the snowy curtain then transformed into a long gown, becoming the same ghostly shade of her porcelain doll-like form. The trio kept their leery sights pinned on the floating woman while she lingered close to her archway, keeping peacefully bound to her dress and with hands clasped out front of her.

"Good evening," said the Ghost, tenderly.

"H-hello," gulped Landon, keeping his eyes on the beautiful ghost.

"I can guess that one of you has come to explore the Hallways of Quinn, correct?" asked the Ghost.

"Yes," said Jade.

"Well then, since you've bravely ascended the Krinzen Staircase, one of you must be holding a Venture Key," said the Ghost, airily. "The one who first held the Venture Key will be allowed to make their lone entry into the halls. Which one of you is the first handler?"

The trio eyed one another.

"I w-was the first to hold the key," said Landon, stepping closer to the ghostly woman.

"I hope my son's creations didn't harm you too much," said the Ghost, "they're only meant to protect the keys from unworthy hands."

"I believe someone might've persuaded those securities before we found the key, I don't think they cared for your son anymore," said Landon, suddenly puzzled, "wait, *your* son?" The Ghost then darted her silvery eyes upon Landon. "Who are you, if I may ask?"

"I am the Quinn's Keeper, and the mother to the maker of many marvels," revealed the Ghost, as Landon then quickly eyed Makari.

"Mother?" recited Landon.

"*You're* Olanna Nicollet?" gasped Makari, "from the unfinished tomb! Don't you remember the name on the stone? It has to be her, Landon."

"Yes, now, if you would please present your key to me for inspection of authenticity," said Olanna. Landon still had the wrapped key in his left hand. Holding out his hand the next, Landon opened his palm as the ghost then reached out at Landon. The trio watched as the cloth began to slowly unwrap itself from the key and gently levitate out of Landon's palm. The ghostly woman never touched the key, but only kept it-a-float between her gaunt hands while she began to meticulously examine the glass key. "And you two must be Makari and Landon Tuolumne: siblings from beyond Revlenion; a new heart strike known as Poplar Drive…and such a curious connection I most certainly do read here."

"That word again, curious," said Landon.

"What's a heart strike?" asked Makari.

"A sanctuary where your heart can never go dark," said Olanna, still closely examining the key until becoming visibly addled.

"Is…is something wrong with the key?" asked Makari.

"The key is genuine, I promise you," said Landon.

"I'm aware that it is authentic, but what I find most fascinating is that the core of the key has been…eternally divided," said Olanna. "Everything I need to know about you has been rooted in this key," Olanna then eyed Landon, "the very moment you touched this, a very small imprint of you was made on this marvel, but in such an unexplainable manner, it has decided to divide its power."

"Has this happened before?" asked Jade.

"Never," assured Olanna, "but sensing from the dynamic shine that comes from this key, it's certain to me—more than ever before as it was in life—that my son's entire philosophy to create such unique marvels is alive and well."

"Is this one truly the last of the Venture Keys?" asked Landon.

"Unfortunately so, and the very last one to enter these halls. The day my son was crafting this very marvel was both a day of triumph and tragedy," said Olanna.

"What happened?" Landon asked.

"Monte never had any children of his own, instead, he found love in creating marvels, like this one. My son was a genius, and he had the divine ability to create such wonderment with inanimate objects, but found his ultimate creation to be the Venture Keys. Monte discovered his secret formula within in the realms of Revlenion. Though, Monte was a very secretive and at times paranoid of others that might steal his formulas, so he devised certain securities—much like the ones you've come across to apprehend your own key—in order to protect his cherished works. Nevertheless, like all geniuses and with all the protections he had created, nothing could protect him from his mistakes or death. It was like any other day in which Monte was working in his laboratory at our home in the countryside. He asked me to join him; he was going to show me how he created his marvels. Seconds before he completed this here key, something went terribly wrong. I could see the failure building in Monte's eyes; it was such a discombobulated look that overcame my son, such a look I had never seen from him in all his years," said Olanna, after she choked on few of her words for only a second more, "and then suddenly...everything went black. I don't blame my son for mishandling the magnificent properties of his keys, not one stride of guilt. I am only heartbroken that Monte could not be with me in this wonderful second life and to see what has become of his brilliant work."

Olanna then began to cheerlessly eye her windowless stone room.

"If you're here as a ghost, why isn't Monte here with you as well?" said Makari.

"As mysterious as the formula Monte created, a phenomena occurred," said Olanna, "the liquid that would create any one of Monte's keys seeped into my body as I was slowly drifting into a different state of mind and being. What my son had unknowingly created was strong enough to send him to his natural grave, but instead my soul surrendered itself to forever remain split between Revlenion and the beyond."

"Against your will?" said Landon.

"I had no will in death, because it was the formula that made the choice and put me here with a purpose. Now here, only to guard the entry to the Hallways of Quinn and deter fraudulent seekers of these halls," said Olanna as she gave Landon back his key, watching him pluck it from floating in the air.

"If you know, could you tell me, how are the keys and Ordinheir related? Was your son a guardian, too?" asked Landon.

"No, not a guardian that was ever in search of a manifesto, but one that believed in keepers of peace, like you two," said Olanna, eyeing our siblings. "You see, Ordinheir found my son's mastery with his magical inventions to be extraordinary and helped guide him to Revlenion so he could create perfect specimens for the venture that ignites every manifesto."

"Wait, *to* Revlenion?" exclaimed Makari.

"Correct," said Olanna, nodding.

"What Ordinheir stood for was, that everyone from anywhere in this universe is born with a magnificence: magic. It's what resonates with the heart and is shared with the mind. To Ordinheir, it doesn't matter if you were born in Revlenion or not—sure the magic could be easier for you to control only because of the sheer brilliance that this country harnesses—but to her, those that were born beyond the stars of this country, she attested, were just as equally precious if one truly believed in the magic that was on the inside. Monte was her proof—"

"—And so are you two," said Jade, eyeing Landon and Makari.

"Exactly," nodded Olanna. "And in the annals of the manifestos, it is my pleasure to say, that you two are the youngest guardians to ever set foot in this room. Now comes the remarkable choice: together, you may enter the halls that you will find just a few steps ahead—or—withdrawal from your manifesto for which you seek."

"We have to go on our own? We haven't done anything on our own in this place; what if we can't protect ourselves from what's behind that curtain?" said Landon, as he and his sister gathered beside Jade.

"But you already have," said Jade, "you two have already proven it not only to me but to yourselves. You two found that Venture Key on your own, brilliant endeavor—regardless of your nameless help. You two still fought your way through, so fearlessly than I will ever know. I've only ever guided you, but here…it's about you two now."

"Together, you're not alone," said Olanna, "and as I see it, you defy the odds."

"Don't worry about me," Jade pressed, carefully adjusting his broken leg. "I'll be fine on my own."

"We've made it this far, Lan," said Makari, ceasing her brother by the chin, almost in way that struck Landon as if his own mother were standing right in front of him and trying to draw his attention. "Whether it's the magic or maybe even the manifesto…or all the clues that have made way into our hands. Whatever it is that may be trying to tell us, it's all made one thing clear…it's always been you and I." Makari then finally tossed herself into her brother's chest when she felt her blue eyes filling with tears.

Landon wrapped his arms around his sister, closing his eyes as he did, and sensed a rapturous halo at the very moment of their kindred embracement. He knew he had only ever felt that heartening warmth once before.

Sitting in the back seat of an old ivory Vauxhall Velox, with a hand-over-hand while their Aunt Marion sat in the front passenger seat beside an odd looking driver they had never met before, Landon and his sister could see dozens of black parasols sprouted in the air. The old car came to a halt; its tires digging into the pebbled road that lined between timeworn headstones that leaned in every which way. Stepping out from the old car, a hand still in his sister's, together they walked, in procession to the crowd that gathered near a leafless yet towering tree. In the provoking memory that was deliberately engulfing Landon's mind at the same trek in time, he could recall a tension around his neck; not exactly was it the black bowtie he once wore with his suit, but it was the suffocating vision of himself and his sister as they approached a fresh plot within some desolate cemetery.

"What's your choice then, Landon and Makari?" asked Olanna, lightly.

"Okay," Landon opened his eyes, facing the ghostly woman again. "Let us enter the Hallways of Quinn." Olanna nodded, blessedly, and her ghostly figure withered back into the curtain that, in turn, revealed an entry for our brave siblings to cross. Together, while hand-in-hand, Landon and Makari strode beyond the threshold and finally entered the Hallways of Quinn.

"Jade…" Makari called, seeing her wayfarer-eyed friend cracking a smile.

"When I get scared, I let a memory of someone I love sink in… one that reminds me of who I am," said Jade, placing a hand over his chest from the floor in Olanna's chamber. "Do that…and you'll see just how much they still believe in you."

Landon and Makari then twisted their heads back toward the darkened hall that rested ahead. Entering a narrow foyer, pits of light fixed in the wooden ceiling along the hallway ahead began to flourish for as long as Landon and Makari could see and wincing for only a second after the sudden brightness that rapidly bloomed above.

"Now, each of the following hallways you'll find ahead house thousands of awaiting vaults that maintain the very purpose to every past, present, and future manifesto," said Olanna, floating between Landon and Makari's shoulders.

"How do we know which vault is ours?" said Landon, eyeing the dimly lit hallway ahead.

"The three numbers on the teeth of your key represent your vault door number," said Olanna, pointing at the key in Landon's hand.

"Six-zero-one," said Landon, reading aloud the numbers on the key. "I've been wondering what these numbers meant."

"Your vault must be really important, for it's in the six hundred zone. You'll find your vault directly at the end of this hall, vault number six-hundred and one—a rather easy find," said Olanna, pointing carefully ahead. Landon began to take a few steady steps forward through the dust laden wooden hall. "Remember this, Landon and Makari Tuolumne, the key that is in your possession embraces every bit of delicate intelligence shared between the both of you; don't let anyone else ever posses it. You two are—and forever shall be—its only master and mistress," said Olanna, forewarning

"It's our key to keep," said Landon.

"And so it is," nodded Olanna.

"So, it's true?" Landon pulled for one more revelation from Olanna before she could wither back into her otherworldly slumber. "Everyone in this universe has a manifesto."

"Absolutely," said Olanna, exultantly, "and a *key* to identify it, but it doesn't necessarily mean *everyone* has come to claim their own. Those that have acquired a Venture Key have a choice: accept the quest of mastering a manifesto or allow it to dwell forever in its vault," revealed Olanna. "The Venture Key may be yours to keep, but until you master your own manifesto, that key can fall into another apprentice's possession."

"If our key is the last one, how can there be future manifestos?" asked Makari.

"Not every apprentice that has acquired a Venture Key has always made it this far," said Olanna. "Understand this, your key will always honestly lead you. Not only is it death that can separate you from your key, but should you desire to turn away from its enchantments, it, too, shall turn away from you and seek another master. Your key might also have been in possession of another guardian once before."

"You mean to say, that the key needs us just as much as we need it?" asked Landon.

"Exactly," said Olanna, nodding, "you're at the helm of the might of the Venture Key, but remember—your manifesto can only exist if you wish to set it free. An honor this has been, Tuolumnes—the Ordinheirs must be very lucky to have found more than one Cherished Guardian this time around," said Olanna, applauding.

"What do you mean?" said Landon, halting their advance by giving Olanna a worried stare.

"Only a few hours ago, another venturing apprentice entered through these halls and might actually still be somewhere inside," said Olanna, as she began to wither back into her slumber, "good luck to you all."

Not another word came from Olanna as her snowy dress became very still again. Landon raced back to the silky curtain, seeing that the walls around him had now enclosed the archway. Landon spun on his heel; there was no other way, but to keep moving forward. Landon and Makari each took a deep breath and followed the circles of ghostly white lamps shining from the old roof above and followed them down the red-bricked hall.

The Tuolumnes had been walking for nearly fifteen minutes already, reading the signs at the entrances of every spidery-webbed hall that housed thousands of circularly shaped vault doors on either side of them.

"Vaults five-hundred and twenty through seventy," read Makari, as they passed another hall entry. The further Landon and Makari trekked down the main hall, they agreed, the colder it became. At one point, a grim radiance of absolute hopelessness slipped into Landon's mind, regardless of his sister by his side. Landon's kept sights were lost upon the lonely hallways around them. At the same time, Landon could feel a tingly, eerie prickle beginning to itch around the back of his neck that made him spin on a heel. Makari tugged on her brother's jacket sleeve, inadvertently replacing her brother's thoughts with a luminous reminder to keep his sights on the promise ahead.

As our siblings finally arrived to the end of the main hall, it was there and like Olanna had said it would be, stood their vault: 601. Landon and Makari basked in its enormity and spotted the banner of embossed numbers above the metal door, but there was something very odd about this particular vault. Our siblings were well aware that all the vault doors could only be opened with a Nicollet Key, but their door had already been opened by some other dark means.

The siblings eyed the short walk-up that swiftly guided to the metal door ahead. Even though they kept a sure notice on the trail of footprints upon the dusty cobblestones that strangely disappeared behind the vault door, there was no chance in sight for them to withdraw from the hall. As Landon and Makari warily approached the door, they could see that something had melted and burned its way through the keyhole until mastering a broken entry. Landon could feel an irritating drop of blood and sweat roll down the side of his forehead. Landon then stepped in front of his sister, noticing that she too was holding her breath, as they together, gently slid through the small opening of vault number, six-zero-one.

Landon entered the humid chamber first, until they both could see that its center was solely lit by the pale moonlight outside that pierced through a jagged hole from the cupola roof. Our siblings kept moving, steadily following mounted rows of lamps that had been fixed upon thin columns that stood along a spiral staircase that directed them to the center of the room.

In the center of the vault now, it was clear to them, they were not alone, and that was because the red-hooded-figure that had its back to them and kept fidgeting and speaking whisperingly into something it held in one of its gloved hands.

The red-hooded-figure then shifted a violet eye, seeing Landon first slowly descending the stairs from behind in the reflection of the hand mirror in its firm grip. Landon kept his eyes on the red figure that persisted to keep its back toward him and his sister, as they could still hear it speak intently to the mirror.

"Lan..." whispered Makari, anxious.

"Get behind me," said Landon, hushed. "Hello?" Landon shook, nervously. "Are...are you an another apprenticing guardian?" Landon was certain to keep a distance from the figure that still reserved its violet right eye on Landon through the reflection.

"Hello there... Landy boy..." the Red Hood spoke softly, "I am a guardian of some sorts." The red figure then giggled, as Landon titled his head.

"I know that voice," murmured Makari.

Only one person had ever called our brave Landon, *Landy boy*, all during his time in Revlenion.

"I'm thrilled to see you made it out of the West Royal Pine, alive," spat Britta Terry, pulling back her hood as she faced Landon and Makari, "and I see you haven't come alone. How perfect."

"But…but the newspapers said you were—" Landon gasped, eyeing Britta's slowly decomposing face.

"—Dead?" grinned Britta, pushing back her head of gold curls, "indeed I am, silly boy. You see, a sacrifice had to be made." Britta then playfully displayed an ugly row of fresh stitches that rounded her neck and was thrilled to see Landon and Makari cringe at the terrible sight.

"Your eyes—you're possessed by one of those creatures, aren't you? But your eyes weren't like that before," said Landon, as the piercing moonlight from above bounced against Britta's dilated violet eyes.

"Correct you are, boy," said Britta, grinning wildly again. Landon found himself unable to remove his spellbinding gaze he set upon the decomposing face that grinned in front of him. It was such a horrid sight. "I was already part of the plan before you ever arrived to Revlenion."

"Just like the plan you and the Holbrooks tried on us, to have us killed in the forest?" sneered Makari.

"*All* part of the plan," said Britta, with a ghastly hymn in her throat. "Though, I wouldn't give those two idiots the amount of credit that I'd give you. I knew those orphans had nothing to lose; I simply bribed them with a handsome chest of solbecks in order to seal the deal on duping you. But again, somehow, the curious Tuolumne siblings," Britta then gritted her teeth, "managed to flee."

Makari then felt an empathetic churn boil in her stomach, reeling at the idea of what other lured deeds Britta had put the Holbrooks through.

"Why are you in our vault?" jeered Landon.

"Whoever said that this vault belonged to you two?" said Britta, seeing our siblings' eye one another. "I'm here to introduce you to the door of your manifesto," said Britta. "I'm glad Vizton didn't harm you too much; I need you both to last for as long as *we* need you."

"You, this is all because of you?" said Landon.

"Almost everything," said Britta. "You see, Landy, I am the product of the next generation of Dark Seethers. I was approached some time ago by a now fellow Dark Seether, she who spoke of many darkly, beautiful things and caught my attention with one movement we both have in common: the unfair ruling of manifestos and the taking down of the Ordinheirs. We will rise at the coming awakening of our father and we shall finish what he started years ago. We, the Dark Seethers, will help carry out what you selfish Guardians have destroyed and stolen!"

"Awakening of your father?" said Landon.

"You must've heard of him by now...the Dark Alman," said Britta.

"It can't be," Landon shook.

"Oh, Landy boy," laughed Britta, "you don't have to act so surprised, but it's true and he will flourish once again, thanks in part to the both of you. The Dark Seethers are already one step ahead of you and your wretched followers," Britta then tilted her head, "can you guess what was once locked away in this vault?"

Landon shook his head, unwittingly.

"I hoped that, after hearing that two have been parading around so extraordinarily wise beyond your years, you'd found that out yourselves," said Britta, shaking. "Very well...My father's body was once held captive in a titanium shell in here, not able to breathe, not able to speak, nor able to use his beautiful mind," Britta then suddenly screamed, "THE VERY PEOPLE YOU CALL FRIENDS DID THAT TO MY FATHER!" Landon felt his sister flinch behind him and then watched as Britta reclaimed a gentle composure. "*However*, other Dark Seethers and myself found a way to rescue our dark father, and in return, we'll be his lovely ones only known as his darkly victors," cheered Britta, "and maybe, he may even give you and your hideous sister some of the glory—since, in fact, you're the ones who've brought us the very key to his release."

"There's no way that I'm going to give you our key," said

Landon, taking a step backward.

"Oh, I'll make you give that key to me," gritted Britta, "Getting in here was difficult enough and I'm *not* about to waste precious time prying that key from your body. Do, do you even realize what I have gone through? I-I had to find the best counterfeit Venture Key from some old, disgruntled tinker in Arkgothin City; convince that depressed ghost back there that I was an apprentice of the Ordinheirs, and break in here, myself."

"It doesn't seem like it was all worth the trouble," said Landon, "sounds like you don't believe in your father after all."

"Oh," gasped Britta, "I do and it was all worth the pain and death," Britta giggled, "because," She chortled, "the plan has still worked and the best part of it is—you."

"How am I the best part of the plan?" said Landon.

"I figure you found out about Mr. Varick?" Britta asked, with a hum as Landon nodded. "Well, the darling evelisk that was within good-boy-Varick did its job to the best of its ability, but it found a little fiery barrier it could not overcome, as you might've figured out by now."

"An evelisk fears fire—" said Makari, carefully stepping beside her brother.

"—NOBODY'S TALKING TO YOU, BEAST!" roared Britta, spearing a stare at Makari and then composing herself again. "The beloveds can die by fire. Vizton and I knew where to find the last Nicollet key, but neither our possessed friend nor us could defeat the Feuer Guards, but while we retreated to re-master our plans of seizing the key—we find out—that somehow two odious children managed to defeat three hundred-year-old creatures. From there on, once we knew of your manifesto and your so-called-plan, thanks to Varick.It was better for us to wait and have you bring us the prize!"

"Say what you want about me, but we're here with the Venture Key on our own behalf," said Landon. "My sister and I claimed the key because of what we believe in...and like you said, two kids found the key? You and your Dark Seethers have been outsmarted...I'd call that, checkmate."

Britta's lips quickly curled.

"I'm going to ask you one last time, Landon, to hand over that key or else…" Britta fumed as she held out a hand that waited for the key; "words cannot describe the harm I will place upon you and your sister if you don't put that key into my hand. Now."

"No," said Makari stepping in front of her brother. Britta then slowly drew back her spare hand and softly placed it behind her back and inhaled a deep breath.

"If I can't convince you then maybe…Father can," said Britta, eyeing the rose-shaped hand mirror she was still holding. "Would you like to meet him? I believe you need to anyway since as I recall him once saying, he's part of your loathsome manifesto."

When Makari attempted to take one step in front of Landon, Britta snapped, whipping from her fingers a malicious ribbon that slithered through the air until it bludgeoned Landon with a force that slammed him on his back. Landon, trying to catch his breath, rolled to his side and watched as Britta's wicked enchantment carefully constricted itself around his sister until it tauntingly dangled her in the air above him.

"Let my sister—!" Landon screamed, as the tail of the ribbon ripped from Britta's fingertips and whipped our boy across his face.

"*Tut tut*," Britta sighed, gleefully watching Landon cuddle his face in agony. "I am terribly sorry about that," she then began to toy with the silver band around her ring finger, "I sometimes lose control of my gifts, but to pardon your request, I only ask for the key—now —before every last breath of air is squeezed out of her mangy body."

Landon could see that his sister was still alive, though most of her tiny body was wrapped in a horrid bind.

"You'll never get away with this," said Landon, seeing that his sister was trying to reach for his touch through the ribbon. Landon jumped to his feet and tried to pry apart the leathery lasso off of Makari while her body remained levitated in the air.

"Uh-uh, Landy boy," snapped Britta, conjuring another whip at

Landon, as a dark ribbon suddenly roped Landon's hands behind his back, causing them to twist until he felt the most unbearable pain. "If you try that again, I'll make sure that the ribbon twists your arms right out of their sockets—promise to me that you won't do that again."

"I-I," gasped Landon, as his arms twisted in such a way he had never felt in his entire life.

"*I can't hear you—*" Britta sang.

"I PROMISE!" cried Landon, as he fell to his knees.

"That's a good boy," purred Britta, as her ribbon loosened its incredible bind on Landon. The ribbon let go, but only enough that Landon could feel the circulation in his arms return and heard a small pop in the joints of his elbows. "Now that you're comfy allow me to introduce to you…my Dark Alman, Evercanezer."

Britta gasped, victoriously raising the rose hand-mirror higher into the air and after calling upon her father, the lamps that encompassed the entire room began to flicker and nearly spark.

Landon's watery eyes watched as Britta's deranged face grinned at the sight of the darkly molten mass that slowly poured from the glass of the rose mirror, like a whirling umbilical pod that tried to take the form of a ghostly man's inhuman shape. Landon locked his eyes on the disturbing molten creature as it then spoke:

"Ah, the Cherished Guardian," croaked Evercanezer, his demonic voice gurgled through the heavy mist and sounded like it was reverberating from the chamber walls. "I must apologize for my daughter's lack of generosity, but here, allow me to make you feel less…vulnerable." Landon could feel Britta's ribbon weaken again until Landon was able to bring his hands in front him to massage his reddened wrists. "She doesn't know how precious you really are to me."

The dark mass swayed its massive head at Britta, burbling a growl; the girl in the red cape quivered, knowing that her master was undoubtedly scowling at her through his dark mist.

"Let…my sister down," panted Landon, eyeing the creature that scrupulously hid in the mist.

"In good time, my friend," said Evercanezer. "First, I want only to talk with you—will you delight me with such an exchange this evening?"

Landon had no choice.

"Yes," sighed Landon, after eyeing his sister once more. Landon had no idea how firm of a grip Britta's rope was tied around his sister, but he recognized it couldn't be stronger than the bond between his sister and himself.

Even though her words were bound, Makari's sights, however, were free and Landon noticed. The way Landon looked up at his sister, he insisted in his mind that he could still hear her every faultless word, every guiding expression.

"Hear me, brother," Makari's voice called inside Landon's head. "Do as they say. We've already won, we've already won."

Landon sighed.

"Well, what do you wish to talk about?" Landon obliged, fixing a sight on the molten creature.

"That not only are you a great asset to me and to the return of my Dark Seethers, but how you could live on to be the most victorious in my realm," said Evercanezer.

"I have no desire to be your help," Landon spat.

"Landon, my brave friend, but you already are," cheered Evercanezer. "You have brought me the very key I need to return to my life's art—subconscious your act might or might not be, but little do you know that helping me has *always* been the unyielding principle to your manifesto."

"That can't be," said Landon, shaking.

"Oh, but it is true, only I would know that myself since I too once had ventured for a manifesto when I was a young boy," said Evercanezer. "We're not that different, you and I."

Landon eyed the dark mist very closely, trying to catch a glimpse of the man that still hid between its dark and misty façade.

"We're nothing alike," said Landon, "all you and your followers have done is cause pain and have tried to kill my sister and me," said

Landon.

"That's only because we are trying to make you understand," grieved Evercanezer, "and those aren't friends, Landon. Ask yourself; do you really believe that a friend has left behind all of those clues up there? Do you really think a friend would lead you into harms way more than three times? No. I would've wholly guided you from the very beginning—held your hand and protect you from the harm every second! But the real monsters are found upstairs—the ones who you should be fearing."

"But why like this, all the suffering and—?" Landon choked.

"It's the unfortunate process that all filthy manifestos feed from…it wants you to suffer, forever," said Evercanezer. "But I'm here to cure you free from it."

"Cure me of what?" said Landon.

"Cure you free from the poisonous clutches of the Ordinheirs," growled Evercanezer, "they're trying to convince you that you were born with the magnificence of magic. Nobody is born that way. They breed this lie all throughout the universe, but *our* world doesn't work that way. Power is harnessed; knowledge for magic is earned and there is no such thing as manifestos. It is all a lie. The truth, Landon, lies with me…and in that truth is the heart and mind we could share, and create the supreme magic."

"I believe in my heart and mind," said Landon, "but the way you speak…the way you act—"

"—Exactly, the Ordinheirs want you to see me at my worst!" howled Evercanezer. "They don't want you to seek the absolute truth that can be discovered on your own—What they've stood for has caused far more pain than any other force within Revlenion, look at what they've made of me. Long ago, when I was just a little boy, I too listened to the manifesto that the Ordinheirs had deemed was so right."

"What other way is there?" said Landon.

"The way of me," Evercanezer championed. "I can guide you to splendors the Ordinheirs would never. Unfortunately, Ingrid and her shallow plinths will only instill lies and doubt that will one day lead you to your own imprisonment. Listen to me Landon, if the Ordinheirs don't get to you first, they'll sacrifice your sister—you don't want that now, do you?"

Landon's eyes shifted around the room and back up to his sister, still watching his every effort.

Could this be true? Landon thought.

"All I ask is for your Venture Key, and in return, I will save you and your sister from the malevolent hands of the Ordinheirs and the others that have displaced the both of you," Evercanezer encouraged, "free me of this bind that the predators we know have bestowed upon me…free me, Landon Tuolumne, and you will live to be my greatest victor, ever." Evercanezer then stretched a long and horribly putrefied arm out from his misty cloud, unrolling an open palm at Landon while Britta tossed a jealous glare at our brave boy. "Just hand…me…that… key."

"My sister, the Ordinheirs and a new friend have all told me that I would and could do great with a manifesto," Landon then reached for the marvel in his jacket pocket as an idea then conveyed his mind, "I've questioned many parts of my journey thus far while in Revlenion, but none has ever tried to hurt or lie to me and my sister," said Landon, as Evercanezer's body shifted in the mist.

"Without me, all you'll ever be is a wandering slave," Evercanezer seethed.

"No," said Landon eyeing the hovering creature, "I'm just a boy with a choice. You said power and magic should only be harnessed by doing it on your own. If you want me to believe that's the truth," Landon then tossed the glass key high into the air, "free yourself."

Britta watched in horror as the sea-glass key spun for a few taunting seconds and could only regretfully remain in place with the mirror still in hand. No matter how many times Evercanezer tried to desperately grasp for the Venture Key it would only continue to slip through his hideous fingers.

Landon watched with unfettering triumph as he and his sister's

Venture Key shattered into dozen tiny splinters along the redbrick floor inside the vault. Britta screamed to the top of her dead lungs as the molten mass containing the Dark Alman then began to swirl and reached with both of its ghastly hands out at Landon, lifting him up into the air.

"KILL HIM NOW!" roared Evercanezer, as Britta then pulled a dagger out from her red cloak. Landon could now finally see two horrifying and green scalene eyes at the moment they emerged from the molten mass. The giant eyes reminded Landon of the shapes that he, his mother, father, and sister would carve out for the eyes of their jack-o-lanterns, every year. Such an ornament that was able to remind our brave Landon of wonderful joys and about the times of boundless happiness that he knew was lost, and for the pernicious eyes that hovered before Landon were strikingly free of ever knowing the kind of joys our brave boy had once known.

Suddenly, Britta let out another terrible scream, but this time, her sights were on something else. Landon could see Britta was keeping a dismayed stare on an entity that was settled somewhere behind Landon and Makari. Landon squirmed to break free from Evercanezer's tight grip and noticed that the ribbon that bound Makari in the air was beginning to unwind. Fearing it was something that would obliterate him at an instant, Evercanezer dropped Landon to the stone floor as his darkly mass stormed back into the mirror, and at that very instant, a prevailing arrow made with such phenomenal light, struck the mirror in Britta's hand and shattered it to pieces across her face. In that same time, Makari could feel the ribbon around her body greatly undoing and ripped it away until she fell into her brother's arms below her. Makari kneeled for only a second to catch her breath until she and her brother quickly endured, surveyed the room and hoped to see that Jade had found them and returned with help.

Our siblings' hopes were trodden when they found nobody else was in the room with them, but only to see Britta was splayed between slivers of the mirror that had shattered around her. Landon and Makari watched Britta bend in pain while sobbing over the pieces of glass and could see curls of thick green smoke spew from the broken handle of the rose mirror.

"Where is my ring, where is my magic?!" choked Britta, crying to herself. Britta let out another terrible scream, provoking Landon and Makari to take another step back. She could see her mangled reflection in the shattered pieces from her mirror. "Look at what your greed has done to me," Britta spun her body back toward Landon and Makari, realizing that they were inching backward to the stairs. Britta pitifully displayed the harsh aftermath that had been lashed upon her body: most of her left hand had been burned away, and parts of her face hung to the side like a torn Halloween mask that revealed the face of a rotten creature that hid underneath.

Landon and Makari spun on their heels and dared to make their escape out of the vault and away from the masked creature that was now in pursuit of them.

"Let him go!" Makari screamed from the top of the stairs, steps away from the vault's exit. Britta had managed to grab Landon by the ankle while the three of them charged up the spiraling stairs. Landon turned his body around; his back pressed hard against the stone steps and could see the foul creature slowly raising its dagger into the air.

"THE DARK ALMAN IS REAL, HE IS REAL!" cried Britta, but out of nowhere, an arresting force struck the back of her crumbling body.

Makari screamed!

Britta gulped for a full breath with every trembling backward step she made away from the stairs. Landon cared not to watch her suffer and instead crawled up the stairs unaware that, whatever invisible force was in the room with them, was powerful enough to imprison Britta by transforming her into a titanium statue. Britta now stood in the center of the vault, beseechingly curling her hands up toward the pale moon that lit the center of the chamber, and for one last time she exhaled a breath as the hardening shell devoured her. Landon crawled up the stairs until he came to his feet, arms out to push the vault door open. With all their might, the siblings made their escape and together pushed the vault door completely open.

Sitting only a few paces ahead of them amongst a blinding shimmer of fantastic light, Landon and Makari could see what they thought was the shape of a slender house cat. Suddenly, the feline's odd silhouette seized our brave siblings off their feet with another brilliant wave of fantastic light. In that precious amount of time, Landon still managed to take hold of his sister by the hand as they flew backward into their vault again and together could sense a collective numbness. Feeling the moment slowly narrowing to black, they knew that their bodies were about to crash against the stone floor within the vault, but somehow that didn't happen. Instead, Landon and Makari embraced the different consciousness of being and felt very peaceful as they were each gracefully slipped into the softest bed either had ever slept in.

CHAPTER SIX

THE MAGNIFICENT TRIO

Landon woke with the warm yet ashen summer morning sun that beamed from one of the tall windows in the spare room. Trailing fingers down his face, Landon could feel a pair of bandages on his forehead and chin. Fighting with himself to open his tired green eyes, Landon rolled on his side away from the irritating sunlight. When Landon finally managed to peel an eyelid, he could see an engrossing front page from the Cappa Gazette that boasted a bold headline hovering close to his face:

THE CURIOUS CAPPA VISITORS SAVE MANOR!
The Famous Tuolumne siblings bring Vizton Eplaville to justice.

"Hello?" said Landon, eyeing the newspaper as he slowly sat up with an ache.

"Well-well," said Dionne, as she folded up the newspaper while sitting on an iron stool beside Landon's bed, "lovely to see you that you're finally awake. If we would've known that the gloomy summer sun was going to do the trick of ceasing your deep slumber—we certainly could have spared our dear McDaniel the worry."

"So, I wasn't dreaming?" said Landon, rubbing his eyes again.

"What do you mean, dreaming?" laughed Dionne. "You're still here in the manor, safe and sound."

"Where's my sister—and Jade?" sparked Landon.

"They're both just fine," Dionne assured, patting the bedside.

"What happened to me last night? My head is throbbing," said Landon, massaging the back of his head.

"That is the result of your astounding bravery, but I could also say, you took one nasty fall last night down in your vault…but I like saying that you were just being brave a *whole* lot better," grinned Dionne.

As Landon then adjusted his back against the headboard of his cool bed, spurts of foggy images from the night before that began to echo in his brain like a terrible dream that he could suddenly remember.

"I met him," Landon eyed Dionne again, "I met the Dar—"

"—Landon, listen to me," said Dionne softly, elating a hand, "you don't have to talk about him. I know everything about what happened in the vault last night."

"How do you know what happened?" said Landon.

"The man that saved you and your sister is an old friend of mine and former mentor of Jade's," said Dionne, "you're very lucky he was able to reach you in time however that brilliant man managed to find you three down in the vaults. Still, he brought you back to us and spoke of such wondrous lengths about how you and Makari were simply divine."

"I…I don't remember seeing anyone else down there with me," Landon fumbled, "Or did I?"

"Are you *positive* you didn't see him? Well, it must have been that nasty fall on the stairs, he did say you and Makari made quite the nasty fall," said Dionne, "*That* might've unsorted your memory, regardless, you two did your best."

"I hope we did our best," sighed Landon, "but, I think I made the mistake of destroying our Venture Key."

"Whether it was a mistake or good idea, *that* is all over now," said Dionne, as she then sat next to Landon on the bed.

"Where's my sister and Jade?" said Landon, as he sat up.

"Jade's fine—he's now using that cane more for walking than

twirling it around, like he usually does, but he'll be okay. However, you'll have to ask Makari how she really feels," said Dionne, as she nodded at someone standing in the room's balcony threshold.

Makari eyed her brother, feeling a whoosh of relief stride between them. With their eyes locked, Makari darted toward her brother and dove into his open arms on the bed.

"*Ooow!*" groaned Landon, as Makari hugged him tightly around his bruised side. "I'm happy to see you, too."

"I knew you'd wake up," said Makari, elatedly, as her big blue eyes began to water.

"I had to, freckle face," laughed Landon, as his sister then pinched his arm.

"Why do you look a little older to me now?" Makari chuckled.

"I…I do?" Landon hummed.

"Here's a get-well card I thought you'd like to read," said Makari, picking up the mechanically typed note that was hidden underneath Landon's stowed armlet on the bedside table. Landon gave a moment to admire the complete stand that was packed with a vase of lavender and peonies; a wicker basket brimming with of all sorts of tantalizing treats from Dingoduns that were either chocolate-glazed, peculiarly boxed or wrapped.

Landon:

Never have I witnessed such bravery and selflessness presented in my life. You stood on your own and I applaud you. However, I must apologize for rendering you and your brilliant sister to sheer unconsciousness, but I know you'll both be up and venturing once again. Until we meet again, my green-eyed wonder.

Helpfully yours,
Simon Feliné

"Helpfully Yours, Simon…" breathed Landon, ecstatic, "*thank you.*" Landon eyed the name on the card again. "Did you get a chance to meet him, M?"

"No, but he sure did leave behind plenty of Dingodun candies for us," said Makari, as she held open a box of *Rolly Zolly Caramel Tears* and popped a tiny, dark chocolate dipped caramel ball into her mouth.

"Simon is…let's just say he's always been on his own venture," said Dionne.

"I can't wait to meet him," said Landon.

"You will very soon, but first," nodded Dionne, "there is one thing I wanted to speak to the both of you about."

"Okay," said Landon, as Makari took hold of Simon's card.

"Yesterday when we spoke in the manor study about the Hallways of Quinn, I told you I wasn't sure of what you would find within the halls—in actuality—I *did* know everything what you would indeed find down there. It's not that I was being maliciously dishonest to you or the rest of the company; I knew it wasn't my place to intervene with the curious properties of your first venture with your manifesto. I believe, that had I told you *every* detail of what you could find down there, I have no doubt that the outcome would not have been in your favor," said Dionne.

"I, I understand," said Landon.

"But I will say this, I had no clue that your bold venture would lead you directly into *that* specific vault or dangerous paths—that just goes to show the risks of accepting manifestos," said Dionne, genuinely.

"I just need to know one thing now…the Ordinheirs said to me, that with my first venture, I would find the purpose of my manifesto," Landon suspected, "then if I met the Dark Alman on this course, is his presence truly the purpose to my manifesto?"

"I'm afraid to guess, but as it seems," Dionne stressed, "that *he* just may be part of the manifesto—one dark significance or another. However, don't give him that satisfaction."

"What satisfaction?" asked Landon.

"The belief that he truly serves a purpose in your manifesto," said Dionne, "allow the bravery and unconditional love you so wildly display win its purpose."

"Where does that leave us now?" asked Makari.

"Knowing of that particular vault, something very dangerous was stolen out of it—Can you recall what that was?" said Dionne.

"His remains," said Landon, after he pondered for a few seconds.

"Yes, and with his remains having been stolen from the vault and possibly somewhere in Revlenion, there's no telling what could happen next, but all you need to remember is that you two definitely crippled every part of his plan," said Dionne, "because you, Jade included, stood for something that he and his followers know nothing of...and *that* is the acceptance of who you really are...the very boy and girl I see before me that were born with not only such bravery, but are both such beautiful guardians at that. When you faced him, Landon, you accepted *every* risk possible and from that moment on, your manifesto blossomed and shielded you and your sister's precious mind and heart from all his darkness."

"He told me that he wanted to cure Makari and I of the manifesto...and ensured he'd churn me into the guardian that I'm *supposed* to be," said Landon.

"No, the stars that made and brought you both to Revlenion, *made no mistake*, my brave boy and girl," said Dionne, as she held onto our siblings' hands, "you two were born perfect the way you are, Landon and Makari Tuolumne."

"I just hope we can learn how to control the manifesto," said Landon.

"You will—There's much to learn from the manifesto, but for now, let your minds rest," said Dionne.

"What about this?" asked Landon, unfolding open the Cappa Gazette in his blanketed lap and rereading the front-page headlines.

"Oh yes," said Dionne, picking up the front page, "that is the work of the R.C.C. and Antoine, to say the least. Late last night, Jade and your sister were questioned by the R.C.C., about what evolved down in the Krinzen and up until the point you both disappeared into Quinn. Your sister and Jade told a rather convincing tale, as the

Chamberlains understood it to be, about how you three defeated Eplaville within the Krinzen Staircase."

"We don't know if Vizton actually died in the stairwell," said Makari, "all we did was lock him in the destructive mess that he caused."

"That's exactly what Jade said, but the R.C.C. somehow found that to be substantial evidence of Eplaville's demise," said Dionne, "even if his body has yet to be retrieved. Then something came to mind—if you three accomplished such a task, like the R.C.C. had requested, wouldn't that call for some sort of recognition?"

"Well, should it?" said Landon.

"Get dressed and I want you two to come join me to see some familiar faces at the bottom of the Grand Cappa staircase in five minutes," said Dionne, as she stood from the bed. "Remember this Landon and Makari, we share the knowledge with ones involved and they know what truly happened during last night's escapade. Believe in what you experienced and not what others dare to say otherwise. I'll see you two downstairs."

The Head Lady then exited from the room with a wink, leaving Landon to quickly slither out of his Cappa crested pajamas and slip into his usual attire that had been cleaned and were awaiting him from inside the wardrobe.

While Makari awaited her brother to finish dressing for their departure, a thought came to mind that sent her to reach for the art deco radio that was sitting silently on its shelf as it had done before. After a quick flick of the radio **ON** switch, a familiar voice began to spew ever so smoothly and crisp through the tiny speaker:

"My-oh-my!" Lately Lynne popped from the old radio, "such a story that's circulating my airwaves! Sounds so reminiscent of a time long ago, as all of us 'ole Revelers know, a story like the Tuolumnes isn't the first time Revlenion has seen such curious wonders. But that's the cool beauty of our even more curious T-kiddos…they're making a name for themselves…"

Landon then stood from his bed, after bow-tying the last lace on one of his shoes, and paced toward the radio to gather every promising word Lynne was about to bequeath:

"I can say this now, I would love to double my bet from before, saying that our T-kiddos would do something of *legendary proportions*, but I'm safe to say that I believe that our Tuolumnes will become the very spine of our lore, the beating heart to every child's wildest dream, and the venture behind the grandest saga our country will ever know…However, kiddos, that with all these heroics, we must remember that they are not only children on quite a fantastic voyage, we must regard them as a value—not just for their victories, but the fact that they are people too. If you can hear me, kiddos, I'll be here cheering your every move and always with a mighty tune. Who knows, maybe one day, the curious tale of the Tuolumne siblings will be regarded as the bravest fairy tale anyone can mention. The Tuolumnes are on one hell of a journey—So, here's a classic number by David Bowie with *Fantastic Voyage*. Hear me now, loud and clear, *this one* is for the kiddos!"

▼

Landon and Makari jumped from the manor's elevator cabin and hurried along the hallway until they reached the top of the Grand Cappa Staircase. Reaching the drop from the top of the staircase, the siblings spotted McDaniel clasped to the back of a wooden wheelchair where a very sickly looking yet very conscious Mr. Varcik (tossing a "grateful" nod at our siblings) peacefully sat. Standing at the near bottom of the grand staircase was the Cappas, Ms. Qwara, and next to her was our siblings' brave wayfarer friend, Jade Cooper, balancing his stance on the staircase with his famous cane. The main foyer below, however, was remarkably cramped with the entire Manor staff, members of the Cappa Gazette, and dozens of zealous Cappamites. As Landon and Makari descended the staircase in unison, the foyer erupted into applause as our brave siblings came side by side with Jade.

"What's going on?" Landon mouthed, as Jade shook his head.

"Good afternoon ladies and gentlemen, we wish to thank you for joining us for this very rare and prestigious ceremony," announced Antoine, eyeing his audience, as they broke into applause again. "I would first like to take a few moments to thank our fine friends…for proving me wrong. Yes, I said it, for allowing me—no—to remind me of what marvelous and fantastic properties this country has to offer our minds and hearts. I was certainly apprehensive of the case these three certainly desired to partake; fearing relentless endeavors, alas in return their strides have returned what the House of Cappa can only wish for—and that is the birth of these fine heroes!" The entire room burst into applause for our siblings and Jade again, as Antoine then introduced his R.C.C. colleague to the Cappa masses. "If Mr. Savini would like to come forward to say a few words." The short Gargoylian Chamberlain then took to the stairs, standing just below the Cappas, with a polished wooden box in his hands.

"There is much to be said about our country and the occurrences that happen within our very own Cappa Valley. These manifestations arrived to our growing metropolis like a dark cloud and have either whirled curious, horrific and even tragic maladies. However, soon after these events, we realize that just under our very noses, swift victories are set into motion to protect what Cappa Valley truly stands for in Revlenion. These victories come in all shapes and sizes, young and old and no matter how loud their fanfare might be, they must never go overlooked. These victories must be given the highest honor of respect and gratitude, as we must gather to celebrate the heroes of our valley. It is my duty and absolute privilege to present the youngest recipients—Landon and Makari Tuolumne with Jade Cooper—to ever receive this honor, the Heart of Revlenion!" said Mr. Savini, as he clicked a small button atop the wooden box and displayed three golden and emerald heart-shaped medallions. A burst of photojournalists' camera bulbs popped into the air as the foyer once again erupted into applause. "Since the entire country will henceforth know of your recent, heroic events," continued Mr. Savini, "upon receiving this badge of the highest merit, Landon and Makari Tuolumne, you are now recognized as citizens of Revlenion, and together you three will forever be known as the Magnificent Trio!"

While the foyer exploded into the loudest cheers and applause yet, Landon traced his sights upon the pool-like mass of faces that smiled and cheered for him, his sister, and wayfarer-donned friend. Amidst the popping flashes from the cameras, and the roaring chants of his last name, Landon felt as though the entire room's volume fell to a faint hum. Drawing his sights on his mother and father standing ahead of the crowd at the foot of the staircase, both very tranquil and hand-in-hand. Aiden and Annette Tuolumne looked just as spirited and smiling tenderly back at their brave son that stood only a few paces away. Landon's eyes gazed at the phantoms that stood there while his father then gave his brave son one more comforting nod and his mother gestured a kiss to him through the air. After another blinding flash from a fat lensed camera, Landon felt his sister slide a hand into his after noticing his pensive stare out into the applauding crowd. Landon then tossed a grin at his sister, returning his sights to the young hazelnut haired and redheaded Cappamite couple clapping feverishly for their magnificent heroes.

It'll be okay, Landon thought, *they'll make sure of it.*

Landon then joined his sister and Jade in waving, in thanks, for the grand honor the R.C.C. and the Haus of Cappa had bestowed upon them.

As Landon, Makari, and Jade stepped back through the rippling glass of the Elddri Mirror, still peacefully hovering in the living room at 1245 Poplar Drive, there was a sense that time had really past that same afternoon from which they had originally departed. Landon and Makari eyed the refreshing room of their new home, sighing at their return.

"Why on earth would we come back here?" Landon moaned.

"We did what the R.C.C. asked for," said Makari, examining her medallion that was pinned to her denim jacket.

"You're absolutely right, you two did fulfill the expectations of the R.C.C. and to some people, like me, you wonderfully surpassed them," said Jade. "But there was one person who ruled that you two should return home."

"Who would do that to us?" said Makari.

"Me," said Jade, as his young friends looked as though they were about to burst into a riot, "but for all good measures."

"Why?" Landon asked.

"You two need time away from Revlenion and there's nothing wrong with that," assured Jade, "and I believe your Aunt Marion would be awfully worried if she came home and not able to find her remarkable niece and nephew, ever again. In time, I think you'll be able to explain to her who you two really are...but it's the reflective time you spend away from Revlenion that'll, I believe, prepare you two for whatever else might come our way."

"You're right," said Landon.

"Use this time away to muse from your visit and remember that your manifesto still lives, well beyond and presently of this mirror," said Jade, as he then spun on his heel, before remembering, "I almost forgot." Jade reached into his coat pocket, "This is a gift from Simon that he asked me to give to you. He said he ruined your last one, I guess?" Makari awed as she then tore into the newspaper wrapped gift.

"A journal! Thank you, Jade!" sparked Makari, hugging Jade, and then examining the craftsmanship of her new leather bound journal. "Tell Simon I said, thank you, the next time you see him, please."

"I believe you'll have the chance to tell him yourself," Jade ensured. "Now you can write about Revlenion, whenever you wish." Jade then drew his eyes upon Landon, "*Ah*, and for you—I believe, that no matter how time was created, human or otherwise, we can believe that it is a real thing. It may separate us, from one dimension to another, however that doesn't mean it isn't something that can't be shared between you and me." Jade then pulled from another pocket an awkwardly wrapped gift and handed it to Landon.

"Wow," said Landon, after ripping away the parchment wrap. Landon gazed upon his new, polished pocket watch and flicked it open to admire its intricate inner-workings; all delicately ticking away and unremittingly measuring the time between Revlenion and where he and his sister stood on Poplar Drive.

"No matter how friends use their time together, know that I'm happy to share mine with you," said Jade.

"And I the same," smiled Landon.

"Me too," grinned Makari.

Jade then nodded in thanks.

"One last thing before I go: I figured it'd be rather difficult having to explain to your aunt where this mirror came from, without her of course freaking-out and convincing her to believe you two did not manage a way to go prying up into the attic," said Jade.

"Oh, I almost forgot about our little addition," said Landon, eyeing the levitating mirror.

"The moment after I pass through the mirror's port, all you have to do is touch the glass," instructed Jade, demonstrating, "while you say these three simple words, *riddle-me-not*. Seconds later, you'll return the mirror back to its cubic disguise." Jade then spun on a heel toward the mirror again.

"When will we see you again?" Makari asked, relishing in one more hug out of her wayfarer friend before his departure.

"Maybe in a few weeks or sometime in the fall," said Jade, "I need enough time to formulate where exactly the manifesto will take us next...as it is still open."

"Jade," said Landon, tossing a hand out, shaking his sleuth's hand, "thanks for sticking up for us the entire time...Detective."

"*Friend*," nodded Jade, shaking Landon's hand.

"A friend, indeed," smiled Landon.

"Until next time, kiddos," said Jade, and then with a nod.

Jade then adjusted his wayfarers the next, but before he made his exit back into Revlenion, he gave the end of his phenomenal cane a quick tap upon the broken box that was still spread on the common room floor. The siblings watched in sheer awe as the cane worked its mysterious magnificence upon the Elddri Cube's wooden box and swiftly reconstructed its broken parts. Jade nodded again as Landon and Makari waved good-bye, for now, to their friend as he slid back through the Elddri Mirror. Landon and Makari continued to gaze upon the mirror for only a few seconds more after Jade disappeared beyond the silvery pool. The siblings each stood before the Elddri Mirror, watching the glass until the rippling reflection was calm again. Our brave siblings remained in front of the mirror, perceiving their brave selves in the mirror's reflection once more.

Landon and Makari then each placed a hand on the still glass and simply recited the three-worded-guise verse, together. And just like when the Elddri Cube had been opened by our siblings the first time, it slowly began to remarkably work in reverse. The siblings watched as the mirror reverted, working much like a massive zoetrope as it spun in the air. After the last tiny cube nestled itself to complete the mirror's disguise, Landon and his sister cherished the phenomenal cube that rested in his hands for a few seconds more until deciding to carefully return the golden cube back into its wooden box. The siblings marched back upstairs, Landon with the box out in front of him led the way into his room that was the same as he left it earlier that day, but only to find that it now basking in the summer sunset that was solely illuminating the bedroom walls with crisp, summery gold and reds.

"There's no turning back is there?" asked Makari, she on one side of the bed across from her brother and the box resting between them.

"Nope," said Landon, after placing the old box on his bed, "and I don't believe we ever will." Landon and Makari eyed the Elddri Cube once again, reveling in its magnificent presence.

"During the ceremony, what were you thinking about when we were standing on the staircase?" asked Makari, watching her brother smile.

"I was imagining that mom and dad were there with us," said

Landon, "cheering...*just for us.*"

Makari tilted her head, absolutely charmed by her brother's words and agreed.

"So was I," said Makari.

"Whatever we do, I just want us to remember them as they were," said Landon, nodding.

"We will," said Makari.

"I know it will be hard not to miss them—" Landon tried.

"No it won't," said Makari, inching closer to her brother on the bed. "Because we still have someone that not only shared a time with mom and dad but wants to retain the love we once knew, all the same." Landon was about to close the box's lid when he heard the rumble of the old red car driving up Poplar Drive. "We need to cherish Aunt Marion as much as any memory of the happiness we once shared." Landon was suddenly overcome by his sister's truth.

"Landon, Makari," Aunt Marion called from downstairs. Aunt Marion entered the kitchen form the garage and placed her purse on the cooker's island while she trekked toward the common room.

Aunt Marion eyed the room and became visibly overwhelmed by a memory that she began to reminiscence within her mind. She circled herself around the radiant room, until the slow spin on her heel wheeled her to the sight of her niece and nephew standing side by side, looking at her from the kitchen stairs.

Landon and Makari smiled.

"Is it me or does this house feel more alive—?" Aunt Marion tried, nearly crushed by Landon and Makari as they embraced their aunt once again.

"It does," said Makari, teary-eyed.

"What's wrong?" Aunt Marion awed, as she held onto her Landon and Makari.

"Makari and I experienced," said Landon, pulling away as he saw his sister gawk at him, "actually, we just had a lot to *talk* about today."

"And we're so thankful for—" Makari said, when her aunt stopped her.

"—Words can't express that kind of thanks, but with our acts I know we've shared can do just that. I will stand by you two for as long as time shall allow and let me be the one to be thankful for *you*," said Aunt Marion, carefully eyeing her niece and nephew, "we may have each lost a part of our hearts, but we've gained another because we are here…together."

"I don't want to be sad anymore," said Landon.

"And you never will be again," said Aunt Marion, gently pinching her nephew's chin. "Now, how about we go watch that spectacular sunset."

Aunt Marion led the way through the foyer, outside and the three of them claimed a spot on the short stoop just before the open front door. The Tuolumnes watched as the silver lamppost popped itself into its pearly illumination as the evening slowly crept along Poplar Drive. Makari then rested her head on her brother's shoulder next to her, as they together, peacefully watched the orangey sky gradually awaken its tiny stars for them through the remaining summer night. Our brave siblings, along with their Aunt Marion, began to try and guess where in the starry blankets above they could find the famous constellations and be able to name each of them. They sat together, laughing at times, and awing at moments when they were able to catch the sight of an occasional shooting star zooming overhead. Aunt Marion then finally stood and excused herself back inside the house and allowed Landon and Makari to savor the night. The magnificent Tuolumne siblings rested there along the stoop and tranquility free of any words. Before deciding to wander back inside, however, it was then that Landon and Makari realized where their manifesto began.

<u>ACKNOWLEDGEMENTS</u>

From a childhood fantasy to conquering the odds, *Revlenion and the Guardian Manifesto* wouldn't exist without the exceeding persistence, nerve, and passion present in the creative hands responsible for fulfilling this dream.

A venture, all of its own, I share the ending of this novel with Rahiem Brooks and the entire Prodigy Gold Books team; without out you, Landon and Makari would still be languishing some place unkind. To my past and present creative realm and members of HAUS LIMITED: Isaac and Michelle Minarik, Luis Briggs, Felipe Flores, Maggie Peck, and Daniel Doperalski– thank you.

My family and closest friends–you are here with me in every page.

And thank you to my Carter–The Sagittarius to my Gemini and the captain of our cosmos.

Forever your storyteller,

-Kalvin Klaus
October 2018

CPSIA information can be obtained
at www.ICGtesting.com
Printed in the USA
BVHW032105221118
533752BV00001B/12/P